Gigi and Banana Wine Before the Fall

A Novel

By

J Michael O'Reilly

And they were behind us, reflected in the pool.
Then a cloud passed, and the pool was empty.
Go, said the bird, for the leaves were full of children,
Hidden excitedly, containing laughter.
Go, go, go, said the bird: humankind
Cannot bear very much reality.

T S Eliot, "Burnt Norton" from "Four Quartets"

* * *

Picture yourself in a boat on a river
With tangerine trees and marmalade skies,
Somebody calls you, you answer quite slowly,
The girl with kaleidoscope eyes.
Cellophane flowers of yellow and green
Towering over your head,
Look for the girl with the sun in her eyes and she's gone.

The Beatles, Lucy in the Sky with Diamonds

* * *

They looking back all th' eastern side beheld
Of Paradise, so late their happy seat,
Waved over by that flaming brand; the gate
With dreadful faces thronged and fiery arms:
Some natural tears they dropped, but wiped them soon;
The world was all before them, where to choose
Their place of rest, and Providence their guide.
They, hand in hand, with wandering steps and slow,
Through Eden took their solitary way.

- John Milton, Paradise Lost

1984

Dr John Thompson drove up to the immensely high grey steel gates of the Central Mental Hospital, stopped his car in between equally high grey stone walls, and waited for Pat the gatekeeper to appear. As he waited, Dr Thompson thought of the case that was foremost in his mind that day, the first interview to be conducted with a new admission. Nasty case of patricide, found guilty but insane and committed. Young man of 26 discovered by a neighbour standing in tears over the body of his dead father with a bloody axe in his hand. Very complex psychology associated with patricide, Dr Thompson thought, and very difficult to treat. Young men kill for many different reasons but when a man kills his own father there is something very deep-rooted behind it. When Pat finally made an appearance, coming out the door in the wall and closing it behind him in quick jerky movements, the doctor wound down his window and held up his ID. Immediately he was hit by a blast of cold air. Pat didn't bother looking at the worn square of plastic with the barely recognisable photo, he just said the usual "Morning Doctor Thompson", got the usual "Morning Pat" in reply, and stamping his feet against the cold he scurried back into the warmth of his gate lodge where he hit the lever to open the gates. On mornings like this, the grey sky suggesting the possibility even of snow, he always wished there was some other system of admitting the staff. After all, he knew the doctor and his car at sight, both men had been working there long enough, but protocol must be adhered to and regulations must be obeyed. He knew well enough they couldn't afford to take chances when it came to security in a place like this - not after that incident last year when a patient had escaped and terrorised the neighbourhood for a couple of hours before he was recaptured.

Once through the gates the doctor proceeded slowly up the avenue and parked his car in his designated spot, his number plate almost touching the little white wooden post with his name on it.

Again he thought of the patricide case he was to interview today. Violent too, likely as not, better be careful, get a couple of the nurses to sit in, he thought, one male if possible. Passing through the three lots of steel and glass doors into the gleaming reception area he was met with the usual greetings and smiles, some admiring, some simply welcoming, from the receptionist and nurses at the desk. He knew by now what most young nurses were thinking when they looked at him, but if he ever gave it a thought he certainly didn't show it. At 42 he was still strikingly hand-some, but having been happily married to Jane for nearly ten years and with two small children, he no longer gave members of the opposite sex as much as a second thought.

In his office he took off his overcoat and hung it on the tubular steel coat-stand beside his secretary's desk, put on his white cotton lab-coat, and went on through to his own private room. Helen wouldn't be in for another half hour so that gave him time for his daily pre-work routine of going through the list. The list told him at a glance everything he needed to know about the progress of every patient under his care: physical and mental condition, date admitted and complete history, medication being received, names of all nurses in charge, future prognosis, and anything unusual he ought to know about. He looked down the list to the case he was most interested in, this recent arrival, straight from the Central Criminal Court, committed to be held in the hospital at the court's discretion. Dr Thompson had appeared as witness in the case, being one of the members of the Panel of Expert Witnesses, and it was largely on his intervention that this new patient was now here and not receiving rougher treatment in the overcrowded conditions of a prison cell. Prosecuting Council had reduced the charge from murder to manslaughter on grounds of diminished responsibility, but before long it was obvious they would have problems making even the lesser charge stick. For it became abundantly clear to anyone witnessing the trial that - unless the young man was a particularly talented and convincing actor - he was clearly insane.

Defence Council had little or no control over his conduct, the two young lawyers being barely able to get him to sit down and be quiet most of the time, as at regular intervals the accused would stand up, raise his right hand in the air as if testifying, and announce clearly to the Court: "I killed him, I killed God the Father, the bastard! I killed God!" And then there would follow a stream of vitriolic, foul-mouthed abuse targeted at the Almighty which literally had some people calling for a priest to perform an exorcism on the defendant right there in court. His lawyers would try and get him to sit down and be quiet and likely as not get an elbow in the face and more abusive language hurled at them for their trouble. At one point he even plucked the wig off Junior Council's head and threw it across the courtroom. Of course there were elements in the public gallery that found this irresistibly amusing and pretty soon, as word got about, the gallery was so full of locals enjoying the best free entertainment they'd had in years, that the judge ordered the court cleared. Dr Thompson was relieved as he didn't consider the accused at all entertaining, nor did he consider that there was any possibility that he was acting, rather he was utterly convinced from the start that this young murderer was profoundly and possibly irretrievably mentally ill. The defence tried their best to make a case but with their client screaming his guilt from the rooftops they pretty soon gave up and talked to the Prosecution about mitigation, whereupon they sought advice from Dr Thompson about advising the Judge to instruct on criminal insanity. And so it was with great relief and not a little professional pride that he heard the jury bring in their verdict and the Judge pronounce his verdict. Due to the defendant's lack of inhibitions in proclaiming his guilt, not many of the details of the case came out in Court and no witnesses were called. In the end the case, which had been hyped up in the press to levels approaching hysteria, and promised to be the most sensational murder trial in years, was all over in less than a day.

When Dr Thompson heard his secretary come into the outer office he put down his papers and went out to her.

"Morning Helen, how are you this fine morning?"

"Oh all right I suppose," was the answer. Helen, an efficient and intelligent girl of 24 with short fair hair, had been a bit under the weather the last few days and a few discrete enquiries among the other staff elicited the information that she was having trouble with her boyfriend. The effect of this was something which Dr Thompson, while not wanting to encourage moodiness among his staff, was at least prepared to tolerate and even to alleviate if at all possible, if only for his own sake and for the smooth running of his department. Dr Thompson was known for his compassionate nature, something which commanded great respect and loyalty from his staff.

"Excellent Helen, big day today, you know we start interviewing the new case, Karl Jones, we'll be in the secure room here, everything will be recorded and I will need a transcript by the end of each day to take home with me and read, so you will be very busy typing for the next few days." That should take her mind off boyfriend troubles, he thought.

"Certainly doctor," she replied.

"Oh yes, and I want two psychiatric nurses in attendance, outside the door, just in case things get troublesome. At least one male if one is available if you please. Have them here before 11.00. Now I'm going up to Professor Jacobson to discuss the case with him. I will be back at eleven with the patient."

Two hours later he returned with his patient, a short and slightly built young man with light brown hair, big dark eyes and a bewildered expression on his face. As Helen looked at him she didn't imagine he could be any trouble but the two nurses were there as instructed, on chairs outside the secure interview room, and they stood up as the doctor entered.

"Oh you are here, excellent, I'll have a word with you in a moment, just let us get settled inside first." And the doctor escorted his shuffling patient past the nurses standing like a pair of personal bodyguards on either side of the door.

Inside the large, brightly-lit, white-walled interview room there was a desk with two chairs and a long psychiatrist's couch, offering a choice of seating arrangements, but nothing else to enliven the white, sterile surroundings. Everything was new and Dr Thompson was now beginning to accept the modern tubular-steel design of chairs, desk and even the couch.

"Now Karl - is it all right if I call you Karl?" the doctor asked. "Fine," he added, even though he had got no reply, as his patient looked around the room suspiciously. "Now which would you prefer, an armchair or the couch?"

"I can lie down on the couch if I want?" Karl Jones asked tremulously.

"Of course, that's what it's there for. Or else you can sit in the armchair if you prefer."

His patient said nothing but got onto the couch and lay back, as if testing it for comfort.

"You prefer the couch, do you? That's fine. Now just stay there one moment and don't move, I will be right back."

Outside the door Dr Thompson, while keeping one eye on his patient through the two-way mirror in the wall, addressed the nursing staff who stood before him, slightly self-consciously, in their immaculately white starched uniforms.

"Thank you so much for coming over, I hope you won't be needed but I would like you to stay here for at least the first two-hour session." He looked at the male nurse first and read his name-badge. "Nurse Ryan, hi – what's your first name, I always like to be on first name terms with my staff."

"Nigel, doctor."

"Well Nigel, I don't think our friend inside would be much of a match for you," and the doctor slapped the well-built six-footer on the shoulder.

"No doctor, I think I could handle him all right," Nurse Ryan replied smiling.

"And Nurse - eh ?" the doctor said, bending to read the name-badge of his female colleague, a fair- almost red-haired, pretty young woman in her mid-twenties. "... Mullen, thanks, yes you have a question?"

"It's the patient, doctor, you see I know him," the nurse blurted out in somewhat of a rush. "I knew he was to be admitted but I didn't expect to see him so soon."

"Are you sure you know him, Nurse?"

"Yes, it's him all right, I followed the case and know all about him. You see we lived on the same road when we were children."

"Did he recognise you, do you think? He showed no sign that I noticed."

"I'm pretty sure he didn't, he hasn't seen me in ten years, but I wouldn't want to do anything to jeopardise the interview process, so I thought you should know."

"Quite right, thank you, but I'll tell you what, stay with us for the moment, if you knew each other as children you might come in quite useful later on, I'd like to hear your impressions of the patient. But we won't take any risks letting him see you again, so if you wouldn't mind staying in the observation room for this and all subsequent interviews, I think that would be best." And Dr Thompson opened a door into another room off the outer office and sat Nurse Mullen down in one of a row of chairs in front of another large two-way mirror.

"You will be able to see and hear perfectly in here, and he will never see you. What's your first name Nurse Mullen?"

"Zoe, doctor."

"Right Zoe, feel free to ask my secretary Helen for anything you'd like in the way of tea or coffee. I'll call back when I have finished interviewing the patient. Thank you."

"Thank you doctor." Nurse Zoe Mullen turned her attention to the young man behind the glass. He was lying quite still on the couch and she couldn't see his face but it had given her quite a fright seeing him in person again after all these years, especially after the publicity of the trial and the details of the murder she had read. She was becoming used to coming into contact with the most mentally disturbed cases every day, some of them violent murderers, but when it is someone you know, someone you have known as a child and grown up with, it is a different matter. So she was very glad when Helen stuck her head round the door and offered her a cup of tea.

Inside the brightly-lit interview room Dr Thompson sat for a moment behind the desk to turn on the door-locking mechanism and the audio recording device. Then he came round and pulled up one of the tubular steel armchairs beside the couch and started talking in a gentle, soothing and very matter-of-fact tone of voice.

"Well Karl, we're both nice and comfortable now, so I'd just like to ask you a few questions, maybe go over your early life, to get to know you a bit better, is that all right?" He got no reply and continued.

"Excellent, so why don't we start at the very beginning, and you can tell me about your childhood, anything at all that you'd like to recall. Can you remember much about your childhood? Some people can, and others can only remember a little about their past."

"I can remember everything," his patient said in a quiet mono-tone. "Where do you want me to start?"

"I would like very much to hear everything about your child-hood, starting with your earliest memories, whatever springs to mind."

"I was born in 1958 but I don't remember much about that. Ha! Then there was 1959, 1960, 1961 - no, 1962 - no... I know, I'll start when we moved house, the new house was better, more funner, I think I'll start there, that was in

1964

because it's nice sitting here on one of the dining chairs on our new front lawn where the men have left them until they have the table out of the big lorry and in place in the new dining room first. Today is warm and sunny, the green leather seat is like a hot water bottle under my legs, and when I sit on it first it nearly burns my bare skin below the ends of my short trousers, the red ones with the stitching on the pockets. The sun is sitting on the top of my head like a warm, fat cat. The chair I'm on is Daddy's, the one with the arms, and the wood is dark brown like chocolate but it looks like it's melting in the sun it's so shiny. There's a different smell here from the last house, something that reminds me of Christmas, maybe it's that big tree next door that looks like a giant Christmas tree. It's so much fun here that I don't mind my sore legs and I like watching the great big removal men carrying everything from the truck into our new house. The enormous lorry is bright blue, it's so big it looks like a whale, it even has whale eyes and a big smiley mouth at the front. It's parked outside the front gate as it's too big to fit in the driveway but that doesn't matter, this road is different from our last one, there's a sign that says Cul-de-Sac which means you can't get out the end, you have to turn round and go back out the way you came in, so there's no traffic, maybe one car dribbles past every quarter of an hour that's fifteen minutes and there's four in every hour. Every time I recognise something from the old house I want to laugh seeing it like that, one of the men is funny he keeps calling me "gaffer" and though I don't know what it means I know he is being funny. He is also a little scary as I can see part of a tattoo just visible on his arm where he has rolled up his shirt sleeves, and Mummy says men with tattoos are dangerous. He's got nice eyes but awful shoes.

"Howaye gaffer?" he says to me as he passes. "Keepin an eye on us are ya, makin sure we does our work proper?" I don't know how to reply and just giggle a bit which makes me feel foolish, but I still like it when he talks to me. On one trip he has the big, tall lamp from the drawing room in his hand and he takes the big orange lampshade off and puts it on his head which makes me laugh even more. When he comes out he's talking to one of the other men.

"It's been a hard day," the other one says and the funny one says something and then starts singing. It sounds like "I've been working like a dog it's been a hard day's night." And then they both start singing the same song but I've no idea what it is; we learn songs in school but not this one. They go back into the truck singing like this and then I notice a couple of small faces scrunching through the front railings, two boys about my age, one maybe a year older and the other a year younger I'd say. The older one can spy over the top crossbar of the railings in between the spikes, the smaller one is poking through the bars holding on with both hands. He looks like the prisoner in the Monopoly In Jail picture but a funny sort of baby one, not scary at all. Each has a flop of blond hair with a fringe down over his eyes.

"Are you moving in here?" the older one asks. I decide not to answer as I really don't know yet if I want to be friends with these boys. Mummy may not think they are at all suitable.

"Is this your house?" the littler one says. I notice he has his jumper on back to front and inside out, with the label under his chin, it's bright yellow nearly like his hair. The other one's jumper is stripy red and green.

"What's your name? Why are you sitting on that chair? Is that your chair?" I go on ignoring them and hope they will go away.

"Course it's not his chair Patrick," the older one says. "It's much too big for him, can't you see? He couldn't even get up on it without being lifted up by his Mummy. He still sits in a highchair and gets fed baby food I bet."

"Do not," I reply before I even remember I'm not supposed to be talking to them.

"Do too," the older one says, and the two boys slope in between a couple of removal men, cross the lawn and slouch in front of my chair.

"Do you want a fight?" the older one asks, boxing the air. The younger one is playing with a purple yo-yo. They both have brown leather sandals with buckles and straps.

"Not really," I reply, unable to think of anything else to say. I wish my brother was there, though he's not much good at fighting at least he's bigger than this boy and might scare him off a bit. But George is back at the old house with Daddy, helping him pack up some stuff.

"Or else ..." He looks around our front garden for a moment and stares at the hedge on the left side between us and next door.

"What?" I ask hopefully.

"Or else we could have a race through that hedge from end to end starting at the house first to reach the railings is the winner. What do you say? Are you on?" This hedge isn't like most hedges, you wouldn't be able to crawl through most hedges, but this one is made up of large branches with lots of space between them, so it's definitely crawlable through.

"All right!" I say, relieved that I wouldn't have to fight. "If you like."

"C'mon then, or do you need a hand getting off the chair?"

"Of course I don't," I say sliding off the green slidey leather.

"Don't mind Barry," says the little boy, his blue eyes visible for a moment as the breeze catches his fringe. They remind me of the bluebells Mummy used to pick from our last garden. Barry's at the hedge already, his eyes are also blue but much darker, like the really dark purple wine gums that are nearly black. "He's all right when you get to know him, sort of. What's your name?"

"Karl. What's yours?"

"Patrick. And he's Barry. Oh yes I told you that. He's older than me, he's nearly eight, how old are you?"

"I'm seven."

"I'm nearly seven too."

"When will you be seven?"

"I don't know, next year some time. Barry's nearly eight – oh. Do you like my yo-yo?"

"Very nice." Patrick is trying to yo-yo it up and down, the only problem is that it goes down all right but he can't get it to go back up again.

"I need to practise some more," he says smiling, and winds up the string and puts it in his pocket. We have reached the hedge and Barry has already found a way into it. He is sitting inside on one of the low branches with his head peeking out looking like a big yellow-green-and-red parrot in a cage.

"This is where we start," he says, "We start here and we've got to go all the way to the end without touching the ground. Anyone who touches the ground is a rotten egg. I'm going first."

"How do we race then?" I ask. "If it's a race we all have to start at the same time - and in the same place."

"That's your tough luck. I'm starting now." And he immediately starts crawling between the branches, Patrick and myself watching him as he wriggles through the smallest gaps.

"What are you waiting for? I'm going to win," he calls out from inside the hedge.

"You always do anyway," his little brother replies, giving me a funny smile and raising his eyes to heaven. "Oh well, I suppose we might as well follow him." And the two of us climb into the space where Barry has gone and start crawling through the branches. Halfway through Patrick gets stuck in a gap too small for even his tiny body. I'm coming up behind him because I let him go ahead to be polite, and I stop and try to get him untangled.

"You go on," he gasps, "Try and catch up that big eejit of a brother of mine."

"You'll have to go backwards. You can't get through that way." I see a gap to his left, nearly at the edge on the neighbour's side, and I head for it. There's a space to stick my head out too and half my body so I climb up to see how far Barry has gone and I can stand here like this it's like being up the mast of a ship in a storm because the mast is swaying and I'm really high up in the crow's nest and down below I can see the sea all green and rough and cold looking I hope I don't fall in I can't see any land for miles but I didn't come up to look for land what was I looking for?

"I've won!" I hear Barry's voice from the end of the hedge.

"I've reached the railings! You two are losers. You're rotten eggs!"

"Drat," says Patrick, finally wriggling backwards into an open space, "We'll never hear the end of this."

But then Barry's voice changes and we hear:

"Hey, how do I get out of here?" Patrick and I look at each other and start laughing.

"Hey, I'm stuck, I can't get out this end." Suddenly there's a gap right beside Patrick which wasn't there before and I watch him drop down onto the lawn and follow him, and soon we are standing in front of Barry down at the railings end trying our best not to laugh too much.

"I'm going to kill you two. Get me out of here. You – this is your hedge, how do I get out?"

"I'm sorry I don't know. You see I've never actually been inside the hedge before so I don't know if there is a way out where you are. Sorry!"

"Right, you're dead. As soon as I get out of here you're dead."

"I think you're safe Karl," says Patrick. "He's going to be in there all day, maybe even all night too."

"I think you should turn around and come back to where we got out," I say, trying to be helpful, and we guide him back out.

"Piece of cake. I knew I'd win," says Barry when he's finally out of the hedge. "Right, in future the game is you have to touch the

13

railings and then get back again to where we started, right? It's both ways, there and back again. That'll be much better." Then he starts laughing and pointing at me. I'm wondering what I've done now. Then Patrick looks at me and starts laughing too.

"What?" I say, "What's so funny?"

"Don't tell him," says Barry but Patrick ignores him and says:

"You look like you've got a bird's nest on your head."

I feel my head and sure enough there's a load of twigs and stuff stuck to the top of it worse luck. I bend over and shake it off and Patrick gives me a hand.

"Right," says Barry when he's finished laughing at me, "Now how'd you like to see a rat?"

"A rat?"

"Yeah, a rat, you've heard of rats, haven't you? There's a nest of them, five or six, maybe even a hundred. They're at the end of our garden, come on I'll show you."

"They're really only mice, they're too small to be rats," says Patrick.

"They are so rats," says Barry, "They're just small coz they haven't grown up yet."

Patrick gives me that funny "my brother's crazy" smile again and we set off across the lawn to the front gate where the removal men are still unloading all our stuff. Before we reach it I realise I can't go out, I'm never let leave home without asking Mummy first.

"Wait a minute. I forgot something. I have to go inside."

"What?"

"I'll be back in a minute." I do not want to lose my two new friends or to let Barry see what a baby I am not being allowed to go anywhere on my own, so I dash into the house and run round all the empty rooms and pieces of furniture left in odd spots till I find Mummy upstairs in what I think is going to be their new bedroom.

"Mummy, I just met two boys from our road, can I go over to their house to play please?"

"Two blond boys, one a couple of years older than the other?"

"That's amazing, how did you know that?"

"I was in the front room and I saw the three of you in the hedge."

"Oh, sorry, you don't mind, do you?"

"Where are they now? Where do they live?"

"They live … across the road I think, and they're at the gate."

"Well, let's meet them then, shall we?" And she takes my hand which I just remember to shake off as we go out the front door and I see the two brothers swinging on our gate.

Mummy smiles her beautiful smile at them. "Hello boys, nice to meet you, but you really must be careful not to swing on gates that have spikey railings on top. It's very dangerous. You see you could get one of those spikes right through your eye and it would go all the way into your brain and come out the other side of your skull and you wouldn't want that to happen, would you?" Mum's friendly warning makes both boys immediately jump down off the gate and stare at her in horror.

"I'm Mrs Jones, who are you two and where do you live?"

"We live in Number 33 over there, I'm Barry Blaney and this is my little brother Patrick."

"We're brothers," says Patrick.

"How nice, are you going to be friends?"

"Oh yes please Mrs Jones," Patrick looks like he wants to give my Mum a hug.

"I saw you climbing through the hedge, was that your idea Barry?" Barry doesn't look so sure if it was his idea after all and says nothing.

"Yes that was his idea," Patrick helps out. Barry glares at him and I can see him mouthing the words, "You're dead."

"Well I don't mind, I suppose it'll get some wear over the coming years, that's only to be expected, but just don't tear your clothes or get too many scratches or I'll have your mother coming over and complaining to me, all right?"

When she says this I can see Patrick's eyes opening ever wider. He looks like he wants to swallow her with his eyes.

15

"What are you going to do now?" asks Mum, "Are you going to your house?"

"Yes please Mrs Jones," says Patrick again. "We live just over there, in Number 33."

"Yes, very nice, just make sure you are home by six o'clock for your tea, Karl. Barry, please tell your mother that Karl has to go home at six o'clock."

"Yes Mrs Jones, I'll be sure to tell her. Thanks Mrs Jones."

"Thanks Mrs Jones," says Patrick and this time he really does give Mum a hug, and boy is she surprised.

"Thanks Mum, see you later," I say. As we go Barry is still talking about the race through the hedge.

"That was cool, that race, I can't wait to do it again, that's a pretty cool hedge. Of course it's not as big as our hedge but then you can't climb through ours so it's not much use. That's where the Mullens live." His voice drops to a hoarse whisper as he points to the house on our left. "That's their house, 32, funny thing is they used to live in our house and they just moved next door and sold our house to us and we moved in to 33."

"Why did they do that?" I ask.

"They wanted a bigger house, my Dad said. They have five children, our house is only big enough for about three: me, Patrick and little Richie."

"Is our house a three-children house and their house is a five-children house?"

"Don't be stupid, it's how many beds the house has so everyone gets their own bed."

"Oh ... I still don't understand ..."

We walk around the side of the house and down the path in the middle of the grass to the back wall where there is stacked a huge pile of firewood.

"You have to be really quiet," says Barry. "It's hard to see but they're in there at the back. You can just about see them moving sometimes."

I look in where he shows me but all I can see is bits of dead tree and wood and strawey stuff.

"Can you see them?"

"Not really."

"There's nothing in there but woodlouses," says Patrick. "One of them's my pet, I call him Woody."

"My brother's the only person in the world with a pet woodlouse. Look, show me, out of the way!"

I pull back to let Barry take a peek and Patrick is there pointing his finger at the side of his head and rolling his eyes wildly. I can't help laughing.

"What are you two laughing at? They are there, I've seen them millions of times."

"Millions of times? Really!" says Patrick, still smiling at me.

"Look – you – what's your name?"

"Karl."

"OK, Karl, you pull a couple of these logs out and we'll be able to see in ok." He points at a log sticking out so I give it a tug and immediately the whole pile comes collapsing down at our feet like an avalanche, we have to jump back to avoid getting our shins whacked.

"What did you do that for?" Barry shouts.

"You told me to!"

"I didn't tell you to knock down the whole pile of logs, did I? You're going to get into real trouble with my Dad when he gets home."

"No he's not," says Patrick. "Don't worry," he adds to me, "I'll tell Dad it was Barry's fault."

"C'mon let's go upstairs," says Barry.

We follow him into the house where we meet their mother in the kitchen making tea. She really is pretty.

"Hi boys, who is this? Have you made a new friend?"

"Oh this is Karl, he's just moving in across the road."

"Oh really? How nice. Into that beautiful house, number 14! Well, it's lovely to meet you Karl, I hope we'll all be great friends." I

17

sort of stare at her a bit and mumble something and then stare a bit more, her prettiness making me feel stupid.

"We're going upstairs," says Barry, "He has to be home at six." And we go out of the kitchen and into the back of the hall. Their house is smaller than ours as it's stuck onto the house next door, I think they call it semi-attached. But it goes back a lot and the boys have a big bedroom at the side with a window looking over the driveway and the fence and the hedge between them and the house next door, where the Mullens live, and straight into one of the bedrooms at the side of that house. When we enter the room I am stabbed with jealousy at the sight of a pair of bunk beds. They even have a ladder at the side up to the top bunk. We have our own room each, me and George, with old beds made of some dark wood not like these bright shiny bunks. Also they have posters all over the walls which we're not allowed – Tom and Jerry, and a big rocket taking off, and some gorillas; all we have is some old dusty pictures of bogs and mountains. The first thing Barry does is to go over to the window and pull the curtains. There's a kind of seat under the window and shelves on either side covered with lots of toys and games, and a big box under it that's filled with more toys and games.

"Don't want them looking in," he says, "Do you want to play a game?"

"OK."

"Cluedo or Monopoly?"

"What's Cluedo?"

"You don't know Cluedo?"

"No, but I know Monopoly. We play that …"

"Monopoly's for kids, it's boring. Let's play Cluedo. Have you ever been murdered?"

"I don't think so …"

"Right then, it's about time you were."

So he takes down a box from one of the shelves and I can't believe how many games they have, including lots I've never even seen before. Then we sit on the floor and start playing Cluedo and it's the best game I've ever played in my life, it's got all these people like

18

Colonel Mustard he's yellow and Mrs Peacock she's blue and Miss Scarlett she's red and there's a big house with a library and a ballroom and someone gets murdered and you have to find out who did it the little rooms are so nice just like a real house you can see every bit of the room only flatter until you get inside them there's a door and a window and a picture hanging on the wall and when I go through this door I'm in the library that's my favourite room all the books on the bookshelves they're tiny but real I can take them down like this one is some poetry book by John Keats there's a picture of him inside he looks nice and that one is a big atlas like the one in school only bigger and there's lovely furniture in here a really old sofa with curvy ends and carved wood everywhere but it's not that comfy to sit on but this other one is it's a little armchair just my size not like the ones at home in the drawing room they're too big for me I can't bend my knees and that looks like Colonel Mustard in the uniform coming in the door and he's got something in his hand oh no I think it's a gun and he's – I don't believe it he just tried to shoot me with the gun in the library – luckily he missed and the bullet went up into one of the books on the shelf behind me I better get out of here he's aiming at me again I'll hide behind the armchair there's a door over there if I run for it I might make it – now! – he's shooting at me again but I'm out and into the next room it's the ballroom and there's someone else here a woman in a purple long dress that must be Miss Scarlet she looks beautiful and she's calling me over what will I do? now she's coming over to me holding out her left hand her right one is behind her back she's trying to take my hand what's she got in the other one it's a knife she's trying to stab me with the dagger in the ballroom I pull my hand out of hers and run and she's after me but I get away out the doors and I'm back in the corridor between the rooms it's really dark here and I don't know which way to go there's someone else down at the other end of the corridor I can't see who it is but it's someone big a man I think it's the Reverend Plum because I can see the white bit on the front of his collar even though the rest of him is all in black what's he got in his hand it looks like the rope oh no he's going to strangle me with the rope in the - he's coming at me I better get into this room here and hide where am I now it must be the billiards room there's a big table with a green surface I've never seen a billiards table before but it's got lots of different coloured balls on it there's lots of red ones but only one of each of the other colours blue and pink and – oh-oh – there's someone coming in the door opening it ever so slowly I better hide underneath the table maybe they won't see me down here and they'll go away but they're -

"Why can't you leave them alone?" says Patrick as Barry goes over to the curtains again.

"Just making sure,"

"What's he doing?" I whisper to Patrick.

"I told you, I don't want them looking in."

"Who?"

"The Mullens. All those girls." He sounds like he doesn't like girls much. "There's four of them, including the little baby."

"C'mon!" pleads Patrick, "we have to finish the game before Karl has to go home at six o'clock for his tea, what time is it now?"

"There's a clock on the wall."

"Karl, can you tell me the time please? I'm still learning. I can tell what the big hand and the little hand are for and when it's something o'clock or half past, but I don't know the rest."

I look at the clock on the wall beside the poster of Tom and Jerry.

"It's a quarter past five, we've got another three quarters of an hour."

"Oh great! How long is that?"

"Long enough to finish the game if Barry can stop messing with the curtains. Come on it's your turn."

Then something silly happens to me worse luck. Waiting for Barry to play again I put Colonel Mustard in my mouth to see if he tastes of mustard, then Barry shouts, "Come here quick, look at this!" and me and Patrick jump up and run to the window saying, "What? What?" When we get there Barry just says, "Oh nothing I thought

20

they were there" but when I get back to the board I can't find Colonel Mustard.

"Where's your piece?" asks Barry. "Where's Colonel Mustard?" Then I realise I must have swallowed it when I jumped up to go to the window.

"I don't know," I say, feeling like I'm going to get sick. So we spend ages looking for Colonel Mustard and I have to pretend to look even though I know he's in my tummy making me feel sick. Then the boys' mother calls up the stairs:

"It's nearly six o'clock boys, Karl has to go home now."

When I leave they're still looking really puzzled and trying to find where Colonel Mustard has gone to so I just say "Bye" and run downstairs. I pass Mrs Blaney in the kitchen and say, "Thank you for having me to play, Mrs Blaney," as I have been taught to do. She turns from the cooker and says, "Why, you are welcome Karl, thank you for coming. I hope we'll see plenty more of you in the future. Wait, I'd better see you across the road." She takes off her apron and hangs it on the back of the door and we walk through the little playroom where the boys' little brother is lying in his cot, and out the back door. On the side passage Mrs Blaney puts out her hand for me to take which I do and it feels really soft. Her shoes and fingernails are pink like the pink of Liquorice Allsorts, the square ones with different layers you can peel off, or the ones like a wheel with the pink on the outside - that pink.

"You've got really soft hands," I say to her, "And I love your nails."

She bursts out laughing, a sound like a bicycle bell ringing, and she looks down at me.

"Oh I think we're going to like having you as a neighbour," she says and she's still smiling a pretty smile.

"Good, me too," I reply happily.

When we get to the gate we see my Mum outside our house just across the road and a little bit up to the right. She's standing on the footpath looking left and right like mad and waving at me to cross the road. There isn't a car in sight. When I run up to her she gives me a

21

big hug which squashes my head against her tummy, I love when she does that. Mrs Blaney comes over the road after me and I go into the house leaving the two Mummies talking. I can't hear what they're saying but I suppose they're asking each other their names and where they live and how old they are and stuff like that.

"We have to go out for tea as there's nothing to eat in our new house and anyway we can't find any pots or pans to cook in even if we had any food. Would you like that?" Mum asks when she comes back inside.

"Oh yes please. It's like when Winnie the Pooh couldn't find any honey to eat isn't it? Where will we go?"

"We'll have to find somewhere."

"Somewhere new?"

"Probably."

"Wow! Brill!"

After Dad and George have come home we all get into Dad's car and drive somewhere to a restaurant and after dinner when I'm licking my vanilla ice-cream because if I eat it too quick my brain turns to ice Mum says, "Karl had a big adventure this afternoon while you two were out. Do you want to tell us all about it?"

"All right, but there's not that much to tell. I just met a couple of boys and we had a race through the hedge and then we went to their house and we looked at a rats' nest but Patrick says it's only mice and anyway we couldn't see any but Patrick's got a pet woodlouse called Woody then we went upstairs and played in their bedroom they've got bunk beds with a real ladder going up and we played a really cool game called Cluedo why don't we have Cluedo it's a great game you can get murdered or murder someone else with a knife or a rope or a candle-stick and I was nearly shot by Colonel Mustard and stabbed by Miss Scarlet."

"Sounds dangerous," says Dad, but he's only joking.

"And the Mullens live next door and you can see into the girls' bedroom so Barry pulled the curtains."

"Good idea," says Dad.

"Next time I'm coming." says my brother George.

****

The new church is really big much bigger than our last one it's like a giant underground cave it's so big the ceiling is miles above my head and there's so many people I can't see the altar or the priest all I can see is the people in front and some statues of saints halfway up the walls in mini-caves so I'm just sitting here looking at the people in front of me there's a woman with nice long hair but I can't see her face she has a son of about three who keeps turning around and making faces and sticking his tongue out at me he's annoying me so much I stick my tongue out at him to make him stop and just then Mum sees me worse luck. Mum and Dad went into the bench first and then me and then George we're on the right side of the church on the other side there's someone looking at us a girl no two girls now they're smiling I look down at my prayer book and nudge George.

"Don't look, but over there," I whisper, "There's two girls looking at us."

"Where?" he says too loud and looks around everywhere.

"Don't look!" I shout-whisper. Too late.

"Stop talking you two. And stop looking around." Mum warns us. "You're making a show of us."

After Mass we're standing around because Mum and Dad have met some people and then suddenly the two girls are there again. They're with the grown-ups Mum and Dad are talking to. And then there's a boy and a younger girl and the mother's holding a baby.

"That would be lovely," Mum is saying. "Wouldn't you like that George and Karl?"

"What?" we both ask together as we hadn't been listening. They tell us it's rude to listen to other people's conversations.

"A party. Next Sunday," says Mum. "These are the Mullens and they've invited you both to a party next Sunday in their house for their daughter's birthday."

"Everybody will be there," says this woman, Mrs Mullen I suppose. "All the boys and girls on the road, and that way you can get to know everybody at the same time. But first here's our lot. That's Kieran - he must be your age I'd say," she says to me, "He's seven, how old are you?"

"I'm seven too," I reply wishing I was a lot older. Then she asks me when my birthday is, and when I tell her she starts screeching like a lunatic.

"Oh that's hilarious," she screeches, "You're one day younger than Kieran and you look so alike - same height, same ears, same hair, same Clarks sandals!" Kieran and me eye each other up. He has green eyes and a freckly face and very short, tousled hair which sticks up in the front. I think he looks nothing like me, and I'm about to say so but I don't get time, one day older than me oh Lord!

"So you'll be great friends. Then there's the girls, Yvonne and Zoe, they're nine and seven - oh Zoe's going to be eight next week, hence the party on Sunday. And Rebecca's five."

"Happy Birthday," says George with a strange look on his face. Yvonne's got really dark blue eyes almost purple, the colour of violets, and Zoe's got eyes like those really big flowers called sunflowers. I know all my flowers because Mum taught me all their names in the garden of the old house. Both girls are wearing white stockings and shiny black shoes. I can't stop looking at Zoe's eyes I've never seen such beautiful eyes in my life and I can't stop looking at them they're so beautiful I think they're the most – then George gives me a dig.

"Well thank you very much, nice meeting you, say goodbye boys," Trust Dad to get us out of it. He hates standing around talking to people nearly as much as I do.

"Bye, bye," says everyone, "See you on Sunday."

"Bye. Bye, thank you," we all say and as we leave the girls are giving us these really nice smiles. George doesn't want to leave.

****

The Mullens' back garden is nice and big but not as big as ours and you can't see any houses at the end only really tall trees and there's

24

blue sky and fluffy clouds like marshmallows but I feel so stupid just standing around where's George? Over there with the Mullen girls I wish I could join them but I wouldn't know what to say and I don't want them to think I'm stupid where's Barry and Patrick? Why aren't they here? They must have been invited they only live next door I love Zoe's party frock or whatever it's called and the sun's shining on her hair it's like wavey gold I wish I could see her eyes again but I can't go over.

"Hi. You're one of the new boys aren't you, the Joneses?" This boy is much older, maybe even ten or eleven. He's got big brown glasses which match his brown hair, and a little freckled nose that doesn't seem big enough to hold his glasses up so they keep sliding down. His eyes are grey I think it's hard to see with the reflection on his glasses but they look like little squirrels hopping about. His shoes are those ones called desert boots.

"Hi. I'm Andrew," he says, holding out his hand. After we shake hands which feels a bit odd he pushes his glasses up his nose. "I live up at the top, in one of the newer houses. They were built in the forties you know. Yours is much older. Early 20th century I'd say, Edwardian. My sister's in college studying architecture, that's how I know all this stuff. You were probably wondering."

"Not really."

"Which one are you? Karl or George?"

"I'm Karl."

"I expect you don't know everybody here do you? Would you like me to bring you round, introduce you?"

"Not really, I'd rather just stay here."

"That's all right. Bit shy are you?"

"No I'm not. I just like it here."

"That's all right. Know how it feels. I used to be shy too. You'll get over it. Will I just point everyone out? I know it's frightfully rude but just this once won't matter. Oh by the way that's their poodle Lulu. We've got a poodle too only it's usually purple, she's called Dilly."

"What do you mean it's usually purple?"

25

"After it comes back from the poodle parlour, but the colour wears off after a while. Mum likes purple, it's her favourite colour, sometimes she gets her hair done the same colour as Dilly."

"I see."

"Right. So the Mullens first as it's their house. That's Yvonne and Zoe talking to what looks like your brother - am I correct?"

"Yes. He likes talking to girls. I don't."

"Can't say I blame you. Yvonne's the older one, dark brown hair, a good bit taller, though there's only a year between them. The other one's Zoe - with the auburn hair, but don't say that to her or she'll go mad, she hates people calling her hair auburn. Who else is there? They have a brother called Kieran but I don't see him, he's probably in his bedroom making his Airfix models. He's about your age. I expect you'll be good friends. He's a nice boy, quiet, studious, reads a lot, looks a bit like you actually." Great, thanks, I say to myself.

"Then there's someone you'll want to avoid. Over there but don't look now. What is he up to - no good anyway."

I look over and see an older boy, in behind the raspberry canes in the vegetable plot at the end of the garden.

"Rory O'Connell he's called, watch out, he's trouble. If he eats those raspberries he'll be sorry, definitely not ripe for another couple of months. It's only July after all."

"What's that over there?"

"What's what over where?"

"Behind the vegetable plot, over the wall at the end, with all the trees. And what's the buzzing noise?"

"Oh that's St Marks - the hospital. All the houses on this side of the road back on to the grounds of St Marks. All you'd have to do is climb over any of the back walls and you'd be in, but I know for a fact that no-one is allowed play there. Strictly out of bounds. And the buzzing noise, since you mention it, that would be the melodious sound of chainsaws cutting down trees to make the hospital bigger. That happens a lot."

"Oh, ok, I was just wondering."

26

"Oh-oh, here comes Rory," says Andrew as this big boy comes towards us with a naughty grin on his face.

"Look what I've got," he says to Andrew, opening his hand. "Look - gooseberries. I'm going to put them down the girls' backs."

"You would," says Andrew. "I'm off." And he leaves me with Rory worse luck.

"They're really hairy and horrible, it'll be a scream – ha! - the girls will scream," Rory says and laughs.

Rory is much bigger than me. I don't really like him a lot. He's got greasy hair and torn-at-the-knees-jeans. He's a bit scary looking. His shoes are just a mess, so wrecked I can't even tell what colour they once were brown or black and the way he blinks his eyes reminds me of those things in the zoo called reptiles.

"What do you think?" he asks me.

My brain can't think of anything to say.

"I'd give you some but I don't have that many."

"That's OK."

"Right, here we go. Who's first? Zoe I think, the birthday girl. Zoe's got to be first." And off he goes. I watch him skulk down the garden to where my brother is still talking to Yvonne and Zoe, and a minute later I hear a scream. Zoe's reaching with one hand down the back of her neck and the other one going up from her waist and squirming madly while Rory looks the other way.

"Did you see that?" says a voice behind me, "I'll kill that Rory O'Connell."

I look around and see Mrs Mullen. I thought she was going to go after Rory but she just says, "Take my advice Karl, and don't play with him. Here, come with me and meet Kieran. He's in his bedroom and I can't get him out. Maybe you'll be able to."

Inside, the Mullen's house looks the same as ours, with two rooms on the left and two rooms on the right. But upstairs it's much bigger with more bedrooms and more stairs. Kieran's room is tiny though, with just enough room for his bed, a wardrobe and a bookshelf piled to the ceiling with hundreds of books and magazines. There are about fifty Airfix model airplanes flying around the ceiling.

They're not really flying, it just looks that way, actually they're hanging on pieces of string.

Kieran is sitting on the floor putting something together with a Meccano set. He's wearing shorts and his shoes are brown leather ones but the laces aren't tied properly and one of them has a black knot.

"Kieran, stop that a minute and say hello to Karl."

"Hello," he says without looking up. All I can see of him is the top of his head.

"Well if you're going to be so unsociable and insist on staying in your bedroom when everybody is having a great time out in the garden, at least be friendly to Karl."

"All right." This time he looks up and I see his green eyes again. His eyes are like ... actually they are just like Rory's gooseberries.

"What are you making?" I ask helpfully, looking at the tangle of tin in front of him.

"It's a nuclear-powered submarine."

"That's nice."

"Well I'll leave you two to get to know each other," says Mrs Mullen. "Come down for food in about half an hour."

"That looks really interesting," I say as Kieran goes on with his kit-making.

"It's a Dreadnought."

"Great. What are all those planes up there?"

"Well that one's a Spitfire, that's a Hurricane, that's a Messerschmidt 262, that's a Lancaster bomber, that's another bomber but a Wellington, that's another Spitfire, that's a Hurricane, that's a Bristol Blenheim and that's a Stuka German Dive Bomber."

"Lovely."

As he has gone back to putting lengths of tin together with a little spanner and tiny nuts and bolts, I turn to his bookshelf and see if I can pass the time there.

"Don't touch any of those please, you'll only get them out of order. They're all in chronological order going back a whole year."

"They're all in what order?"

"Look." He gets up off the floor and joins me at the shelf. "See - Model Aircraft April 1963 to April 1964. Meccano Monthly September 1963 to May 1964. Then there's the Children's Build-Your-Own-Weekly Encyclopedia. Forty-nine volumes, I've nearly got the full set. And then I have some of my Dad's - Irish Dentistry cause he's a dentist, Nature, Science, and Scientific America - that one comes from America. Oh, and that's a copy of the Irish Medical Journal. What do you get?"

"I get the Dandy and my brother gets the Beano."

Kieran looks at me funny.

"Did you make all these models yourself?" I ask him.

"Of course, but that's just a few of them. I've got hundreds more outside."

"Outside? Where?"

"In the garage of course. Where else? Can't fit anything in here. The girls get all the big bedrooms. I'm going to work on my submarine now, you can watch if you like. But don't touch anything."

"I think I'll go and find my brother."

"OK. Bye."

"Bye."

Back downstairs I find a room with glass doors that lead straight out into the garden without having to go the way we came in through the kitchen and a kind of scullery I think it's called and the side door. Outside I see Barry and Patrick have just arrived. Barry is heading over towards Rory but when Patrick sees me he comes running over.

"Hi," he says. He's got the same yellow jumper on as he had last week but this time it's on the right way round. His hair has been brushed and it's nearly flat and over to one side, though I think it's really dying to stick up.

"What's the party like?" he asks, taking out his purple yo-yo and giving it a twirl. It goes down but it doesn't come back up.

"Don't know really, I've been up in Kieran's room."

"Bet he was making a model - Airfix or Meccano?"

"Meccano. Nuclear submarine."

"That's all he ever does. All his old ones are in there." He jerks his head at the garage beside us. This garage is enormous, it's nearly the whole length of the garden and there are lots of windows in the side. It must fit about ten cars.

"Is that your brother there?" Patrick is pointing down the garden to where George is still talking to the older Mullen girls, what about, I cannot imagine.

"That's him. He likes talking to girls. I don't, do you?"

"No way, except my little cousin Sally, though we don't really talk much. I just tickle her and she laughs."

"Here's the food anyway. Brill!" he adds as he sees Mrs Mullen behind me bringing some paper plates and cups out of the house and putting them on a table Mr Mullen has just put in the middle of the grass.

"It's easier to do it this way," she says, "Yvonne, Zoe, come give me a hand please." The two older girls go inside with their Mum and soon the table is full of food and drinks - sandwiches and buns and sausage rolls and big jugs of ... water and milk!

"Mr Mullen's a dentist," Andrew explains, reappearing at my elbow. "He says all fizzy drinks are bad for children's teeth and Coke can take the rust off a rusty nail."

"That's useful," I say.

Everyone rushes over to the table and we all stand around but George has already started stuffing food into his mouth, I can't look. Rory finds another use for his gooseberries by throwing them into the girl's drinks and splashing them. This is stopped quickly by Mr Mullen giving him a slap on the head.

"That's enough of that," he says crossly. "If you want to stay you can learn to behave yourself. Otherwise you can go home."

We all look at them and at each other and no one talks for a minute. I feel funny inside, a bit sorry for Rory and a bit scared of Mr Mullen.

"Great food," says Andrew, "Thanks very much Mrs Mullen," and everyone starts saying the same thing:
"Thanks very much Mrs Mullen... Thanks very much... Great food... Thanks very... Mrs much... Thanks Mrs... thanks very Mullen... Mullen very much."

And then there's a second's silence and Patrick says on his own, "Thanks very much *Mister* Mullen," and we all laugh.

Then we all go into the kitchen where Mrs Mullen has the cake with eight candles on it and Mr Mullen lights them and Zoe holds her hair back with her hands on both sides of her face and leans over a little to blow out the candles and I can see the candlelight reflected in her sunflower eyes making them shine and glow and the little freckles on her nose are golden and they're alive and dancing in the candlelight and we all cheer and start singing "Happy Birthday" then her mother asks her did she make a wish and I know what I would wish if I could have a wish I'd wish ...

Just one kiss.

The food was yummy but it's finished now so we're all sitting round in a circle in their big playroom Zoe's over there and she's sitting beside Rory worse luck which makes me feel bad in my tummy and the magician is in front of the fireplace and he's dressed in a black suit and he's got a thin moustache it's not real it's only painted on and he's got a black top hat I think it's called like in that film that was on one Sunday afternoon that Mummy liked because she loved the dancing and he has a little round table with stuff on it and a magic wand that he waves and flowers come out the end of it and millions of different coloured hankies come out of his sleeve that keep on coming out for ever and he can make every single animal in the world out of balloons but his best trick is to pull a little white rabbit out of his hat for this he wants a volunteer from the audience that means a helper and we all put our hands up saying "Me, me!" but because I'm in front of him he chooses me so I'm standing here holding the hat and he's waving his magic wand around it a few times saying some magic words but it's not the ones everyone knows like Abracadabra because everyone knows that one and anyone could just say that and make

31

rabbits appear out of hats all over the place no it's real magic words that no-one else can understand and after a minute I can feel a kind of wobbling in the hat and he puts his hand in and pulls out a little white rabbit it's really tiny and I can't believe it and everyone goes, "Aaahh!" and they look at the rabbit and the magician and some of them are looking at me too because I helped do the trick didn't I Mummy and wasn't that amazing Mummy?"

"Yes dear, that was amazing." says Mummy, tucking me into bed.

"And I really helped the magician pull the rabbit out of the top hat didn't I Mummy?"

"Yes you did darling."

"And it wasn't my fault the rabbit did a poo in the magician's hat, was it Mummy?"

"No lovey, it wasn't your fault."

"I want to be a magician too when I grow up."

"That will be nice," says Mummy kissing me and turning out the light.

Billy will help me become a magician if I ask her because she can help me do anything she usually just comes during the day but tonight I know she's here and I ask her to make me able to do magic and I'm not scared of the cold dark bits down at the end of the bed usually I'm afraid to put my feet all the way down to the bottom because I think sometimes there must be something down there in the corners where it's really cold and dark something like a snake or a small dinosaur that bites your toes or a cold hand that would grab your foot and pull you all the way down to the end of the bed and even further and then down through the underneath of the bed to places where it's even darker and colder that you can't ever escape from but I'm not scared tonight. Not when Billy's here.

****

I like baths because the water's nice and hot but not too hot or it will burn you and I'd maybe even boil like an egg so Mummy's testing the water with her elbow before I get in she does it with her elbow because it's pointy and she can just tip the water and the pointy bit tells her how hot it is when she runs the bath that means turning on the tap and filling the bath it doesn't really run anywhere that's just a joke the bathroom fills with steamy clouds the steam disappears the ceiling and you can't see anything in the mirror it's all fogged up and now I'm getting in the bath the water's boiling I can't get down into it only one little bit at a time till I get used to it and even then it almost hurts it's so hot but after a while now it's lovely and I'm just lying here and it feels like I'm dissolving that's like when you have a cold and have to take the fizzy medicine it dissolves in the water I feel like that like my body isn't there any more I'm just part of the water and all I have is a head and what's inside my head that's me because I'm inside my head and the rest of me is just my body and if I lie really still and don't move for ages the water goes calm like a pond and I can see the reflection of the taps in the water near my toes left is Hot and right is Cold it's written on them but if I move a muscle even just one little toe it makes a ripple and the ripples are coming up towards my face like little baby waves and I can count them as they come one mini wave every time I move a toe I like when I've been in for a while the water gets not so hot so Mummy turns on the hot tap again and I pull up my legs and then I swirl the water round and round me until the water behind me gets hotter because that's the coldest bit I've got a brown spot on the side of my hip just there and it's really big nearly a quarter of an inch I measured it with my ruler but it's all right no-one can see it even when I've got my togs on so no-one in the whole world knows it's there except me and Mum I can lie flat out in the bath because I'm so small and even spin around and pretend to swim when I close my eyes I can put them under the water to rinse my hair after Mummy washes it and I don't get soap or water in my eyes but I have to close them as tight as I can like making a fist with my eyes Mummy's going to wash my hair now with the shampoo that smells like apples I wonder how they get the apples inside the bottle they must have to shove them really hard or maybe they use apple juice she's got her sleeves rolled up and she squeezes some shampoo onto her hand and now she's rubbing it into my hair and she says:

"Sit still can't you?" But I can't because she's rubbing too hard she's pushing me around and I keep sliding on the bottom of the bath because it's really slippery and now she's pushed me right down and I slide down to the end of the bath with my feet up in the air and my head goes under the water and for a moment I think I'm in my dream the bad one I keep having where I'm under the water in the swimming pool and I'm trying to get to the surface but I can't and I'm running out of breath and I'm sure I'm going to drown though I always wake up before I drown but this time Mummy pulls me straight out of the water and I can breathe again.

"Sorry!" she says and pulls me up and even though I want to cry I don't because I know Mummy didn't mean it it was just an accident she didn't do it on purpose and her eyes are happy. Mummy's eyes are the bluest blue ever, light blue like the summer sky on a really sunny day.

"At least that's got your hair rinsed," she says and we have a laugh together which is nice.

"Can I play now?" I ask her and she always lets me play with my boats and things I have a little yacht with a sail that really moves from side to side and I can blow it like this and make it go all the way down to the end of the bath but it doesn't come back on its own then I have a dingy my uncle gave me and you blow it up and it floats and I put my soldiers and some animals in it so it's like Noah's Ark only smaller Noah had two of every animal in the world but I've only got a lion a horse an elephant and a giraffe the elephant is like the one in the Zoo and he can float so when I hold him down at the bottom of the water and let him go he bounces out of the water right up in the air like this that's fun but he's fallen overboard and the soldiers have to rescue him because he fell off the Ark after he had a fight with the giraffe and he's the only elephant left in the whole world so if he drowns there'll be no more elephants ever again so this soldier jumps overboard and swims to the elephant and saves him and they pull him back up onto the dingy I mean the Ark and he's saved Mummy's

34

coming back in now to get me out and she's taking the big huge towel off the radiator it's nice and hot and I stand up and she wraps me up in it and lifts me out of the bath while I pull my legs right up and puts me on the bath mat that's the best part then she pulls out the bung from the bung hole I won't let her do that while I'm still in the bath I know I'm not going to go down the bunghole I'm too big but the water goes down so quick in a whirlpool and it makes a scary noise when the last bit goes out. Then she says:

"Hurry up and get dried now I'll be back in a minute." But I don't dry myself I just kneel down on the mat and curl up into a ball with the towel all around me and over my head and it's so warm and cosy in here like this like an eskimo in an igloo because the air in the bathroom is a bit cold and I'm a bit cold too so it's nicer to stay wrapped up like this until Mummy comes back then I'll get dry and into my pyjamas so I'm just going to stay here in my igloo.

When Mummy comes back she says, "Come on now, up!" and lifts me up then she takes my pyjamas off the radiator where she put them to make them nice and warm and rubs me dry and puts on my pyjamas first the bottoms then the top and buttons me up I run into her bedroom and sit on the bed on the lovely white bedspread with the lines like waves on it and a minute later Mummy comes back in to finish drying my hair and cut my toenails she says the best time to cut toenails is after a bath because then they're nice and soft and easy to cut and I don't mind her cutting them any more like I used to because I know it doesn't hurt it just tickles a bit then we go into my room and we kneel down and I say my prayers God bless Mummy and Daddy God bless George and Karl God bless Little Pop Big Pop and Auntie Penny and I have to concentrate really hard and not get distracted if you get distracted when you're saying your prayers and start thinking about something else like what you had for dinner it's a sin and you have to start again then she puts me into bed and the sheets are all fresh and clean and white because it's Saturday night and they're new and the pillow case doesn't even have a wrinkle in it and getting into bed is like lying down in a bed of snowdrops.

****

The sun slinks down behind our house at the end of the afternoon before tea-time and when I stand right here and look up it's hiding behind the chimney and I can look up at it without hurting my eyes but not for long and the sky is all different colours like Smarties no more like Jelly Tots the sun sets further up the road probably in the Blaney's garden that's funny it doesn't really set in their garden or it would be all burnt up and maybe the house too but when you stand on the road or look out from my bedroom window that's where the sun goes down right behind his house over the wall in St Mark's and in the morning it comes up in the wild overgrown garden behind us and so does the moon it sits there in the sky really low down between the houses behind us and when I stand here I can see it through the first apple tree and when I move over here it moves too and I can see it through the third apple tree and when I move back again it moves back again too that's funny that it moves around so much and sometimes the moon is really big like one of those big silver coins that looks like a real money coin but you can take the silver wrapper off and it's chocolate inside Mum must have hung a clothes line between the apple trees once and one end of it hangs down by the first apple tree and there's a kind of loop at the end like a hangman's noose and I can stick my head inside the noose like this and hang on to these two branches and take my feet off the ground like this and all I have to do is let go and I will be hung or hanged which is it and die and then I'd be dead that apple hanging right in front of me has got little freckles on it just like Zoe's little freckles on her nose I don't want to be hanged I better get down.

****

Sometimes I miss my old house it was so big you could get lost in it there was a whole storey we didn't even use storey is a part of a house like a floor like two-storey or three-storey and it's also a story you read in a book like Mummy reads The Wind in the Willows that's

36

what she likes to read best and it's my favourite too I love Ratty and Mole and Mr Toad and she used to read to me in the old house but she doesn't read to me here so much that's why I miss the old house George fell out of the tree in the back garden there and broke his hip so we had to go to the hospital with him and he stayed there for ages and we had to visit him every day in the rain sloshing through the traffic I remember sitting in the back seat of Mum's Mini looking out at the traffic and the rain and there was so much rain on the window-screen I couldn't hardly see hardly anything except the raindrops running races down the glass and I'd give them names like Blobby and Drippy and try to guess which one would win the race but Mummy was scared because the wipers wouldn't work fast enough to clear the rain off the window-screen and she couldn't see out and there was floods on the roads so it was dangerous to drive and our little Mini was so small I thought it was going to float away like a little boat in the flood and we'd have to just sit there while we floated away down the road just the two of us in our little Mini-boat till we reached the river and then we'd float down the river till we floated out to sea that was scary but it was funny too at the same time because we didn't float away at all we just stayed stuck in the traffic looking out at the rain.

****

I can't wait to get to Andrew's Halloween party we're not allowed go to anyone's house who has fireworks because they're too dangerous even if we don't touch them even if we don't go near them because you can never trust fireworks they can just go off any time even in the box they can just explode and kill everyone so we go to Andrew's and his Mum has these things called table fireworks and they're great gas they're tiny mini-fireworks and all they do is make smoke and the odd little bang and stink out the kitchen so we're all sitting round his kitchen table in his little kitchen there's him and George and me and his Mum is lighting all the fireworks there's a mini-volcano which pours out lots of gooey lava and a thing called Flash Gordon which doesn't even flash and a dragon called Puff the Magic Dragon but it's really just a box with a straw with smoke coming out of it and we're let hold little sparklers called Wizard Wands which look great in the dark and tickle our hands and then there's a disgusting big snake though it's more like a worm and it's made from burning something that turns into what looks like a big pile of dog poo and lots of little mini rockets that don't go anywhere they just make a bang when you light the fuse with a match and wait about five minutes we're not allowed light any matches but Mrs O'Brien looks more scared lighting them than we would be my favourite is the Volcano because it makes such a mess when all the lava starts flowing out of it and it looks like it will never stop and Mrs O'Brien is getting really upset and keeps saying "Oh dear oh dear" a lot and me and George can't stop laughing it's a scream then we have to play bob the apple and pass the orange until it's time for tea we all get a slice of Barm Brack though I always call it Barn Brack because I don't know what a Barm is it doesn't make any sense anyway and I don't even like it because of all the raisins and currents and things in it and they all drink tea but I don't like tea actually I hate tea but Mummy says it's not nice to say "hate" so I just have milk and then there's the nonsense about the ring and whoever gets it is going to be married within a year and I get it and they all shout at me "Who are you going to marry?" and I say "Zoe" because I can't think of anyone else and Andrew and George say they're going to tell her and make her give me a kiss I hope they don't but I hope they do too then we dress up and go round the neighbours for sweets and those little oranges there are some houses where the people are really nice and they have big bowls or bags of stuff inside the door on a table or a chair and they give us loads like the old couple at number 26 they're really sweet but some houses you have to avoid like our next-door-neighbour who goes mad if you ring his doorbell and Mummy says we're not to go near him we have to pass his gate to get to Andrew's but that's not really going near him.

****

38

The bin men come on Fridays. They drive really slowly up the road in their little green and yellow truck with the sliding roundy roof that they slide up to put in the rubbish and then slide back down again to keep in the stink and they stop at every house. The men walk up our drives and collect the bin. Some of them put it right up on one shoulder and hold onto it with just one hand and some of them bend over with it on their backs. We stand around outside at the gates and sometimes follow them round and have a chat. Some of them are old and some of them are young but they're all really dirty. Mummy says it's not their fault they're dirty it's because they have to do dirty work. But they all seem happy cept for one who calls us "posh kids" and says "Wharaya lookin at?" when we look at him. We don't mean to be rude it's just that he's interesting looking. He's got a black jacket with shiney bits on the shoulders, his shoes are more like work boots and he's all black from head to toe - except his eyes which are really white and pale blue. They look like a couple of diamonds at the bottom of a coalmine.

"How'd you like to have to do this work?" he asks us as he passes up the Blaney's drive and Barry and Patrick and me are standing at the gate. We just look at him. He looks really cross which makes his face look even dirtier than usual.

"Ya wouldn't would ya?" he says coming back with the bin.

"No sir," I reply because Mummy tells me to always be polite to everyone no matter who they are and Daddy always tells me to call grown-up men "Sir".

"Well make sure yis learns yer books, yer readin and writin so yis don't end up like us."

"Yes sir," I say and one of the other bin men starts laughing.

"Did ya hear what the youngfella says to Jackser? Calls him Sir if you don't mind! Jayses Jackser, that's the first time yiv ever been called Sir in yer life!" And they all start roaring laughing. Barry and Patrick start laughing too but I don't know if everyone's laughing at me or at Jackser the bin man so I join in anyway. Then another bin man gets a brush handle and puts the end of it on Jackser's shoulder and says:

39

"Arise Sir Jackser, you have been knighted!" and everyone laughs again. Even Jackser gives a sort of funny grin. They go off down the road still laughing and me and Barry and Patrick look at each other and we're laughing too.

"That was funny," says Patrick.

"Yeah," I say.

"Jayses Jackser," says Barry and we can't stop laughing.

****

This is the best day of the year we have dinner in the dining room that's at the front of the house and it's where we put the Christmas tree so there's this lovely incredible smell off the tree we decorated it the weekend before the weekend before Christmas Eve we bought it from a place in Rathmines me and Mummy and George and took it home in the boot with a piece of string holding the boot closed so it wouldn't fly open and let the tree fall out then Mum put it in the bucket with the peat briquettes in it to stop it falling over and put wrapping paper round the bucket so it looks nice and not like a dirty old bucket which it is and we all decorated it that night the tree I mean not the bucket even Dad helped he put the star up on the top because he was the only one who could reach but that's all he wanted to do he had to read the paper so then Mum put on the lights because we're not allowed and me and George put on the little horses and the trapeze girls from the circus and the birds with the real tail feathers and the little presents tied up with gold string and the Santas and the glass mirrors with our names on them and then we put on all the balls and the tinsel and other stuff till it was finished and Mum was nearly crying it looked so beautiful she said so I gave her a kiss to make her happy again Grandad is here for dinner we call him Little Pop sometimes because he's Mummy's Dad not Daddy's and Daddy's Dad is bigger so he's Big Pop and he lives in a big house even bigger than ours it's on Ailesbury Road with Auntie Penny and Auntie Rosemary who look after him as well as Bridie the housekeeper Little Pop has a housekeeper too but she went home for Christmas so he was on his own and had no-one to cook his turkey and he didn't know how to cook it himself so he came to us he's really nice but his pipe is very smoky and makes me cough it's really annoying it makes him cough too even worse like he's going to choke and the study fills up with thick smoke when he's in there it's like the house is on fire and we can hardly see the telly there's so much smoke but Mummy says we have to be understanding because he's very old and one day I'll be old too but I don't even know how anyone gets to be that old he must have lived forever and I don't know why he does it smoking the pipe I mean he doesn't even seem to enjoy it himself he's sitting on the other side of the table beside Mum and I'm on this side beside George and Dad is at the top little Pop lives in a bungalow and we visit him a lot Mum and me and George and it's nice he's got a picture on the wall of Mum when she was about two and she's got lovely curly blonde hair it's hard to imagine she was two and then she was three and four and five and then the same age as me and then she grew up and met Dad and got married and George was born and then me all that time she was alive just like I am but I wasn't even born and she never even knew that I would be born and if she hadn't taken the medicine after the other babies died then me and George wouldn't ever have been born and then I wouldn't be alive where would I be if I wasn't alive Kieran says he remembers being in Heaven before he was born and driving around in an ice cream van in God's pocket but I don't remember anything like that at all Little Pop's so old he doesn't have to work anymore his back garden is very small and his house is nice 'cept I don't like if I have to do a poo there because he has funny toilet paper not soft pink paper like ours but hard and crinkly and brown like what Mummy puts on the baking tray before she bakes buns grease proof paper it's called why does he have grease proof paper in the toilet I don't know but he does Mum is carving the turkey and asking us all what we want and there's so much food on our plates even George won't finish it all Daddy is opening a bottle of wine and Mummy gets a glass but Little Pop has milk like me and he makes a joke about us having white wine and Mum and Dad having red wine and George has a Fanta I'm not allowed have Fanta yet I'll just have to wait till I'm older and we'll both have to wait till we're much older for Coke I don't have any of the extra stuff they all have on their plates they call it trimmings but I think that's a silly word I really don't like that word it's a stupid word so all I have is turkey and roast potatoes I eat the potatoes first and then the turkey on its own but it's a bit dry so I have to take a drink of milk with every bite Mum and Dad are talking to Grandad and George just never stops eating so I'm just sitting here looking at the picture of the Jocund Peasants on the opposite wall and the Christmas tree by the window and my candle-house which is nearly halfway burnt down now so I can see the light through the stain-glass windows like in a church and it's so pretty the pictures are all different there's four of them one of Santa one of a snowman and the other two are a Christmas tree and a robin but I like looking at the snowman one best because he's funny looking he has a big red face with red cheeks and a big smile so that side is facing me and I keep thinking he's going to melt when the flame gets near him but he hasn't yet which is nice I'm wearing a funny hat we got in the crackers and so is everyone else they look funny but I don't like mine it keeps falling down over my eyes and I wish I could ask to take it off after turkey we're having Plum Pudding but I don't like plums so me and George are getting ice cream I can't wait but there's so much food still on everyone's plate it'll be ages before they're finished and then they're going to have seconds the robot is cool I've never had a robot before and it walks and makes robot noises and its eyes light up with real little lights because it has batteries inside which make it go my new black shoes are so beautiful exactly what I wanted with the elastic at the sides and the smell off them is so gorgeous I didn't want to wear them this morning they're so perfect so Mum said I could wear my old ones and I lay in bed with one of them on the pillow beside me and the boxing gloves are brill I really love them except George wanted to start a fight right after we went outside and he started hitting me before I was ready that's all I just wasn't ready that's why I started crying he didn't hurt me at all and I won't cry again because I could see Daddy was cross with me for crying but the next time I'll be ready and put my fists up and defend myself and he won't hurt me again they're great the boxing gloves and

42

I'm going to get really good at boxing and no-one will be able to hurt me ever again we opened the presents after Mass before breakfast me and Mum went to the Convent where I will be serving Mass when I'm older and Dad and George went to Rathgar because that's where George serves Mass I don't mind getting up so early because it's Christmas Day and Mass in the Convent is at eight o'clock and it's so cold out and still really dark and it's almost like snow on the walls and the car and the grass but Mum says it isn't real snow just frost when I walk on the frosty grass it makes a scrunchy noise and I can see my footprints where the grass is squashed down flat the moon is there over the houses on the other side of the road and there's a fuzzy ring around it like a sherbet lolly looks when you put it in a glass of Coke you can just see the round lolly through the glass and the Coke is all black around it like the black sky around the moon the boy beside me did that at George's party and it went all fizzy for ages and when he took it out it was nearly all gone and then he drank the Coke but he said it didn't taste too good so I won't ever do it the Convent gates are open and there's the little gate-house and we're driving up the long drive between the trees up to where we park the car and walk along the crunchy gravel to the little front door inside it is really warm and there are lots of candles lighting and the nuns have started singing already and one of them must be playing a little organ the music is so beautiful like a choir of angels we walk up the aisle that's the bit between the benches where you can walk and my shoes make squeaky noises on the wooden floor because it's polished so much it shines and Mummy is going into the front bench on the left I can nearly see some of the nuns from here they're behind bars like a sort of cage and I wonder why and there's a big black curtain on a pole sticking out in front of their cage I think they don't want anyone to see them so I'm trying not to look Mum said they don't want to see anybody from the outside world because they live in a closed order I don't understand what that is but I think if they see you or you see them it's bad luck and when it's time for Communion Mummy goes up to the altar rails they're marble like my marbles but much nicer with little pillars and a white marble step to kneel on and in the middle there's a beautiful brass gate but it looks like gold it's so shiny the gates of heaven are like that too I bet only a million times bigger and covered in pearls too that's why they're called the pearly gates she kneels down on the marble step she's got a little black hat on with some black lace around and her hair is curly and brown under it it looks like Dad's chocolatey chair only nicer and her shiny black shoes with the pointy heels I have to stay sitting here because I haven't made my First Communion yet that'll be next year in Miss Carey's class then I'll be able to receive Communion it's called the Host and the priest puts it on your tongue so you have to stick your tongue out but you're let do that it's not rude and then it melts on your tongue and you're not allowed eat it or chew it or even touch it with your teeth or it's a sin I can't wait I wonder what it tastes like George said it tastes just like turkey and it's really dry too I know I'll cut a piece of my turkey into a round shape like this flatten it down and then pick it up and put it on my tongue and - "

"Karl, what on earth are you doing?"

"Oh nothing really. Just eating my turkey it's really nice thanks Mum. Happy Christmas everyone."

And everyone says Happy Christmas back to me which is nice, best day of the year, it's just the best ever, and the end of the best year ever I love my new house and my new friends are great especially … and maybe next year I'll … you know… Zoe, maybe in

1965

The circus is called Fossett's and it's on in a place called Booterstown which I think is a funny name but no one else does. We're going with the Mullens, and Patrick and Barry and Andrew are coming too. Mum and Mrs Mullen are both driving but we swap cars so me and George and Patrick and Barry and Andrew go in Mrs Mullen's car and Kieran and Yvonne and Zoe go in Mum's car. That's fun because Mrs Mullen calls Patrick Paddywax like the shoe polish but that's Padawax and she keeps saying things like:

"Paddywax you're the smallest so you have to sit on somebody's knee. Karl I want you here in the front beside me." That makes George and Barry cross because they both want to sit in the front and don't want to have Patrick on their knee. So there's a big argument but I say nothing and Mrs Mullen puts me in the front and the three big boys are on the back seat with Patrick bouncing around on top of them. I have to put on my seat belt because I'm in the front and Mrs Mullen shows me how to do it. When she reaches over to get it I can feel her chest against my arm and it's soft and squashy against me and she smells nice.

"Everyone all right in the back?" she asks. "Paddywax, are you all right?"

"Yes thanks Mrs Mullen," Patrick says and then says, "Ow!" when he gets a dig from who do you think Barry. Then we're off.

We arrive at the Circus and park the cars and Mum and Mrs Mullen go to the ticket desk to get tickets then we all go in and I'm sitting between Patrick and George and the girls are together with the two Mums but sometimes I look over to where Zoe is sitting and I can see her face in the half dark of the big tent and her face looks different in the strange circus light I think she's really pretty and she's looking happy and I try to get her to look back at me but she never looks back at me and then George says:

"What are you looking at?"
"Nothing. Just the tent."
"It's not a tent it's a Big Top."
"Big Top, yeah."

So we watch the clowns and the trapeze people and the women on the trapeze are wearing outfits like swim suits but all glittery and really high up at the sides so you can see their hips and their legs are so long and so beautiful it makes me feel funny inside and the jugglers and the horses are cool with the girls standing on their backs as they ride round and round the ring that's amazing but my favourite is the magician when he makes the girl disappear in the Vanishing Cabinet he calls it and then puts her in a box and sticks swords through the box but when he takes her out she's not cut at all not even a scratch and none of the swords went through her even though it really looked like they did then this guy spins plates on top of sticks he's got about twenty going at the same time and he keeps coming back to each one to give it a spin so he keeps them all going forever and they nearly look like they're going to fall off the sticks and just at the very last minute when a plate is wobbling like mad and slowing down and it's just about to fall off the stick and you think it's impossible for the plate to stay on another second then he comes running back to it and gives it another spin and it stays on the stick and goes on spinning again and everybody cheers then there's some tumblers and little men like the Seven Dwarves doing somersaults off see-saws and landing on each other's shoulders and tightrope walkers without a net so high up but they never fall not once and then it's the Intermission that's when they stop and you can get ice cream and popcorn and the two Mums and Andrew because he's the oldest and Yvonne go to queue up and tell the rest of us to stay there and a few minutes later they come back with popcorn and drinks and we all get some and Yvonne gives me mine saying "There you go little Karl" but she's smiling so I don't mind her calling me Little Karl and then we sit eating and drinking and waiting till the second half starts and I say to Patrick.

"You know what?"

"What?"

"This is just the best ever."

"You bet!"

When we come back from the circus the first thing we all try to do is somersaults.

"Are we allowed up here?" I ask because we've never been in the girls' bedroom before we're never even been upstairs in Mullen's before.

"Course we are, why not," says Yvonne, "As long as we all take our shoes off. Anyway, Mum's gone out again and Dad's still at work." She starts taking off her shoes, they're the black lace-up boots that I like, and pretty soon we all have our shoes off in a big pile. It feels really funny but nice having my shoes off in the girls' bedroom. I try to put my shoes beside Zoe's they're the ones with the big rubber soles but then Barry pushes mine out of the way worse luck.

Their bedroom is huge and it's got two beds in it and a chest with drawers beside the window and a big long wardrobe with sliding doors all along the wall where you come in.

"This is perfect for a circus - look," says Kieran and jumps up on one of the beds and does a head-over-heels tumble and lands feet-first on the floor.

"Hey get off my bed," says Yvonne, "You've wrecked it."

"It's not wrecked," says Kieran getting up on it again, "Not yet anyway." And he does another head-over-heels finishing up with his feet neatly on the floor.

"See, I can somersault," he says.

"That's not a somersault," says Barry, "Anyone can do that."

"Like to see you try," says Kieran and Barry pushes him out of the way jumps on the bed and rolls over but when he reaches the end of the bed he doesn't have enough room because he's bigger than Kieran and he ends up falling off the bed and landing on his bum on the floor. We all burst out laughing, even Yvonne who doesn't mind any more about her bed.

"Hey stop laughing, that wasn't funny," Barry says.

47

"Oh yes it was," we all shout and Yvonne gets up on her bed but she's too big and she ends up on her bum on the floor too and we all laugh. Then Zoe's up on her bed and Yvonne's doing it again and pretty soon we've got a pair of lines with Barry Kieran George and Yvonne on her bed and Patrick and me and Zoe on Zoe's which is the one nearest the window. When I do my head-over-heels I end up standing beside the window and I can see my house across the road and up a bit past Rory's and suddenly Zoe is standing right behind me because she was next and:

"Look you can see my house from here," I say, "And that's my bedroom window at the front on the left - see?"

"I know where your bedroom window is," Zoe says and when I look at her she is smiling. Then she takes one step away from me, turns towards the room and does a perfect handstand. She even walks a couple of steps on her hands. I've never seen anything like it in my life.

"All right Zoe, that's enough," says Yvonne. "We all know you can do handstands but can anyone else?" Immediately everyone is on their hands with their feet in the air, it looks like the whole bedroom has been turned upside down and they are all falling from the ceiling. Some of them are trying to do cartwheels but there isn't enough room and everyone keeps bashing into each other.

"How did you learn to walk on your hands?" I ask Zoe.

"Gymnastics of course. I've been going to gymnastics classes for two years."

"I never even knew you could go to gymnastics classes. I must ask Mum to get me into one."

"Do you like gymnastics?"

"I love it."

Have you ever done it?"

"Not really – I mean sort of. We do PE in school."

"So what do you do in PE?"

"Actually all we do is jumping up and down exercises waving our arms and running around the hall carrying a sandbag." Zoe laughs and I add, "But pretty soon we're going to be doing somersaults - they have the mats."

"When it's better weather we can do some in the garden. I can show you how to do handstands."

"Brill," I say and then something gets into me and I have to go and ruin everything by saying "I bet I can do one now" and I suddenly throw myself onto my hands in front of Zoe and kick my feet up in the air. I suppose I was hoping she'd grab my feet and help me do a handstand but instead I accidentally kick her in the face worse luck and I hear this yell and when I get back up on my feet she's holding her nose and Yvonne and George are around her asking is she all right and I'm saying, "What happened?" and I can't believe I've just done that and I ask her is she all right but she doesn't answer she just goes on holding her nose and looking like she's about to cry. I'm so embarrassed I have to get away from her so I grab Patrick and start wrestling with him and everyone joins in except Zoe and pretty soon we all end up in a tangled heap on the floor.

"Vanishing Cabinet!" Kieran suddenly screams and we all look at him as he wriggles out of the pile and stands up. He's pointing to the big wardrobe with the sliding doors.

"See - look, slide the door open and someone goes in, look I'll show you." And he slides open the wardrobe door nearest the end and gets inside and there's a lot of banging and rattling for a minute.

"Now open the door." We can barely hear him but someone slides it open and there's no sign of Kieran until we hear him again.

"See - I've disappeared, vanished into thin air." Then he pokes his head round the opening. "See? Brilliant huh? Wait, I've got an idea." And he runs into his own room next door and comes back with a black stick with white bits of paper sellotaped to the ends.

"Magic wand," he explains. "Now empty all your clothes out of this side of the wardrobe."

"We're not emptying all our clothes out, Mum'll kill us," complains Yvonne.

"Where can we put them?" asks Zoe.

49

"Come on, it'll be fun, here, just leave them on the bed." And Kieran is already grabbing armfuls of clothes and hangers and shoes and piling them on Yvonne's bed. Then we all help and pretty soon the wardrobe is empty and everything is piled on the two beds apart from all the stuff all over the floor.

"Now, I'm the magician and I need an assistant," says Kieran and I wish I'd thought of it it because I really want to be a magician but it was his idea and anyway I've got a better idea that'll be ever more amazing than Kieran's Vanishing Cabinet about putting someone in a box with holes in it and sticking pokers in through the holes so I let him and he's got Patrick and he's whispering to him while we all sit in rows on the two beds on top of the piles of clothes. A minute later they're ready and Kieran says, "Now ladies and gentlemen boys and girls" in a big booming voice just like the man in the real circus with the top hat and funny red suit and shiny leather boots and I have to admit to myself that he's good at this. "Pray pay attention to the most amazing magical vanishing disappearing act you have ever witnessed in your lives. I will put my assistant Patrick here into the Amazing Disappearing Vanishing Cabinet, slide close the door and say the magic words Abracadabra, wave my magic wand and hey presto" - then he slides open the door - "My assistant has completely disappeared." And sure enough there is no sign of Patrick because he's moved down the wardrobe to where the next door is and Kieran rattles his stick against the side and back of the wardrobe just like the guy in the circus and we all pretend to be amazed and impressed and go "Ooooh!" and "Wow-wee!" but we're all looking at each other and smiling like we know he's really not fooling anybody. Then he slides the door shut again.

"And now ladies and gentlemen boys and girls observe very closely now while I will make my assistant reappear again - " and he taps the door and opens it again and we all roar laughing because it is still completely empty. So he looks in and we hear some muttering and Patrick saying "I didn't hear you" and he closes it again, taps it twice really hard with his stick and this time when he opens the door there is Patrick with a silly grin on his face.

"That was deliberate," he says, "The first time I reappeared I was invisible." And we all say "Wow" again and "Amazing" and "That's incredible" even though we know it really wasn't. And then we all take turns being made to disappear and reappear in Kieran's Amazing Disappearing Vanishing Cabinet.

"What else can we do?" Zoe says, "Anybody else got any ideas?"

"Yeah," says George, "Why don't some of us dress up in these clothes and pretend to be clowns?" I can't believe he's just said that because he means the clothes on the beds and they're all girls' clothes but they think it's a good idea and Yvonne grabs me and says:

"Little Karl would make a great clown, come on," and she starts putting her shoes on me a which are too big and baggy trousers and lots of multicoloured stuff and pretty soon I'm dressed head to toe in girls' clothes and then she shouts out:

"Make up! He needs make up!" and they're all screaming laughing and standing me in front of the tall mirror so I can see myself and Yvonne's got her mother's lipstick which she's putting on my nose to make it red and even though I'm struggling and telling them to stop I'm sort of enjoying it so I don't struggle too much and we are all laughing and making so much noise we don't notice the door opening and Mrs Mullen coming in.

"What is going on in here? Oh my goodness what are you doing and who is that? Karl is that you? What are you doing to the poor boy? And why are your clothes out of the wardrobe and all over the place? Right, out - everybody, you Patrick and Barry and George out and go home. Girls you can start tidying up here and get all your clothes back in the wardrobe, I will sort out poor Karl." And she gets some tissues and starts wiping the lipstick off my face and taking off the silly clothes I have on.

"I'm sorry Mrs Mullen, I didn't mean to - "

"Oh it's not your fault at all Karl, it's these two girls letting you all into their room and dressing you up and making such a mess - "

"We were playing Circus, Mum, it was fun!" Zoe says.

"Yeah it was your fault really for bringing them all to it," says Yvonne. "Now they all think they're Circus performers."

"Right that's it Yvonne Mullen, you are in serious trouble, just you wait till your father gets home!"

By now I am out of all the girls' clothes and my face is clean so I pick up my shoes and sneak out the bedroom door behind Mrs Mullen while she's still giving out to the girls and just when I reach the door I turn and say:

"Thanks very much Mrs Mullen," and I'm gone.

****

Opposite my room is the big spare room it's got two old beds in it but no-one ever sleeps there the little spare room is half-way down the stairs at the back beside the bathroom there's five steps down and then a little landing with a little window out to the side of the back garden and a lovely picture of a river and trees beside it on the wall sometimes Mummy sleeps there if Dad is snoring and she can't get to sleep one time when I couldn't sleep I went into Mum and Dad's room and got into Mum's side of the bed then I realised she wasn't there it was only Dad and he was snoring like mad so I couldn't sleep there either so then I went down to the little spare room and got in beside Mum but she said the bed's too small so we both got out and went back up to my room and we both got into my bed which was funny and I said to Mum "I've been in three beds tonight and I still haven't got to sleep" and she stayed there until I fell asleep then she went back to her bed because Dad had stopped snoring then that's what she told me next morning anyway and we had a bit of a laugh together which was nice the big spare room has lots of old dark brown furniture like the two beds and a huge wardrobe that's nearly the size of the whole wall that's where we hide when we're playing hiding games I used to be small enough to fit in the drawers underneath and George used to put me in and push it closed but not the whole way because then I wouldn't be able to breathe and I'd be dead but I don't fit anymore so now I'm standing in the left side because they always look in the right side first because that's nearest the door and Yvonne's on and we're playing Hide and Seek this time because last time it was Sardines and I can hear Yvonne counting really loud down outside the bathroom door so everyone can hear and she's going "Five ten fifteen twenty twenty-five thirty thirty-five forty forty-five fifty" and I've got this funny excited feeling in my tummy like I'm scared but I'm not of course it's just that I'm standing here in the dark waiting to be caught and it's really exciting and I'm smelling the funny smell from the old coats and Mummy's fur coat is in here too and that weird fur thing that's like a scarf with two foxes' heads on it and they're tickling my ear they're furry and tickly but really soft and nice the others are all over the place upstairs I don't know where they are but I know where Zoe is she's in the other side of the wardrobe because I saw her going in and she saw me too and I wanted to go in with her but I didn't dare and now I can hear Yvonne she's finished counting and she's coming up the stairs and now she's coming in the door and I'm holding my breath and I can see just a tiny bit through the crack in the door because if you close it completely you can't get out and Yvonne's there and she's opening the other door and she's found Zoe and Zoe says:

"Aw-oh, why did you have to look in here first?" And Yvonne says:

"Anybody else in there?" And Zoe says:

"No, I looked before I got in my side, it's empty, come on, let's find the others." And then she closes the door on my side so it clicks shut and I want to shout out but I can't because I get a fright and now they've left the room and I can hear them across the hall looking in my room and George's room and they're finding Kieran and Andrew and George why did Zoe say there was no-one else in the wardrobe and shut the door didn't she know I was in here if I'm last to be found I win the game but I don't like being in the complete dark and not able to get out so I don't know if I should call out and get them to let me out or wait and win the game they're sure to come looking for me in the end so I'm standing here in the complete darkness it's so dark I can't even see if my eyes are open or closed and the fur coat beside me is tickly and now it's scary too because there might be something in it or the furry fox heads might still be alive and something is touching my leg it's trying to get a grip on me and I'm trying to open the door now because I think I've had enough of being in the dark wardrobe but it won't open there's a sort of screw and a catch but I can't turn it and the thing gripping my leg won't let go it's like the thing at the bottom of my bed come alive it really exists and it's eating me so I'm trying to shake it off by shaking my leg and there are shoes under my feet and I fall over and try to grab for something I grab the fur coat and scarf and they come right down on top of me and one of the foxes is biting my face I can feel its teeth on my face and it's scratching me and trying to eat my nose and I'm crying now I can't help it I start yelling "Help!" and "Let me out of here!" and stuff and I can hear voices outside and some of them are laughing and I go on yelling "Let me out, let me out" and start banging on the door the other fox head is eating my ear and I can hear George's voice outside saying "Who's in there? I didn't know there was anyone else in the wardrobe" and Yvonne is saying "There can't be, Zoe said it was empty, it must be our imagination."

"That's a pretty loud imagination," says Andrew.

"Or maybe a ghost," says George.

"That's not imagination or a ghost, that's Karl," says Patrick. And then the door opens because Patrick opened it and I'm lying at the bottom of the wardrobe covered in mummy's fur coat and scarf and I have a foot in one of her boots so I jump up and roar like a big grizzly bear with the fur coat covering me and fall out of the wardrobe and Patrick gives a little yelp like a dog but nobody else is scared and Patrick's the only one who laughs.

"Well look who's in here, it's little Karl," says Yvonne. I hate when she calls me that but I like it too which is weird.

"Who would have thought that," Zoe says smiling at me but I don't know if it's a nice smile or not.

"Typical Karl getting locked in the wardrobe - cry baby," says George.

"I wasn't crying!" I shout and I try to explain that someone locked me in I don't want to say I was Zoe but they're leaving the room and no-one's listening.

Andrew picks up the fur coat and puts it back on the hanger in the wardrobe because he's the only one who can reach the hook and the others have gone off but Patrick's still there and he's going "Roar!" like a bear at me and trying to cheer me up and he's funny and nice and so is Andrew but I can't understand why Zoe locked me in the wardrobe and I wish I knew if she did it on purpose.

"Who's on?" We're all back on the little landing. Yvonne 's in the bathroom and I can hear her saying the poem that's on the top of the toilet:

> *"Please remember don't forget*
> *Never leave the bathroom wet, "*

She comes out holding the frame with the picture and poem in it and we all start joining in. I know the poem off my heart so I don't need to look:

> *"Nor leave the soap still in the water*
> *That's a thing we never oughter;*
> *Nor leave the towels about the floor*
> *Nor keep the bath an hour or more*
> *When other folks are wanting one*
> *Please don't forget IT ISN'T DONE!"*

And we all shout the last line and start laughing and I feel better and someone else says again:
"Who's on?"
"Must be Karl, he was last to be found."
"Karl, you're on!"
"Go and count."
"Bet you won't find me."

"Anyone want to hide in the big wardrobe?"

"Better not," said Zoe, "You can easily get locked in there and it's scary in the dark isn't it Karl?" And then Zoe gives me a funny kind of smile and I don't know if she's laughing at me or not. All I know is that the sunflowers in her eyes are dancing and waving at me.

****

There's another thing in the big spare room that I don't like but I can't stop looking at it it's a sort of big dresser with sides on it with mirrors so you can see the side of your head and the back of your head if you swivel the mirrors in a certain way I can look straight ahead and see my face in front of me or now I'm looking in the left side mirror and I can see the right side I think of my head yes if I wink my right eye that's it I can see it but it doesn't look like my left eye like it does in the mirror straight ahead it really looks like my right eye that's cool sort of but the thing I don't like is I can see how short my hair is because Dad always makes me get my hair cut really short sometimes I really hate him for making me get it cut so short he comes with me on a Saturday afternoon to Donnybrook and the barber puts me up on a kind of padded plank he puts across the arms of his chair and he sharpens his long blade on a leather strap that's hanging on the wall and he holds it up and says:

"Will we give ya a shave?" but that's just a joke he's not really going to shave me and I can see him laughing in the mirror behind me but it's not funny and then he asks Dad how much to take off and Dad's telling him to take it all off it's so long but it's not long it's really really short because it's only three or four weeks since it was cut last and the barber says "Right-o" and gets out his buzzy shaver thing and starts at the back of my head I'm sitting here looking at myself in the mirror and I want to cry he's taking so much off even though there's hardly any there to begin with but he's taking it all off anyway and it's falling on the floor to be swept up and thrown in the bin my lovely hair and some is falling on the white sheet he's put around my shoulders and I want to pick it up and take it home and try to stick it

56

back on with glue but I know that's impossible and I know that when I get home I will come in here and stand in front of the three-way mirror and look at myself and hate my hair and hate myself and hate my Dad for making me like this even though I know I really love him because he's my Dad and it's a sin to say you hate your father it's the fourth of the Ten Commandments Honour thy Father and thy Mother but if I ever have any children I'll let them grow their hair really long as long as they like like that boy in Miss Lynch's class he's only five but he's got really long hair like it was never cut and Miss Carey said he looked like a girl but all the girls in my class think he looks gorgeous and say he's so cute there's that spot just in front of my ear my hair should cover it but when the barber cuts it so short there's no hair there to cover it and everyone can see it if my hair was long like that you wouldn't be able to see my ears and the way they stick out and you couldn't see the spot at the side there either if I cover it with my finger it goes away and I look normal but I can't cover my ears or the back of my head where there's no hair except right up at the top and I look like that picture of Hitler I saw on the telly and everybody hates Hitler because he started the War and died in a bunker though at least I don't have a moustache but my hair looks just like his at the back of my head with a cap on that's not my school cap it's more like an army cap like a military cap with a hard black brim but I can't see the front just the back and the side this is a good shot standing up like he is I'm getting him and the street ahead and a bit of the car the bonnet and the Mercedes badge we're on the Rue de l'Opera now that's the Opera House up ahead I wonder has he recognised it yet he knows every major building in Paris studied them all drew them all as a student knows them all inside out, his greatest dream come true he said to me this morning, the greatest day of his life that makes two of us I felt like saying to him I can't believe I'm here with him doing this shooting this film official film-maker to the Third Reich I'll remember this day all my life the 23rd of June 1940 here we are stopping outside the Opera he can't wait to get in and doesn't even wait for the car to stop there he goes up the steps come on quick get him walking in the front entrance up those steps and into the foyer but I don't want to look like Hitler not even from the back but I do and now everybody is going to hate me and it's all my Dad's fault I wish I could stop looking at myself.

****

There are loads of ways to make yourself dizzy you can just hold your arms straight out like an aeroplane and spin round the garden we call that helicopters or if you're sitting in class and you're bored you can move your head round and round like you're doing loop-di-loops with your head and pretty soon the whole class will be spinning round like mad I did that one day and Miss O'Driscoll looked like she was flying all over the ceiling it was hilarious then Dan beside me tried it and got sick all over our desk worse luck. I had to put my hand up and say "Excuse me Miss O'Driscoll but Dan's just been sick" and everyone turned round and stared and some people made "yucky" noises which made Miss O'Driscoll cross and she said "You should have some consideration for others who aren't well" then I had to go downstairs and tell Christie to come up with his bucket and mop and it took ages for him to move all the desks and mop it all up and he kept talking to himself saying things like "I don't know ... kids these days ... gettin' sick ... disgustin' it is ..." then in Senior Infants the boy beside me said something funny and we couldn't stop laughing and even when Miss Lynch caught us and told us to stop we still couldn't stop and we just went on laughing and laughing our heads off and even when she put us outside the door we still couldn't stop laughing like mad it was insane you just can't laugh like that anymore when you get older.

But one thing happened to me in Senior Infants that wasn't funny and I hope it never happens again Miss Lynch asked me where my writing copy was and I'd left it at home so I said my brother had it thinking that would get me off but Miss Lynch said go up and get it from him then and sent me upstairs to Miss Carey's class because that's where George was it was his last year in my school so I'm walking up the stairs and wondering what I'm going to say and how to get out of the mess and wishing I'd just told Miss Lynch the truth that

58

I'd left the copy at home anything would be better than this and what's George going to say anyway he won't have a clue what I'm on about and maybe I should just sneak out of the school and go somewhere and hide but that would only make it worse so I'm knocking on the door and the boy nearest it opens it and looks at me like he knows I'm going to get into trouble and Miss Carey sees me coming in and stops teaching and says "Yes, what is it?" in a real unfriendly voice and she's so big and scary in her green housecoat with the row of biros in the top pocket and some of them are leaking so there's a big red stain like blood just over where I think her heart is so it looks like she's been stabbed through the heart like in Cluedo or that body in the movie that I wasn't supposed to see and I get scared and say the first thing that comes into my head:

"Please Miss Carey, can I borrow a rubber from my brother please?" And she says, "You don't interrupt my class just to borrow a rubber, you could have borrowed one from someone in your own class, go and stand in the corner." And everyone looks at me and some of them laugh and I can see George and he's just looking down at his desk like he doesn't even know me and I have to go and stand in the corner between the old fireplace and the big double doors that have Miss   O'Driscoll's class on the other side and I'm standing here now with my face in the corner and she's going on with her class I don't know how long I'll have to stand here and I don't know how long I've been here already it feels like forever and I don't know if I'm really standing here in the corner of Miss Carey's class now or am I remembering it later this couldn't be happening right now it's not real I must be thinking about it later and remembering it no I'm really here standing in the corner but I can't believe it's real it must have happened earlier or yesterday or to someone else I wish this wasn't happening.

****

I don't often play with Rory any more he seems to have other friends from his school that he goes to play with can't imagine why because my friends on the road are the best friends ever much better than my school friends but we're playing now at the drain just outside his gate and we've pulled it up and inside it's all black it's like looking down into that place where bad people go when they die I'm not supposed to say the word and there's water in it I can see our reflection the drain cover was really heavy when we lifted it up we both had to hold it in both hands and now it's standing up and I hope it doesn't fall Rory has a big long leaf from one of those trees like palm trees you see in films on a desert island I think it came off that one over there in that front garden I don't know who lives in that house beside Mullen's and he's poking it into the drain I'm holding the drain cover up though it can stand up on its own all right so I don't really need to hold it.

"Do you want a go?" he asks me.

"What do I do?"

"Oh just poke it in the water and see how far down it goes, it's fun." I don't really see the point of it but I say "OK" and take the leaf. He takes hold of the drain cover and immediately says:

"That's really heavy." I'm about to tell him he doesn't need to hold it up that it stays up on its own but I think I can see something moving down in the drain and I poke my leaf in as far as it will go.

"I think there's something in here," I say but he's not listening because he's started saying something himself:

"I don't think I can hold it it's too heavy." And suddenly the drain cover is falling down and as soon as I notice it I pull my hand out and I nearly get it out in time but it just grazes the back of my hand as I pull it out and the drain cover slams down on the drain with a huge noise like a big iron gate closing in a prison and I look at my hand and it's a bit grazed and I'm looking at Rory to see did he do it on purpose and his eyes are as black as the water in the drain and I don't know if he did or he didn't and now my hand is beginning to hurt but I'm not going to cry not in front of him so I say:

"I think I better go in and wash my hand in case it gets an infection, hadn't I?"

"Oh it's nothing, it'll be all right. I couldn't hold it any longer it was too heavy for me it slipped out of my hand."

"That's all right, but I think I'll go in and wash my hand anyway. See you round."

"Yeah, see you."

When I go inside and show Mum my hand she says I shouldn't play with Rory any more he's too rough but I tell her it wasn't really his fault the drain cover was too heavy he couldn't hold it any more it slipped out of his hand though I know when I had it it was able to stand up on its own all right so I think he might have been telling a fib.

****

The Mullens call the big room at the back of the house the sunroom because it gets the sun. That means it faces south and the sun shines in all day. They have a door out to the garden from that room, a double glass door with a steel frame and lots of glass above and on both sides. But it's not called a door at all, they call it the French Window. Don't know why, but I remember having this argument with Kieran once.

"Why do you call it a French Window?"

"That's what it's called in France."

"So what? We're not in France, are we?"

"Well it's called a French Window here too."

"It's not a window. A window is something you can open or look through but it's not something you can walk through, so it can't be a window. What you can walk through has to be called a door."

"But it's a French Window, not an ordinary window."

"It's not a window at all - it's a door."

"That's the style of window they have in France, ones you can walk through, they're all like this."

"So you can walk through all the windows in France? They must have a lot of burglaries, you know everyone just walking into people's houses through the windows." I start to laugh but Kieran doesn't think it's funny so I stop.

61

"That's their problem."

"Why not call it a French Door? That would satisfy everyone."

"It wouldn't satisfy the French."

"So what? We're not in France are we? I'm going insane!"

This argument went on for a while and got nowhere. So that's what they call it, the French Window, it's a silly name but it's pretty useful really because if we're in the house and we want to get out into the garden, instead of going round through the kitchen and the scullery where they keep the deep freeze and the washing machine, out the side door and past the garage, we just have to go through the sunroom and out the French Window. To be honest I wish we had one but the back of our house faces the other way, north, and doesn't get any sun, that's why our drawing room is always dark and chilly. I suppose you have to have a sunroom before you can have a French Window.

Anyway we're all there in the sunroom and Yvonne is playing the piano, just messing really she can't play, but I can see the veins on the backs of her hands through the skin and they look nice. Funny thing is, they're blue, so they look like the rivers on the map of Ireland in my school atlas. Zoe is better and gets piano lessons. They play a duet, that thing that every child knows, no one ever teaches us, we just know it. I can play it myself though I've never had a piano lesson, I just know the notes. It goes C, A, F, G in the left hand, and the right hand goes C E G - A C E - F A C - G B D. Over and over again. Then the other half of the duet plays a tune higher up if they know it but it's harder. Then we get bored and go outside.

Most days we play all the time but sometimes we just lie on the grass and look up at the clouds and see what shapes we can see. Barry always sees guitars and the girls always see hairstyles and Andrew sees countries and George and Patrick see animals. I just see what everybody else sees. Kieran doesn't see anything but clouds and likes to tell us about the different types of clouds and their names and then tells us what the weather is going to be like. He says things like:

"The wind has veered round to the south-east today and there is a scattering of cumulonimbus clouds there showing that it will remain fine for the rest of the day and into tomorrow." He sounds like the weatherman on the radio. Then Andrew joins in and says things like:

"Viking Forty, visibility moderate to good, five miles, one hundred and ten millibars rising slowly."

"That's incredible!" I shout, "It's the Shipping Forecast, it's exactly the way they say it on the radio after the news. Dad always makes us be quiet while he listens to this stuff when we're down in the Cottage. Say it again."

So Andrew puts on a really posh radio announcer English accent like on the BBC and says:

"Mizen Head to Slyne Head and the South Irish Sea, fair, three miles, one hundred and five millibars, falling slowly."

"Oh that's brilliant I love that, but what's Slime Head? - it sounds horrible," I say but Andrew doesn't have a chance to answer me because Kieran is getting cross.

"That's all wrong," he says, "It's not Mizen Head to Sline Head and the South Irish Sea. And by the way Karl it's Slyne with an N not Slime with an M."

"I think Slime sounds better," says Patrick, "You know - Slimey sea and slimey fish and eels and things."

"It's nothing to do with slimey sea it's Slyne Head and anyway The South Irish Sea isn't anywhere near Slyne Head. It's Howth Head to Carnsore Point and the South Irish Sea." Kieran's really getting mad now.

"It doesn't really matter Kieran, I was just joking," says Andrew. "It doesn't have to be perfectly correct if it's just a joke."

"Yes it does, it should be right, you can't just make stuff up and say it all wrong. That's stupid."

"The whole thing is stupid if you ask me," says Barry.

"Well no-one's asking you Barry," says Andrew and now he's nearly getting cross which never ever happens so I think we better start something else like ...

"Let's play school – Andrew come on, give us some questions."

"Yeah, yeah," everyone agrees.

"Oh not stupid school again," - except Barry.

"OK. Everyone has seen the letters WC on signs in public places, but does anyone know what they stand for?"

"It's a toilet," says Yvonne.

"That reminds me, I need to go," says Zoe with a little laugh, and she gets up and runs into the house.

"Yes, it is the sign for toilet," says Andrew, "But what do the actual letters stand for?"

Nobody knows so Andrew explains it's Water Closet and when Zoe comes back we all says things like:

"Did you have a nice time in the Water Closet?" and: "Was it wet in there?" and we all laugh but poor Zoe doesn't know what we're on about and gets really embarrassed until Andrew explains. Then he says:

"Now we're going to have some puzzles," and he stands up in front of us as usual like a teacher.

"Oh God," says Barry, "Not this again!"

"Drop dead Barry," says Yvonne. "We all want to play so you can scram if you don't." We all look at each other because Yvonne hardly ever gets cross either and Barry just shuts up.

"Right," says Andrew. "First, who can answer this simple question: which is correct - the yoke of an egg ARE white or the yoke of an egg IS white?"

"That's too easy," Barry scoffs, "It's the yoke of an egg IS white of course. Stupid question."

"Wrong!" says Andrew and Barry stares at him and shouts, "What?"

"The yoke of an egg is *yellow* not *white*!" And we all fall about laughing.

"Next: which is heavier, a ton of feathers or a ton of bricks? George?"

"Eh, a ton of bricks?" George guesses.

64

"Wrong!"

"No I meant to say a ton of feathers, it's a ton of feathers."

"Wrong!" By now everyone has got it and we're all laughing.

"What?"

"They're both the same!" we all shout.

"That's impossible, bricks are heavier than feathers; it must be a ton of bricks."

"Wrong!" everyone shouts and George is getting really upset.

"They both weigh a ton," explains Andrew quietly. "You see?"

"Oh," says George in such a way that for a moment I almost feel sorry for him.

"Next, let me see," says Andrew. "A really hard one for Karl: What gets wet when it dries?"

"A towel?"

"Well done, now Yvonne: Which would you rather – be nearly drowned or nearly saved?

"Nearly saved of course. No wait – that's a trick question, I mean nearly drowned."

"That doesn't make any sense," I complain. "Who'd want to be nearly drowned?"

"No, Yvonne's right," says Andrew, "it is a trick question. If you are nearly drowned you're not actually drowned, but if you're nearly saved that means you're not saved so you are drowned."

"Oh yeah, I get it!" I say.

"I don't get it," says Patrick. "If you're nearly drowned do you drown the next time?"

"Idiot!" says his brother, giving Patrick a thump.

"I'll explain it later," I whisper to him.

"Here's another one, what about this: what's another word for a dirge?"

"A dirge? it's something to do with a funeral I think. Is it a hymn at a funeral?" I read this somewhere.

"Yes, it's a lament," Andrew says. "Anybody know where the word 'posh' comes from? What do the letters stand for?

"Didn't know they stood for anything," Zoe says.

"What's he talking about?" asks Patrick.

"POSH – Port Out Starboard Home," says Andrew, and then he starts going on and on about something to do with sailing on a cruise in the Mediterranean and not wanting to be too hot in your cabin but no one is really listening to him any more we're all just lying on the grass looking up at the clouds and feeling the sun on our faces and the grass tickling our bare legs.

"Let's play Queenie-I-O," says Kieran and we all agree. So we line up at the house end of the garden as usual and George is on because he won the last game and Kieran goes to get a ball but the only one he can find is an old tennis ball that was in the flower bed for ages and it's really mouldy and damp.

"Yeuch," says Yvonne, "I'm not playing with that!"

"Have you not got anything else?" says George.

"*We* have," says Patrick, "Hang on and I'll get one." And he runs down to the end of the garden to where the wall is lowest and climbs over into his garden. A minute later a tennis ball comes flying over the wall and lands in the middle of the grass. It bounces a couple of times and Zoe walks lazily over to pick it up. When she bends over her hair falls down over her face and when she straightens up she puts it behind one ear. She's wearing her jeans with the pockets at the side but none at the back and her red sneakers and she looks so beautiful. She throws the ball over to us and starts doing some handstands and other exercises in the middle of the garden and I can't stop watching her I just love the way her body moves.

"These are my stretching exercises," she says swinging from side to side, "I have to do them for gymnastics."

Now we're all lined up again and George has started with Queenie-I-O but he doesn't say it very well, he says it like he couldn't care less:

"Queenie-I-O who has the ball
Is she big or is he small
Is she fat or is he thin?
Is he like a rolling pin?"

66

He always says it like this I've no clue why.

Yvonne has the ball to start off and she passes it along the line. I'm at the end beside Zoe we're standing right beside each other and when George picks her she passes the ball to me and holds up her hands to show him they're empty. When she gives me the ball her fingers touch mine and it feels really incredible. I look at her but she doesn't look back and now everyone is going wild and shouting and jumping up and down because - yes, I can hear it too, it's Mr Whippy - and everyone knows what to do, the first thing is we need money. The Mullens are running into their house to get some and Patrick is climbing over the wall into his garden and me and George have to run down the side of the Mullen's house, down the drive out the gate across the road and into our house to find Mum and beg her for some money for ice creams.

"Quick, quick, please Mummy, hurry up," we plead as she takes forever fingering the inside of her purse.

"How much do you want?" she asks.

"It's sixpence for a sixty-six and ninepence for a ninety-nine." I say. "That's got a Flake in the top."

"I want a ninety-nine," says George.

"It's rude to say I want," says Mummy and gives us sixpence each.

"Aw!" says George but I just say, "Thanks Mum" and run out the door. It's parked up at the top of the road near Andrew's and I run as fast as I can and there's other children running too and I think I'll never get there but I'm faster than all of them and much faster than George so I'm at the van and in the queue before him.

"A sixty-six please," I say when the ice cream man asks me what I want and he's asking me if I want raspberry ripple on it but I don't but he doesn't hear me and puts in on anyway so I have to lick around it and Patrick's here now but not the Mullens and we walk back down the road together the two of us when he gets his he's got a sixty-six too and we're standing outside my gate and I say: "Here's the Mullens."

"Why aren't you getting ice creams?" I ask them as they come across the road to us.

"Mum's out at work and Bridie won't give us any money," says Yvonne. "She says we got our pocket money on Friday and she can't give us any more."

"But that was a week ago."

"I know. We'll get this week's today when Mum and Dad come home."

"Here, have a lick if you want," I offer and Yvonne and Zoe take turns holding my ice cream to their mouths and licking a little. Zoe looks at me over the ice cream and I can see her sunflower eyes are happy.

"Thanks," they both say. I don't offer any to Kieran but as soon as I get it back from Zoe I lick the exact place where she just licked.

"How much do you get?" asks Patrick but I wouldn't say that because Mummy said once it's rude to ask others how much pocket money they get. They don't seem to mind.

"I get eightpence because I'm eight," says Zoe.

"And I get ninepence because I'm nine." Yvonne makes a face at her younger sister.

"Hang on, does that mean you get sevenpence Kieran?" asks Patrick.

"Patrick is really quick at sums," I say and the others laugh but I didn't mean it to sound mean and Patrick laughs too.

"I'm only six, I wish I was older," Patrick says. "How come I'm always the youngest, it's not fair. Andrew's twice as old as me, he's 12. I would love to be that old."

"Yes, Kieran gets sevenpence, and he never spends a penny of it, just saves it all in that stupid tin money-box of his," says Zoe giving him a dig.

"And he won't ever lend us any not even for an emergency like now when we've no money for ice cream," adds Yvonne.

"I'm saving up for an Airfix model of a destroyer. They're really expensive."

"That's all he ever spends his money on - stupid Airfix models."

"They're not stupid - you take that back!"

"Won't - they are stupid."

"I'm telling Mummy on you."

"Tell away you big baby."

And now Kieran tries to hit his two sisters but they're much too big for him to get anywhere near so he starts kicking them and when he gets a kick on the shins himself he starts crying and turns and runs across the road and into his driveway yelling, "I'm telling on you, just you wait," and stuff. He's really mad.

"You're lucky you don't have a little brother," says Yvonne.

"I *am* a little brother," I remind her.

"Hey - so am I." Patrick remembers.

"I have a little brother," says George arriving with a ninety-nine in one hand and the Flake in the other hand and starts using the flake as a scoop to shovel it into his mouth. "And they're a real pain I can tell you."

"Thanks," I say. "Hey - where'd you get the money for that? Mum only gave us sixpence."

"I found another three pence in my bedroom."

"Huh! Why don't you offer the girls some of your ninety-nine then? They don't have any money to get an ice cream."

"I've hardly any left, I need it all myself." He says, licking like mad to make it disappear quicker. I look at the girls and shrug as if to say I tried and they smile back.

"He needs it all himself," says Yvonne.

"His need is greater than ours," adds Zoe.

"I can see that," I say as we all stare at my brother who's stopped shoveling the ice cream into his mouth and is now sucking it out of the end of the cone.

"You should get your pocket money on a Thursday because Mr Whippy usually comes on a Friday and then you'd still have money to get ice cream," I suggest.

"Good idea. When do you get yours?" Zoe asks me.

"On a Saturday," I say and Patrick starts laughing. Then the two of us can't stop laughing even though it's not really funny and the others are just looking at us. Patrick's laughing so much his ice cream is all over his face.

"See what I mean?" says George. "Kid brothers, huh!"

I look at Patrick and we smile because we don't mind being kid brothers and it makes us feel the same. But then Rory comes out of his gate behind me and just as I'm taking a lick of my 66 he shouts "Watch out Karl there's a wasp on your head" and pretends to slap the back of my head. I duck and stick my face into my ice cream cone worse luck.

Everybody laughs and Patrick says, "You look like a snowman with a carrot nose" and everybody laughs again, even Zoe. Rory just smirks and says, "Must have flown away, lucky you weren't stung" and goes up the road to Mr Whippy. I try licking the ice cream off my face. I don't mind the others laughing at me, I couldn't care less, but why did Zoe have to laugh?

"Your Mum is home," George says, looking down the road to where the Volkswagen Beetle has turned the corner, its orange indicator still sticking out on the left side just under the roof.

"Oh that's really cute," I say to distract attention from my ice-creamed face. "Did you see that? It's got a little orange arm."

"Got a little orange arm!" George snorts. "That's a stupid thing to say."

"No it's not. I think it's cute too," says Zoe and I look at her and we smile which makes me not feel so bad about her laughing at me earlier.

"What little orange arm?" asks Patrick.

"It's the winky-willy," says George. I can't believe George has said this because I'm pretty sure that's just what we call it and not anybody else. My Mum and Dad have a lot of funny words for things that other people don't use, like picture house instead of cinema, silver paper instead of tin foil and windcheater - that means anorak. I've no idea where they get them all, it's like they have their own language that nobody else uses and I have to try really hard not to say any of these words when I'm with other people. But the worst of all is definitely winky-willy.

"What?"

"The winky-willy, that's what it's called."

"I think it's called the indicator," says Yvonne looking at George a bit funny.

"Yeah all right, it's the indicator too, but we call it the winky-willy." I really want to murder him now for embarrassing me so much as the others are all laughing and repeating "winky-willy! winky-willy!" like it's the funniest thing they've ever heard.

"I think that's a good name for it, winky-willy," says Zoe, "I think it's cute."

"Oh you think everything is cute today." Yvonne says.

"What's wrong with that?"

"Your mother's there, I think she wants you," I point to Mrs Mullen at their gate.

"Better go then, see you round." they both say.

"All right, see you round."

"See you square," says Patrick and gives a little laugh.

****

"That's a nasty cold you've got, I hope you'll be better soon."

"Oh I'll be fine by tomorrow, don't worry. Mummy?"

"Yes lovie?"

"Will you be going out soon?"

"Yes, I have to go to the shops, would you like me to get you anything while I'm out? Maybe a comic or two?"

"Oh yes please. Can you get the Beano and the Dandy? Please?"

"Of course I can. Anything else?"

"No that's all – oh can you bring in Dad's radio before you go?"

"Of course, I'll get it now. We have to look after a little chap who's sick don't we?"

"Yes Mummy. Thanks Mummy. I love you."

"I love you too son."

"Mummy?"

"Yes lovey?"

"You won't have to put the nose drops up my nose will you? My nose isn't really blocked, I mean it's not too bad and those nose drops are just the worst thing ever and they don't even make it any better they don't clear it or anything please?"

"No, I don't think so, not this time anyway."

I don't often get sick and I'd never make it up and I don't really like being sick but when I am too sick to go to school it's the most fantastic feeling in the world not having to get up at ten to eight and get dressed and have to go to school on the bus but just be able to stay in bed and go on lying here and then Mum gets the radio and I can listen to Jimmy Young on Radio 1 with his *"Nice cup of tea in the morning and a nice cup of tea with my tea"* and Mum goes out to the shops and comes back with the comics and all I have to do is lie in bed and read them unless I'm really sick then the doctor has to come with his black bag that has his things in it like his something scope I can't pronounce that word that's really cold when he puts it on my chest and listens to my lungs and tells me to cough and then puts it on my back and it's even colder on my back and I have to lean over and pull up my pyjama top for that and he taps my back with his knuckles on his hand why does he do that and then he tells me to stick out my tongue and he puts the flat thing that's like a huge ice-pop stick on it and tells me to say "Aah" that's really funny then he writes out a perscription for Mummy and tells her to give me one three times a day or something and to ring him if I'm not better in a few days but I always am I like the doctor but I don't think I'll need him today it's just a cold and thank God I won't have to have the nose drops they're horrible I have to lie back on the bed with my head falling over the side and Mum sticks the glass tube with the rubber squeezy thing at the end up my nose twice once each side and I nearly feel like I'm drowning with the stuff and it goes right into my head like it's gone inside my brain I can't stand it it makes me want to scream I hope she never ever gives me those again all I've got is a bit of a cold but I can't stop sneezing and blowing my nose it's like my brain is melting and turning to slush so I'm better off in bed I'd only spread it around if I was let up that's what Mummy says at least I don't get asthma like Kieran that must be awful not being able to breathe it's bad enough when it happens in my dreams but to not be able to breathe when you're awake must be awful and then last year all the Mullens got whooping cough I don't even know what that is but they said you can't stop coughing and it's the worst cough ever and it feels like your lungs are going to turn inside out and come out of your body and you make a noise like "Whoop! Whoop! Whoop!" poor Zoe getting that I hope it wasn't too bad maybe she didn't get it too bad please God don't let her get it again and don't let me ever get it when I'm lying here in the daytime I'm never scared of what's at the end of the bed I can even go right down there with my toes so my head is under the blankets and I know there's nothing there sometimes I wonder if I talk to myself too much I wonder does everyone talk to themselves or is it only me? I heard Dad say to Mum once that talking to yourself is the first sign of madness does that mean I'm going mad or was he only joking? the funny thing is when I talk to myself sometimes I say "Me" and sometimes I say "You" like sometimes I might say to myself "Come on you have to hurry up" but sometimes I might say "I have to hurry up" but saying "You" would mean there's one me doing the talking and another me that I'm talking to that would mean there are too me's that can't be right that would definitely mean I'm going mad when I close this eye my left eye I can see the right side of my nose like this and when I close my right eye I can see the left side of my nose that proves that I'm inside my head looking out and the eyes are like windows and if I hold my finger up to my eye I can see through it even though it's still there I can see it and see through it at the same time like it's a ghost finger but if I close one eye it goes solid again and I can make it disappear and reappear again that's weird I'm really going mad but why am I inside this head anyway? Mum says there are two Princes in England nearly the same age as me and George and they live in a castle and a palace called Buckingham Palace I'd love to

73

be a Prince why can't we be the Princes? or why am I me? why am I not George? I'm not saying I want to be George – God no! I wouldn't wish that on anybody – not even George - no I'm just wondering why I'm inside my head and not inside his head or somebody else's like one of the Princes in the Palace I mean I could have been born inside anybody's head but I wasn't I was born inside this one and I'm stuck inside it the round head with the stupid sticky-out ears and the spot in front of the left one I'm definitely going mad I think I'll go stick my head in that noose again oh brill here's Mummy with the comics.

****

"Keep on your own side," says George, giving me a push.

"I can't help it, the seat's so slippery. Put the arm rest down like I said."

"Do put the arm rest down George," says Mum turning around in the front seat.

I love driving in Dad's car sitting in the back seat looking out the window it's an Austin Princess I know because it says Austin on the front and it says Princess on the boot lid - the boot is where we put stuff like suitcases when we go away it's not like a boot that you wear like wellies it's got two colours dark green on the top half and grey on the bottom half and the seats are red leather and on the back of Mummy and Daddy's front seats are two wooden trays that fold down for picnics I love that though we never really use them much 'cept sometimes me and George play cards on them when we're driving along which is fun but the cards keep slipping off onto the carpet I always sit on the right and George always sits on the left no idea why it's just always been like that always the seats are wrinkly and I love the smell especially when I stick my head inside the space where the arm rest comes out of in there it's really dark and the smell of leather is amazing it fills my head like music the only thing I don't like about the seats is that they're slippery so when Dad goes around a corner really fast me and George slide along the back seat and if the arm rest isn't down he'll deliberately slide all the way over to my side and

74

crush me up against the door Mum and Dad have seat-belts in the front but they forgot to put them in the back seats worse luck that's why I keep telling George to put down the arm rest but sometimes he won't but now he's just put it down which is a good job because it's been a long journey on all these twisty windy country roads and we've been sliding all over the place for about two hours so far and we're still not there yet in fact I don't know if we're ever going to get there because no-one seems to know exactly where we are supposed to be going I think I better ask again:

"Where are we going anyway, does anybody know?"

"I told you already three times," says Mum, and it's probably true but anyway, "We're going to look at a cottage."

"Why?"

"Because we might want to buy it if it's nice."

"Why?"

"So we can have a holiday home to go to," says Dad. Well if Dad says it it must be true so I make a face at George who said we were just going for a picnic.

"Really? Our own holiday home?" I can't quite believe it.

"Yes, wouldn't it be lovely?" Mummy turns around and smiles back at us. "This one we're going to now has stunning unobstructed sea views from the front of the property in an easterly direction."

I wonder why she has started speaking so funny and then I see she's reading from a piece of paper she has, it must be one of the sheets the man in the office in Wexford gave her.

"It also has four beds, a living, dining, kitchen and numerous outhouses and stores."

"Where's the bathroom and the toilet?" asks George.

"There aren't any," Dad says, "No running water at all."

"No running water?" I ask, "No bathroom? Does that mean we don't have to wash?"

"Brill," says George, "I love it already."

"You can wash in the sea," says Mum.

"Sure thing," says George.

75

"What if the soap floats away?" I wonder. "We'd never get it back."

"I think it must be down this one, judging by the map," says Dad trying to look at the map and drive at the same time because whenever Mummy looks at the map he tells her she's reading it wrong, upside down or sideways or whatever, and they have a row.

"Couldn't be, it's a dead end," Mum says.

"How do you know?"

"Didn't you see the sign?"

"No I didn't see the sign if there was one which I doubt as I was trying to read the map and drive at the same time. Let's just see how far it goes."

"I'd go back if I were you," says George, "I think Mum's right, I think there was a sign."

"When I need directions from a nine-year-old you will be the first to hear about it George thank you very much." But just as he says this the car skids to a stop and me and George go sliding forwards off the seats and nearly end upon the floor.

"Daa-ad!" says George.

"Sor-ry! Guess what - it's a dead end. Well who'd have thought that?" Mum just looks at him and says nothing.

"So we'll just turn around and go back, no harm done."

"You can't turn around, there isn't enough room, you'll have to reverse," Mum is right as usual, there's a gate in front of us and another one on the left but definitely not enough room to turn. But Dad doesn't like being proved wrong so he gets out of the car and has a look around. Then he calls George.

"George be a good chap and open these two gates so I can turn, then close them behind me."

"Sure thing," says George. That's his latest phrase, he got it from a western we were watching. So he gets out and Dad gets back in but a minute later he's back at Dad's window with a very worried look on his face.

"I'm not opening that gate, there's a bull in the field," he says pointing at the one on the left.

"Oh you saw that did you? No it's not a bull, it's only a cow, quite harmless, now the gates please."

So George opens the two gates and Dad starts to turn the car, driving forwards into the field straight ahead and then reversing into the other one George is in. As we reverse into this field I look out the back window and sure enough there's what looks like a pretty big bull pawing the ground and staring at George as if he'd like to eat him.

"Eh, Mum, Dad, can you see what I see?" They both turn around.

"I think George might be right," says Mum, "That does look rather like a bull."

"George, quick, get into the car!" shouts Dad out the window just as the bull decides to charge.

I open the back door and George comes flying in as the car takes off, its rear wheels skidding madly and churning up the mud in the field trying to get a grip. Some of the mud is splashing the bull in his face which makes him even madder. We make it out the gate, round the corner into the lane and head off at full speed with the blackberry brambles scraping the sides of the car.

"What about the gate?" asks Mum." We can't leave it open."

"What about the bull?" I ask. "We can't leave a bull wandering around."

"Oh I wouldn't worry," says Dad, "He'll probably go back into the field himself."

"And close the gate behind him," Mum adds, and Dad gives her a funny look.

So then Dad stops the car, reverses back to the gate where the bull is standing, maybe he's been trained not to leave his field, and then Dad does something really brave that I'll never forget. He gets out of the car, closes the first gate and walks over to the field with the bull staring at him, closes the gate right in front of the bull's nose, I can even see the ring in it, and gets back into the car. Me and George just look at each other in amazement.

"Wow!" I say.

"Cool," says George.

"You stupid idiot!" says Mum and starts hitting him on the shoulder really hard. "You could have been killed!"

Dad just looks at her with a funny smile on his face then looks at the two of us in the rear-view mirror, gives us a wink and drives off.

Back at the beginning of the lane we notice another lane with another dead end sign on it.

"I think we should have taken this one," says Dad.

"That's a dead end too!!" we all shout.

"Yes, but can't you see the house down at the end? I think that's it. And this one faces the right direction, towards the sea."

This time Dad is right and the third house along this lane turns out to be the one for sale. We stop at a gate and all get out of the car. Inside the gate we can see a run-down cottage with white plaster walls, small windows with lots of tiny little square panes of glass in them, and cute little red barrels at each corner catching the rainwater from the gutters. We have stopped at the back gate and when George and me run round the front we can see the sea right in front of us and a cliff about fifty yards from the house.

"Hey! Mum! Dad! Come round here, look at this!" we shout and a minute later Mum and Dad come round the side of the house and now they're looking at the sea and they've both got these big grins on their faces and they've got their arms around each other and their hair is blowing in the sea-breeze and I've never seen them look so happy together.

"Yes," says Dad, "this is it."

"Oh it is just perfect, absolutely perfect," says Mum and we all just stand there looking at each other while Mum stares out to sea with her blue eyes even bluer than the sea and the sky.

"Come on," shouts George and we go and look in all the windows along the front but can't really see anything inside except some old dirty looking furniture.

"Did he not give you a key?" asks Mum.

"No, he said he didn't have one."

"So how are we going to see inside?"

"I have an idea. I think there was a window open at the back."
So we go back around the side of the house and Dad starts banging at
one of the little square windows. Then he opens it up a bit of the way.

"What use is that? We can't get in through there," says Mum.

"You're right, *we* can't, but I know someone who can," and he
looks down at me.

"Oh no, it's all dark and dirty and scary in there," I say.

"Let me go, I'll go," says George.

"No you're too big, it has to be Karl, come on son, do it for
your old Dad, it won't be so bad."

"For you - really? All right, I'll try."

"Good boy, here I'll give you a push up. When you're inside
go to the back door here and see if you can open it."

"All right." And he gives me a push up and I'm in through the
window.

Inside the house is really dark and smelly and full of cobwebs
I can hardly see where I'm going and I'm really scared it's like being
in a haunted house but I want to do this for Dad so much because I
want him to be pleased with me this room seems to be a bedroom
there's a bed there and a wardrobe against the wall over there and the
door is here into a kind of dining room there's the table that's the front
of the house on the right I can see the sea through the little windows
even though they're so dirty I'm going left and here's the kitchen but
it's not very nice full of junk I don't think Mum'll like it much there's
an old cooker and a sink and some cupboards I think I saw something
moving under the cooker and there's the back door I can hear them
outside but I can't see them the windows are too high and that thing is
moving around again under the cooker it must be a mouse or even a
rat a real one not like Barry and Patrick's but yippee I can see a key in
the back door lock so I'm turning it but it won't turn so I try turning it
the other way but it still won't turn and Mum and Dad are outside
saying "Open the door" and I can hear Dad's getting cross but it's not
my fault the key's too stiff I'm not strong enough to turn it or maybe
it's rusty and stuck in the lock I don't know but that thing is still
moving around under the cooker and now it's come out I don't believe

79

it it's definitely a rat I've got to get out of here and now I'm running out of the kitchen and back through the other room and the bedroom and I'm climbing back out through the window and Mum's there and I'm crying because I'm so scared and so ashamed that I couldn't open the door but it wasn't my fault except it was really and Dad's looking at me the way he does and I can't look at him. So I say quickly, "I'm going back in again" and I jump up on the window-sill and I'm in the window and across the two rooms and at the back door in no time and this time I grab a cloth that's hanging by the sink and wrap it round the key so I can get a better grip and with one big turn it opens and the door creaks open and Mum and Dad are standing there in the sunlight and smiling at me.

"Well done son," says Dad, "I knew you could do it!" And in they come. I go back out into the sunshine and pretty soon they're back out too because it's dark and gloomy in there and there's a rat.

"It'll be fine once we clean it up a bit," says Mum. She's like that, Mum, always looks on the bright side and I'm so proud that I let them in.

****

It's cold here at night in the winter because there's no central heating in the Cottage just fires in the living room and the dining room and this old Kosengas heater in our bedroom that smells but I like the smell it's not like any other smell and it's not like gas on its own which I don't like and if you smell it anywhere you have to tell an adult because it means something is left on and it's going to either blow up and explode or we'll all die from being gassed like in the War there are no curtains on the front windows the ones that look out at the sea only those tiny yellow cotton ones on the back windows that don't keep out the cold on the plastic cord that we pull across and on the front windows all we have is the Venetian blinds I love them I love pulling them up in the morning in the summer when the sun is shining on the sea like the sea's on fire and it's so bright it blinds me I wonder is that why they're called blinds Venetian means they come from

Venice that's a town in Italy where there's no roads or streets only rivers and canals right outside your front door imagine that walking out your front door and you have to get into a boat called a Gondola to go anywhere we'd have to get a boat to school instead of walking wouldn't that be cool but in the winter there's no sun on the sea only rain and cold wind and it blows straight in off the sea it's ferocious Daddy says but I like to lie down behind the bank that used to be another cottage in front of our cottage but it fell down and now it's just a grassy bank with prickly yellow gorse bushes around it and grass growing on the top when I lie down behind the bank I can feel the wind rushing over my head as it blows in off the sea and I can hear it whistling really loud like the kettle we have to boil water for Daddy to wash and shave in and sometimes Mummy washes her hair in the rainwater barrels she says it's soft and good for her hair how can water be soft I mean it's either cold or hot and ice is hard but soft is like a pillow or a cushion or Mummy's cheek when I kiss it that's soft but not water I don't understand that but if Mummy says it it must be true I'm going to go to sleep now so if I stop thinking of stuff and just lie really quiet I'll be asleep in no time did I say my prayers I can't remember do I need to do a wee yes I think so I'll get up and say my prayers and have a wee at the same time because I have to kneel down for the potty it's the easiest way like this just take it out of my pyjamas and point it at the high bit where the handle is because then it doesn't make so much noise and if I hold the potty like this when the bottom fills up it doesn't make splashy noises and splash me the potty is blue and my wee is yellow and when it's in the bottom of the potty it looks green because yellow and blue make green Miss Lynch told us that when we were painting and mixing colours now the potty's safe back under the bed far enough in so no one will kick it and spill it again and I can get back into bed George is still asleep good I didn't wake him or he'd give out and Mummy and Daddy are asleep down the other end of the Cottage they can hear us when we talk because the sound travels along the roof I don't understand how but Mummy comes and tells us to be quiet and go to sleep if we're talking after lights out she's not really cross I know but I think Daddy is and even though he's lying in bed far away I can still feel that he's cross oh no I forgot to say my prayers when I was having the wee I'm not getting out again it's too cold I'll just say them here God bless Mummy and Daddy it's raining really hard now I can hear it battering on the window and on the roof because the roof is made of what's it called car-gated iron I remember that word because it's like a car and a gate when it's raining we can always hear it on the roof so we know when it stops too then it goes all still and quiet the roof used to be thatched years and years ago maybe even a hundred years ago but now it's car-gated iron and inside the cottage you can see the wooden beams going along the ceiling and when I lie in bed in summer I can see faces in the wood some of the faces are scary and some of them are nice it's scarier here in winter because we're so close to the cliff sometimes I think the Cottage will be blown off the cliff right down into the sea every winter the sea eats away a bit more of the cliff and every time we come here the first thing we do is run to the edge to see how much has gone since we were here last sometimes it's only a foot or so that you wouldn't even notice but sometimes it's much more there's a wall on the far side of the grassy bank and there used to be about twenty feet of land there when we came here first Dad says and now there's only about six feet and soon the wall will fall down the cliff and then the grassy bank and then our house and sometimes I lie in bed at night and worry the house is going to fall into the sea if I go to sleep and when we wake up we'll all be in the sea floating around in our beds the wind comes in under the door it's very drafty so we have that big old screen to keep the drafts out but they sneak under it and round it anyway and the wind makes the fire go smoky and the living room fills up with smoke like when Grandpa's smoking his pipe at home only worse and sometimes the rain comes straight down the chimney and lands in the fire and goes hiss hiss when the fire burns the rainwater and makes it into steam tomorrow is New Year's Eve and we are going into Wexford Town to have dinner tomorrow night and we're going to the Talbot Hotel it's really nice there we go to the bathroom before dinner the three of us and have a wee and wash our hands and when we come out there's Mummy in the lobby it's called where they have the big

armchairs and the nice paintings that Mummy likes and now we're
going in for dinner and sitting down at the table and looking at the
menus and I'm going to order steak and chips that's my favourite and
ice cream for dessert and afterwards we're driving home in the dark
with the wind blowing the car around and the rain on the window-
screen with Dad's squeaky wipers trying to clear it away I look at Dad
in front of me but all I can see is the back of his head and his hat and
even when I look in the rear-view mirror I still can't see his eyes I
think it's because I'm too small there are dark hedges and darker fields
flashing by me and hundreds of raindrops landing on the window right
beside me but they don't last long before being blown into long streaks
and blown right away with the wind the sea's on the left on the way
into Wexford that's George's side and you can see it some places if it's
still bright but it's on the right now driving home that's my side and I
can't see it but I can feel it really close beside me it's scary because if
we took a wrong turn we'd drive straight into it and the car would fill
up with water and we'd all drown I like it when there's a moon shining
on the sea in the summer when it's calm but in winter like now there's
no moon only dark clouds and you can't even see the sea but you
know it's there all right even at night and just here near Curracloe
there's only one field between us and the sea it's so close I can hear it
roar all stormy and deep and cold and it feels like it's the sea splashing
over us not the rain it's so heavy and I'm afraid a huge wave is going
to wash over the car and drag us out to sea I wish I was back in the
Cottage we're nearly at Curracloe then it's five minutes to Ballineskar
and then ten minutes to Blackwater when we come home I have to go
out to the barn in the rain to the Elsan to do a poo and the wind is
coming in that hole in the wall where the plaster is falling off and
there's some rain coming through the roof I can see the wooden beams
and in daytime I can see a tiny bit of sky there's my mouse trap in the
corner maybe a shoebox wasn't the best thing to make it out of I still
haven't caught him yet maybe he doesn't like the cheese it's old and
hard now it's really cold out here so I better be as quick as I can I don't
like it here not at night in the winter though it's all right in the summer
and I don't mind the smell of the Elsan it's sort of nice it's like tar kind

of but the toilet paper goes damp and falls apart in the winter and when I'm finished I'll go back inside with the raincoat over my head and wash my hands in the kitchen sink and go straight to bed it's so nice to get into bed after being outside in the stormy night that was a really nice dinner tonight but the rain is still pouring down it's really awful and I'm glad I'm back home and tucked up all cozy and safe in bed and not outside in the storm I like the smell of the gas heater and the sound of the rain on the roof and Mummy's reading a bit more of The Wind in the Willows about the snow and Badger's house under the tree and that's what it feels like here all cozy and warm and safe with the wind howling outside it's like I'm in Badger's house inside the tree and before that she did Incey Wincey Spider for me putting her hand up my back and tickling me because I could hear the water pouring down the drainpipe and into the barrel at the corner of the house and that's what made me think of it tomorrow we are driving home to Dublin it will be New Year's Day and it will be a new year and I'm excited now because I'll see Zoe before we go back to school and I'm definitely going to kiss her this year definitely in

1966

I wake up early because there's a funny light in the room, not like daylight or sunlight, different, a light I've never seen in my bedroom

84

before. I sit up in bed and pull the curtains. The first thing I notice is the roof of the house opposite ours is white instead of red. The sky is also white like a big dirty white sheet and there are big soft flakes appearing out of the white. Our grass is white instead of green and even the road is white instead of black. Everything has gone white as if someone spilt an awful lot of milk all over the place like that time I knocked over the milk bottle at breakfast and Dad got cross.

"I don't believe it!" I whisper to myself and pick up Big Ted.

"Look Big Ted, it's snowing."

Big Ted says, "Wow!"

"Wow is right. Thank you God, thank you Billy." I am up out of bed in a flash and running into George's room next door.

"Look - look - out the window, it's snowing! It's really snowing!"

"Goway, leamealone." George isn't good in the mornings.

"No really - you've got to get up," I tug at his blankets but he just grunts and moans again: "Leamealone! Goway!"

I give up and run into Mum and Dad's bedroom. They're still asleep and I don't want to wake Dad as he doesn't have to go to work today and doesn't like being woken up too early. So I just tiptoe over and touch Mum on the shoulder.

"What is it love? Can you not sleep?"

"No, it's morning and it's snowing. Can I get dressed and go outside?"

"Snowing - it couldn't be, you must be dreaming."

"No it is, really," I whisper, afraid of waking Dad.

"Really? What time is it?"

"Eh - nearly eight." She has a little gold clock on her bedside thingy and the hands are difficult to see as they're all scrolly like old-fashioned writing also it's still dark in their room but as far as I can see it's time we were all up.

"Wait a minute, I'll get up." Mum gets out of bed, grabs her silver-blue dressing-gown that's all padded - 'quilted' she calls it like a quilt - from the back of her door and we both go downstairs holding hands. Her hand is big and warm and ever so soft like a big soft pillow.

We reach the playroom and that has the same strange light in it I never saw before. I look out the window and the same big soft flakes are drifting down and landing on our concrete drive. Just then the big white square boiler starts up with that familiar rumbling sound and the little flame that you can see inside the little window lights up. Mum looks at the clock above it.

"Eight o'clock, is it that time already? Well all right, but wrap up warm. Put on your scarf - and your new gloves - won't you?"

"Yes Mummy, thanks Mummy."

"But only in the garden. Not out on the road. I'll try and get your lazy brother out of bed to join you so you're not on your own."

"That's all right, I don't mind, I'm going to make a snowman."

George's curtains are still pulled so Mummy mustn't have been able to get him to get up I can hear some voices out on the road further down near Mullen's or Blaneys but I'm not going to go even as far as the gate the snow is still falling it'll be here all day and we can go out at ten o'clock as usual the back garden's nicer anyway so big and there's so much snow in it plenty for me to make the biggest snowman ever the way to do it is you have to start with a little snowball like this and then roll it over new fresh snow until it sticks and starts getting bigger and bigger like this Mum and Dad's curtains are still closed too Dad must be still asleep I wonder what Mum's doing is she in bed too or maybe she got up and is having her breakfast that's funny she's having cornflakes and if I open my mouth like this I can have snowflakes when I look up I can see the snowflakes coming straight down at me out of nowhere just out of the whiteness but I can't see where they start they just appear a few feet over my head and there they are then they get bigger and bigger as they get closer it's like travelling through space with the stars coming at you except it's white space not black space and it's never bright out in space always dark and always cold if I was out in space in a rocket I'd be cold and all alone and all the stars would be flying past me and I'd have to fly for ever to get to the end of the universe it's so big and it'd take me for all eternity that's like when you die and you're in heaven and time goes on and on for ever and ever and never stops or if you're bad then you'll go to Hell for all eternity and you'd be burning and suffering with the Devil but I don't want that to happen that's why I say my prayers and try to be good and when I make my First Holy Communion this year I have to go to confession first and tell the priest my sins and he'll give me absolution not a solution that means he absolves me from my sins which means he forgives them then my soul is clean and white just like all this snow or like Mummy's sheets when she washes them and hangs them on the line in the summer only not so big as a sheet there's nothing on the clothes line now except an old rag that Mummy uses for the floor and it looks like ... yes it's completely frozen solid and as hard as a piece of wood that's so funny I'm going to bring it in and show it to Mummy but first I have to finish this snowman one big snowball for his head and another one even bigger for his tummy he doesn't need legs I'll just give him some feet later.

"That's the worst looking snowman I've ever seen." Oh great - George has woken up at last.

"I've never made one before and I can't roll the snowballs any bigger because then they get too heavy to push."

"Here - let me, I can make them much bigger." One good thing about George is he is a lot stronger than me so he's useful like that sometimes. Pretty soon he's rolled the snowballs twice the size I had them and then together we get the littler one on top of the bigger one, put on an old hat that's been in the garage for ever and give him two pieces of coal for eyes, another three bigger ones for buttons on his tummy and a twig off one of the bushes for a mouth. Then I run towards the house.

"Where are you going? We're not finished yet."

"He needs a nose, I'm going to ask Mummy for a carrot." I'm pretty sure that's the best thing to use as I saw it in a picture once. When I get back Yvonne and Zoe are there.

"I like his nose - good carrot," says Yvonne when I stick it on. She's got her Balaclava on, the navy one, and there are bits of her hair

87

sticking out all round her face. She's wearing her blue anorak and she's got her jeans tucked into her wellies.

"What's his name?" asks Zoe. Zoe doesn't have her Balaclava on but instead she has the hood of her anorak up. It's got fur around the edge and she looks like Gerda in the Snow Queen picture book I have and I've never seen her look so beautiful. In fact I've never seen anyone look so beautiful. She's got her wellies on too but only one trouser leg is tucked in, the other must have fallen out. I really want to tuck it in for her.

"It doesn't have a name," George snorts, "It's a snowman."

"He has to have a name. What about Snowy?" she suggests.

"Snowy the snowman, that's ridiculous." George says.

"I think it's a nice name, he's my snowman and I'm going to call him Snowy." I look at Zoe and she gives me a nice smile.

"He's not your snowman, how is he your snowman?" says George.

"I made him."

"You just rolled a couple of snowballs, I turned him into a proper snowman," he argues.

"But I started him, you just made him bigger."

"Karl's right," says Zoe. "You just made him bigger. That's like Bridie saying that Debbie is her baby just because she feeds her and makes her bigger when it's obvious that Debbie is Mum and Dad's baby because they started her."

We all stare at Zoe, not knowing exactly what to say to that. Except George.

"That's the stupidest thing I've ever heard," he says. "Yvonne, is your sister completely nuts?"

"Have you only noticed that now?"

"Wooly gloves are no good in the snow, they get all wet," complains Zoe, ignoring the other two.

"I know," I agree, "Then your fingers get all wet and cold. My hands are freezing. Anybody else out on the road?" I ask to stop me thinking about my cold hands. "Let's go see who else is out."

George and Zoe go on arguing about what to call the snowman as we walk down the side of the house but as soon as we reach the front gate George suddenly shuts up when a snowball comes flying over from the other side of the road and hits him in the face. I want to laugh but another one just misses me by an inch and suddenly we're all shouting and there are snowballs landing all round us.

"It's the Blaneys - "

"And Rory - "

"Take cover - "

"Get some ammunition - "

The four of us duck down behind our front hedge and George and myself start scooping up snow to make snowballs. He's handing his to Yvonne and I'm doing the same for Zoe. Pretty soon we realise this is a big mistake as neither Yvonne not Zoe can throw snowballs for toffee. I mean it's pathetic as Dad says, the boys are on the far side of the road and the snowballs are barely making it over the hedge. They go up in the air for a bit all right but then they fall down and land on the footpath. I think I better do something.

"OK we're going to swap now," I shout. "Yvonne and Zoe, you can make the ammo and me and George are going to throw."

"At last. I thought you'd never take over, my arm's falling off," complains Yvonne.

"Me too," says Zoe.

So they start making the snowballs instead but that's not much better as they're so slow me and George are getting blasted by the guys across the road and we've never got enough ammo to fight back pretty soon they cross the road and they're on top of us and it turns into hand-to-hand combat and then it gets worse the boys are in our garden now and Yvonne and Zoe instead of fighting them suddenly join with them and start rubbing snow into our faces Zoe is on top of me pinning me to the ground with her legs and she's grabbing as much snow as she can and throwing it at me and rubbing it into my face I'm looking up at her and she's laughing like mad and her face looks a bit funny darker sort of because she's facing downwards and her sunflower eyes are darker like they're in a storm and bits of her hair

89

are hanging out of her hood and falling down towards my face a long curling wave of golden auburn hair and suddenly everything in the world changes and I can't see anything except her face and her hair and I can't hear anything except her laughter and the feeling of having her sitting on top of me is amazing but I don't know if she's doing it because she likes me or because she's really fighting me all I know is I don't ever want it to stop I want her to go on sitting on me pushing snow into my face and laughing at me forever then everyone is on top of us and I'm being crushed underneath their bodies till I can hardly breathe I can't even yell out because I've no breath to even speak and I wish they would get off and I'm scared now I might even die and I try to wriggle out but it's impossible Zoe's chest is right on top of my chest and her face is up against mine though it's not her face it's the side of her head with her hood and her hair under it and I could kiss her now but I can only touch her hood and she wouldn't even feel it but I can smell her hair and if it's the last thing I ever smell before I die I will be happy because it's the most beautiful smell I have ever smelled in my whole life though I know I like a lot of smells like the garden swing that we had in the last house and the Christmas tree and marzipan icing and Mum's perfume and the caps in our guns when we're playing cowboys and Indians but this is really the best so I stop wriggling because now I just want to stay here forever with Zoe's body lying on top of mine smelling her bodysmell forever even if I die.

But now it's over and she's getting up and we're all laughing at each other and saying what a great snowball fight that was and the boys are saying how useless me and George were but I couldn't care less I just want to go on feeling what I was feeling when Zoe was on top of me I've no idea what it was but I don't want the feeling to stop but when I look at her she's not even looking at me and I don't know what she's thinking and if she felt anything like I did.

"Thanks Zoe," I say, "You've got snow everywhere, even down my neck." But she doesn't answer.

"The road!" Barry shouts suddenly. "It's really slippery where the cars have been. We can make a slide! Come on!"

Out our gate and onto the road which is mainly white but has two or three dark tracks where a couple of early cars have been up and down already.

"This is good here, outside our house," says Barry.

"No, it's better round the corner," says Kieran. So we're all walking up and down looking at the road for the best place to slide as if we know what we're doing. I think this is funny because we've never been sliding anywhere in our lives. There's ice in the gutters where there's usually rainwater and as I stand on it some of it breaks into a million little pieces like glass and some of it just cracks but won't break because it's so thick and no matter how hard I kick it with the heel of my boots it stays solid. The only other one not interested in finding the best place to slide is my brother. All he seems to want to do is eat snow. You'd think he'd have had enough of that in the snowball fight but not at all. He's going along the wall outside where Coleman used to live before he moved round the corner sliding his gloved hand along it and scooping the snow up into his mouth.

"Having fun there?" asks Yvonne.

"Yeah, it tastes good - snow," he says, what an eejit, I can't believe he's my brother sometimes.

"OK we'll have the slide between our house and the corner," says Barry, "But we start at my gate and we go in that direction. This is the best place to start."

"My brother thinks he knows everything - he's never even seen snow before," Patrick says to me with his usual grin he puts on when talking about Barry.

"I was just thinking that," I agree. "But at least he's not addicted to eating the stuff."

A few minutes later we are all sliding along a stretch of road between Blaney's gate and the corner. We run along for about five giant steps then it's really slippy, slippy enough to get us nearly as far as the corner. Sometimes we fall, sometimes we bump into each other and hang onto each other's scarves or anorak hoods. I try bumping into Zoe a couple of times but it doesn't work so I give it up and just have as much fun as possible. It's the first time we've ever done anything like this on the road and it's incredible. Then I think of Andrew.

"Where's Andrew? Why doesn't someone go up and see if he's in?" Nobody even replies so I go up the road myself amazed at how different and how beautiful every familiar house and tree and car looks with snow on it they look like houses you'd see in a picture on a Christmas card but they're actually on our road everything is the same but different and now I'm at Andrew's house Number 20 and I open the porch sliding door ring on his doorbell but there's no reply maybe he's still in bed and I ring again and wait but there's still no answer but at least I tried and I can go back now and slide some more till it's time to go in for lunch. I'm sorry Andrew wasn't in, he would have enjoyed sliding.

****

"He said he never thought he'd live to see the day. He's so proud."

"Well he's right to be, your father was one of the heroes of the Easter Rising. If it wasn't for people like him we would never have achieved Independence." Mum has her hand on my Dad's arm and the two of them have this funny look on their faces like they're going to kiss or cry – one or the other. I think I might cry too as this fifty year anniversary of the 1916 Rising is very emotional and everybody in the street is cheering and lots of people are crying too.

"Is he in a good seat?" asks Mum.

"One of the best, right at the front just a few seats away from Dev."

"Granddad's just a few seats away from Dev? That's fantastic," says George beside me.

"Who's Dev?" I ask without thinking, I'm so caught up in the sight of the army with all their gun carriages and tanks.

"Who's Dev?" George shouts, giving me a dig in the ribs. "Who's Dev? Devalera, the President stupo!"

"You do know who the President is, don't you son?"

"Yes Dad, sorry, I couldn't really hear, the parade is so noisy with all the tanks and marching."

"That's all right," says Mum. "Can you both see out all right?"

We can see everything because we're on the top floor of one of Grandfather's offices on Parnell Square overlooking the Gardens of Remembrance where the Parade is starting from and there's office chairs and desks all around with office stuff on them like little rubber stamps hanging on a round rack and we're standing by the window and there's even a swivelly chair beside me but if I sit on it I can't see out and I can't even swivel it because Dad's behind me but it's really exciting because it's exactly fifty years since Granddad and the leaders of the insurrection not resurrection that's what Jesus did what's their names Padraic Pearse and James Connelly and Joseph Mary Plunkett he was Granddad's Commanding Officer even though his name was Mary they all fought the British in the GPO that's a big building half way along O'Connell Street on the far side it's got lots of pillars in front that's how you recognise it and that's where Granddad is in the Stand they were barricaded in there for the whole of Easter week in 1916 being fired at by the British "Ta saighduiri na Breathanach ag teacht anios Sraid Sackville" I can't believe he just said that only Pearse would take his schoolroom Irish into battle with him typical he never misses a chance to teach everybody the rest of us just want to survive I wonder sometimes if it's all just a game for him playing at being a Revolutionary I wonder if he's a bit mad all those speeches about a blood sacrifice nothing else will do God almighty what are we doing here he'll make a blood sacrifice out of all of us before we're finished but Jesus if we ever get out of here in one piece we'll live off it for the rest of our lives independence or no independence what are we going to do here anyway sitting around all morning waiting for orders when they do come they're just going to blast us to hell and back with their 18 pounders and we're supposed to defend the GPO with a few old rifles and pistols we might as well have pea shooters and catapults and -

"Look boys - can you see - the army is marching down the street!" Mum is pointing down to where there are lots of soldiers marching past and I feel like I want to cry but I don't know why I just feel really funny sort of happy and proud and there's a strange feeling in my throat and then suddenly there's a roar and another roar and a plane flies right over our heads and then another one. The noise is like a Halloween rocket makes when it takes off only a million times louder.

"They're jet fighters," says George, "What kind of jets are they Dad?"

"I don't know exactly, son."

"I bet they're Spitfires," I suggest, remembering the models in Kieran's room.

"Don't be stupid, Spitfires were in the War, there aren't any Spitfires around anymore are there Dad?"

"No son I don't think so." I'm hoping Dad would give out to George for calling me stupid but he's too busy looking up at the sky for more fighter jets and looking down at the ground at the soldiers and I suppose Mum probably didn't hear him with the noise from the planes or she'd have said something Mum is pulling me over to the window and letting me stand in front of her and when I look out the window I can see the soldiers marching down the street and the flags flying over the Garden of Remembrance thank God that's over and we won't have to stand at the flagpole again when we go home and salute the flag like we had to this morning that was so embarrassing though at least there was no one on the road but there might be now and if anyone saw us standing there it's bad enough that we have a 40 foot high flagpole in our front garden I mean it's OK for Grandad to have one he's really important he really fought in the GPO and he lives on Ailesbury Road where loads of houses have flagpoles because they're embassies but Dad didn't fight in the GPO and neither did Mum or me or George so why do we have to stand there in the front garden saluting the flag with Mum taking pictures of us George is in his school uniform and Mum's in her best new pink suit with the little jacket and short skirt and Dad's wearing a suit and I'm wearing what I always wear and I'm just praying that they'll get it over with before someone comes out on the road like the Blaneys or the Mullens and

94

see us all saluting the flag like eejits Oh God I'd die Oh God I'm sorry for saying Oh God I'll never forget when the huge flagpole arrived on the back of that big lorry that took up nearly the whole road and the neighbours standing outside the railings watching as the men put it up and I can hear them talking the little old ladies trying to figure out why we're putting up a great big flagpole in our front garden and what it's for saying made-up things like:

"Perhaps Mr Jones has been made Ambassador to some foreign country, he is a JP you know" and:

"I think they've sold the house to an Embassy" and:

"Yes I hear it's the new Nigerian Embassy oh I hope there won't be lots of black men coming to live on the road" and:

"No it's the new Arab Embassy."

"Well they're worse all heathens, at least some of the Africans are Christians now after all our wonderful Missionary priests going to darkest Africa and baptising all the black babies and converting them to Our Lord Jesus Christ."

"Amen".

And the men are digging a huge hole and mixing cement and then planting the pole like an enormous gigantic tree with no branches or leaves and they're saying things like:

"What's with the flagpole youngfella - are yis expectin a visit from de Queen of England or wha?"

And then when it's stuck in the ground safely Dad produces this giant flag that he had in the bottom of the big wardrobe and ties it onto the rope that's on the pole and starts pulling it up till it's up at the very top and flying in the breeze, and it looks nice all green white and orange but then he looks up and gives it a big salute and starts showing me how to do it:

"Hold your hand flat like this and bring your arm up moving it from the elbow until the fingers of your hand touch your right eyebrow at the corner like this look - that's a proper salute."

"Yes Daddy." And I do a perfect one.

"No - not like that - like this," he roars. "Look - I just showed you - look." And I have to do it again and again until I get it right.

95

Down on the street there are tanks and some guns being pulled by armoured cars and soldiers on horseback they're nice the horses and pretty soon it has passed and then we go back down all those stairs we climbed up and get in the car to drive home and we have to go round lots of back streets because of the traffic and it takes ages and no one says a word all the way home until we're nearly there and then Dad goes into one of his long sort of talking to himself talks:

"You know I've been thinking. We never got one of the whole family because you were taking the pictures my dear and therefore you weren't in them you see. We need someone else to take a picture of the four of us and then we'd all be in it wouldn't we? If we could just find somebody else to hold the camera." And then when we turn into the drive he says, "I think just one more photo by the flagpole with all of us if we can find someone to take it for us before we go in," and I can't believe it's going to happen again.

"No Dad please," I say before I can stop myself.

"What?" he turns around and looks at me, one of his really scary looks. "Are you not prepared to salute your own national flag, the flag your own grandfather fought and risked his life for, so that you could live in a free country and not be ruled by the bloody British?"

"No, I mean yes, I mean it's just that we've done it haven't we, I thought we'd done it all already, this morning."

"What we really need is to get a photo with all four of us in it," he goes on, ignoring me, "If we could find someone, one of the neighbours perhaps, who could hold the camera and take a picture for us then we could all be in the picture together. Look there's a boy, who's that, one of your friends I dare say, grab him there and get him to take a picture."

I half-turn around and look out the back window. It's Rory worse luck. George has seen him too but doesn't seem to mind and starts getting out of the car. I wish I could stay here and hide in the back seat of the car but Dad is out already at the gate calling:

"You there, boy next door, sorry I don't know your name, come here and make yourself useful, do you know how to take a

96

picture with a camera?" I can't believe he's saying this and I'm down on the floor looking for a way to actually get under the seat.

"Come on everybody out, one last photo with all four of us in it, this young lad's going to take it for us. Come on."

We're all out of the car now and walking over to the flagpole again and Rory's there with a big smirk on his face but at least it's only him and not the others unless - Oh God no there's Barry at his gate what is he doing I can't look we're all lined up now at the flagpole and Dad's giving Rory a long lecture on how to use the camera Oh God hurry up and just let him take the thing before - Oh no! It's Barry and Patrick - and they've seen us and they're heading up the road and now Kieran is with them that's who Barry was waiting for at his gate and they've all seen us and they're on their way up ...

"Nice salute everyone now," Dad's standing beside the flagpole then Mum George and me all of us in a row like four real soldiers saluting the national flag only we're standing in our front garden and my friends are looking.

"All right young chap, you can take the picture now, is everyone saluting? Watch the birdie, you can take the picture now have you taken it yet does he know how to do it I've explained it to him is he a bit unintelligent or what?"

"Calm down dear, he knows how to do it ..."

I can't look and have my eyes closed but I can hear the boys laughing and something else, a kind of stamping noise on the footpath outside the railings, what are they doing? I finally hear the click of Dad's old camera which means Rory's finally taken the picture I open my eyes and yep there they are marching up and down the footpath, Barry, Patrick and Kieran, their hands up to the sides of their heads in perfect military salutes.

"What are those scallywags up to?" Dad is grabbing the camera from Rory who can't stop laughing really nastily and the other three are still marching up and down saluting like mad and now they're doing the goose-step like those German soldiers you see in old movies of Nazis and Dad's raging and I don't know whether to laugh or cry the boys look so funny I want to laugh but they're laughing at

97

me so it shouldn't be funny Oh God why does he have to do this to me I can't take any more I'm going to scream I'm going insane just let me out of here and upstairs into my bedroom but the front door is locked so I'm running down the side of the house but the back door's locked too so all I can do is hide in the garage and sit here on the stupid peat briquettes I'll never be able to face them again marching up and down and saluting like that and laughing at us but they were funny too I never knew you could laugh and cry at the same time this has never happened to me before I think I'm going mad.

****

I can't believe I have to wear this. I look like a girl 'cept I've no hair. I'm all white - white sandals white socks white shorts white jumper white shirt and white tie. Why don't they just paint my head white too?

"Ow!" I know I shouldn't make a sound but that hurt. I can see Dad standing behind me when I look in Mum's dresser mirror while he rubs hair-oil into what's left of my hair - just the little sticky-up bit at the top as I've just had it cut again for my First Communion. Extra short, so there's hardly anything left at all. He looks really cross and he's giving my hair a good spanking.

"Have you got your Missal?" he asks me, stopping at my hair for a sec. I resist the temptation to make a joke about missal and missile, not a good idea at the moment, and just say:

"Yes Daddy."

"You know Mummy bought the Missal specially for you for your First Holy Communion today. I hope you're grateful."

"Yes Daddy, thank you Daddy." But even though I look like an overgrown baby in a white babygrow and even though Dad's rubbing my hair so hard I can barely stand up and even though I have to make my Communion on my own in some Convent instead of with my school friends, I'm still the happiest I've ever been in my life because when I went down for breakfast this morning Mum was standing in the kitchen with a big smile on her face and said she had a

98

surprise for me. George was there too, he's dressed the same as me even though he's not even making his First Holy Communion he made it two years ago and I can't remember what he wore but I'm sure it wasn't what he has on now because it wouldn't still fit him. Right now he's got the same white outfit as me same white shirt same white shorts same white jumper even the same white Clarks sandals and white socks and because he's about twice the size of me he looks a complete idiot he looks like a snowman or something but I'm not going to tell him that not yet anyway. Everyone else in my class - I mean the other boys - they all had suits, little three-piece suits with shorts and a waistcoat, or else grey shorts and a blazer - that's a sort of jacket nothing to do with going on fire - at least none of them are going to see me because they'll all be in Rathgar Church and we'll be in some Convent somewhere not even the one I went to on Christmas Day and where I'm going to serve Mass next year but another one somewhere else I've never even been to so they'll never see me if they ever saw me like this I'd be dead.

Downstairs Mum takes both my hands in hers and:

"Close your eyes," she says, "We've got a surprise for you." So I close my eyes and I can feel her leading me through the kitchen and out the back door and turning me left and I want to open my eyes because I can't wait for the surprise I've no idea what it is but I don't want to spoil it for Mummy so I squeeze my eyes really tight shut so they don't open even by accident until Mum says:

"You can open them now," and I open my eyes and there in front of me leaning up against the red brick wall of the side of the house beside the kitchen door is the most beautiful bicycle I have ever seen it's blue and white with a white saddle and a silver bell and it's even got a back carrier and a front light and it's even got three gears with the lever on the handlebars I can't believe my eyes and I can't even tell Mum how much I love it I just give her a hug and get up on it and cycle up the drive to the front gate then turn round and come back down again and I can see Mum standing there in her best outfit the pink suit and hat and her high heels looking so pretty and happy so I ring the bell to show her it works but it comes right off the handlebars and falls on the ground worse luck and Mum looks shocked but I pick it up and pretend to fix it back on so she's not upset the screw just came undone I can fix it later the bike is perfect it's just the right size for me not too small and not too big like the one I learned to ride on in the garden where that little girl lives who keeps saying "never mind your own business" that was so funny the last time we were there with Barry asking her questions about private stuff to get her to say "never mind your own business" she's got a really big lawn and it must have been her mother's bike because it was so big and we were all taking turns riding round the grass but when they found out I couldn't ride they helped me pushing me round and round and even though I couldn't reach the saddle to sit on and it was really hard to get it going on the grass though that was useful when I kept falling off about twenty times in the end I managed to get it going and keep it going long enough so that everybody cheered and said I'd learned to ride and I never even used those little wheels at the back that Patrick still has stable-riders I think they're called and when I came home I told Mum I'd learned to ride and she was amazed and that must have been when she got the idea to buy me a bike for my First Communion but when I come back to her and get off the bike she says "Oh no look at your sock" because my right sock is all black it must have got oily from the chain and if Dad sees it he'll go mad so Mum says to take it off quick and she'll get me another one so I'm standing here in the hall with only one shoe and sock on holding the other shoe and oh no Dad's coming down the stairs he's going to kill me if he finds out I got oil on my white sock I better hide the shoe behind my back and stick the bare foot behind the other one and stand on one leg so maybe he won't notice.

"What are you doing with your foot son? Why have you one bare foot? Where's your shoe and sock?"

"I … I …eh…I had the wrong sock on so Mummy's gone to get me another one." This is the best I can think of.

"What do you mean the wrong sock? They were fine."

100

"Eh … you see I had two left socks on …"

"Two left socks? There's no such thing as two left socks, they're both exactly the same."

"I mean – two right socks. I had two right socks on so Mummy's gone to get me another one."

"Two left socks … two right socks … unbelievable! Children!" and he goes off down the back stairs to the kitchen shaking his head. I'm feeling relieved that I didn't get into trouble with him until I realise what I've actually done. I'm supposed to be making my First Holy Communion in an hour and now I've just lied to my father! Oh my Lord! And it's too late to get confession my First Confession was last week and there isn't any Second Confession I have to go straight to Mass now and get Communion and I've told a lie - that's a sin - and going to Communion with a sin on your soul is a mortal sin, Miss Carey told us, so that's it, I'm finished I'm going straight to Hell! But if I'd told him I got oil on my sock he would have killed me. Oh Lord! What will I do? I need a priest to hear my confession quick. Maybe I can ring one up, there must be one in the phone book. Mum's still upstairs I can use the phone in the study. Ok, phone book, but what do I look up? Priests? - LMNOP - There aren't any listed, just a Mrs Priestly who lives in Delgany she's no use she can't hear my confession. What about churches? CH - Here's one, Church of the Sacred Heart Donnybrook what's the number 694537 ok here goes. If a priest answers I'm just going to say the same confession stuff we did last week.

"Donnybrook Parish, Fr Cleary speaking, may I help you?"

"Bless me Father for I have sinned this is my First Confession no sorry it's actually my Second Confession I lied to my father about the sock because I thought he'd be mad at me for getting oil on it and I have to make my First Holy Communion in half an hour and for all my sins I am heartily sorry."

"I beg your pardon?"

"Karl! What on earth are you doing? Who are you talking to on the telephone?"

"Oh – no-" I'm about to say 'no-one' but realise in time I better not start lying to Mum on top of everything else so instead I just start bawling and she takes the phone from my hand as I run upstairs to my bedroom. After I've finished crying I wonder if I just pray to God for forgiveness will it be all right but then I remember what we learned in Miss Carey's class about the Sacrament of Penance and what we have to get that only a priest can give us at first I wasn't really paying attention I had my head down with my ear to the wooden desk because it comes alive and buzzes and I can hear every noise in the whole class and it's like I'm a million miles away but still here and I can -

"Karl Jones, what are you doing?"

"Oh-oh! Nothing Miss Carey, I was just listening to the desk."

"Listening to the desk." Everyone is laughing and I'm pretty sure they're laughing *at* me.

"I mean I was just taking a rest. Sorry, I'm a bit tired today."

"Karl, do you want to make your First Holy Communion?"

"Oh yes please Miss."

"Well then I suggest you pay attention during religion class so you know about the Holy Sacrament of Penance and the Holy Sacrament of the Eucharist. Can you explain the Holy Sacrament of Penance to the class please."

"Yes Miss that's Confession, when you've done something bad and you have to tell the priest all about it."

"And why do you tell the priest your sins?"

"Eh, because he likes hearing about them?" Everybody is laughing again but this time I think they're laughing *with* me.

"No you silly child, the priest doesn't like hearing your sins, he's got far better things to do with his time, he hears your confession so he can give you something, what does he give you?"

"Oh I know, Our Fathers and Hail Marys Miss."

"Yes you have to say prayers for your Penance, and what does that grant you?"

I really haven't a clue what she wants to hear now so I look around at my classmates. Most of them don't seem to have a clue either because they're looking up at the ceiling like they're trying to think really hard but then I hear something whispered behind me and repeat it immediately:

"I know Miss, it's a solution."

"*Ab*solution, child, *ab*solution!" The priest absolves you of your sins, that mean he cleanses you of your sins and forgives them. Now sit down and pay more attention in future."

"Yes Miss."

George was right - it does taste like dry turkey and now it's stuck to the roof of my mouth and I'm kneeling on my own at the altar rails and everyone's waiting for me to finish my prayers but I can't get up until I've finished my Communion and I can't get it off the roof of my mouth Oh God I think I'm going to get sick Oh God I'm sorry for saying Oh God I think I closed my mouth too quickly after the priest put the Host on my tongue I nearly bit his finger off I was so nervous and I'm pretty sure I blessed myself the wrong way round it's supposed to be forehead heart left shoulder right shoulder but I think I went forehead heart right shoulder left shoulder Oh God does that mean that I'm not properly First Holy Communioned? I mean that I haven't received the Sacrament and it's probably a mortal sin and I'll go to Hell when I die should I tell someone I'll tell Mum tonight when I'm going to bed she'll know what to do I hope the priest didn't notice or he'll tell Dad and then I'll be in big trouble still it was nice of him to hear my confession before Mass that was a good idea the priest on the phone told Mum and for Penance he made me promise never to tell a lie to my father again so I better try not to it's still stuck to the roof of my mouth and everybody's waiting for me to finish and sit down so they can say the last prayers like they told me in the practice we had yesterday everybody else finished their Communion ages ago but I mustn't chew it even if I could get it down that's a real mortaler as Ronan Tinney said in class and I can't stick my finger in my mouth to get it off bet that's a mortaler too so I just have to wait for it to melt but it's not melting because it's too dry up there on the roof of my mouth this could take forever we could be here all morning I better just pretend I'm finished and sit down.

Thank God that's over I mean it's a nice convent and the priest was nice and the service went fine apart from getting the host stuck on the roof of my mouth Dad gave me a real look when I finally sat down but I won't be happy till we're home and I can get out of this silly outfit. Daddy's talking to the man at the gate and he's opening it up to let us back out.

"Just imagine," says Mum, turning around in the front seat as we drive off. "The priest said he had never given the Blessed Sacrament to such a holy and prayerful child. He said he had never seen anyone take so long over their post-Communion prayers. Isn't that nice?"

"Very nice," I agree.

On our road and nearly home thank God oh-oh who's this Mr Mullen standing outside his gate and waving at us no don't stop Dad please I can see Kieran getting out of his car and he's wearing his Communion suit a nice tweed three-piece and the others are there too oh God Dad's stopped to talk to him and Mr Mullen's inviting us to Kieran's party and Dad's saying:

"Yes, we'd love to come in for a quick drink to toast the two Communicants."

"No, no Mum," I shout-whisper trying to slide down in the back seat so no-one sees me and Mum is waving at me to be quiet.

"We'll just park and be straight over," says Dad and we drive in our gate.

"No Dad please, Mum please, we can't go in looking like this, not into the Mullen's – please, not in these clothes!" I beg them.

"No way," George joins in.

"Yes you're right there's no need for you to be dressed like that," says Dad turning round in the front seat and I can't believe what I'm hearing I'm so happy but then I realise he's only looking at George.

"You take your Communion suit off quick now George and we'll all go over. You can put on your school uniform."

104

"But me - what about me? I can't go like this!" I protest.

"Nonsense. It's your First Holy Communion Day. You have to stay in your vestments." I can't believe he's calling it that, he's calling my white outfit "vestments"! I really want to die.

"Yes but I've made it now, let me change too - Mum please!"

"No lovey, you look perfect as you are."

"But ... but ..."

"No buts." Dad turns full around to me and glares in a way I know means I better shut up.

Walking across the road I'm looking left and right to make sure nobody else is around. I look like the chicken crossing the road all I need is a red beak. In their gate and up to the front door thinking if it's just the Mullens who see me like this it'll be not too bad, as long as there's nobody else - "

"Hi Karl, nice outfit," says Patrick as soon as Mr Mullen lets us in the hall door.

"What are you doing here?"

"Oh we're all invited."

"Oh God no!"

"Come on through to the sunroom, we're all in here," says Mr Mullen in his usual friendly manner. Then I hear a snort I recognise.

"*What is that*?" God no it's Barry and he starts his most nasty laugh, the one he usually uses for Patrick but now it's all for me as he points at my all-white outfit and roars.

Then Yvonne, hearing the howls from Barry, comes and just stands there in front of me looking in disbelief.

"I think you're taking this too far," she says, "You look like a giant Communion Host."

"Or an ad for Persil," says Kieran, joining us.

"I think he looks like a boiled egg," says Patrick.

"Thanks Patrick."

"I think he looks cute." I can't believe it but Zoe has just pushed through the crowd around me and is smiling at me. She's wearing a nice party dress and looks really pretty. Then she tousles

105

my hair which Dad spent ages trying to get to lie flat with his hair oil this morning. That makes it stick right up and she pats it and smiles.

"You're all white," she says laughing a little but not meanly. "You look like a ghost."

"Yeah," says Patrick, "The Holy Ghost!" And we all laugh.

****

It's not just the size of the gates that's so scary though I've never seen such high gates before in my life they're ten times taller than me and George and all covered in twirly bits and there's the school badge on one of them the same as on my blazer pocket only it's huge and they go up for ever right up to the top of the underneath of the arch that joins the two enormous buildings which George is explaining to me are the Junior School on the right and the old house where the priests live on the left. These gates are the biggest scariest gates I've ever seen and because they're all black I think I know what they remind me of and it's not the gates of heaven like the ones in the Convent more like the gates to the other place that I'm not supposed to mention. But they're not even the scariest thing I'm seeing right now - the scariest thing is the thousands of boys I can see at the far end of the passage filling up the yard everywhere I look. I want to turn around and leave and run down the street I just came up from Parnell Square where we got the bus in from Palmerstown Park it took ages and all the time I was getting more and more scared sitting beside George with him telling me loads of stories about how the priests slap the boys on the hands with leather straps called biffers when they haven't done their homework and I'm looking at my skinny knees sticking out of the end of my grey shorts and my socks held up with elastic bands that Mum made and my new black leather shoes that Mum polished this morning before we left the house and I want to go home and take off my white shirt and school tie and school cap and the whole uniform all of which me and Mum bought last week in Clery's and go back to Miss Carey's though when I tried them on I was excited and looking forward to big school and leaving Miss Carey's was fine I was sad to go but I felt

106

grown up to be leaving and I thought big school would be an adventure but now I just want to cry and go home to Mummy and the worst thing is I can't feel Billy anywhere I've no idea where she is and I really need her now and here's a priest stopping us halfway along the passageway and:

"Hello Master Jones, welcome back," he says.

"Thank you Father Crawley," says George. This priest has the longest feet I've ever seen in my life his shoes must be size 20 and his face is really long too but I don't want to look at it it's so scary and I really don't want to see his eyes.

"And is this your younger brother by any chance? Hello young man, is this your first day in Belvedere?"

"Yes Father Crawley," I say copying George.

"Well, well, I hope you'll be very happy here. You know, I can remember my own first day here as if it was yesterday, and that was a very long time ago. Well off you go now, don't be late for class."

"Thank you Father," says George.

"Thank you Father," I repeat.

"He seems nice enough," I whisper as we enter the yard.

"Naw, he's one of the worst for sending you out to be biffed, really bad. He's not called "Killer Crawley" for nothing. Now you're going to have to line up over there when the bell goes. Your line is first then Rudiments then us in Grammar so you better just hang around there that's the toilets there but you won't have time to go now so you'll have to wait till break time so just stay there till the bells goes I've got to meet my friends. See you."

For the first time in my life I actually want George to stay with me the yard is ginormous and I cannot believe the number of boys in it there must be a thousand and one and they're all bigger than me every single one even the ones in my class I bet are all bigger than me because I know I'm small and the noise is unbelievable and I wish George hadn't said anything about the toilets as now I really want to go and I've no idea how I'm going to last till break-time whenever that might be this is definitely the worst thing that has ever happened to

107

me in my life how could Mum and Dad do this to me they must really hate me to send me here help me Billy where are you oh God Billy where are you now when I need you help me please!

****

"So you know where you are going don't you?" Mum says as we drive up the drive between the tall trees in the dark.

"Yes Mummy, I go in the little brass gate onto the altar, then go left and - "

"First you have to genuflect, in front of the altar, don't forget that."

"Yes Mummy."

"Then what?"

"Then I go in the door at the side and say hello to the priest."

"Yes, if he's there, I don't see his car. If he's not there just go on through to the back and put on your surplus and soutane."

"Yes Mummy,"

"And then wait for the priest to come. There won't be many at mass today so it won't matter if you make a mistake, I'll let you know if there's anything you've forgotten."

"Yes Mummy, thanks."

"Now go in and remember to genuflect. And concentrate on what you're supposed to be doing. Love you."

"Love you too." I'm getting out of the car and walking over the crunching gravel to the little doorway at the end of the stone building. Inside there's a tiny porch and then I'm in the warmth of the church I press my fingers against the spout of the holy water font and feel a little come out father son holy ghost amen and up the aisle the rubber soles on my shoes squeaking again on the polished wooden floor there's the nun's cage on the right with the curtain in front there's a little handle on the little brass gate and I'm opening it though it's so small I could easily jump right over it if I took a run because I'm good at jumping but I better not and I'm inside and close the gate behind me the altar looks beautiful with the six really tall candles and the flowers

108

and the huge painting of Our Lord on the cross behind it with his Mother Mary and the other Mary and the soldier and remember to genuflect then left around the steps and open the door to the Sacristy no one here yet but the light is on so I'll just go in there's a little sort of altar there where the priest gets ready and puts on his vestments and I have to go round the back to this little room where they showed me to go there's a little bench and hooks for the surpluses and soutanes there's my surplus and soutane where the nun said it would be I have my own hook with my name on it and they even sewed on name tags with Karl on them I take my jacket off and put it on the bench the soutane goes on first over my jumper and button up all the buttons there must be eight nine ten and then the surplus with all the creases I think they're called pleats Mummy said millions of tiny pleats and the nuns iron them all one at a time every single one until the surplus looks perfect just because they love God Mummy said imagine loving God that much but I can't and I'll just sit here on the little bench and wait for the priest to come it's so silent here there isn't a sound and there's a nice smell of polish and incense and something else I don't know what and here's the priest I better go in to him and tell him I'm here because I'll have to light the candles that's one of my jobs they told me the priest's nice he's got eyes like black marbles and his shoes are black too and shiny he knows it's my first day serving and he says not to worry everything will be fine and gives me a really long pole with a kind of candlewick at the end which he lights and sends me out to light the candles the candles are so tall I can't see up to the top to see if they're lighting yet some of them light easily and I can see the flame but this one won't light what will I do Mum's there in her bench the front one on the left where we sat together on Christmas Day and she nods to let me know when each candle is lighting but now she can see I'm having trouble with this one and she has a worried look on her face like she doesn't know what to do either I'll just have another go the thing I'm lighting them with that the priest lit inside still has enough wick on it I'll just reach up again and I think it might be yes it is lighting now and Mum's nodding and has a smile on her face so I can blow this thing out and bring it back inside all I have to do is ring

109

the bell at the Offertory that's when he raises up the Host and the Chalice bring up the water and wine in the little glass jugs on the glass tray just before Communion take the paten from him when he's finished giving the nuns their Communion and go around with it holding it under everybody's chins when they get theirs just concentrate now I know when to sit stand and kneel but it's hard to stay kneeling on the step for a long time without anything to lean against I'll be glad when I can sit down over there on the chair when he reads the Lesson the pattern on the carpet looks like a dragon it is red on a sort of green background with all swirly bits that look like claws or scales or spines and a tail and there's a stream of fire coming out of its mouth right there the priest's giving his sermon better pay attention it's about the Good Samaritan and who is thy neighbour Rory on one side number 13 that weird old fellow on the other side number 15 hate when the ball goes in there George always makes me go in for it he'll never go in himself the garden's all tangled up those strange boxes with glass tops for growing vegetables in though there's nothing in them but weeds the cricket ball broke one of them once and it was inside I cut my hand trying to get it out then he came out of the house in his dressing gown roaring at me and I had to jump back onto the wall and I grazed my knee trying to get over and he was chasing me I thought he'd kill me if he caught me he was so mad by the time I got back into our garden I was covered in blood I looked like I'd been through a mincer Mummy's mincer minces up the leftovers from the Sunday roast for Monday's dinner don't like mince in fact I looked exactly like Jesus on the cross in that painting over the altar of the crucifixion oh-oh the priest is looking at me he's finished his sermon and I'm supposed to do something what is it ...

****

"But how do you know which one is which? They all look the same."

110

"Look - it's obvious!" says Barry, in his usual way like he's lost his patience, "That's George, that's Ringo, that one's John and that's Paul."

I look at George and think of my brother but they don't look a bit alike. Still, I like having a brother with the same name as one of the Beatles. Rubber Soul is a joke I think because you have a sole on your shoe and it might be made of rubber and your soul is when you die and go to heaven. It sounds the same but they're spelled different.

"Why doesn't it have their name on it?"

"What do you mean?"

"There's no name of the band on the cover - only Rubber Soul."

"Of course there is, show me - " and he grabs the album out of my hands. "I knew that, I knew there's no "Beatles" on it."

"Why not?" I ask.

"Oh that's because, that's obvious, can you not see why not?" he thinks for a while. "That's because they're so famous they don't need to put their name on the cover. That's how famous they are."

"Oh." I know he hadn't even noticed the Beatles name wasn't on the cover and he's just pretending, but I couldn't be bothered arguing as the music is filling up all the inside of my head and there's no room for anything else. All jangly guitars and droning voices that sound like they've got a bad cold and drums that are like fireworks exploding.

"Carve your number on my wall
And maybe you will get a call
From me ..."

"Why don't you have any Beatles records?" says Barry.

"I don't think my Dad likes them. He says they use drugs and that's bad. And their hair's too long and that's really bad."

"I've got a single by Elvis, we can listen to it after this," Barry says. "Guitar Man, it's brill."

"Who's Elvis?"

111

"Who's Elvis? Are you serious?"

"Ow, that hurt."

"I'll show you my Elvis impersonation. Do you want to see it?"

"I suppose so, if I have to." Then he stands up pretending to hold a microphone and starts shaking his left leg like mad and singing:

"Well it's a-one for the money

A-two for the show

A-three to get a-ready now go cat go..."

And then there's a load of stuff about blue something shoes but I don't really get it, I've never even seen Elvis, I've no idea what he looks or sounds like so I don't know if Barry's impersonation is any good but when he's finished I say "Great" because I don't want another slap on the head.

****

"I think Daddy has something to show the two of you, a surprise. He's up in the drawing room."

"What is it?"

"Why don't you go up to the drawing room and find out?"

We're sitting in the playroom doing our homework and the last thing in the world we expect is a surprise from Dad I mean he's just not that type he never has surprises for us which I suppose is why this is such a surprise. It's a few weeks before Christmas and one of those days in December when it's so cold and damp that I would happily trade places with the cat I mean look at her there on top of the boiler on her rug, all she does is sleep all day and eat when she's really worked up an appetite and then sleep some more.

"All right," we agree doubtfully and leave what we're doing and go out the door. We stop for a second outside the drawing room, unable to quite believe what we're hearing coming through the door; It sounds like rock music. We open the door and go in.

My Dad is sitting there in his usual armchair beside the big old Pye gramophone, out of which is coming the unmistakable sounds of

112

John, Paul, George and Ringo performing She Loves You. He's got an album sleeve up in front of his face as he's reading the stuff on the back. The picture that we can see is a colour drawing of a man with a striped jacket and trousers with those white things on his shoes that they used to wear years ago and he's sitting on a drum. Behind him there's a car driving up a hill and there's all sorts of other stuff in the picture too. As George and myself approach we can read the title of the album – "A Collection of Beatles Oldies" and when Dad turns it around we can see it says "But Goldies" on the back cover. And even though I don't really like The Beatles (I mean Dad was the one who put me off them, telling us they were drug addicts) I've a feeling, looking at this album cover and listening to the music coming out of my Dad's record player (in Stereo please note Barry Blaney!) I've a feeling that that is about to change. I cannot believe this especially after what I said to Barry yesterday.

"So - what do you think?"

I can tell you we don't have a clue what to think except that our Dad has lost his marbles but we're not about to tell him that.

"Great," I say as George and myself look at each other in disbelief.

"Eh, Dad - where did you get the Beatles album?" George asks.

"I bought it of course, what do you think?"

"You just bought a Beatles album?"

"Yes, I thought it was about time I got acquainted with what the younger generation are listening to. Don't you agree?"

I wanted to say, "Absolutely not, are you mad?" as the last thing I really need is a father who is trying to act young and trendy like Mr Blaney. But instead I say:

"Great. What songs are on it?"

"All the hits: She Loves You; From Me to You; Yesterday; Eleanor Rigby; Yellow Submarine - that's my favourite. All of them."

"Can you put on I Wanna Hold Your Hand?" says George, "That's the greatest!"

113

"Eh, let me see the cover, where is it? Let me see now," and he's peering at the list of tracks on the back cover because he can't see very well unless he has the right glasses on, and George is pointing and telling him:

"Look, it's there, can't you see, it's the last track on side two - look!"

"Of course I can see son, but I can't put that song straight on, it's the last one, I have to put on side two from the start."

"No you don't, you just lift the needle over and put it down at the start of the last track, we do it all the time, look I'll show you - " and George makes a grab for the needle and Dad tries to stop him and the next thing I can hear is a nasty scratching noise a bit like the screech the Griffin's cat made that time Barry stood on its tail.

"You idiot!" shouted my Dad as George pulled his arm away looking pretty guilty. "Look what you've done now - you've scratched my brand new record."

"Sorry Dad."

"Sorry!? Sorry?! That's not going to do any good. Now I bet it's going to be scratched and every time I play it there'll be a scratch on it and we'll be able to hear the scratch!" I think Dad is getting pretty upset so I sneak out of the room leaving George to face the music haha but Dad was right about the scratch and now we have the record in the playroom because Dad didn't really like The Beatles after all and every time we play side two of that album now you can hear the scratch and there's even a place in Eleanor Rigby where the needle sticks and keeps repeating the same bit over and over with Paul singing: "socks in the night when there's - socks in the night when there's - socks in the night when there's ... " which is quite funny really and we all sing along to this bit over and over again until we get tired of it and someone pushes down on the needle arm to get it to go on. But that was how we got into The Beatles and since then we've been hooked and pretty soon after that we changed the name of our Club from The Secret Seven 'Cept There's Eight which was the old club to:

****

114

"The Beatles Club. That's the new name," says Andrew as we all sit around in our garage.

"Who says? Says who?" says Barry.

"Why? Have you any better ideas?" asks Andrew.

"Yes, I want it to be the Elvis Club."

"The Elvis Club, well we can put it to a vote. All those in favour of changing the name to The Elvis Club raise your hands." Barry puts up his hand and stares around at us.

"All those in favour of The Beatles Club?" Everyone else puts up their hands except Patrick.

"You didn't vote Patrick. You have to vote for one or the other," explains Andrew, sitting on his little pile of books in front of our garage door.

"I think the old name is better, why can't we keep the old name?"

"Because that's only for babies - the Secret Seven - it's a really stupid name," explains his brother.

"Not as stupid as Elvis - Ow! That hurt!"

"That's enough of that," Andrew says. "The motion is carried and from now on the official name of our club is The Beatles Club."

"God he's so - " Yvonne beside me whispers.

"Pompous?" I suggest under my breath, using a word I learned recently which makes her smile and nod at me but immediately I regret it as I feel disloyal to Andrew and hope he didn't hear me. I think I better say something out loud to cover up.

"So what do we do in the Beatles Club?"

"Same stuff we did in the old club I suppose," says Patrick.

"So ... in other words – nothing?" I say to him and we both break up laughing.

"We can collect things to do with The Beatles like posters and put them on the wall," says Andrew.

"And records. We can play records here if we bring out the record player." George's idea has a problem which I just notice.

"Eh George, you forgot there isn't any electric socket in the garage."

"Isn't there? I didn't know that."

"That's why when Dad vacuums his car he has to plug it into the socket in the kitchen, remember?"

"Oh. Never noticed."

"We've got electric sockets in our garage, maybe we could move the Club there," says Yvonne.

"Good idea, it's too cold here," says Barry.

"And it's really uncomfortable sitting on these Paint Tins," adds Patrick. "it's really digging me having to sit on them."

"You mean the tin is digging into you?" I ask him. Everyone's stopped talking now and they're listening to me and Patrick.

"No, I mean it's digging me - or is it bugging me, I get confused between those two." And now they've started laughing.

"What you mean is it's bugging you," I help out.

"Yeah that's right, it's really bugging me having to sit on these tins."

"That's my boy," I say patting him on the back

"What's digging then?" he asks quietly.

"That's if you like something or someone, you really dig it," I explain.

"Oh yeah, thanks. I dig you."

"Great."

"Can we move on please," says Andrew.

"The Peat Briquettes are worse than the paint tins. Our Mum gives out about getting our trousers dirty," says Kieran. "Look!" And he gets up from where he's sitting on a couple of briquettes, turns around and bends over.

"See, my bum's all dirty isn't it?" And he laughs.

"Yeah why didn't you wipe it properly?" says Barry.

"Shut up Barry," says Yvonne. "I'm going to ask Mum and Dad tonight can we use our garage."

"Well that's a major change of location you are proposing and you know all proposals must be put through the chair," says Andrew.

"Put through the chair – what does that mean?" asks Patrick.

"I am the chairman of the club, all proposals must be put through the chair, through me."

"If you're the chair, can we sit on you?" asks Patrick, his face lighting up. "I'm getting really sore sitting on this paint tin."

"Yeah and I'm all dirty from the Peat Briquettes," shouts Kieran, "Let's all sit on the Chair!" and we all rush over to where Andrew's sitting on his little pile of books, knock him off and sit on top of him. When he gets up his glasses are crooked and he's covered in dust but he doesn't seem to mind, he's the best ever. If we move the Club into Mullens' garage it'll be dark up there and if I was sitting beside Zoe in the dark when no-one's looking I could kiss her quickly on the cheek and no-one would notice that's what I'll do definitely next year will be the year coz it'll be

1967

"How long have you been coming in here? I thought no one was allowed," I ask.

"We weren't when we were younger, but they don't seem to mind now," answers Yvonne. I can hardly believe what we are doing I never thought I would get in here and I'm feeling half excited and half really guilty though Mum and Dad never actually told us we couldn't come in here in fact I don't know if they even know about it or maybe they just never imagined we would be let by the other parents or maybe they don't actually mind if we come in I hope not and anyway I'll tell Mum tonight when I'm going to bed that'll be all right then. The Mullen's wall is so easy to climb over we just went to the corner of the vegetable patch where they burn the rubbish just like we do in

117

the corner of our bit behind the hedge but on the other side of the wall it's much higher and we had to half climb and half jump down and then we were in. The first thing I can see is that big tree that I can see even from my bedroom window it's not a chestnut but something much bigger and Kieran has already fallen out of it once and nearly broken his arm or so he says. Yvonne has gone first then George then Zoe then Kieran but he's running off on his own now and I'm last. I'm glad the Blaneys aren't with us and thank God Rory isn't here or even Andrew he wouldn't approve I'm glad it's just us and the Mullens.

"There's that noise again," I point out. "Andrew said it was chainsaws, that they're always cutting down trees in here."

"Yeah, I've heard it before but you get used to it," replied Yvonne.

"I hate it," says Zoe, "I wish they'd stop." I look at her sympa-thetically but she's not looking at me so I change the subject.

"How far can we go?" I ask, thinking that the grounds of St Marks look so enormous that we could easily get lost.

"Anywhere we want," answers Yvonne half turning round to me. She's wearing her long skirt and her new zip-up leather boots, the ones she got for Christmas. Zoe's wearing her duffle coat that's nearly too small for her now she must be growing.

"But we've only been over to the pond so far, it's beautiful there," says Zoe. She has waited for me to catch up with her and she's walking beside me now which, when I think of where we are, makes me think I've gone mad and I'm in some other world maybe the world of my dreams but this is the real thing and I'm here now and I'm awake and it's really real.

"Where's the pond?" I ask her.

"Oh it's over there on the right past those trees. But first you have to see this, let's show them the hut!"

We have crossed though some fallen branches and undergrowth and come out onto a path. When I look back I can see the top floor of the Mullen's house with Rebecca's bedroom and the bathroom windows. I follow the others across the path and through some more bushes till we come out at an open place with a very big

118

tin hut shaped like one of those barrel chocolates with the green gooey stuff inside from a box of Milk Tray only much bigger and not so nice looking.

"It's a Nissen hut," explains Kieran, "It's been here since the war - imagine!"

"What's a Nissen hut?" asks my brother.

"That is - a hut like that, that shape, it's called a Nissen hut. They used them during the war for living in - barracks they're called."

"So who lived in it? Why would there be soldiers here - we weren't even in the War." I don't know much about history but I know that.

"Army hospital," Kieran says, making it sound as if he's just discovered some big secret, "Though I'd say this one was just for storing stuff."

"What's stored in it then?"

"That's what we want to know," says Yvonne. "We want someone to go inside and have a look."

"We're all too scared to," adds Zoe.

"No we're not," Kieran says, "It's just that we can't reach up to get in that window see - " And he points at an opening at the side of the door that is almost completely boarded up.

"We can see in but we can't climb up. George, you're the only one tall enough. If you took away those boards you'd be able to get in easy." Kieran is looking at my brother with this look on his face like he's just caught a fish and he's going to reel it in.

"I'd never get in there," says the fish, wriggling off the hook, "The gap's too small and these boards - " and he starts poking at them " - are too nailed on, you'd never get them off. Anyway," he adds, putting his face up to the gap and sniffing, "It stinks in there. It's probably full of dead stuff."

"Maybe there's dead soldiers there from the war - dead Nazis," I suggest but I'm only joking.

"Uuugh!" says Zoe, "Don't say that."

"Don't worry," I say to reassure her, "There aren't really any dead Nazis in there, they never even came to Ireland."

119

"They could have parachuted in when those bombers bombed the docks," Kieran suggests.

"Yeah and landed in our back garden and hid in St Marks for 25 years," adds Yvonne.

"Well - you never know."

"What are Nasties anyway? Why are you always on about them?" Zoe asks Kieran.

"Nasties!" snorts her brother. "There not called Nasties!"

"That's what you said - Nasties."

"I didn't say Nasties, I said Nazis - it's German for National Socialists, it's what German soldiers were called. Don't you know anything about the War?"

"It doesn't matter what they're called, there aren't any here. Now what else is there to see here? Where's the pond?" I say.

"Come on then," says Kieran, giving up on his Nazis idea, "It's over here."

We go back onto the path and turn down to the left so we're walking along behind the Blaneys'. After a couple of minutes we follow Kieran in through some bushes and small trees, climbing up a raised bank where there are some little stone steps in a gap in the trees and suddenly there below us is a large ornamental pond about twenty feet wide and curving round to the left for another fifty feet or so with rockery all around it. On the far side is a building with lots of windows but I don't see anyone at them.

"Wow!" I say.

"Cool!" agrees George.

"How deep is it?" I ask.

"Nobody knows," says Kieran mysteriously. "Down this end it's only a couple of feet but it gets deeper as you go over there."

"You could still drown if you fell in so we have to be careful," says Zoe.

"If we had a raft we could sail over to that island over there," I suggest.

"That's not an island, it's just a bit that sticks out in the middle before you get to the other side." Kieran.

120

"Oh! Well, it looks like an island. What are those plants and stuff?" I ask.

"They're water lillies I bet," says Zoe. "They make really lovely flowers in the summer with big pink petals."

"How do you know?" says Yvonne.

"I recognise the flat leaves. I've seen them in the garden centre, remember? We went with Dad."

"Oh yeah. Is that what they are?"

We start walking around the pond as far as we could go. There are some places where we could sit, some flat rocks in the rockery. Zoe sits down on one and looks at the water. She's got her duffle coat on with the collar turned up to keep her warm.

"You can't see it from outside," Yvonne says, "You wouldn't even know it was there, it's like a secret garden."

"I was just thinking that. How did you find it then?" I ask.

"I found it," Kieran boasts, "I've been all over the grounds here, I know where everything is, I'll show you."

"Can't wait," says George and he shuffles off, poking at his ear with his finger.

"Isn't it beautiful," says Zoe, "It's so peaceful here."

"What about those windows over there!" I ask, "Can't they see us from there?"

"No-one's ever there," says Yvonne. "I've never seen anyone."

"Anyway it doesn't matter, we could be anybody, visitors' children who didn't want to go inside," Zoe adds.

"Why would they not want to go inside?" I ask.

"Have you ever been in hospital?"

"George was in hospital a few years ago and me and Mum visited him every day in the rain. I remember driving across the city with Mum in her little Mini and it was raining so much I thought the car was going to be swallowed up by the floods there was so much water on the roads."

"What did you do when you got there?" Yvonne asks.

"I stayed in the car."

121

"Exactly," says Zoe. "Everybody hates hospitals. I remember when I had to go in for my appendix. Temple Street Children's Hospital. I'll never forget when Mum and Dad left me there and went away. I stood at the window overlooking the street and I could see them walking to the car and I banged on the window I couldn't stop crying but they couldn't hear me and a nurse had to drag me away and put me in bed."

"Stop, you're making me cry," says Yvonne.

"You wouldn't have liked it."

I want to say something to comfort Zoe but I can't, not in front of the others, but I try to catch her eye to show her that I sympathise but she's not looking at me.

"Have you got a scar?" asks George with his finger in his ear again.

"Yes she has, it's really big," Kieran answers for her. "Show them your scar Zoe, go on!"

"No!"

"Go on! Show us," says George. "I'll show you the scar on my hip from when I fell out of the tree."

"Nobody wants to see the scar on your stupid hip," I tell George.

"I'm not showing anyone my scar so stop it." Zoe is beginning to get a bit upset now.

"She never shows anyone, but I've seen it, it's a real beaut," Yvonne adds.

"Leave me alone!" She's nearly crying now so I have to think of something quick.

"Kieran!" I shout suddenly, "Where else do you know about here? Come on, show us some place else."

"Ok, what do you want to see - there's a big wood and a field and a big house and a bicycle shed and a gate lodge and - "

"What's a gate lodge?" I ask, thinking this could be something and Zoe has just been looking at me as if she's grateful for me changing the subject.

"It's the little house beside the main gate where the gatekeepers used to live."

"Show us then."

"All right, come on."

We turn away from the pond and head back the way we came until we pass the Nissen hut again and as we pass it Kieran asks:

"Sure you don't want to try getting in?"

"Yep," replies my brother. "But look at that tree."

"What tree?"

"That one there," my brother replies pointing to one, and I know what this one is, it's a chestnut.

"What about it?" asks Yvonne.

"It would make a brilliant tree for building a treehouse. You see those branches, the way they spread out like that? You could easily get some planks onto them and make a floor. Then you could build some walls and put a roof on it, and hey presto, you've got a treehouse."

"We'd never be able to build that," say Yvonne. "Where's the gate lodge?"

"Over here," says Kieran. No-one seems very interested in George's idea for a treehouse.

We continue along through a wide open grassy area with a few of those tall skinny trees with white trunks and branches called silver something, silver beeches I think they're called, while over in the distance to the right I can see the chimneys and roof of a big old house.

"We have to keep over here among the trees or they'll see us," Kieran says quietly, almost whispering.

"Who'll see us?" I ask.

"Not so loud - the Greeners of course," he replies.

"What are the Greeners?"

"Kieran thinks there are men in green coats all around the grounds," explains Yvonne.

"He's seeing little green men," adds Zoe with a giggle.

123

"There are - I've seen them," he says. "They're the grounds-men. If they see you they'll chase you."

"Yeah sure." George isn't impressed.

"Look, is that it - the gate lodge?" I ask as a little cottage comes into view between the trees.

"That's it all right," says Kieran.

"Oh it's so pretty," says Zoe, "I've never seen it before."

"It's like a picture on a jigsaw," her sister agrees. It is indeed, with its sloping roofs, and windows with tiny square panes, some of which have coloured glass in them. Zoe goes up to one of the windows and tries to peer in.

"And over here is Vinegar Hill," says Kieran.

"What's Vinegar Hill?" we ask.

"You know, like the battle in Wexford, when the French helped us and we tried to defeat the British but we lost again." I had heard something about it in Irish History.

"Yes 1798," I say. "Boolevogue and Father Murphy and all that, but what's that got to do with here?"

"Nothing really, it's just a hill but I called it Vinegar Hill because it reminded me, that's all."

"Well it looks like a good place for battles all right," I agree, as we approach the little mound surrounded by grass. "Some of us could be on the hill and the others are trying to capture it and - "

"Bo-ring," I hear George say behind me but I ignore him. "But we'd need a few more, we'd need Andrew and the Blaneys."

"Yeah, we could have a real battle with guns and swords." Kieran runs up to the top of the hill and starts chanting:

"I'm the king of the castle, get down you dirty rascal." I chase after him and try to push him off.

"You get down! You're the dirty rascal!" And we start having a pretend fight and both of us end up falling over and rolling down the hill just as the girls and George arrive. Of course George has to copy us and runs up the hill and starts rolling down too. Zoe's looking at us shaking her head.

124

"What are you at, you're covered in hay," she says. And we look at each other and at our clothes and sure enough, someone has been cutting the long grass here recently and we're covered in it. It's like the hay you get on the haystacks down near the Cottage but not so much of it. We get up and start picking it off our clothes.

"You better get all this off you before Mum sees it," Zoe says to Kieran and she's picking it off his jumper. "You too," she turns to me and George and pulls a few wispy bits of long grass off my back. Then she starts pulling all the hay off George's back.

"Stand still," she says, "Stop wriggling!"

"I can't help it, you're tickling me!"

"That's not tickling, how is that tickling?" And then she's suddenly got her hands under his arms.

"This is tickling!" she says, and he screams and starts running but she's after him and he trips and falls and I cannot believe it but Zoe is on top of him, sitting on his chest and tickling him everywhere she can reach. Me and Yvonne are just standing here looking at them. I can't believe she is doing this to George just like the way she sat on me and pushed snow in my face I thought that was something special she did just for me and now she's doing it to him I can't believe it.

"Come on, we better go back, we've got our homework to do," Kieran says, "Tomorrow's Monday." And I'm so glad he said that because I don't want to stay here any longer because right now I'm really sick of the place and all I want is to go home. Walking back through the fields Kieran is beside me talking about something or other I'm not even listening to him and I turn around and see that George and Zoe are walking together; the setting sun is on the top of Zoe's hair and it's all gold and so beautiful I stop and stare for a second but then I have to turn back again quickly so she doesn't see the look on my face.

****

Why does time go so slowly when I'm sitting here in class like this we get a half an hour for lunch but it never feels like that it's more like five minutes the time flies and I can't slow it down but when we're back in class time just stops and each minute is like an hour why is that? after lunch is the worst we get a break in the morning at half ten then we get lunch at twenty past twelve but when we go back into school there's no break until we get off at a quarter past three that's nearly three hours but it feels like a week and today we have Irish then writing then religion and it's the worst afternoon lunch was nice today Mummy gave me chicken sandwiches because we had a chicken for dinner last night and an apple which wasn't one of ours from the garden they're all gone now it was a supermarket apple they're not bad but they don't have the freckles like on Zoe's nose and then a Club Milk which I ate with my bottle of milk over in the gym biting the chocolate off first then eating the biscuit those jam tarts and cream cakes look really nice but I'm never allowed buy one because Mummy won't give me the money she says they make us fat well I don't want to be fat like Tubby Ryan anyway he's so fat he's got real boobies like a girl so I don't mind but the gym always smells of spilt milk when we go there for PE especially when we have to do push-ups and we're lying face-down on the floor it's yucky it used to be the theatre that's why there's a stage at one end and it slopes down in that direction so it's easier to run with the sandbags towards the stage but really hard to run back up to the end and that time Chris Shannon did a wee in his shorts it started at his shoe and went downhill along the floor towards the stage in a little stream and Mr Dempsey stared at it like he couldn't believe his eyes and followed the stream up to where Shannon stood his face was red and everyone was staring at him and he even had wee running down his bare leg and over his shoe and Dempsey told him to go to the toilet immediately and get cleaned up and as he left Chris turned round and said "The river Shannon" and everybody laughed even Mr Dempsey I love PE it's my favourite and I'm really fast because of Billy the fastest in the whole class and even when we share with Rudiments there's no-one faster than me in the whole of Rudiments too pretty soon I'm going to be the fastest boy in the whole

Junior School but I'm not strong I can only carry two sandbags and some of them can carry three or four like Eamonn he's really strong and that time when they measured our chests and we had to breathe in deep breaths and hold it while Dempsey put the measuring tape around us he said my chest with a full breath was the same size as most boys when they breathed out that wasn't a very nice thing to say and he didn't have to laugh when he said it because then everyone around started laughing but I don't care because I know I'm the fastest in the class and that means something it doesn't matter how big your stupid chest is anyway what does that matter you can't run fast with a big chest like a barrel who wants that unless you want to be a weightlifter or something but I don't I just want to be able to run really fast like Billy and when we have races in the gym she's always there right beside me running up and down beside me and she always helps me win I've never lost a race there and I never will she's the best ever -

" - writing Karl Jones?"

Oh God Mr Naughton is talking to me I'm supposed to be doing something.

"Sorry Sir? I didn't hear you."

"That's because you are staring into space. Are you having a nice daydream?"

"Yes Sir, I mean no Sir, I wasn't dreaming Sir I was just thinking."

"Thinking, were you?"

"Yes Sir."

"And what exactly were you thinking about?"

"About the question Sir."

"And what was the question?"

"Eh ... well you see Sir that's just it, I couldn't really understand the question so I was thinking about what it meant and wondering if you would explain it a bit more Sir if you don't mind."

"And what part of the question do you not understand?"

"Eh, the first part ... and the last part ... and the bit in the middle ... well, all of it really Sir."

"Look - it's very simple, you just have to write down your favourite five activities that you do outside school. Now start writing!"

"Oh yes Sir, that's easy, running, taking my bike to the park."

"Yes, yes, just write them down please!"

Going into St Mark's with everyone, serving Mass, watching TV - and then, looking out at the dismal smoke-stained two-hundred-year-old buildings outside the classroom window, my heart leaps up because I remember the one thing that makes during the week bearable, the one thing I live for all week, that oh yes brilliant, it's today, today is Thursday and tonight at twenty-five past seven on BBC is:

"Top of the Pops is on now Mum, can we watch it?"

"Is it that time already? Have you finished your homework?"

"Yes Mum. I have finished everything."

"Nearly," says George beside me, "I just have my poetry to learn."

"All right, you can turn it on then, but only for Top of the Pops and then it's off again." Mummy's doing the ironing on the kitchen table a pile of washed clothes in the tub on one side of her and another neat pile of finished ironing on the other side. "I don't mind listening as long as I don't have to look at them. I can never tell if they're boys or girls anymore."

I watch every song hoping The Beatles would be on next or even the Monkees but they aren't so when it's over George goes back to his homework and I read a book. Another week before it's on again I can't wait that long and I'm really disappointed. But then there's Pick of the Pops on the radio on Sunday evening if Dad lets us we're always having our tea in the dining room at that time and we miss most of it but if we hurry sometimes we can get the end of it listening on the gramophone in the drawing room if we're let and we can get there in time for the top thirty count-down and listen to who's number one.

****

128

"Tadpoles?" asks Mummy, sitting at her desk in the study. She has her microscope out and is looking at something in it.

"Yes tadpoles, they're baby frogs," I explain.

"Yes I know what tadpoles are, I do have a PhD in science, what I'm wondering is, why do you want them?"

"It's for Environmental Studies, we have to find some, collect them in a jar, we can bring them in to school if we want, or just leave them at home."

"And where do you think you are going to find tadpoles?"

"There's a pond in St Mark's, there should be some in there, right?"

"That's something I've been meaning to have a word with Mr and Mrs Mullen about, since you seem to get in there through their garden. I don't know if I like you going into the hospital grounds, you could get into trouble there."

"Oh no it's perfectly safe, and we never see any staff or any patients so they don't mind."

"Well if you promise not to fall into the pond, there's a jam jar beside the sink, I just washed it, you can use that for your tadpoles. Oh and put on your wellies."

"Great Mum, thanks, I love you," and I'm out the door, down to the kitchen, and sure enough, there's the jam jar sitting on the draining board, just waiting to be filled up with tadpoles. I change into my wellies in the cloakroom and walk out our gate because you can't really run in wellies your socks keep falling down inside the boots and going under your feet, across the road and into the Mullen's drive.

At the Mullen's back door I knock and wait. Their doorknob is really funny, round and kind of silvery but I suppose it's steel and if I put my hand just up against it like this but not touching it I can see the reflection of my hand all curvy and really big and I can see my arm and the rest of me all tiny and far away it's so cool and when I move my hand closer to the doorknob and then move it away like this it goes bigger and smaller bigger and smaller it's so funny -

"Oh hi Kieran, do you want to come out to play? I have to go into St Mark's and collect tadpoles for school."

"What's that?"

"It's a jam jar to put the tadpoles in."

"Sure, let me get a jam jar too. Have you asked Patrick?"

"No, but it's a good idea."

"We can climb over the wall. Hang on a minute."

"Brill!"

A few minutes later we are climbing over the wall at the end of Kieran's garden where it's low and you can get into Blaney's easy but it's still tricky with the jam jars and we have to take turns holding them for each other. At the glass door at the back of Blaney's house we can see Mrs Blaney in the kitchen and we knock and ask her nicely can Patrick come out to play but we don't say anything about going into St Mark's because he may not be allowed so we hold the jam jars behind our backs where she can't see them.

"What have you got behind your backs, boys?"

"Oh nothing, just a jam jar." Kieran says.

"And what are you doing with them? You're not thinking of going into St Mark's are you? Because you know Patrick isn't allowed in there don't you?"

"Oh no," says Kieran, "We were just going to make some jam." I can't believe he's just said that and I stare at him wondering how he's going to get out of this one.

"You're going to make jam?"

"Collect some fruit I mean, for jam, from the raspberry bushes in our vegetable patch."

"It's only May, Kieran," Mrs Blaney points out, "I don't think you'll get any raspberries yet, seeing as they don't appear before September."

"Oh well, we better put the jam jars back then," I say.

"Is it ok if we just jump back over your wall?" Kieran asks. "Thanks Mrs Blaney, oh and if Patrick wants to come out we'll be in our garden." At that point Patrick does come out and looks at his mother hopefully.

"Please let me go into St Mark's Mum!" he says.

"We'll look after him, we promise," says Kieran.

130

"I'm putting Karl in charge," says Mrs Blaney looking at me. "You're responsible Karl, make sure you don't get up to any mischief."

"Yes Mrs Blaney."

"Go on then, and be careful."

"Thanks Mum," he says and two minutes later the three of us are in St Mark's heading for the pond. Patrick is excited and has a few questions.

"I can't believe I'm in here. What's a tadpole? It's my very first time. What do they look like? How do you know where to find them? What are you going to do with them when you get them home? Will they grow into frogs in the jar? Can I have some to put into Barry's lunchbox? I think he'd like some for his lunch."

"Yeah, a tadpole sandwich, that'd be nice," adds Kieran.

When we get to the pond we stop at the bushes where the entrance is between the big laurel leaves.

"Here," says Kieran pulling a hanky out of his pocket. "For security reasons you have to be blindfolded." And he starts tying the hanky over Patrick's eyes.

"What? Why do you have to do that?" Patrick objects.

"I told you - security reasons. We have to keep the entrance to the pond top secret."

"Kieran," I say, "It's Patrick, I think we can allow him in."

"No way. Too risky. He has to be blindfolded." One of the things I like about Patrick is that he's always good humoured so he doesn't seem to mind when Kieran ties the hanky around his eyes and we go through the bushes to the pond where he unties the blindfold. Patrick looks behind him to see where he has come.

"Yeah, I'd never be able to find my way through those bushes again," he says and we both crack up.

"Top secret," I agree very seriously, and we both laugh again.

"Yeah well," says Kieran. "You can't be too sure."

"Cool pond, where are the tadpoles?"

"We have to look for them," says Kieran, "They could be anywhere."

"They've probably seen us coming with the jam jars so they're hiding under a rock," I suggest.

"Yeah, they've got this top secret hiding place that none of the other frogs know about and they have to be blindfolded when they go in there," says Patrick.

"I wonder if it's shallow enough to walk in." I really want to put my foot into the dark green water and see how deep it is.

"Why don't you try?" says Kieran. "You've got wellies on, your feet won't get wet." I'm standing at the edge of the pond looking down and I can see the sky reflected in the green water and my face and Kieran's and Patrick's beside me.

"Hold my arm," I say and they both hold onto me as I put my right leg over the edge of the pond and my wellie goes down into the water. It's really hard to push it in at first and as it goes in deeper the water grips it on all sides and squeezes the rubber wellie all around my leg. It feels like the water has got hold of my leg and it's trying to pull me in and drag me under and suddenly it's scary and I pull my leg out of the water real quick and it comes out with a funny squelchy noise but my wellie nearly gets stuck in the water because the pond was grabbing hold of it so tight it didn't want to let go like it was grabbing my leg and trying to suck me under and drown me.

"Whatcha pull it out for?" asks Kieran scowling. "You weren't all the way down yet."

"I couldn't put it any further in, the water would have gone over the side of my boot."

"No it wouldn't. You weren't all the way down yet," Kieran says again. "You could've gone in further."

"Come on, let's look for tadpoles," I say and start walking around the edge of the pond. I don't look at either of my friends because I don't want them to see that I was scared. "Is that some there?"

"Where?" says Patrick, "Oh yeah, there they are."

"That's not tadpoles it's just some dead leaves," Kieran says, joining us. "You don't even know what they look like. Follow me, I'll find some." And we start walking the other way around the pond and halfway along Kieran runs into the bushes and come out with a long stick which he starts using to poke in the water. Me and Patrick are looking at him and into the water and I couldn't really care if he finds tadpoles or not it's just fun being here with my friends in the sunshine beside the pond it's just the best fun ever.

"Have you seen the haunted Chapel?" asks Kieran suddenly. "Bet you haven't!"

"Course I have. What's the haunted chapel?"

"Knew you hadn't seen it, come on it's over here." And he starts off through the bushes.

"What about my tadpoles?" I ask.

"Oh we'll get them later, come on."

On the far side of the bushes we see Kieran heading up the path to the left, behind the gardens. A short way along there's a little wooden building in the middle of the path, dark and strange looking. Me and Patrick follow Kieran round to the other side.

"There! What did I tell you?!" Kieran points at the front which is a small shrine with candles burning inside, flowers and a tiny altar with a statue of the Virgin Mary on it.

"It's a shrine, not a haunted chapel," I tell him. "Probably for the patients or their relatives to pray at and light candles at."

"Yeah," says Patrick, agreeing with me as usual, "Who says it's haunted?"

"Yeah," I say, agreeing with Patrick as usual, "Who says it's haunted?"

"It just is."

"It just is! You can't just say that."

"Well I bet you wouldn't come here one night at midnight and run around it three times and sprinkle the blood of a dead cat around it."

"Why would I want to do that?"

"They say if you do that you'll meet the Devil."

"Wow!" says Patrick. "That's scary!" And I don't know if he's being serious or not.

"I don't really want to meet the Devil to be honest," I say.

133

"I bet you wouldn't do it anyway," Kieran repeats.

"I bet *you* wouldn't," I reply.

"Let's try it some time and see who's scared."

"OK let's!"

"Where are we going to get a dead cat?"

"You're not killing our Puss that's for sure," Patrick says. "I love our Puss, she's so soft and cuddly and when I tickle her tummy she purrs."

"We'll just have to wait for a cat to die," I say, "There's lots of cats on the road, one of them is bound to get run over some day. If not we'll have to wait for one to die of old age. What's over there?"

"No-one knows," Kieran answers, sounding mysterious the way he likes to.

"What do you mean, no-one knows?" asks Patrick.

"No-one has ever been past the haunted chapel, we've never gone over there, it's too near the hospital buildings, too near the humans."

"Too near the humans?" I repeat and me and Patrick are starting to laugh.

"I mean, too near all the people who work there, and the patients and people who visit, you know?"

I take a look inside the shrine again, with the little candles burning in front of the statue. It's nice and safe looking, not at all scary. "Come on, let's get out of here before the Devil appears," I say.

"Yeah – or some humans," adds Patrick and we both crack

up.

★★★★★★★★★★★★★

Left side back right side I can see the whole of my head in the side mirrors and I think it's even worse than the last haircut Dad said to cut it really short and it will last till Easter the spot seems bigger I wonder do they grow is it going to get bigger and bigger till it covers my whole head or will it get hairy like Paul Kelly's in school on his neck

134

it's horrible but I shouldn't say that it's not his fault it must be awful having something like that but at least he doesn't have sticky-out ears that's why they call me that and when my hair is so short it makes my ears stick out even more that's why they call me monkey face in school but if they knew that here they'd start calling me that here too and then my life would be finished why do they call me that? I must look like a monkey or they wouldn't call me that if I had a wig with long hair I could cover them or a hat with flaps over the ears like that boy was wearing in the yard that's it - that would be perfect I could just pull the flaps down and no-one would see my ears then Zoe might really like me I'll have to ask Mum to get me one that's all I need and she won't ever laugh at me again like that time in the zoo we're at the elephant enclosure and there's this baby elephant called Jumbo and he's really cute I love the way me and Zoe say things are cute and he's small but still ten times bigger than me and I have to stand here and feed him with this strawey stuff and my friends are throwing monkey nuts at Jumbo but some of them are hitting me which I bet they're doing on purpose I bet that's Rory and Barry I wish they weren't here Mum's taking millions of pictures with her old Kodak camera in the brown leather case and all I really want is to get upstairs and have the tea and the ice-cream cake and get this birthday party over with oh brilliant now the elephant has his trunk on my head and he's sort of sniffing me and his trunk is all wrinkly and rough and hairy up close and my friends are all laughing at me even Zoe and I'm too scared to move or else I'd just run and not stop where's Billy when I need her I'll just close my eyes and pray Billy Billy where are you are you there what will I do will I run? and now she's beside me and we're running as fast as the wind out of the elephant house and past the sea lions with their funny mustaches and past the cold penguins in their big swimming pool and the crazy monkeys on the island in the middle of the lake and there's the hippos and the rhinos and we don't stop until we're back at the shop and the restaurant where were going to eat upstairs and there's some benches so I'm just going to sit here until they all come back thanks Billy for rescuing me.

"Happy Birthday to you
You live in the Zoo
You look like a monkey
And you smell like one too!"

I try to smile again for Mummy when she's taking pictures of me blowing out the candles on the cake but I don't feel like it and I bet I know who it is singing that *"You look like a monkey"* stuff I bet it's Rory and Barry the other children are too nice to make up a song like that though those two are supposed to be my best friends here and the others are just from school and people Mummy invited because she knows their Mummys I wish Yvonne didn't have to go to that other party then she'd be here with Zoe instead of Zoe sitting down there beside Rory and laughing at his song and Kieran and Patrick couldn't come either anyway I'll blow out all the candles so here goes Mummy's slicing up the cake and then I can put some ice-cream in my Fanta and it'll be like a what's it called a float or something next year I want to go to the pictures for my birthday I don't like the stupid zoo.

****

Yvonne's hair is straighter and darker than Zoe's and she has a fringe but I prefer Zoe's because it's a bit wavy and she has a side parting that comes down nearly over one eye - her left eye girls part their hair to the left and boys to the right - they're lying face down on the grass and letting us sit on their backs like we're horse-riding and when we brush their hair that way it goes nearly all the way down their backs sometimes they let us plait it but mostly we just brush it I love doing this in the sunshine because there are so many different colours in their hair when the sun shines on it it's not just that Yvonne's is dark brown and Zoe's is auburn there's so many more colours like in Yvonne's there's the colour of the chestnuts in the hockey pitch on Temple Road where they lie on the ground in their shells like the big brown eyes of a spikey-skinned dinosaur and there's different shades of purple and brown and black and even really dark dark blue and one

136

or two strands of gold and in Zoe's I can see more gold and yellow and light brown and dark brown and even that orangey colour I loved so much that was in the garden swing in the last house and if I go close enough to it I can smell their shampoo – apples and oranges and I think peach or melon – and their hair shines so much in the sun it's like those pieces of silk material Mum has in her sewing room if they have their hair tied up they take out the elastic thingy and shake it out and let me or George brush it and then they put it up again they give out about having split ends but I've no idea what that means I just think their hair is so beautiful the French windows are open and we've put The Monkees on their record player which is just inside and right now it's playing "Last Train to Clarksville" which we all love and we're singing along to it *"Take the last train to Clarksville and I'll meet you at the station ..."* before that we were measuring each other back to back George and Yvonne first and George is the tallest but Yvonne's nearly as tall and then me and Zoe and she's so much taller than me three inches Yvonne said I really better start growing the hula-hoop is lying on the grass and after we've done their hair Zoe stands into it and pulls it up her legs up to her waist we've all had a go at it but Zoe is the only one who can do it properly if she wanted to she could make it spin all day she starts by giving it a little twirl with her hands but once it's going she just moves her hips a little round and round and the hula-hoop goes on spinning orbiting her hips like a planet orbits the sun we learned that in Science only much faster it's like the hula-hoop is in love with her and likes hugging her around her hips and won't let her go I could watch her hula-hooping all day long and I'd never get tired of it looking at her I think it's the most beautiful sight I've ever seen in my life she's wearing her tight jeans the really old faded ones and her old runners and the new stripy top that her mother bought in town last week and when she twists her body her long auburn hair flies around and when she looks down at the hula-hoop it falls over her face but every now and then she pulls her head up and looks up at the sky and the sun and shakes her hair out of her eyes that's when she looks around at us for a second and sometimes she smiles like she's concentrating too hard to speak but

137

she knows we're all looking at her because she's so good we can't stop it's like we're hypnotised and we can't take our eyes off her even the hula-hoop looks like it's hypnotised it can't stop twirling round her body it just doesn't want to stop it loves her so much I know how it feels it's the first week of our school holidays and there's no school for another three months nearly and it's like time has really stopped and we've gone into eternity sitting on the Mullen's lawn like this with the blue sky up above and the green grass underneath us listening to The Monkees singing "I'm a Believer" now and watching Zoe swinging her hips making the hula-hoop go spinning round and round her skinny body for ever and ever this is it this is what they mean when they say that when you die you go to heaven and live in eternal happiness for ever and ever amen for all eternity.

****

"When does Wimbledon start?"
"In a couple of weeks."
"Do you think they'll qualify?"
"Sure to qualify, I mean look at them, they're so brilliant."
Me, Patrick, Rory and Barry are sitting on the footpath outside Andrew's house watching Yvonne and Zoe playing tennis on the road in front of the gates of Maggiore. George isn't here because he's playing cricket and when I called over to Blaneys' Rory was there but I wish he wasn't. The girls take their tennis seriously even though they've nowhere proper to play, wearing little white skirts and white tops and their tennis shoes, and they even keep their racquets in wooden frames that you screw shut so the racquet doesn't go bendy if you leave it out in the rain. I know because I have one of them in my hand which Zoe gave me to mind and I'm playing with the little screws, opening them and closing them, it's fun. There's never any traffic up here and there's plenty of space today because even Andrew's Dad's car isn't parked outside their house as they've gone away for the day. It's hot and sunny and we couldn't be bothered doing anything except sit here and watch the girls playing.

"Where's the net?" Rory shouts over to them.

"It's there in the middle – can't you see it?" Yvonne replies.

"It's a magic net," says Barry, "Woven by the fairies, of such fine material that it's invisible to humans."

"Is it really?" asks Patrick.

"No you idiot, I'm being sarcastic! They don't have a net."

I'm looking at the side of Barry's head and his hair is growing down in front of his ears and it's getting really long, nearly to the bottom of his ear they're called side-locks and there's even bits covering the top of his ear and it's all blond and cool looking and I don't know if I like him or hate him for having such long beautiful hair I just wish more than anything in the world that I was allowed have my hair that long and that it was his beautiful blond colour.

"What are you looking at?" he suddenly says, turning to me.

"Nothing really. I was just wondering - do you not have to get your hair cut, it's getting really long."

"That's not long, except compared with yours of course but then you don't have any hardly. I'm going to grow it even longer than this, not getting it cut all summer."

"Does your Dad not make you get it cut?" I ask, thinking of my own trips to the Barber's.

"Of course not, his hair is even longer. Hey man it's 1967, be cool!"

"It's the summer of love," says Rory, "That's what they're calling it. Love and peace man!"

"The summer of love, yeah sure, what do we know about the summer of love?" I reply looking at Patrick. Even his hair is longer than mine. So is Rory's, it looks much longer because it's black and thicker.

"We could find out," says Rory looking at the girls, and he and Barry start laughing but I have no idea what they're laughing about. Now the girls are up close to each other hitting the ball to each other without letting it bounce, that's called volleying.

Sometimes one or other of them misses the ball and it bounces past them and either goes in the big gates of Maggiore or else way on

139

down the road, and whoever missed it has to turn round and chase after the ball and pick it up. Funny thing is, any time one of them has to bend over to pick up the ball Rory and Barry start making all these weird noises sort of like laughs only worse.

"Why are we watching them?" asks Patrick. "They're not even any good, they keep missing."

"That's the best bit," says Barry, and Rory and himself start their snorting-laugh again.

"Why don't you at least help?" asks Yvonne. "Why can't you be ball boys?"

"Yeah OK," I reply, about to get up.

"No you don't," hisses Barry beside me grabbing my arm, "Let them do it themselves."

"Why? Why can't I?"

"Just stay there," says Rory.

"Did you say you would?" Zoe asks, smiling over at me.

"Uh, no, sorry, changed my mind," I mutter, looking down at her racquet frame and twiddling the screws. I wish I could be her ball boy and save her the trouble of having to run into the bushes in Maggiore to get the ball every time she misses but I don't want to go against Rory and Barry. And so I sit here, ashamed of myself for being such a coward, and missing the opportunity of helping Zoe, and I am no longer enjoying watching them play tennis.

"Why don't you two get your bikes and go for a ride?" Rory says.

"All right, come on," says Patrick. I don't want to leave Rory here with Zoe because I don't trust him but I have to now so we get on our bikes which are propped up on their pedals against the footpath outside Andrew's and start off down the road. The air is lovely and cool on my face as I cycle along and it feels really nice. We go all the way down to the end of the road but we're not allowed out on the main road so we turn and go back up.

"Race you to the corner," Patrick says.

"Sure, you've no chance." I know I'm much faster than Patrick on my bike because it's bigger than his and has three gears and

140

he doesn't have any, but I let him nearly win just to make him happy. As we turn the corner and cycle up the road there's no sign of either the girls or Barry and Rory. Then we see them coming out of the gates of Maggiore.

"What were you doing in there?" I ask.

"We lost a ball," Yvonne says. "It went into the bushes and we couldn't find it for ages."

"Yeah so we had to help them," says Barry with a funny smirk on his face. I look at Yvonne and Zoe and notice their faces are red, like they're blushing, but maybe that's just from the tennis.

"Did you get it?" asks Patrick.

"Get what?" says Rory.

"The ball of course, did you find the ball?"

"Oh – no, couldn't see it anywhere." And then Barry and Rory start laughing.

"What's so funny?" says Patrick. "You two are really nuts sometimes you know." He laughs and I join in but I don't feel like laughing because my stomach is tied in a knot and I know there's something wrong.

****

If I slipped now or if this little piece of cliff I'm sitting on broke away and slid down and over the edge there I would fall - how far is it a hundred feet? – to the beach below it's funny that I'm not afraid and what's even funnier is that when I lie in bed at night just before I go to sleep and think about walking along the cliff path and about sitting here then I am afraid and then in my imagination I am unable to stop myself from being pulled over the edge of the cliff and falling down to the sand a hundred feet below now that's scary why am I more scared by thinking about it than actually doing it? is it because I am alone in bed at night and things are always scary when you're alone in bed at night and you can't get to sleep? why is everything so scary then? maybe it's just me maybe other people don't get scared so easily I mean I used to be scared of everything even the cold dark bits at the

141

end of the bed I bet no-one else is scared of that I told George once ages ago I was scared of what's at the end of the bed and he laughed and called me a stupid baby and a coward and everything else he could think of and I remember telling Mum too and she called me a silly goose though she said it in a nice way not like George and then she said there was nothing down there and nothing to be afraid of but I can't help it I'm still a bit scared of it and then there's my bad dream where I can't breathe I wonder should I tell Mum about it maybe there's something wrong with me I'm sure it's not normal it always starts with me jumping into a swimming pool but I go so far down that I can't get back up to the surface and I keep swimming and kicking my feet as hard as I can and holding my breath but I can't reach the surface though sometimes I have my eyes open and I can just see the surface but I can't get up there and just when I think my lungs are going to burst and I will have to open my mouth and drown that's when I wake up and I'm really out of breath like I've been holding my breath in my sleep or not able to breath because I was under the blankets or something I hate when it happens it's so scary but it's not nighttime now it's daytime and the sun is shining on the waves making them go all glittery like the waves are on fire and I don't want to think about scary things what I want to think about is what it would be like if she was here I know it's impossible and we'll never get them to come but if we could invite Yvonne and Zoe here for a week in the summer then maybe I could come here with just Zoe and sit here like this looking out over the sea and maybe even hold her hand because she'd be scared of falling over the cliff or maybe she'd slip and nearly fall and I'll save her like this by reaching out my hand and grabbing hers just before she goes over the edge and I'll pull her up onto the field and save her life and then we'll walk back to the Cottage together and she's holding my hand like this and just before we climb over the last grassy bank she stops and turns and looks at me and the sun is shining on her face on the little freckles on her nose and the sunflowers in her eyes are dancing and on fire like the waves of the sea and she says "You saved my life." And then she kisses me not just on the cheek like a friend or an auntie but right on the lips and I can feel her lips so soft against my lips and when they touch I –

"Ka-arl! Ka-arl! Where are you?!"

Oh-oh that's Mummy calling it must be time for lunch I better go home I don't want her to get worried thinking I fell off the cliff or anything I better run back now watch out for the cow pats there are loads of them and watch out for that clump of nettles I better go left no right no left no – oh Lord that's brilliant – I've fallen right in the cow pat! and it's all over my t-shirt and my shorts it must have been a new one it's really runny not hard like when they've been baked in the sun Mum's going to kill me.

At least I missed the nettles.

At night we play cards and Monopoly at the dining table and the huge moths try to get in the window because Mum says they're attracted to the light they keep flapping their wings and banging their heads against the window pane and in the morning I find their bodies lying dead on the outside window-sill like little pieces of torn-up carpet and I nearly feel sorry for them they must really be afraid of the dark that they died trying so hard to get into our house to the light sometimes one of them does get inside the Cottage somehow maybe down the chimney and it starts flapping about all around the ceiling light and George starts screaming then Mum or Dad will have to kill it and throw it into the fireplace because you can't open a door or window to let it out or the house would be full of them and really they're so yucky we wouldn't want that when I wake up in the morning the sun is shining in through the Venetian Blinds because the Cottage faces West no East and that's where the sun gets up so it's shining in and reflected on the sea at the same time so there's twice as much sunshine and Mummy says one day she'll wake us up really early about six or maybe four and actually watch the sun getting up over the horizon that's the line between the sea and the sky though on rainy cloudy days you can't see it all you can see is grey and that means we won't get a swim but if you can see the lighthouse on the horizon that means we'll definitely get a swim probably even two one in the morning down at the bottom of the cliff and one in the

143

afternoon at Ballineskar we wear our old togs in the morning and don't stay in long because it's stony there so we get out and sit in the sun under the cliff where we're sheltered from the wind but in the afternoon we wear our new togs and sit in the sand dunes but it's just as windy there it's always windy when I get up and it's a lovely sunny day like today I just put on my shorts and a tea shirt and my old runners or sandals I don't even bother with socks so I look just like the children in the Famous Five books which is really brill then we have breakfast outside sitting in the sun I can see the sun shining on the milk in my bowl of corn flakes and the bubbles are like little tiny suns themselves because they're round and yellow and they shine like the sun when the sun shines on my eyes and I close them nearly up completely I can see the light on my eyelashes and they're kind of blurry and they make little rainbows I can see all the colours of the rainbow in little sparkly dots like coloured stars millions of miles away cept they're right in front of my eyes and they're so beautiful the sun shines on the sea the same way with little sparkly circles Mum is sitting in her favourite chair the one with the stripy canvas back that folds up and she has her head back like she's looking up at the sun but I can see her eyes are closed and she's got a little smile on her face she looks so happy and that makes me happy too because she's never as happy anywhere or anytime as here in the Cottage.

****

"This meeting is called to order," says Andrew banging our hammer – the little one not the big one - on a block of firewood. "Order! Order!"

"He likes being Chairman doesn't he?" Patrick beside me says.

"Yes, he does it very well, he really has a knack with that hammer."

"Be quiet you two and listen to Andrew," Kieran is sitting on the other side of Patrick and he's taking this very seriously.

"This meeting is called to order. There are two items on the agenda. Since we don't have any written minutes I am going to say what they are and then look for a proposer and seconder. Right, order!" Andrew is getting a bit cross because Yvonne and Zoe won't stop talking about some clothes they saw in a shop and Barry is giving George a lecture about someone called Eric Clapton and what a brilliant guitarist he is but George is looking bored. So Andrew bangs his hammer on the block of wood a couple more times as hard as he can and then something funny happens - the block of wood breaks in half and we all laugh.

"Order! Order!" Andrew shouts and he's getting so upset we feel sorry for him and try to be quiet though me and Patrick are finding it hard to stop laughing.

"First item on the agenda: moving the premises of the clubhouse from the Jones's garage ground floor to the Mullen's garage roof space. Mr Mullen has very kindly said he will fix it up for us with floorboards and carpets and a ladder. Who is going to propose the motion?"

"Propose the what?" Yvonne says. "That sounds rude." And we all crack up again.

"What's a motion?" asks Patrick.

"It's like a proposal or a suggestion," I explain.

"Oh thanks."

"It's also when you do a poo," I add.

"Oh thanks – uuugh!"

"Who proposes that we move to the Mullen's garage?"

"I do," says George. I can see he's just hoping to get closer to Yvonne, he'd move in to the Mullen's house if he could.

"Who will second the motion?"

"Seconded," says Barry, probably for the same reason.

"All in favour say Aye." We all say "Aye" except for Kieran.

"All against say Nay."

"Nay!" says Kieran very loudly. "I don't want everyone up in my garage loft. That's my space."

"Not any more brother," says Yvonne, giving him a dig in the side.

"The Ayes have it," says Andrew. "Motion carried." Then we all start talking at once.

"Brilliant! When do we move?"

"What kind of ladder? Is it a rope ladder?"

"Where did you get the carpets?"

"Your Dad's great."

"Can't wait, it'll be brill!"

Andrew starts banging the hammer again. "Order! Order! We now come to the second item on the agenda." As we all calm down he puts on this really serious face and pushes his glasses up his little nose.

"As we all know the tragic death has taken place recently of The Beatles' manager Barry Epstein.

"I know."

"That was very sad ."

"Who's going to look after them?"

"Order! Now as everyone knows, a successful pop group needs a manager, they simply cannot survive without one."

"Why not?" asks Patrick. "What does a manager do anyway?"

"Well he manages them doesn't he?" Andrew tries to explain. "He gets them concerts and recording deals and takes care of their money and stuff like that."

"Oh ok, thanks." Everyone is looking at Patrick as if he's stupid but we're actually all glad he asked because none of us really knew either.

"So if we want the Beatles to continue being the Fab Four and making great records and touring and maybe coming to Ireland again like they did in 1963 but we were too young to go see them then we have to make sure they have a proper manager."

"So are you going to apply for the job?" Asks Yvonne and everyone laughs.

"No I'm not," replies Andrew. "We all are."

"What?"

146

"You're joking!"

"Good one!"

"Very funny!"

"Order! No I'm serious. The Beatles need a manager and we are going to write to them and offer our services."

"Oh yeah they're really going to want us as a manager, we're just a bunch of kids!" Barry says.

"Yeah, what do we know about managing a pop group?" agrees George. Then everybody joins in and there's bedlam for a while. That's a good word bedlam, it comes from Bethlehem which was a madhouse in London a few hundred years ago, I read about it in History.

"We could learn," says Andrew.

"We'd have to go and live in Liverpool."

"They don't live in Liverpool any more."

"Where do they live?"

"I don't know. London I think."

"Well we can't all go and live in London."

"Maybe they could come and live over here."

"Yeah sure, the four of them are going to come and live with us, I don't think so." - Barry.

"I want Paul," Zoe says immediately. "He can have your bed Yvonne so we can share a room."

"He's not getting my bed. Anyway I want John – so he'll have to have *your* bed."

"George can stay with us." George of course.

"I don't want any of them, especially not Ringo," Patrick says, making a face. "It's bad enough having to share my room with Barry, the last thing I want is to have Ringo there too, imagine the noise from his drums."

"Yeah," I add. "You'd never get any sleep."

"Order! Order! They don't have to come and stay with us, we're just going to write and offer to help, to show that we care and want to support them in their hour of need."

147

"Hour of need!" says Barry, "Are you nuts? It's the Beatles we're talking about. They don't need us!"

"Order! Let's put it to a vote. Those in favour of writing to the Beatles and offering to manage them raise your hands." Zoe and I put our hands up, and when no-one else does apart from Andrew, we look at each other and laugh.

"Those against raise your hands." Everyone else puts up their hands.

"The motion is defeated. But I have a secondary motion. I propose that we at least write to the Beatles and express our sympathy for their loss and offer the sympathy of all their young fans in Ireland. All in favour raise your hands."

This time we all put up our hands except Barry.

"The motion is carried," Andrew says, "Now who's going to write the letter?"

"YOU ARE!" we all shout at once.

"All right, all right, keep your hair on," says Andrew. "Now, what's their address?" Nobody really has a clue about this so I say something.

"Just send it to: The Beatles, London, England. That should get to them."

"Right," says Andy, "Meeting adjourned."

"The next time we have a meeting will be in your garage," I say to Zoe as we leave.

"I hope it's more comfier than sitting on your hard peat briquettes," she replies, which reminds me to ask Patrick:

"Is that paint tin still digging you?" He has to think for a minute then he replies:

"Now you're trying to get me confused! I don't dig it, it's bugging me!"

"That's it, now you've got it. Are you really getting carpets?" I ask Zoe.

"So Dad said."

"Wow – luxury!"

"I know!"

"I can't wait."

"Me too," says Zoe and smiles really nicely at me and just when I'm about to say something about her Dad being great to do up the garage for us she walks away worse luck.

****

"What good is that going to do?" I ask Barry as he sets up the record player on his bedroom window sill. Patrick is doing one of his "He's crazy" signs with his finger at the side of his head.

"I know," I agree with him.

"Look it's very simple," says Barry, "We just keep playing it till she comes to the window. She's bound to come when she hears it. You have to see her, she's so beautiful." Beautiful? That's what my brother said this morning, when we were having breakfast.

"Have you seen the Mullen's cousin?" he says in between shoveling cornflakes into his mouth.

"Didn't know they had a cousin. Why? What about him?"

"Noh a im, a er," he replies, tilting his mouth upwards trying to stop all the cornflakes and milk from falling out as he speaks.

"A her?"

"Yes. And she's beautiful," he adds, before taking another huge spoonful.

Beautiful? I'm wondering what on earth he is on about.

"And guess what her name is. You'll never believe what her name is."

"Is it Arthur?" I ask.

"Don't be stupid. Go on, guess properly."

"Albert? Alouisius? Look George, I've got to get out to school, and even though it's Saturday I don't want to be late. Drama first, then Art, all my favourites. So if you want to tell me her name hurry up."

"Michelle," he says with this really smug grin, as if he had just revealed the most amazing secret of all time.

"Michelle. So what?"

149

"Michelle ma Belle. Don't you get it? The Beatles – Michelle, isn't that amazing? Wait till you see her, she is absolutely gorgeous."

"I can't wait. No I really I can't wait, I've got to go to school." That was this morning and now I'm hearing the same stuff all over again from Barry.

"So what? What do we do then?" I ask. "This is just going to be embarrassing."

"Really embarrassing," agrees Patrick, "I'm getting away from the window, I don't want to be seen."

"Go on then, who cares, don't need you anyway." Barry has now got the record on the turntable, it's not the same one that we have "Michelle" on, Dad's one that he bought, A Collection of Beatles, it's not even the version that's on the Revolver album because, according to Barry, that wouldn't work, no it's the single.

"See, I can make it keep playing over and over just by having this switch on." And he turns a switch beside the turntable and, sure enough, when the record is over and the pickup arm picks up, it goes all the way back, drops down into place, and then gives a click and starts again. Barry has the window open and each time the record plays he turns up the volume until it's at the highest it will go and I'd say everybody on the street can hear The Beatles singing "Michelle". Everybody except Michelle the Mullen's cousin that is, as there's still no sign of her from the next door window. I pick up a big cardboard tube that's sitting there and say:

"What's this?" and start looking at it from both ends.

"It's a kaleidoscope of course, what do you think it is?" Barry shouts.

I make signs at Patrick that I haven't a clue what a kaleidoscope is and he shows me how it works, putting it up to my eye and twirling the end bit.

"Wow!" I say, too amazed at the whirling colours and patterns inside to care what Barry thinks of me. "That is incredible!"

"Have you really never seen a kaleidoscope before?"

"No I haven't, that is amazing!" And I keep turning the end bit to make the colours and patterns twirl around until I come to one image that is exactly like Zoe's sunflower eyes. And then the words of that song on Sgt Pepper's come into my head: "The girl with kaleidoscope eyes … look for the girl with the sun in her eyes and she's gone." And I realise that it's Zoe the Beatles are singing about, that she's the girl with kaleidoscope eyes. Lost in my own world I say:

"Wow! That's just like Zo- " and then I remember in time where I am so I shut up.

"What? It's like what?" asks Patrick.

"Oh – nothing, it's like the pattern in our hall carpet that's all." I twirl the kaleidoscope a bit more but I can't find the bit that looked like Zoe's eyes again so I put it down and start wandering around the boys' bedroom looking at their posters, all of which are new since the last time I was there. There's all the stuff from inside Sgt Pepper's on one wall, then a poster of Bob Dylan in really funny colours, loads of pinups from the inside of magazines and even some stuff from the Beatles Monthly which Barry cut out. It's not all of the Beatles either. Most of his favourite bands I've never even heard of like Tangerine Dream and the Yardbirds. I'm looking at a poster of some guys called Pink Floyd thinking they all look the same when Barry gives a shout from the window and me and Patrick look over.

"Look – they're here! Yvonne and Zoe and look there's Michelle and they're going to – Oh!"

Me and Patrick make it over to the window just in time to see the curtains on the girls' bedroom opposite being drawn very firmly.

"Yeah you're right, that Michelle really is beautiful," I say and Patrick cracks up.

****

"We were chatting for ages, in the Mullen's kitchen, just me and Yvonne and Michelle. Mrs Mullen was there for a while all right but it was mainly me and Michelle talking to each other, Yvonne was helping her mother with some stuff, cooking or something, so it was really just the two of us, we got on so well, she's such a fantastic bird."

151

"'She's such a fantastic bird'!?" I repeat but he just says, "Yeah" like he thought I was agreeing with him. I can't believe my brother sometimes. We're just finishing our homework, sitting at our places at the worktop in the playroom, him on the left me on the right, books on the shelves over our heads, toy cupboard on my right with the cowboy box and Lego box, another toy cupboard on my left with the cars, paints and other stuff, Mum's upstairs somewhere I think she might be on the phone, and Dad hasn't come home yet.

"Yeah she is, I think she likes me too. It's a pity she couldn't stay longer but I don't think she'll forget me." Then he starts picking his nose so I can't look at him.

"No of course not, how could she?"

"Yeah you're right," he says, and then actually sighs. I want to get sick. "Well she's gone now," he goes on, pulling himself together. "Did you not see her at all?"

"No, just someone pulling the curtains very quickly."

"And how many times did he play the record?"

"About twenty I'd say."

"That's really funny, you really made an impression there I can see."

"Who cares?" But in spite of myself I am curious about the Mullen's beautiful cousin, I mean I would have liked to have seen her once at least.

"Where is she from?" I ask George.

"Clonmel I think it's called but I don't know where that is."

"It's in Tipperary."

"If you say so. Yvonne said she's going to visit more often in future."

"Now that she's met you I suppose," I say, trying to be funny.

"Yes I suppose you're right." George doesn't always get when I'm being sarcastic. I look at him and try not to laugh. I'll say this much for George, he keeps me amused. The radio is on and it's playing "Hello Goodbye".

"Do you think they'll be number one for Christmas?"

"Who? He asks. He really doesn't pay attention sometimes.

152

"Who? Tom and Jerry. Who do you think?"

"Huh?"

"The Beatles! Hello Goodbye! Then I start singing: *Hello hello! I don't know why you say goodbye I say hello!*".

"Oh yeah that. I dunno. I suppose so."

"I think they will. It's such a great song, I'm going to buy the single when I get my pocket money."

"Yeah, so am I." He's still not paying attention.

"We don't both need to buy it you know. Then we'd have two copies."

"Oh yeah, right." My brother – sometimes I wonder where Mum and Dad got him.

****

This is incredible! This must be the first time in my life I've stood in front of this mirror and not felt bad. I've got my new wool waistcoat, my new hat with the flaps pulled down over the ears, and new leather gloves, they're the best of all, the most beautiful gloves I've ever seen and the first pair of real leather ones I've ever owned. I'm not going to wear the hat when I go out because I'm not sure what they will think of it but later on I'll put it on when nobody's looking. All for Christmas. All Christmas presents either from Mum and Dad or from Santa though I don't really believe in Santa any more but I don't want to say anything because I think George and Mum and Dad do. It's nearly ten o'clock we'll be allowed go out at ten and I can see the others out on the road already maybe we'll go into St Mark's it's so beautiful in there in the winter sometimes there's frost on the grass and the bushes and the last time we found all these spiders' webs with frost on them they were so beautiful like fairies' wings even though they were made by spiders and Zoe hates spiders and she wouldn't even look at them but then I showed her the ice on the surface of the pond and we poked at it with a stick and some of it broke up and I took a big piece of ice out of the water and gave it to her she said it was like really old glass all bubbly and uneven like you see in ancient buildings before they knew how to make glass properly which is something no-one else would ever say and we looked at each other through it like a window and the ice had little bubbles in it and bits of leaf and twig and the sun was shining through it too and as she held it up in the sunshine it started to melt and drip down onto her gloves and our shoes so I took it from her and threw it right across the surface of the pond and it splintered into a million little pieces and they all went skating across the frozen surface of the pond and she said "Wow! That's amazing!" and when I looked at her the sun was shining in her eyes making her sunflowers light up and it really was amazing standing there with her in the sunshine with the frost all around us and the ice in the surface of the pond and the sun in her eyes and –

"Karl, come on, it's ten, we can go now!" George downstairs. Yes it's time! I take a deep breath, make a wish and fly downstairs. Out on the road we meet the Mullens, the Blaneys, Andrew and even Rory worse luck and they're all talking about what they got for Christmas.

"You won't believe what Patrick asked Santa for," Barry is saying. "And he actually got it. Show them Patrick, show them the most important thing you wanted for Christmas."

Patrick has this look on his face as he reaches into his pocket and pulls out a yo-yo and we all laugh.

"The old one broke," he says in this baby voice that he puts on sometimes.

"Idiot!" says his brother and pretends to give him a whack.

"Leave Patrick alone you big bully," says Zoe. "I think it's cute."

"That isn't all I got," Patrick goes on. " I also got a book and a pair of socks with reindeers on them. All he got was some hard rock albums that made us all deaf when he put them on yesterday."

"Yeah they're so brilliant – Jimmy Hendrix Experience 'Electric Ladyland' and Cream 'Wheels of Fire'" and we all look at each other like we haven't a clue what he's on about. Then he starts pretending to play guitar and making weird guitar noises like "Doyng! Woyng! Oyng! Weeng!" and everybody starts laughing.

154

"Shut up! They're the greatest!" he says. "Do you want to see my Elvis impression?"

"NO!!" We all shout.

"I got a book on Dinosaurs," says Kieran.

"Bo-ring!" says Yvonne. "I got some really cool clothes."

"So did I," says Zoe. She's standing in the driveway clapping her hands in front of her then behind her, in front of her and behind her and kind of rocking to and fro. "New shoes and a cool pair of jeans but we're not allowed wear them yet in case they get dirty."

"I got an Airfix set too," Kieran adds.

"Nobody cares about your stupid Airfix sets Kieran," says Yvonne. "That's all you ever want."

"Yeah well at least they're more fun than clothes." Just then a car horn hooting makes us look round and see the Mullen's Volkswagen Beetle reversing out of their drive. Mrs Mullen is rolling down the window and waving for someone to come.

"Go on, you're the oldest," says Zoe and Yvonne runs over to the car.

"Actually that should be 'eldest' as it's the oldest member of a family," says Andrew as we're all looking down the road at Yvonne talking through the window to her mother. "You say 'eldest' of a number of siblings."

"A number of what?" says Patrick.

"Siblings – you know what siblings are, don't you?" Patrick obviously doesn't so Andrew turns to his brother.

"Barry – do you know what siblings are? If so, you can explain it to your sibling."

"Of course I know what siblings are, they're baby rabbits," says Barry.

I laugh because I think he's being funny but it seems he just hasn't been listening.

"No they're not baby rabbits," Andrew says seriously, "Try again."

"Look, I couldn't care less what stupid siblings are, all right?" Barry is fuming. "You're not our teacher, so stop acting like one!"

155

"Just trying to help," says Andrew softly.

"Well don't. I don't need your help."

"All right, I won't bother then."

"Good, I couldn't care less."

"I'd hate to have you as a pupil."

"I'd hate to have you as a teacher."

"Long-haired hippie."

"Specky four eyes."

"Juvenile delinquent."

"Same to you."

"Same to you with knobs on."

"Same to you with knobs on and brass buttons." By this time they're not really cross with each other and just joking and Yvonne is back saying:

"What's up?"

"The sky is up," says Patrick.

"Barry and Andrew were just having an interesting discussion," I say.

"Where's your Mum gone?" George asks.

"Oh just to visit some people but we have to go soon Bridie's made us lunch."

"Did you say 'Where's your Mum gone'?" I ask George, "That's wrong – it's 'Where's your Mama gone?'" And then I start singing the song:

"Where's your Mama gone? Where's your Mama gone?
Little baby gone – little baby gone
Where's your Mama gone? Where's your Mama gone?
Far far away .... Far far away.
Last night I heard your Mama singing a song"

And then everyone joins in:
"Ooh-wee chirpy chirpy cheep cheep!"
"Woke up this morning and my Mama was gone
"Ooh-wee chirpy chirpy cheep cheep
Chirpy Chirpy Cheep Cheep Chirp!"

We do that kind of thing a lot, it's the best ever.

"We also got something really amazing," Yvonne goes on, "But we have to share it. Me and Zoe. Will we tell them?" She looks at her sister. Zoe has this look on her face that I've never seen before, like she's really pleased with herself maybe but I don't really understand it and I don't know if I like it.

"Hair curling set," she says.

Everybody is silent for a second because either we don't know what a hair curling set is, or we can't think of anything to say about it.

"Lovely," says Andrew at last. "You can both have nice curly hair then."

Then Rory starts messing with his hair and going "Oooh – hair curlers!" and walking round like a girl with his hand on his hip pretending to be a model like in that Miss World competition Dad likes to watch but Mum doesn't.

"Can I borrow it?" says Barry and we all look at him thinking he's mad.

"Hendrix!" he says. "I can make my hair really frizzy and look like Jimi Hendrix, that'd be cool."

"As far as I know Jimi Hendrix has black hair, he is a black man isn't he?" I point out.

"Yeah – so? I could die it too."

"Yeah and paint your face," I add and we all laugh except Barry who's really mad at me.

"You could make yourself look like a Black and White Minstrel," says Patrick and he can't stop laughing until Barry whacks him.

"There's a Black and White Minstrel Show Christmas Special on tonight," says Kieran and everybody looks at him. "I like the Minstrels," he goes on, "I think they're really funny."

"Are you serious?" Barry says. "I wouldn't watch that rubbish if it was the only thing on TV. Anyway do you not know what's on tonight?" Kieran obviously doesn't know what on tonight as he looks blankly at Barry.

157

"The Beatles new movie you idiot – Magical Mystery Tour of course."

"Ah yes," says Andrew, "But only if you have BBC2 and not everyone has you know."

"We don't."

"We don't."

"Neither do we."

"Well, we do!" says Barry, "And since we seem to be the only household who have BBC2 - " and he stops and looks around at all of us, until we all think we know what he's going to say next, I can tell from everyone's faces that they're expecting an invitation to watch the film in Blaneys' until he says – "We're going to be the only ones who'll get to see it!"

"Thanks Barry."

"Very nice of you."

"Hope your aerial falls off the roof."

But in the middle of this something terrible happens. Zoe is looking straight at me and asking:

"What did you get for Christmas Karl?"

"Well you're looking at most of it," I reply smiling. "Waistcoat, gloves, and - " Feeling confident enough even though everyone is looking at me I pull the new hat out of my pocket and put it on, pulling the flaps down over my ears.

" – Hat!"

I'm looking at her face wondering what she's thinking and I can't believe it but I think she's trying not to laugh, and now somebody beside me is laughing I think it's George or Barry and Zoe has her hand in front of her mouth and I can't think of anything to say my stomach is tying itself into a knot and I can feel my face going red.

"Sorry," Zoe says, "I don't mean to ... it's really cute but it's just that ..."

"What?!" I ask in desperation.

"Well, it's just the flaps, they make you look a bit like a poodle."

"A poodle?"

158

"Yeah – sorry – like Lulu."

"That's a rotten thing to say," says Barry beside me, "And totally untrue." I look at him and wonder why he's sticking up for me. "He doesn't look like Lulu ... he looks like Dilly!" And he bursts out laughing grabs the hat off my head and throws it to Rory who starts running round with it then everyone joins in and suddenly they're all playing catch with my hat throwing it to each other while I run after it trying to get it back every time someone has it and I run over to them they hold it up as high as they can so it's out of reach and then they throw it to someone else I know I shouldn't go after it but I can't stop myself and I can't believe this nightmare is happening and my friends are treating me like this and then it gets worse because I can feel tears coming to my eyes and my face is burning and I'm full of tears of frustration and rage and mostly shame that they are doing this to me I've never felt so angry in my life and I really hate Barry and Rory as it's mainly those two who are throwing the hat to each other and holding it up out of my reach because they're so much bigger than me I thought my hat would be great for covering my ears and making me look better but now it's turned into this nightmare that I don't know how to stop but in the end it is Yvonne who feels sorry for me and gives it back to me.

"Here, Karl, have your hat, I think it's nice." As I take it from her I feel grateful to Yvonne and I wonder for the first time if Zoe even likes me at all that she could say that to me and laugh at me and I wonder how I could have been such a fool to think that she liked me.

"Who saw Christmas Top of the Pops?" asks George and for once I'm grateful to him for changing the subject as I roll up my hat and put it in my pocket.

"Yeah, brill!"

"Fantastic!"

"I knew the Beatles were going to be Number One for Christmas," George says and I can't believe he's said that but I couldn't be bothered to remind him that it was me who predicted it.

Then out of the blue Rory comes out with:

"Have you heard this one? Julius Caesar let a breezer off the coast of France. Hitler tried to do the same but did it in his pants." Then he starts roaring laughing.

"That's disgusting," says Yvonne, "Come on Zoe, we have to go in for lunch." And the two of them go off. After they've gone it's just the boys left and I don't really want to hang around. I'm still feeling really hurt about the way they took my hat and laughed at me. But now that I think about it again lying here in bed I remember that it was Barry and Rory who first took my hat and wouldn't give it back and then started passing it around but I don't remember if Zoe did that too and maybe when she said I looked like a poodle she was only joking and didn't mean it yes that's probably it she was only joking I hope. Anyway the hat's up on the shelf in the cloakroom now and I don't know if I'll be wearing it again.

****

Another New Year's Eve another year wasted another year gone when I didn't kiss her how can it happen and that Rory always there maybe she likes him more than me no that's impossible maybe she just doesn't like me at all I'm getting old I'll be ten next year and I still haven't even kissed a girl if I don't do it next year I don't know what I'll do and next year it will be

1968

I'm supposed to do something what is it oh yeah the cloak or cape thing I don't really know how to pick it up properly why didn't I check it why didn't I have a good look at the way it's folded over the kneeler so I would know how to pick it up I don't want to pick it up at all because I know I'll get the wrong corners and there won't be a catch there and when I hand it to the priest he won't be able to fasten it and it will fall off him but now Ken is nodding at me to go over and get it Oh God I better pick it up the right way genuflect in front of the tabernacle where are the catches I can't see them is that one which one is it left or right I've no idea if I pick up this one in my left hand and this side in my right hand will that work here goes back into the middle up the altar steps no need to genuflect he said why didn't he just do it himself he's much older than me and he's done it before why did he make me do it Oh God up the steps and the priest's got his hands over his shoulders reaching out for the two corners with the catches on them I've done it he's got them and he's fastened it around his neck now back down the steps genuflect this time and kneel down back where I was everything went fine so why is Ken scowling at me and making faces and pointing at the priest Oh God no he's got it on inside out it's supposed to say IHS I don't know what that means all I know is it's not I Hate School that's just a joke I heard and it's supposed to have lots of gold embroid-ery and padded bits but there's nothing but some loose threads and stitching well who's going to notice anyway but now Ken's going back up the steps and taking it off the priest and turning it around and putting it back on the right way Oh God that's so embarrassing now everyone knows I did it the wrong way how was I supposed to know I got the catches and gave it to him it's not my fault except it is I should have checked will I look at Mum oh she's got a funny look on her face now she's giving me a little smile doing her best to make me feel better she's so good but she knows I messed up and so does everyone else what's next – concentrate - Communion after the priest gives it to the nuns he turns around and holds out the patten I have to take it and hold it under the people's chins when they're receiving Holy Communion now he's starting the Eucharistic Prayer that goes on forever but I have to pay attention because I have to ring the bell at the end at the what's it called the Consecration all these strange religious words like Transubstan-tiation and Ceborium and Paraclete and Tabernacle and my favourites Cherubim and Seraphim in unceasing chorus praising and all the rules like fasting that's a funny word to fast it's like running fast that was a brilliant match we won 36-6 and I scored three tries the last one was unbelievable the ball came out of the scrum and Dec kicked it way over their heads over to my side I could see it was going to bounce and anything could happen but it bounced right into my hands and I just had to cross the line and run round under the posts for a try between the posts that's the first time I scored between the posts it was amazing and – now what? – Ken's scowling at me again oh God the priest's raising the Host I have to ring the bell - there - that's giving it a good twist there's all these little bells four of them on one big bell and when I twist it they all ring at the same time it's a great bell I better pay attention now because after the priest's given Communion to the nuns I'll have to take the patten and the church is full for these Easter Ceremonies it's never been so full well that wouldn't be hard usually at Sunday Mass at eight o'clock there's no-one except Mum and the old man who can't sing for nuts and maybe a couple of others but today is Holy Thursday and it's packed I wonder will that girl with the blond hair and the blue hat be there if she is I'll try and touch her neck with the patten just the gentlest touch to make her look at me and see if it works she's so beautiful there goes the priest over to the nuns they have a little hatch behind a screen so no-one can see them but I can see them as they come up to get Communion some of them really old but some are young and pretty even with the black habit and the head thing I think it's called a dimple or a wimple and they all sing so beautifully like angels Mummy says and it's true that painting of the crucifixion over the altar is amazing it's so big it takes up the whole wall I love it but I hate it too I can see the two thieves in the distance but if I stand here I am beside them and the other cross is lying on the ground waiting for the next one to arrive he's going to be nailed on proper not just tied Praetorius said I could do it nice job I'm going to enjoy that and I get to arrest him too choose my own men need twenty in case he puts up a fight he's got his personal bodyguard I hear they're useless pacifists the lot of them don't believe in fighting suits me fine but you never know he's tricky that one people say he can do magic raise people from the dead and cure them load of bloody rubbish orders are to proceed to Gethsemane and arrest him I know it that old garden place with the old olive trees on the other side of town there he is in the garden with his men – about a dozen of them but all unarmed the idiots - what a ragbag of a bodyguard I don't believe it they're all asleep this'll be the easiest arrest I've ever made now the priest is finished giving the nuns their communion and I've got to take the patten here goes…

I can't believe it she didn't even come up to Communion why would she not come to Communion the only reason someone doesn't receive Communion is if they've committed a sin she couldn't commit a sin she's too beautiful and nice looking unless - oh yeah maybe she ate something if you eat something within an hour you can't go to Communion that must be it she must have had her tea first - I wonder what she had for tea?

I can't believe this we're actually here at the gates of Aras an Uachtaran   where the President of Ireland lives. These gates are so amazing and so big and so ... locked.

"Why won't they let us in?" says George beside me. "Do they not know we have an invitation to visit the President? Are they not expecting us?"

"Yes of course they're expecting us," says Mum, "Be patient, here he comes now."

"Who's he? Is he the gatekeeper?"

"Shush George," says Dad, rolling down the window. "Hello, we have an appointment at 11 o'clock to meet President DeValera." Dad sounds all posh when he says this and I wonder do we all have to talk posh when we go in here.

"Eh, Mr Jones is it?" says the gatekeeper looking in the car window and checking a list he has on a piece of paper. "And that'd be Mrs Jones? Right. And the two youngfellas. Right you be mister. Just keep on to the end of the drive till ya come to the house and yis can park anywheres ya like."

This chap certainly isn't bothering to sound posh so maybe it's just Dad. I hope he's not going to keep it up.

"Thank you very much my good man," says Dad and I shrink down in the back seat.

We drive up the long winding driveway which seems to go on forever then suddenly Dad is looking all around him and opening the glove compartment and:

"Oh Lord I haven't forgotten them have I?"

"What?" asks Mum.

"The calendars of course – where are they? I thought they were here."

"They're in the boot, remember?" says Mum patiently. "They were too big to fit in the car so they're lying down flat in the boot. Are you nervous?"

"Nervous? What makes you say that? We're only about to meet the President of Ireland that's all. What's there to be nervous about?"

"That's funny Dad," says George.

"What are we doing with the calendars?" I ask because although I know I've been told I've forgotten.

"Oh Lord," Dad groans, "Don't you ever listen? They're commemorative calendars to mark the fiftieth anniversary of your grandfather's company. He wants all the original founders of the company to sign them."

"And Dev was one of the founders right?" says George looking smug.

"Yes but for God's sake don't call him Dev!" says Dad trying very hard to control his temper. "You have to address him as Mr President."

"Aw!" George moans, "I was going to go in and say, 'Howaye Dev!'"

"It's OK Dad he's only joking, he knows what to say." Dad's glaring at the two of us in the rear mirror so I'm trying to calm him down.

"Now here we are," says Mum perfectly calmly. "Everyone on their best behaviour now, don't let us down."

"Is Grandfather here yet?" I ask as we get out of the car.

"I think that might be him now," says Dad and we turn to see a big black Mercedes coming up the drive. I can tell it's a Mercedes because of the star on the bonnet and the radiator grill it's like a gate with bars across. The car stops beside ours and the driver gets out but it's not Grandfather, he's in the back, and the driver is his chauffeur from the office. He opens the back door and helps Grandfather out. He has a stick because he's pretty old now, he was born in the last century and he fought against the British in the GPO in 1916, I'm so proud of him. Dad is getting the calendars from our boot and Mum and George and me go up to Grandfather and shake hands with him. He's wearing a big old black wool coat with a row of medals on the left side.

165

"Well boys," he says, "This is a big day, you're going to meet the President of the country, what do you think?"

"Yes Grandfather," I say, being unable to think of anything else. Then George says:

"When you fought in 1916, was President Devalera in the GPO with you?"

"Dev in the GPO? No fear, he might have been shot at. No, he was in charge of a biscuit factory. But don't tell him I said that." He winks at us and smiles. He may be old but he's pretty smart I'd say.

"Have you got the calendars son?" He says to Dad as we head for the front door of the big white house which I notice has been opened by what looks like the butler. He's wearing a funny looking black jacket that's short at the front and long at the back and his trousers are black with thin white stripes. He's even got white gloves.

"Hey look," says George to me under his breath, "It's Jeeves."

"Yes Sir, I have them right here," says Dad. He always calls his Dad Sir which I think is really funny but nice in a way.

"Come on then, let's meet the old soldier, there aren't many of us left."

Inside the door the butler takes our coats and Mum's little pink hat that matches her pink suit and leads us through a couple of enormous empty rooms until we come to one with closed double doors. He knocks, opens both doors and walks in. Then I hear this:

"Mr M W Jones senior; Mr M W Jones junior; Mrs Jones, Master George and Master Karl Jones." I look at George and we're both trying not to grin. We're in a library or study, not as big as the rooms we've just passed through but pretty big anyway. It's got bookshelves from floor to ceiling on three walls, the fourth being nearly all glass, with enormous French windows in the middle like the Mullen's sunroom only a million times bigger. There are also a number of sofas and armchairs, and in the middle of the room is an enormous desk at which is sitting the most important person I have ever met. He gets up as we arrive and I can see he's even older than

166

Grandfather but very tall and he stands up really straight. He looks quite blind with eyes that are just slits behind little round gold-framed glasses just like the ones John Lennon is wearing on the cover of Sgt Pepper's but somehow I can't imagine him singing Lucy in the Sky with Diamonds.

The President greets us all in turn but doesn't say much. Then we all find somewhere to sit and the butler asks us what we would like to drink. Grandfather says he'd like a Brandy, Dad asks for a gin and tonic, Mum would like a glass of sherry, and then he comes to me. Feeling brave I ask for a Coke and George says the same.

Dad and Grandfather are sitting on hard chairs up at the desk and they are showing Dev the calendars and the three of them start talking about what's on them. There are other signatures there already and Dev's will be the last one. Mum's looking round at the room like she'd really love to get up and look at all the books and when I catch her eye she smiles and I know we're both thinking the same thing that we can't believe we are actually there. A couple of minutes later Jeeves comes back in with a tray of drinks and starts handing them out. Then he comes to us.

"I am afraid we do not have any Coca Cola at present. Would you care for some MiWadi orange instead?"

"Yes please, that will be very nice," Mum says before either of us can start complaining, but really how disappointing not having any Coke in the Aras I'm thinking, and MiWadi? I mean that's just for babies. But then from the other side of the desk comes a voice that is like nothing I have ever heard before in my life.

"We'll make sure we have some for your next visit," the President says. I know he was born in County Clare in the West of Ireland where they have a lot of limestone rock I read about it in Geography and saw pictures of this place called The Burren where there is nothing but these smooth flat rocks for miles around and that's what his voice sounds like – smooth, hard, cold and ancient as the limestone of his native County Clare.

After we get our drinks a man comes in with a big camera and we have to get out of the way while he takes pictures of Dev signing the calendar with Grandfather and Dad standing on either side of him, then some more of Dev on his own then another one with Mum in it.

"We mustn't neglect the ladies," Dev says. "And what about the boys? Let's get one with the boys, come on." And he waves George and myself to come up to him. I'm in such shock that I forget I'm still holding my drink and have a slight accident when George pushes me sideways round the huge desk and I sort of trip over the carpet and spill a bit of MiWadi on one of the calendars. Dad's about to go ape but luckily Dev just takes out a massive hankie, wipes it off and says, "At least it's not blood, there's been enough of that spilt, isn't that right Michael?"

And my grandfather puts his hand on Dev's arm and says, "You're right there Chief, God knows you're right."

After the calendars have been signed (one is for Dev to keep which he seems pleased about) and we've finished our drinks, we are all ushered out through the French windows to admire the gardens which go on forever. We have a stroll around and then the same chap turns up again with his camera on a stand which he plonks down facing the house and we all have to line up in front of it for our photo. So here we are, George, Mum, me, Dev, Dad and Grandfather all standing in a row, Mum in her best pink suit, me and George in our school uniforms and the three men in their dark suits. Dev's standing a little behind me, because I'm smallest they've put me in front and he's got his arm around me with his hand resting on my shoulder and I can feel him there like a great pillar of strength and power behind me and the photographer is telling us all to look at him now and holding up his hand and clicking something in it and as we stand here looking out at the gardens with the great white house behind us I'm thinking that whatever happens to me in my life I will always remember this moment and I will always feel the strength of this mighty Irish warrior at my back. Then when we're going back in through the French windows George trips me up again and I end up on the rug but I don't think anybody really noticed.

168

****

"Ow! The water's freezing!" This water really is freezing in the swimming pool in Blackrock, but it's so brill being here, the Mullens and us.

"I've got a warm spot underneath me," says Kieran.

"What do you mean? Oh!" Zoe.

"Kieran! Uhhh!" Yvonne.

"Yeuch!"

"That's disgusting!"

"What wrong? What's the fuss?" Mrs Mullen's here too.

"Kieran's just peed in the pool."

"That's a terrible thing to do, I'm getting out." So is Mr Mullen.

"I was only joking - I didn't really pee."

"Yes you did! You always do that." Well, his sisters should know.

"It was only a little bit."

"Well don't do it again," says Mrs Mullen, "There's a toilet in the changing room."

This is nice, just us and the Mullens, Mr and Mrs Mullen brought us all here in the big car, the Mercedes, all five of us squeezed into the back seat and even little Debbie in the front on her mother's knee, Kieran telling us all the time he was going to get sick because he wasn't allowed sit in the front, me squashed in between George and the door he was beside Yvonne all right but I was nowhere near Zoe and couldn't even see her but I can't wait to see her in the pool in her swimsuit and show her how good a swimmer I am.

"Hey! Don't splash it's freezing!" That was Kieran just splashed me and now I'm splashing him back but he ducks and I get Zoe by mistake worse luck.

"Hey - Karl! I'll get you for that!" And now she's turned her back and is scooping the water backwards at me with her hands and I'm getting pelted with the freezing cold water but I couldn't care less

I'm so happy Zoe isn't a very confident swimmer she keeps holding on to her Dad it's really cute like she's a little girl Yvonne can swim all right so can Kieran but they're not very good I don't imagine they could swim very fast or very far not like me and George we've been swimming for years all those lessons in that Iveagh Baths pool every Tuesday night then down in the Cottage for years swimming in the sea where you have to be really strong or you could get sucked out to sea Zoe's really funny she won't let go of her Dad or maybe she just likes holding onto him I really wish I was bigger she might want to hold onto me her swimsuit is white with red cherries it's so beautiful and when she turns around and bends over to splash me with the wet swimsuit sticking to her body I can see the outline of her -

"Watch this," says George getting out of the pool, "Everybody look at me!"

"What's he doing?"

"Where's he going?"

"I think he's going to jump." I explain. This pool has a separate diving pool with lots of diving boards and the highest top platform anywhere we've ever been and though no-one would ever actually dive off the top unless they were mad, some people do jump, including my brother. We're all standing in the shallow end and have no intention of joining him but we can see him walking along the side to the ladder at the base of the diving tower.

"Is he safe doing this?" asks Mrs Mullen.

"Has he ever done it before?" asks Mr Mullen. "Which board is going to jump from?"

"No board. He jumps from the top, from the platform."

"What? No! It's impossible!" They can't believe it and stare up to the top platform. It seems a long way up all right.

"Is the water deep enough to break his fall?" asks Yvonne.

"Of course it is, they would have tested it wouldn't they?" says Kieran. "They would have built it deep enough for people to jump and dive into from the very top."

"It's OK," I say, "He's done it before when we were here with Mum."

"Well if your mother allows it then I suppose it's all right," says Mr Mullen, and we all stare up as George climbs the ladders all the way up to the top which takes ages because it's so high and when he gets there he walks straight out to the edge of the platform where he balances on his toes on the very edge and for a moment as he stands there outlined against the blue sky like a stick-man I'm almost proud of him because what he's doing is very dangerous and he's very brave to do it and no-one else I know could do it and now he takes one step forward and he's falling but not the way most people jump into a pool with their arms and legs flying and waving all over the place no way George has his arms straight down at his sides and his legs are dead straight too with his feet together and his toes pointing downwards so he looks like a falling knife and when he hits the water he slices the surface open like a sharp knife and then he's gone and there isn't even a splash not even a ripple hardly on the surface he just cuts the water open like a knife and in he goes and the water just closes tight over his head swallowing him up.

"Wow!" says Yvonne, "That was amazing!" and when I look at her she's actually got her mouth open and then she runs over to meet George getting out of the diving pool, making little baby running steps so she doesn't slip.

"Why don't you show them your dive?" he says to me when they come back. "Karl learned how to dive off the springboard in Butlin's – go on show them, it's about the same height here." But it isn't it's much higher here but I really want to do it and show Zoe I can dive and maybe she'll stare at me with her mouth open too and come running up to me afterwards so I walk over to the boards and climb up the steps and I'm standing here now at the very edge of the springboard looking down at the water and it's miles away I can't even see the surface it's so far away and I'm wondering should I just jump I mean all he did was jump that would be ok but he told them I was going to dive and Zoe will think I chickened out if I jump but it's so far down I've never dived that far down before it's more like the high diving board in Butlin's than the one I dived off maybe I'll just jump or will I dive the springboard is starting to spring and it's bouncing me up and down will I jump or dive it'll be ok to jump no I better dive or will I jump but the boards bouncing too much and I can't stay on it I'm going to fall I better dive no jump no -

"Are you sure your tummy's all right?" asks Mrs Mullen in the car on the way home. "That really looked like it hurt, the way you hit the water like that."

"No it's fine really," I reply, holding my sore tummy.

"That was the funniest thing I've ever seen," says George, "What a belly-flop – Splat! – you really hit the water flat out."

"Yeah what were you trying to do?" asks Kieran, "A dive or a jump?"

"Looked like a bit of both," says Yvonne. I really wish they'd all stop talking about my belly-flop but at least Zoe hasn't said anything.

"When you hit the water you made such a huge wave you nearly emptied the pool," says Zoe.

Oh Lord!

****

"What are we going to see again?" I ask.

"Goldfinger!" Everyone shouts.

"All right - Goldfinger. Is it a cartoon?"

"NO!"

"Why don't we go to a cartoon?"

"Because this is better. It's James Bond," Yvonne, standing beside me in the queue, says gently.

"Who's James Bond?"

"Who's James Bond? Somebody hit him!" Rory's here too worse luck.

"My pleasure." And I get a slap on the back of my head. So is Barry.

"Yeah it's a million times better," says Kieran. "I've seen it already, went last week with the school, and I can tell you - "

"Exactly!" interrupts his sister. "And if you open your mouth about anything that's about to happen or give anything away you will be so sorry."

"Yes but I still don't know who's James Bond," I ask again, risking another whack from Barry.

"Who's James Bond? Who's James Bond? Please excuse my younger brother he's just an idiot."

"Thanks George."

"James Bond, for your information," Andrew helps out, "Is the greatest British spy ever. Double-O Seven - that means he's licensed to kill. Played by Sean Connery. This one was actually released a few years ago but we were all too young to go."

"And now it's out again," adds Barry. "Can't wait to see it, they say it's the best."

"Better than cartoons?" I am almost afraid to ask though I'm actually looking forward a bit to seeing this famous spy now and just want to be sure it's going to be better than Tom and Jerry.

"Much better!" A few of them shout.

"I like cartoons too," says Patrick, "Tom and Jerry's my favourite."

"Hey - mine too!" I say as Patrick joins me beside Yvonne. The queue's not going anyway so we don't really have to stay lining up.

"I love when Tom's chasing Jerry and then he runs into something in the garden like the bird bath - "

"Yeah, or he steps on the rake and it hits him in the face."

"D'ya remember the one with the big dog and his pup and Tom keeps waking up the puppy."

"Yeah or the one when Tom locks Jerry out in the snow and when he takes him back inside he's all frozen like an ice pop."

"Yeah his tail is the stick and he thaws him out in front of the fire. That's the Christmas Eve one, that's my favourite."

"Yeah, me too. What about Bugs Bunny?"

"Yeah and Daffy Duck!"

"Look will you too stop going on about cartoons, we're not going to see cartoons all right?"

"What a pair of morons!" Sometimes I think the only thing George and Barry agree on is how stupid their younger brothers are.

"How long do we have to wait in the queue?" says Patrick.

"Just until they let us in," says George and nobody knows if he's joking or not.

"Hey I think it's moving," says Kieran. But it's not so we wait another ten minutes but now they're definitely letting us in and we're nearly at the Box Office that's where you pay I've no idea why it's called that but Andrew might know.

"Why is it called the Box Office? I mean it's not a box and it's not an office so it's a stupid name really isn't it?" But nobody answers because they're too busy being excited about going into the picture house I mean the cinema don't call it a picture house that's the wrong name for it nobody in the world calls it a picture house except my Mum and Dad and they'll only laugh if I do like they did once already when George called it that in the bus on the way in.

"What picture house is it on in?" he says.

"What what?" Barry is sitting on his own in the second row on the right and so is George on the left with Yvonne and Andrew is behind because we gave him all our bus fare and he paid for all of us and got a big long roll of a ticket from the ticket machine that the grumpy old bus conductor has around his neck and the rest of us are in the front row upstairs of course because you get a better view I've no idea where we're going or what picture house I mean cinema but I can see we've passed over O'Connell Bridge and we're starting up O'Connell Street so we're either going to the Savoy or the Carlton or the Capitol they're all on O'Connell Street or the Adelphi that's on Abbey Street.

"What picture house is it on in?" he says again because he hasn't even realised that he said something wrong.

"I think he means cinema," I say before things get any worse.

"Picture house! Picture house! Nobody calls it a picture house!" scoffs Barry.

174

"Actually that's an old American expression," says Andrew. "The word cinema is an abbreviation of the French word Cinematograph so it depends on whether you believe the French or the Americans invented it."

"Invented what?" asks Patrick.

"Moving pictures of course. The Lumiere Brothers in Paris are usually credited with creating the first moving pictures but the Americans believe it was someone in Hollywood."

"Yeah Charlie Chaplin," says Kieran. "His pictures are so old they move at the wrong speed that's why they look too fast."

"Yeah," adds Rory, "And they're all in black and white too!"

"Is this one in black and white?" asks Zoe.

"Of course not silly, it's in colour," Yvonne answers.

"Yeah technicolor," says Kieran, "The colour is amazing, when I saw it it was - "

"Gotta get off! Next stop - press the bell, come on!" Andrew is up out of his seat first and we're all rushing towards the stairs and shoving each other till we're down the stairs past the conductor standing at the bottom in his little space and out onto the footpath.

"Down here," says Andrew and it's the one on the side street called the Capitol which looks really old-fashioned and nice outside and inside it's all red velvet seats and curtains on the walls and little lights with frilly shades and we've all got popcorn 'cept I don't like popcorn so I've got jellies and we're trying to find our seats in the dark because it looks like the picture has started already but then I hear Kieran saying really loudly:

"This isn't the start it's the end, we've just come in at the end of the last show, I remember this bit it'll be over soon."

"I don't want to see the end first," someone says I think Yvonne and then George says:

"Shut your eyes then. Where are our seats? Who's got the tickets - Andrew?"

"I can't see in the dark and the usherette's way over there but they should be around here somewhere - yes here we are row D, seats seven to fourteen."

Now everyone behind is saying things like, "Sit down!" and "Be quiet please!" and the usherette has come over saying, "Take your seats quickly please children."

"I want to sit in fourteen that's my house number," I whisper hoping Zoe will sit beside me. Instead when my eyes get used to the light I find I'm beside George.

"I don't want to sit beside you. I want to swap," I tell him, hoping I might get to sit beside Zoe.

"Swap with Yvonne then she's sitting beside Patrick," says George because he obviously wants to sit beside Yvonne. Then we all start swapping around and making a real nuisance of ourselves till the usherette comes back over and tells us all to sit down and be quiet or else, but I still don't end up beside Zoe, I'm between Patrick and Barry, oh well could be worse. I can't see in the dark but I have a dreadful feeling Zoe might be beside Rory.

"It's over now that's the end except for the credits," Kieran says from somewhere on my right.

"Have we missed the whole film? Do we have to go home now?" That's Patrick beside me.

"No they're going to start all over again," says Kieran but Barry has already reached across me and given his brother a thump.

"Hey what's that for?"

"It's for being stupid, now be quiet and watch the movie."

"Hey look, the Producer's name is Broccoli," Yvonne calls out.

"I'm not watching this, I hate broccoli," says Zoe which I think is quite funny and I laugh but she's too far away to notice. Rory's down that end too I just hope to God he's not beside her.

"The other Producer's name is Saltzman," says Andrew, "That sounds like salt, you could put it on your broccoli and maybe it won't taste so bad."

"Hey look, the Director's name is Guy Hamilton," I add.

"What's so funny about that?" says Barry beside me.

"Nothing really."

176

"I think it's funny," says Patrick. "He's a guy and his name is Guy, that's funny."

"Thanks Patrick."

"No it's not. You're both idiots."

"OK be quiet now, it's starting," says Andrew.

"When I saw this the first time - " Kieran starts.

"Shut up!" we all shout-whisper and Kieran goes quiet.

This film IS amazing, I've never seen anything like this car with the bullet-proof screen and the smoke and the rockets and the ejector seat and when he rips the girl's tyres with the spiky things that come out of his wheels we all scream. Of course in spite of Yvonne's warning Kieran keeps up a running commentary about what's happening until Barry whacks him really hard on the head and he shuts up.

Where are they I wish I hadn't gone out now but I was dying to go to the loo and now I can't find them the cinema's so full I can't remember where we were and I can't see in the dark there's an empty seat in that row is that it where's Patrick I should be able to recognise his blonde hair and Barry's two seats away but everything looks like it's in black and white here in real life I can't tell any colours or anything is that them oh God I can't stand here any longer I'm missing the film and I'm in people's way where are they where are they I'm completely lost I can't see anything in the dark have I gone too far did I pass the row they're in or is that them up there no it's not what's that noise is it someone laughing it sounds a bit like Barry and George and some others but where's the laughing coming from I don't want to turn around everyone will be staring at me but it's definitely coming from behind me this is so embarrassing I better turn round who's that there is that them and now someone's pulling my sleeve and Andrew's beside me he's come out of his seat at the aisle and he's bringing me back and Yvonne and Zoe are standing up to let me past and Rory *is* beside Zoe which makes me feel sick why couldn't it have been me beside her I could have held her hand in the dark and no-one would've see I could even have kissed her on the cheek the year's half over and I haven't kissed her yet oh God what if he kissed her what if he …

then past George and Kieran and Barry and they're still laughing and George is saying 'Did you get lost in the dark little brother?' but at least it's so dark no one can see my red face and finally I'm back in my seat beside Patrick.

"Did I miss anything?"

"Not really, James Bond just got killed that's all."

"Oh no that's terrible - really?"

"No, only kidding."

"Great!"

"Did you get us any popcorn?"

"No sorry."

"That's all right."

I can see Patrick smiling at me in the darkness of the picture house I mean cinema and he looks really funny in black and white at least Andrew found me he's so great always there when you need him and I begin to feel a bit better and afterwards going home on the bus we're all talking about the movie and I say:

"That was the best movie ever, I want to be a spy when I grow up." And everyone agrees with me but George says:

"You wanted to be a Pirate after watching that movie on TV, what was it - Gene Kelly in The Pirate!"

"That was ages ago."

"It was yesterday!"

"I know, that's what I mean."

****

One summer afternoon, too hot to do anything, we are all lying around the rockery beside the pond, smelling the flowers and throwing little bits of twigs and stuff at each other, looking at the water hoppers on the surface and the lilies trailing their long stalks down into the dark water. There's a buzzing sound in my head but for once it's not the chainsaws – it's a big bumblebee zooming around some flowers beside me. I'm not afraid of bees so I lie there just listening to it. The sound is quite different from the chainsaws, it's softer and warmer and more musical. As the bee comes and goes, so the sound rises and falls like a melody, like it's humming a little bee song to itself.

"It's hot," says George

"Tell me something I don't know," says Yvonne. She's got her new blue and white stripy top on which makes her look like a sailor.

"Eh, ok – the capital of Peru is Lima," says Kieran.

"What?!?"

"You said tell you something you don't know, well I bet you didn't know that."

"Look," says Zoe suddenly,"There's someone at that window." We look up at the building overlooking the pond and there at the window is a man in pyjamas and a dressing gown. He's just standing there staring at us, he doesn't look really old but he does look sick.

"Maybe we better get out of here," says Kieran.

"No, stay here," I reply.

"What if he calls the Greeners?"

"He won't, he just wants to look at us."

"How do you know?" asks Zoe.

"He likes looking at us."

"Why?"

"Because he's dying and we're young and full of life." I don't know why I say this, I've never thought of it before, I just sort of know that it's true and looking out the window over the pond those children are here again the pain is much worse today I can't have long left I feel really tired more tired than I've ever felt in my life but I'm happy too in a way looking at the children playing and talking I wonder what they're talking about it must be nearly tea time they always leave just before six nurse will be here soon to take me in yes here she comes and he goes on standing there staring down at us until a hand appears from behind him and is placed on his shoulder. Then he turns around very slowly and disappears inside.

"Do you really think he's dying?" asks Zoe.

"Do you really think he liked looking at us?" asks Yvonne.

179

"I think they know we're here, they can see us better than we can see them, and they let us play here because they like watching us."

"How do you know?" George argues. "You're just saying that."

"I don't know it, that's just what I think."

"Are they all going to die?" asks Zoe. "All the patients here?" But nobody wants to think of that.

"I wonder what happens when we die," Yvonne says.

"One two three four five six seven," Patrick says.

"What?"

"All good children go to Heaven."

"When they die their sins are forgiven," Zoe joins in and then we all say the last line together:

"One two three four five six seven."

"Well that answers that question then doesn't it?" I say and we all laugh.

"What's heaven like I wonder," says Zoe, sitting up and hugging her knees. She's got her old blue jeans on, they're nearly worn through at the knees with just a few white threads going across and underneath I can see her skin.

"It's like the best time you ever had on earth only it never stops, it goes on and on forever," Yvonne says.

"But they told us in school there are no animals in heaven, what kind of heaven is that, without our pets?" Zoe complains.

"Of course there are no animals in heaven," says Kieran. "They can't let them in because animals don't have any souls."

"That's silly," his sister replies, "It's not their fault they don't have a soul, it's not because they did anything bad. I think they should let them in, how could anyone not let Lulu into Heaven?"

"Then they'd have to let them all in," my brother objects. "Every dog on the road, even that horrible boxer in the house at the end, and that one in number 25 that growls every time we go past the gate."

"Yeah the place would be full of dogs in a minute if you started letting them in," agrees Kieran.

180

"And don't forget cats," I add, "If they let dogs in they have to let cats in too and then the dogs would chase them all over heaven, it would be mad."

"Yeah you're right, and then what about other pets like rabbits and tortoises and hamsters and - "

"Goldfish!" yells Yvonne.

"Yeah and what about horses and cows and pigs and other farmyard animals?" I add. "Imagine all that manure - the place would be a mess."

"Well I don't care," says Zoe when everybody has run out of animals to mention. "I don't want to go there if Lulu's not there, it wouldn't be heaven without her. I'd rather go to - "

"Don't say that sis," interrupts Yvonne.

" – the other place – I'd rather go to the other place, I would, I'd rather go to Hell!" And she gets up and runs round the side of the pond where she sits on her own.

"Zoe!" I can see Yvonne's really shocked and it takes a heck of a lot to shock her but I don't care about that, all I care about is how upset Zoe is and I wish I could go over to comfort her but she probably wouldn't want that. I look at her sitting on a rock at the other edge of the pond with her arms around her knees and her chin resting on her wrist staring into the water looking really sad. I want to tell her that it's all right, that Lulu will be let into heaven, but I really don't know if it's true.

✶✶✶✶✶✶✶✶✶✶✶✶✶

"How long will you be gone?" George is asking Mum but I don't know what he's talking about because I've just come in from school and they're standing in the kitchen talking about something serious. It must be serious because George has this really pained look on his face and Mum looks really unhappy as she turns her head to see me coming in the back door.

181

"What?" I ask, "What's up? Gone where?" Now I know there's something wrong from the look on Mum's face and I'm getting worried.

"Where are you going?"

"I wanted to wait till you were both here to tell you so come in here and sit down now." And we all go through to the breakfast room and sit at the table which is really strange because we're not eating anything.

"It's all right Karl, don't look so worried, it's only a holiday. Your father and I are going away for three weeks - "

"Three weeks!!! How can we survive here for three weeks on our own? How will we eat?" Now George is getting worried.

"If you just wait a minute please George and stop interrupting I will tell you the plan."

"You've got a plan?" I say, "Brill! What is it?"

"Well, obviously you can't stay here on your own while we go halfway round the world - "

"Halfway round the world? Where are you going?" George again.

"It's a Junior Chamber trip to India and Hong Kong. Now to get back to the arrangements - "

"Hong Kong – wow!"

"India – wow!"

"So George is going to stay with the O'Dwyers – you can go into school together - and Karl, since you're the same age as Kieran you're going to stay with the Mullens, it's all arranged."

"Aw! Why can't I stay with the Mullens?" George moans .

"Why would you want to do that? Donal O'Dwyer's in the same class as you, it makes more sense."

"Yes George, why would you want to stay with the Mullens?" I ask, giving him a look. "Maybe you think I should stay with Donal?"

"Anyway it's all settled, we leave in two weeks, you'll have a great time, it will be like a holiday for all of us, for you too." And with that she left the two of us looking at each other.

182

"You planned this," George says accusingly. "You made sure you got to stay in the Mullens."

"How on earth could I have done that?" My brother really has some imagination.

"I don't know but I bet you did. I can't believe you're staying with the Mullens."

I can't believe I'm staying with the Mullens. I can't believe I'm standing here at their window looking over at Rory's house straight across and our house further up with my window at the front and George's at the side and I'm just waiting for Kieran to come back from the bathroom. We're in the girls' bedroom and I'm going to be sleeping in the bed nearest the window which is just unbelievable because it's Zoe's bed – I'm actually sleeping in Zoe's bed! Somebody wake me up I must be dreaming and I haven't even gone to sleep yet! My suitcase is on the floor beside the bed, Mum got us a new one each, it's only made of cardboard but it looks real and it's so cool, I can't believe I have my own suitcase. Here's Kieran.

"It's your turn now, go on hurry up before the girls come upstairs, they take ages in the bathroom and if you don't get in before them you'll be standing outside all night."

This is so funny, creeping down the landing, down the little stairs to the bit in between with my washbag I love my new washbag I've never had one before it's like a pencil case only bigger and waterproof it's got my toothbrush and toothpaste and a sponge which I use for washing my face and my brush and comb and my very own bar of soap that says PEAR'S on it but it doesn't smell like pears or even apples it just smells like flowers - like roses I think. The Mullens' bathroom is really dark because it's got all black marble in it the walls are black and so is the bit around the wash hand basin and around the bath too. There's loads of toothbrushes here I can't imagine how everyone remembers which one is theirs so it's a good job I have my washbag so I can keep mine in it otherwise it would go wandering off with theirs and I'd never find it again. But as I'm standing here looking at them all, all the different coloured toothbrushes, I can't help won-dering which one is Zoe's. If I knew which one was hers I'd

... well I don't really know what I'd do. Better get out of here before someone else -

"Who's in there? Can you hurry up please?" It's Mrs Mullen!

"Sorry Mrs Mullen, it's me, Karl, I'll be out in a second."

"Oh sorry Karl, I didn't know it was you, that's all right, take all the time you want, it's the other lot that spend hours in here if I don't chase them out." Mrs Mullen's really nice, I like her. A minute later I'm back in the bedroom and in bed – Zoe's bed – I can't believe it!

"Well look who's in here, it's little Karl!" Yvonne and Zoe have just come in in their pyjamas and we were about to put out the light and go to sleep.

"This is like Goldilocks and the Three Bears," says Zoe. "Who's been sleeping in my bed!" And she starts walking round to me. Her pyjamas have little red teddies on them.

"We came to say good night to the two little boys," says Yvonne smiling.

"And tuck them in to their beddy-bys," Zoe is right beside my bed now, well her bed really, and now she's pulling back the blankets and I don't believe it she's getting in!

"Zoe! Get out of there or you're going to be in big trouble!" says Kieran.

"What's wrong? I'm just getting into bed, it is still my bed isn't it? It's not my fault Karl is in it." I just lie there afraid to move or speak as she slides into the bed beside me.

"Better get out little sis, I think I hear Mum on the stairs." And Zoe jumps out of the bed and dashes across the room.

"Goodnight then boys!"

"Sleep tight!"

"Don't let the bed bugs bite!" And they disappear out the door. Kieran says, "Good night" to me and I say the same and he puts out the light. I'm lying here in the dark and I cannot believe that a few minutes ago Zoe was actually in bed with me. Is it possible? But I suppose it was just as a joke with her brother and sister there too, it couldn't have meant anything special. Still it was the nicest thing she's ever done to me.

What on earth is that noise? I was nearly asleep it's taken me ages after the shock of having Zoe in my bed and then this rustling, shuffling noise starts and I'm pretty sure it's coming from Kieran's bed. It was nice of the girls to give up their room and I can't believe that I'm actually sleeping in Zoe's bed she's got a couple of posters of the Monkees over it and Kieran's in Yvonne's bed so she's sleeping in his little room over the front door and Zoe is in the other spare bed in Rebecca's room but right now I'd give up Zoe's bed for a room of my own even though I'm pretty sure I can smell her smell from the pillow the smell of her shampoo and her soap and just the smell of her - that smell that I know so well now and love more than any other smell in the whole world, it's hard to know what it smells like, all I can think of is the sunflowers in her eyes and that's what the smell is like – her sunflower eyes - but I'd give it all up now because that noise is definitely coming from Kieran and I know what he's doing although I cannot believe it. He's rocking his head from side to side on the pillow and that's what's making the unbelievable noise. This is driving me insane, I'll have to get him to stop.

"Kieran!" I whisper, "Are you awake?"

"What!" he mumbles, and the rustling stops.

"What's that funny noise you're making?"

"What? Oh you mean this?" And he starts again.

"Yeah, that noise. What are you doing?"

"I have to do this to get to sleep."

"What? Are you nuts?"

"I have to do this, otherwise I can't get to sleep."

"Yes but when you do it *I* can't get to sleep!"

"Oh well, I'll be asleep soon and then it'll stop," he says, and he goes on with the mad head-rocking thing again. I can't believe it.

"Kieran?"

"What?"

"If you don't stop I'm going to get my pillow and I'm going to come over there and suffocate you with it."

"Oh, ok."

I think he's stopped now. I have to get up for school tomorrow and if I don't get to sleep soon I'll be wrecked. I think he's asleep now because the noise has definitely stopped. It was funny getting into bed here and looking across at my own room in our house across the street. It feels like I should be there in my own bed trying to get to sleep instead of here in Zoe's bed trying to get to sleep. But maybe I am, maybe this is all a dream and I really am asleep in my own bed over there and not here and when I wake up I will be at home and Mum will be there pulling my curtains and telling me I have to get up and go to school and even though I'm actually in Zoe's bed and I can smell her smell from the pillow I just wish I was back home in my own ... bed because then I'd be able ...then I'd be able to get ...

****

"And then you put the lid behind it like this and it stands up and it's the speaker – see the wire? That brings the sound from the needle to the speaker. This is the speaker see?"

"Yeah, I get it Kieran. But what records have you got? I mean apart from Sgt Pepper's, I know you have that."

"Oh and it turns itself off automatically so you can put on a record and then go to sleep and it will turn itself off automatically when it's finished. You don't have to get up and turn it off if you're asleep." I look at him like he's a complete idiot but then I have an idea.

"Now that does interest me, so that means we can put on a record when we go to bed and it will send us off to sleep so I won't have to listen to you and your head-banging. But what records have you got?"

"And it plays singles or LP's – see there's the control for 45 or 33 and a third. The only thing it doesn't do is stack records like our

186

other one cause this thing isn't long enough."

"No problem, but tell me Kieran, what records do you have?"

"You mean apart from Sgt Pepper's?"

"Yes, apart from Sgt Pepper's."

"Well, apart from Sgt Pepper's all we've got is the Monkees and Danny Kaye singing The Ugly Duckling."

"Do me a favour then and go downstairs and get Sgt Pepper's, will you please? Maybe I'll get some sleep tonight."

I'm still awake and I've listened to the whole album twice, it's too noisy to send anyone to sleep especially the end of side two with all those weird noises like an orchestra playing sideways and the twenty pianos, that just keeps waking me up again. Tomorrow night I'm going to try The Ugly Duckling.

****

What date is today – the 12th right? They're not home till the 30th, that's another 18 days, that's two weeks and four days I don't believe it I can't stand living here. I can't sleep, the food isn't at all like at home, and I can't get my homework done properly. We have to do our homework in here, I've never been in the dining room before, it's really dark and this table is much bigger and much darker than ours it's nearly black and Kieran's got all his books spread out over half of it and he keeps sucking his pencil and making a sucking noise which is really irritating, nearly as bad as his head rocking on the pillow. I wish I *had* stayed with Donal O'Dwyer now and let George stay here that would be hilarious, see how he'd like it and at least I'd get to sleep. But we got to see Top of the Pops this evening and when we saw who was No.1 we all screamed. The camera was on Paul's face, really close, and he just started singing almost on his own – "Hey Jude" – and then the camera went back a bit and you can see he is playing the piano, just a small upright one, not even a grand like ours, and the others are sitting around on blocks and there's lots of ordinary people right up beside them and standing all around them and Paul is wearing a purple jacket and John has this little t-shirt on with buttons

187

and an orange bow tie it looks like and he chews gum all the way through and we're watching it on the telly in the sunroom all the Mullens and me and when it starts someone says, "Turn it up" and Rebecca goes up to the TV and turns it up real loud and we all start singing along even though we don't really know the words because it's only been out a week and we haven't heard it yet hardly at all but at the end there's this bit that's got no words just "Na na na na-na-na na!" over and over again and it goes on for about ten minutes so we can all sing to that bit and it's the best ever it's just incredible and when it's over Mrs Mullen comes in and switches off the TV and tells us all to do our homework still I'll never forget that song I can hear it now in my head and I'm going to just listen to it in my head again tonight if Kieran does his stupid head rocking thing and I can't get to sleep I'll just –

"Oh there you both are, aren't you good, doing your homework. Karl I've got good news for you. Your mother's been on the phone and she's arranged for a baby-sitter to come and stay with you – you know Orla, she's looked after you before? – well she's going to live with you and cook your meals until your Mum and Dad come home so you won't have to stay here. Orla wasn't sure if she could do it before they left and your Mum didn't want to say anything earlier in case it didn't work out and you were disappointed. So that's good news isn't it?"

Good news? I want to kiss the woman. Instead I just say:

"When do I go home?" And Mrs Mullen says:

"Right now if you want, the girl's there already. George is going home too."

I can't believe this is happening and I'm so happy I could cry and all I can do is pack up my school books into my bag and Kieran's looking at me funny so I better say something.

"See you Kieran. Thanks for letting me stay." And he says:

"Any time. Come and stay again any time you want." And I say "Yeah, will do" even though I'm a bit embarrassed about giving out to him for his head-banging and I leave with Mrs Mullen before she changes her mind or I wake up and find it was a dream. But as we go upstairs and Mrs Mullen helps me pack she's really quiet and I wonder is anything wrong and then I remember what I said to Kieran the first night about suffocating him with my pillow when I couldn't sleep I didn't mean it I was only joking and I wonder did he tell him mum and is that why – and suddenly I realise what is happening – Mum didn't ring up Mrs Mullen, it was the other way around, Kieran did tell and Mrs Mullen rang Mum and told her I said I would suffocate Kieran and she asked her to take me away because she didn't want me there and then Mum had to organise for Orla to come and stay and what is really happening is I am being sent home. We finish packing and the last thing I pack is my washbag. I think how stupid I was being so proud of it when I arrived and now here I am a few days later being sent home. There is a terrible pain in my chest I'm really scared my head is full of something and my eyes are staring like mad and I can't close my mouth as I follow Mrs Mullen out of her house across the road and into our drive. She's carrying my little cardboard suitcase and I have my schoolbag. Orla's standing at the back door and she's smiling but then she always does. Mrs Mullen gives her my suitcase and says goodbye nicely. She says I was a perfect guest but she's probably just being polite and then she's gone. I go upstairs with Orla with the fear and pain tearing my heart. All I want is to be alone because I know I have to cry and when she leaves I lie on my bed crying for ages. When I stop crying I start thinking again. I know I can ask Orla if Mum really asked her to come before she left or was it only after I said that to Kieran. That would prove it one way or the other. But I know I won't because I'm afraid to know the truth. Maybe I'll ask Mum when she comes home.

****

"You know what that is?" says Andrew, pointing to a large tree, the type that grows cones and has spikey things instead of leaves, like a giant Christmas tree. We're all here in St Mark's, walking along the path that goes behind the houses on the Mullens' side.

"What?" asks someone without much interest.

189

"That's the Hanging Tree," says Andrew importantly.

"What's the Hanging Tree?" Kieran asks.

"That tree – it's called the Hanging Tree, that's what it's called."

"Yes but why is it called the Hanging Tree?"

"A man was found hanging from it one Sunday morning, he hanged himself from a branch. With a big rope."

"Why did he hang himself?"

"Because he was dying."

"Why was he dying?"

"He had cancer."

"How do you know?"

"Because this is a cancer hospital. They're all dying of cancer in here. Everyone has cancer in here - except us."

"What's cancer?" asks Patrick in a little voice.

"It's a disease that eats you up inside. All of your insides rot."

"I don't want to be eaten up inside."

"You won't be, you're only a kid. Kids don't get cancer." Barry says.

"But what if we get it from being in the hopsital?"

"It's 'hospital' not 'hopsital', I tell him, laughing. "And we're not in the hospital we're only in the grounds. Anyway you can't just catch it, it's not like a cold, you have to make it yourself."

"Actually Barry's wrong about kids not getting it," says Andrew. "Children do get cancer, it's called childhood Leukemia and it kills lots of children every year."

"I don't want to get Loo-keemy. I wanna go home!"

"Well done Andrew, now look what you've done."

"Sorry. Look Patrick it's all right, nothing's going to happen to you, you're not going to die." Andrew tries to explain.

"Yeah I know, I was only joking, I'm not scared."

"Yeah sure," says his brother.

"Did he really?" I ask, looking up at the high tree.

"Hang himself? Yep. You see that big long branch sticking out there? That's where he did it. Just tied the rope around the branch

190

and put the noose around his neck, pulled it tight and jumped." I remember what I used to do with the clothesline by the apple tree but I don't think I'll mention it.

"Why a Sunday? Why did he do it on a Sunday?"

"I said they found him on a Sunday morning. He might have done it the night before. I think he wanted to be found on a Sunday so they could say Mass for him as soon as possible. You know the way the priest comes here on a Sunday morning?"

"I know that priest," I say. "That's my priest, the one who says Mass in my convent. Sometimes we have to give him a lift out here after Mass."

"How do you know all of this anyway Andrew?" says Yvonne.

"How long have you lived on this road?" Andrew pushes his glasses up his little freckled nose.

"Five years – why?"

"I've been here ten. You know there were people here before us, other children, much older than me, I used to know some of them when I was little. They used to tell me things – stories, legends. Some of them true, some I'm not so sure. But you know a lot of stuff went on before we came here. We aren't the first."

I wonder what it's like to be hanged, how could he do such a thing to himself climb up the tree there are little half broken branches there all right get you all the way up to that branch then stand on that one get up to the next one then onto this really big one I have the rope from the gardener's shed the noose is done it'll slide just enough to tighten what if I chicken out and try to get it loose it won't open I won't be able to it'll be too late anyway I want to die there's no choice there's no other way out it's driving me insane I'll be dead soon anyway I can't stand the pain I've no one to live for no one will care they'll all be delighted to get rid of me here give them a spare bed save money on those useless bloody drugs never helped me a bit just made me sicker and sicker every day what a waste of a life there's a nice view from up here I can see into those gardens nice houses really big not like home the cottage in the front field up forenst *cnoc na*

191

greine that's all gone now never get it back father gone mother gone worked every day of their lives and for what to bring us up all emigrated except me I should have gone too all the good it did me staying here waste of a bloody life I bet that's where those kids live that are always in here I bet they think we can't see them it was nice watching them play they have their whole future ahead of them their whole lives please God none of them will ever get cancer and have to suffer what we suffer in here maybe some day someone will find a cure and no one will ever die of it ever again God forgive me for doing this I know it's a sin but they'll find me tonight or tomorrow morning when they see I'm missing then tomorrow's Sunday they'll say a Mass for me that nice priest who comes every Sunday and God will understand and forgive me I'm in such pain I can't stand it nobody could I have to do this just put it on sit on the edge of the branch and slide off say a prayer first now at the hour of my death amen the roofs of those houses are red I never noticed that be-

We walk on in silence, each one of us impressed by Andrew's superior knowledge and experience. Maybe it's true what he said, that we're not the first though I cannot believe it. It has never occurred to me before that anyone else was ever in our world.   It always seemed as if we were the only ones ever. I can't let it go like that.

"Hang on a minute," I say, "Maybe there were others before us," I stop on the path, and my friends turn and look at me. "Maybe there were others here, playing here and doing stuff in St Mark's, but they weren't like us. They didn't have what we have, do you know what I mean? They didn't have the Club, and the music we have, you know - the Beatles and the Monkees and the Stones and Top of the Pops on a Thursday night and Pick of the Pops on Sundays, and they didn't wear the clothes we wear, and talk like us and they didn't have us! There wasn't anyone ever like us!" And I look around at my friends and we all look at each other and I know I've said what needed to be said and they all understand and Zoe looks at me and smiles her special smile.

192

"What about the treehouse?" says George as we go on walking. "When are we going to build the treehouse?" Nobody says anything.

"A rope-ladder would be good," he goes on, as if to himself, "And a trap door to pull the rope-ladder up from inside when enemies come."

"What enemies?" Yvonne says, "We don't have any enemies."

"George could get us some," I suggest, "He's good at that."

"And a roof in case it rains when we're inside."

****

"Which side do you want to listen to? It's a double album so there are four sides."

"I don't know, I haven't heard any of it yet, have I?"

"We better start at side one then," he says, taking the disc out of the left hand sleeve. It's called a sleeve but you couldn't get your arm into it, only your fingers. With it out come four colour photos and a big sheet of something.

"Wow, what are all these?"

"Yeah it's amazing, you get these brilliant photos with it and look - " He opens out the sheet " – it's got all the words to all the songs on one side and – look at this – on the other side all these pictures. Look at this one - Paul with no clothes on, you can nearly see his micky."

"Great," I say, not able to think of anything else. "What's the first track then?"

"Oh this is incredible, it's called Back in the USSR and it starts off with the sound of an actual airplane taking off or maybe landing, listen -" And Barry puts the record onto the turntable, flicks the switch and we watch the arm pick itself up, move over and drop the needle down at the start. We look at each other in silence, I can't wait to hear this, then it starts and Barry turns the volume up to full and sure enough there's this almighty roaring sound of a jet taking off or maybe landing I don't know which but it's really incredible and then the drums and guitars starts and then Paul we think it is starts singing, *"Flew in from Miami beach BOAC didn't get to bed last night"* and when it's over Barry says, "What do you think, isn't that the greatest song they've ever done, the greatest song ever, and the rest of the album is even better. There's one song called "Why don't we do it in the Road?" You know what that means don't you?"

"Yeah sure," I reply, not having a clue what he's talking about. "Is it better than Elvis?" I ask him.

"Way better than Elvis, wait till you hear this one, it's called 'Dear Prudence'. And there's one later on called 'Obladi-Oblada' where he keeps singing 'bra'".

"Bra? Really? That's funny." And for the next two hours we listen to the whole album and then some favourite tracks a few times more until it's way past lunchtime by the time I remember to look at my watch and I have to dash home. Everyone's already sitting down for lunch when I come in.

"Sorry I'm late, I was over in Barry's listening to the new Beatles album."

"Really," says Dad, "And what is the new Beatles album called that is so important it makes you miss your family dinner?"

"It's not called anything, it doesn't have a name," I reply.

"Really," Dad says again slightly sarcastically.

"But there's a song on it called 'Obladi-Oblada'.

"Really."

"And another one called 'Everybody's Got Something to Hide Except for Me and my Monkey'."

"Really."

"And another called 'Why Don't We Do -"

"Yes Karl, that's enough, I don't need to know every song on the album thank you."

We go on with our dinner and Dad says sort of to himself: "I had a Beatles album once," and then he glares at George.

"It got scratched!"

****

194

"What Panto is it?" asks Yvonne. We've just passed the hanging tree and I'm still looking up at it as we walk along the path behind the houses on their side of the road. It's really cold because it's New Year's Eve and we're all wrapped up in coats and scarves and boots. Yvonne and Zoe have new wooly hats on which they both got for Christmas. I'm wearing my new double-breasted blue wool coat that stops just above my knees. I got it for Christmas too and I'm mad about it. It's the nicest coat I've ever had. Zoe said it was really nice as soon as she saw it. And we're both wearing our new cowboy boots that came from Uncle Jim in Canada.

"What what is it?" says George in front of me.

"What Panto. You said you were going to the Panto tonight. You're so lucky going out tonight, we're not doing anything. Imagine, New Year's Eve and we have to sit in and watch TV."

"Yeah, I wish we could go to the Panto," says Zoe.

"Oh you mean the Pantomime," says George. "Do you call it a Panto?"

"Everyone calls it a Panto," says Barry.

"Why? We don't. We call it a Pantomime."

"Yeah well you call the cinema the picture house, and a car indicator the winky willie so I wouldn't mind that."

"The word Pantomime means 'mimic all' as originally it was all a mime – you know with no words." As usual Andrew is the one with the answers. "Then music and songs were added but it kept the name Pantomime."

"Yeah thanks for the history lesson," says Barry, "All she asked was which one is it."

"Who's 'she' - the cat's pyjamas?" Yvonne demands.

"It's not 'the cat's pyjamas', it's 'the cat's mother'," Kieran corrects her.

"What does it matter?" Yvonne shrugs.

"Cats don't wear pyjamas," says Zoe.

"That's a good point," I agree and Zoe smiles at me.

195

"That's not the point at all," says Kieran, "There is another expression called 'the cat's pyjamas' but it means something completely different."

"Kieran's right," says Andrew, "'The cat's pyjamas' is a different expression. It means something special, like 'the bee's knees' or 'the monkey's uncle'."

"The monkey's uncle," repeats Patrick, "That's so funny – the monkey's uncle" And he can't stop laughing.

"Monkeys don't have uncles," says Zoe.

"Yes and bees don't have knees," I agree and she smiles at me again. "But we're not really getting anywhere here. What Yvonne wanted to know was the name of the Pantomime the Jones family is going to tonight and the answer is: Puss in Boots."

"That's a stupid Panto," says Barry. "It's only for babies."

"No it's not," says Zoe. "We saw it a few years ago and it was great, wasn't it?"

"I can't remember," says Kieran. "I was too young."

"What did I tell you," says Barry, "Only for babies. I bet Maureen Potter's in it, I can't stand Maureen Potter."

"I like her," says Zoe, "I think she's funny."

"That's cool that you're going to Puss in Boots and you've both got your new boots," says Yvonne. "Are you going to wear them tonight?"

"Don't think we'll be let," I reply and I look down at my new cowboy boots again. They just arrived after Christmas. Mum was hoping they'd come in time for Christmas presents but it takes a long time for parcels to come all the way from Canada by boat, so they were a couple of days late. That's what Mum was doing last summer measuring our feet with the cut-out brown paper to send to Uncle Jim. Everyone noticed them as soon as we came out and they all love them, even Barry. Mine have got square toes and George's have pointy toes and they've both got real stitching all over them and different coloured leather and they go down in a sort of "V" at the front and back. They're real cowboy boots and probably the only ones in the whole country.

"They're really cool," says Barry, "I'm really jealous. You know what they remind me of?" And he starts singing –

"These boots are made for walkin'
And that's just what they'll do
One of these days" – And we all join in –

"...these boots are gonna walk all over you." Then Barry continues on his own imitating a guitar sound, going:

"Ner-ner, Ner-ner, Ner-ner, Ner-ner
"Ner-ner, Ner-ner, Ner-ner, Ner-ner"

"Yeah that's enough, we get the picture," shouts Yvonne to shut him up.

"Mum wants to see it because she likes cats," George says. Where he got this idea from I haven't a clue.

"You don't even have a cat," Yvonne objects.

"Yes but we're thinking of getting one," he explains.

"Oh so you're going to see Puss in Boots to get an idea of what cat you should buy, that's really clever." Barry says and starts laughing. I look at my brother who's looking down at the ground and can't think of anything to say. I feel sorry for him which makes me feel really sick inside.

"Shut up Barry, you're so mean," says Yvonne.

"What? What did I say?"

"Oh forget it," says George. I suddenly remember something.

"Hey – did anyone see Dad's Army last night? It's a new comedy programme on BBC. It was really funny."

"Oh yeah," says Patrick, "It was brilliant. I love Corporal Jones, he's always late standing to attention. And - "

"What is it? We didn't see it," asks Yvonne. "We were watching The Forsythe Saga."

"It's a stupid programme about the war," says Barry. "I didn't think it was funny."

"It's not really about the war, though it is set in wartime," Andrew says. "It's about the Home Guard, an amateur unit set up to defend the British coastline against German invasion. It was made up mainly of those too old or infirm to join the regular army."

197

"What's infirm?" asks Zoe.

"That means they're not fit for active service. And that's what makes it so funny. They've no proper equipment or rifles or anything, they don't even have uniforms to start off with, and they all really old and - "

"Yeah, one of them is always wanting to go to the loo," Patrick butts in.

"And another one is always trying to sell stuff on the black market," I add.

"The Captain is the local bank manager, Captain Mainwaring," says Andrew, "I like him. And there's one soldier who's much younger than the rest and the Captain keeps calling him, 'Stupid boy'."

"Did anybody see Meet Me in St Louis?" I ask.

"Oh yeah it was great," says Yvonne and then Zoe adds: "But so sad when they had to move house and the girl smashed all the snowmen because she didn't want to move."

"Yeah it was sad," I agree, happy that no one else seems to have seen it but Zoe and me have.

"I'd hate to have to move house," says Yvonne.

"I can't imagine moving from here, I just couldn't live anywhere else," Zoe says, and as we all look around at each other I can see we are all thinking exactly the same thing. This is home, this is us, it's where we belong, to live anywhere else would be unimaginable, just … just wrong.

We're just passing the back gardens of the last house on our road and when we turn right we are behind the houses of Orwell Park.

"Isn't this the house with the model railway?" I ask as we turn the corner.

"Oh yeah!" Patrick says and we run up to the shed at the end of the garden which we can see through the fence. There's a big window in the side of the shed and inside we can see the most enormous model railway.

"That's amazing," says Patrick, staring in at it. "Look at all the little people and cars and houses and everything."

"That's a steam locomotive and that one's diesel," says Kieran joining us. "And look – that one's The Flying Scotsman."

"Wow!" says Patrick beside me, "What's The Flying Scotsman?"

"The Flying Scotsman was one of the earliest steam engines." Andrew has joined us. "It got its name from the fact that it was the fastest train on the London to Scotland route."

"Jack Bruce is from Scotland. He's the bass player with Cream in case you didn't know. I'd love to go to Scotland," says Barry.

"I wish you would," says George, "In fact we'll all chip in to buy you a ticket." And everybody laughs which makes George happy and makes me feel better and I'm still smiling thinking about it sitting here in the Gaiety looking at Puss in Boots which probably really is only for babies but I've just spotted something which has taken all my attention off the stage so I couldn't really care less about the big cat in big boots because up in a box way over to the right I'm pretty sure is the girl from Mass in the convent, the one in the blue hat. Obviously she's not wearing the blue hat now but the blonde hair is the right length and even in the dark her face looks familiar but I can't see it properly because she's looking at the stage. I'm dying for the interval when I can see her stand up and turn around and I can make sure it's her and maybe see her in the bar when we have our drinks Dad's looking at the programme and reading out bits of it as we sit at the corner table near the long wooden bar sipping our drinks. Dad's got the usual gin and Tonic and so has Mum for a change because they didn't have her favourite sherry. Me and George have been let have Cokes but there's no sign of the girl.

"Did you know the cat is really the Marquis of Carabas?"

"Eh, yeah," says George, "That's the whole point of it isn't it?"

"Just making sure you were able to follow it that's all. Now in the second half the cat *'happens upon a castle inhabited by an ogre who is capable of transforming himself into a number of creatures. The ogre displays his ability by changing into a lion, frightening the*

199

cat, who then tricks the ogre into changing into a mouse. The cat then pounces upon the mouse and devours it'."

"Thanks for telling us the whole story Dad," moans George, "Now we know what's going to happen."

"Don't speak to your father like that George. He was only reading what's in the programme. It's there for everyone to see."

"That's right, I haven't given away any state secrets son."

Suddenly I wish my family was a million miles away because into the bar has just walked the girl. I just look up and she's there, coming in with her mother and father and brother and sister and as she passes she notices me and I think she smiles. I can't be sure if she really smiled at me or if she was just smiling anyway from something one of her family had just said or because she was happy but she definitely looked at me and smiled at the same time. I stare after her, willing her to turn around but she doesn't and they go so far away that I can't see her at all.

"Sit still and stop staring around you," says Dad. "What are you looking at?"

"Nothing really."

"Then sit still. There's the bell, we better drink up, don't want to be late for the second half do we?"

"But we've just arrived, that's only the first bell. There's no hurry!" I exclaim. "What about our drinks? We're not finished yet." George picks up his Coke and knocks it back.

"I am," he says smugly. Then Dad does the same with his Gin and Tonic and Mum takes a little sip from hers and puts it down.

"Can't be late for Puss in Boots. It's your mother's favourite," says Dad, "She loves cats."

Oh Lord, I say to myself.

When we get home Mum and Dad let us stay up till midnight and we open the front windows of the study to hear the foghorns of the ships in the docks and the church bells ringing out over the city before going to bed I can still hear the odd foghorn sounding but the street is quiet and all the lights are off in the Mullens house and Zoe must be fast asleep in her bed by the window just across the road I'm beginning to shiver I should get back into bed but I'm sure I saw the curtains move I forgot to say my prayers that's why I got out of bed but this is more important I know she's over there I just want to see her and then I can go to sleep when I stand so close to the window my breath makes a little round patch of fog on the surface and I can't see out so I wipe it with my pyjama sleeve and it clears and then it doesn't fog up again so bad is that her I thought I saw it move why doesn't she come maybe she's asleep already - the curtain! - I'm sure I saw the curtain move yes there's someone there it's Zoe I can see her quite clearly in the light from the streetlamp she's stepped between the curtain and the window and she's standing there she's giving me a little wave again and now what's she doing she has her hands up in front of her face with the first finger of each hand crossed to make an X – I can't believe it but I think she means a kiss – yes now she's blowing me a kiss and making another X with her crossed fingers but before I can respond she is gone I wait a bit longer with my breath fogging up the cold winter window-pane but she doesn't return a feeling surges through me like nothing I have ever felt before in my life Zoe my lovely Zoe I love the way the sun shines on her golden auburn hair and the way she sits so still and never moves when she's watching TV and her special smell the smell from her pillow and the way she got into bed with me I'll never forget that as long as I live why am I even interested in the blonde girl at Mass forget about her it's Zoe that I want it's Zoe that I love and now I know for definite that I'll kiss her next year because if she's sending me kisses from her bedroom window that means she wants to kiss me and I could probably just go over there right now and go up to her bedroom if I could get in the front door and just kiss her right now coz I can't wait till it's

1969

I've been living in this house for five years I think and this is the first time I've ever really been in here. I wouldn't be here now if George hadn't kicked the ball over the goal-hedge and right over the wall. Why can't he kick the ball at the goal? Or anywhere near it? When I'm in goal it's easy for him to score because the hedge is so big and I can't reach up to the top or get anywhere near the sides of it though Andrew isn't much better he can't really play football at all with his glasses and he can't really run at all with his funny leg and George isn't much better we're all pretty useless I suppose that's why I enjoy it so much when it's just the three of us playing three and in. But I don't like the overgrown garden it's like a wilderness and in the dark in winter it's even worse the bare trees are outlined against the grey sky and they're making weird shapes like witches' skinny arms and fingers or enormous birds' claws and it reminds me of that film "Journey to the Centre of the Earth" where they're in this prehistoric world full of dinosaurs and monsters and it's all overgrown with massive plants it's nearly as bad in here and the briars and weeds are getting tangled around my feet and trying to tie me up and maybe drag me down into the undergrowth I've never been this far in and it's getting so dark I can't even see where George is Andrew's over there but none of us can find the ball it's our best one too the leather one with the stitching and the laces where you stick the adapter in that you attach to the bicycle pump to pump it up when it goes down it's getting a bit wrecked from playing on the road but it's still the best football we've ever had and if it's gone forever please God don't let it be gone forever I better keep looking but it's getting darker it's after five and it's very cold and this place is really scary in the dark all overgrown and you have to watch out for the nettles or you'll get stung and those thorny things that raspberries grow on but they're wild and you couldn't eat them and –

"Karl – are you going to help look for this stupid ball or not?" George shouts over to me.

"I am looking, but it's getting so dark I can't see anything," I reply. "Maybe we should leave it till tomorrow."

"No, we have to find it now, it may not be here tomorrow."

"Why? It's not going to go anywhere is it?"

"Someone might find it and take it."

"How's anyone else going to find it? We can't even find it ourselves and you're the one who kicked it in." I really want to go inside and get warm it will be time for Dr Who soon and then The Flintstones and then Mum will start frying the tea in the big frying pan first she puts in the rasher skins to grease the pan and when they're all crispy and nearly burnt she takes them out and puts them on the side thing that's attached to the pan to let them drain and we get three each on a little saucer and they taste incredible all crispy and salty and chewy then she puts in the rashers and sausages and a tomato for Dad and then the eggs at the end it's always a fry for tea on a Saturday that's why it's the best day of the week with no real school and maybe a match in the afternoon and then my favourite tea but if we don't find this ball soon we're going to be late for tea and   -

"Found it!" I hear Andrew shout though I nearly can't see him it's getting so dark. "It's here!"

Thank God, I say to myself.

203

"How did it get all the way over there?" says George. "I didn't think I kicked it that hard."

"Just try and get it somewhere near the goal in future," I tell him though I'm so happy we found it I can't really be mad at him. Andrew is coming over towards us with the ball in his hands and he looks really pleased as he tosses the ball to me and I catch it and he pushes his glasses up his nose. I can't see his eyes because of the dark but I can see he's smiling at me. He's got lots of twigs and briars and things on his clothes and some even in his hair. As he passes I pick off a couple of sticky-backs from his jumper and throw them away.

"Knew we'd find it," he says, "Just had to keep looking."

"Well done," I say, "Thanks a mil." And then I have an idea. "Do you want to stay for tea?" I ask him.

"Better not," he says, "I'm expected home. Thanks anyway."

The three of us climb back over the garden wall at the low bit where the wall is crumbly like the inside of a Crunchie and we're back in our garden, all dark now and I can see the light in the kitchen window where Mum has started cooking the tea. The thought of it is making me hungry. Andy gets his coat from the bench under the tree where he left it when he was getting too warm and we say goodbye. George goes in the side door and I hear him ask Mum is tea ready yet and I stand for a while watching Andy walking up the drive and out the gate, with that funny walk he has as if one leg is longer than the other and he has to stretch it out further.

****

There's a house on this road, Grandfather's Road, Ailesbury Road, that I want to own when I grow up. It's got two entrances so you can drive in one and out the other - that's so cool, two big sets of gates, that's what I really want in a house, it has to have two entrances, there it is there on the right - on my side, George has probably never even seen it, he's looking out the other window at one of the embassies that has a flagpole with a white flag with a big red eagle on it and as I wonder what country that is George sees me looking over his side and –

"What did you think of Michelle?" he whispers to me. She had been in the Park after Mass with the Mullens that morning. I say nothing.

"Who's Michelle?" asks Mum in the front; George's whispers can usually be heard a mile off.

"You know, the Mullen's cousin, she's up again from Clonmel, staying with them for a few days," I explain.

"Oh, what's she like?"

"She's all right," says George. The words "fantastic bird" come into my head for some reason.

"What do you think of her Karl?"

"She's all right," I say.

"Very informative," says Mum to Dad who shrugs as we slow down to turn into Grandfather's driveway, up the gravel drive and park in front of the door. Dad has his own key because he grew up in this house, lived there until the day he was married imagine that, so we all go in, me and George standing back to let Mum in first we learned that the hard way through the little porch then we're in the massive hall with a huge staircase going up the left side by an enormous stained-glass window. There's even a fireplace in the hall and while Dad hangs up his coat on the coat stand I look at the picture over it, a huge portrait of Auntie Eire who was an actress on the stage and died of cancer when she was quite young. Her two daughters Judy and Jane live in England and we don't see them very often they're my first cousins. Into the drawing room I love those cut glass door handles they match the chandelier inside everyone's here, all the uncles and aunts they're all in their Sunday best and we're in our school uniforms we just go straight through to the back of the room, say hello to Auntie Penny who's wearing her tweed suit she's standing beside the piano as usual smoking a cigarette it's in the ashtray and it's got lipstick all over the end of it, give her a kiss say, "Very well thank you how are you?" when she asks me how I am then go and stand with my other cousin's husband Liam beside the cocktail

205

cabinet they're much older than us but not as old as the uncles and aunts he gets us a Coke each and some nuts and we stand around while everyone goes on talking. Mum and Dad have sat down on the big sofa. After a while the door opens and in comes Auntie Rosemary with Grandfather. He's got his stick but he still needs someone to lean on in the morning. Everyone stands up, except we're standing already so we don't have to, then after he's settled in his big armchair by the fireplace we all go over one by one to shake hands with him. When it's my turn he smiles and winks at me and, imitating President Devalera's accent, he says:

"We'll make sure to have some for your next visit," and we both laugh. Then I go back to Liam and Grandfather explains the joke to everyone in the room and they all laugh and look over at me so I laugh too but I'm not sure if they're laughing with Dev or at him but I don't think they're laughing at me anyway. Still I don't want anyone to laugh at Dev because of something I said, I can still remember how it felt to have him standing behind me so big and tall and strong and famous that day in the back garden of the Aras.

After a while George and myself excuse ourselves and leave the drawing room, go out through the side door and outside. The garden is so long you can't see to the end of it because halfway along there's a big wall and on the other side of that there's a row of sheds and then the vegetable garden and orchard which go down as far as the river at the end. We go down the gravel path and through the door in the wall. Then we're in the vegetable garden with the potting sheds just behind the wall. George immediately goes in to the first one of these and starts rooting around in some drawers and I cannot believe it but he has pulled out a packet of cigarettes – ten Rothmans, they're the ones the airline pilots smoke when they're flying their planes in the cinema ads – and now he's found a box of matches and he's put a cigarette in his mouth and he's lighting it.

"What are you doing?" I shout.

"What does it look like?"

206

"You can't do that. Where did you get those? Whose are they?"

"They're mine, I hid them here last week."

"But you don't smoke – you can't – you're too young!"

"Oh yeah? Just watch me."

I do watch him and it's worth watching because it's a pretty funny sight all right as he doesn't look at all the way an adult looks when they smoke, his eyes are half closed and his face is all scrunched up to one side and he's even holding the thing wrong, between his thumb and first finger with his hand underneath instead of the way I see Auntie Penny smoke, with the cigarette gracefully and elegantly balanced between her first two fingers. Then I notice his finger has gone a kind of dirty orange colour.

"Oh God," I say, "You look ridiculous." Then he starts coughing.

"You know they'll be able to smell it off you, you'll stink of smoke when you go in." He says nothing as he's still puffing on the cigarette but he puts his hand in his school blazer pocket and takes out a new packet of Silvermints and waves it at me.

"Oh Lord," I say, "What kind of a brother have I got?"

"Do you want to try it? Go on, take a drag."

"No thanks it's disgusting. Anyway if we go back inside now we'll have time for another Coke and some Twiglets. I saw a new box there."

"Oh ... OK...I'll just stub this out and keep it for later." And he flicks the lit end off his cigarette with his thumbnail and puts the half-smoked thing back in the box. It really stinks.

All the way home in the car I'm sniffing in George's direction though all I can smell is Silvermints - he must have about three in his mouth - while he opens the window and tries to crouch closer to his door until Mum turns around and says:

"What's wrong Karl, are you getting a cold?"

"Yes I think I might be Mummy, and George has the window open letting in a draft."

"Yes close the window George, there's a good chap," says Dad, "I can feel it on the back of my neck."

Myself and George exchange looks as he winds up the window. He still hasn't forgiven me by the time lunch is finished and we're heading across the road to the Mullens. They told us this morning everyone was going to be playing in their house this afternoon since Michelle is there.

"Don't even try talking to Michelle," George is hissing at me as we wait at the back door for someone to answer our knock. "I want her to myself."

"Suits me fine."

Here's Bridie letting us in and saying, "They're all in the sunroom."

"Thanks Bridie," I smile at her and she smiles back. Doesn't hurt to be nice, I think, just because she's only the maid. In the sunroom they're all sitting around on cushions on the floor, the Blaneys are there as well as Yvonne, Zoe, Kieran, and of course the star attraction, all the way from Clonmel County Tipperary, the Mullens' most famous and beautiful cousin – Michelle! We join the circle, George of course sitting beside Miss World while I go round the other side beside Patrick which happens to be opposite her. I have to admit that Michelle does have something about her. It's funny but she's like a cross between Yvonne and Zoe. She's exactly halfway between the two in height, her face isn't as freckly as Zoe's but is more freckly than Yvonne's, and her hair is Zoe's colour but Yvonne's shape and style. Her eyes are different though, not violets like Yvonne's and not sunflowers like Zoe's. I'm staring at them to try and figure out what her eyes are like but I can't, they're just brown. She doesn't say an awful lot and when she does speak it's in a very low tone without moving her lips so you have to listen hard to hear what she's saying. But the funny thing is, they're all talking about something really serious. Yvonne fills us in:

"We were just talking about telling lies, whether it's ever all right to lie to somebody, ay if you want to avoid hurting them. What do you two think?"

"Right," I say, collecting my thoughts. "George should be good at this because this very morning in our Grandfather's back garden he was doing something that he definitely shouldn't have been doing, and if Mum and Dad found out there'd be big trouble."

"Oh really?"

"What was he doing?"

"Tell us!"

"What were you doing?"

This is George's moment of glory and he's not going to waste it. He looks around suspiciously then gets up and checks that the door is closed – he even looks outside to make sure no-one is listening at the keyhole – and when he comes back and he's just opening his mouth Yvonne says:

"Why don't we all go up to the Clubhouse?" Me and Patrick laugh at the look on George's face.

"Oh yeah brilliant, have you seen our new Clubhouse?" Zoe asks her cousin.

"We used to meet in the Jones's garage but Dad fixed up the top of our garage." Yvonne explains.

"Wait till you see it, it's fab," says Kieran.

"Couldn't be any worse than Jones's anyway," Barry complains, "I hated sitting on those Peat Briquettes."

"C'mon so, show me," says Michelle.

We all head outside through the French windows and a couple of minutes later we have climbed up the ladder through a trapdoor and into what is now a kind of loft in the roof of their enormous garage.

"Your Dad's done a great job here for sure," I say, and he certainly has, with sheets of wood nailed down to the rafters and covered in old carpet. There's enough room for all of us.

When we are settled in roughly the same order as we were sitting in downstairs except for Kieran who has gone up to his bedroom, George looks around at all of us and in a big dramatic whisper says:

"*I was smoking!*"

There is mixed reaction to this revelation, some people like Patrick going "Wow" and others like Yvonne and Barry saying, "So what? I've done that."

"I was trying to get Mum and Dad to notice the smell from him in the car on the way home, it was really funny. But the point is," I continue, "If he was asked if he had been smoking would it have been all right for him to lie and say "No" because it would hurt his parents to know the truth – right?"

"So what would you have said, George?" asks Yvonne.

"I – I don't know. I never thought about it," he says.

"You should never tell a lie," says Patrick.

"You're just a baby," his brother remarks. "What do you know?"

"I think it's Ok to lie in that situation," says Yvonne, "because if you told them they'd be really upset and that would be worse."

"Well he shouldn't have been smoking in the first place," Zoe objects, "If he wasn't, he wouldn't need to lie." Then I notice Michelle hasn't said anything so I ask her:

"What do you think, Michelle? Do you think it's OK to lie sometimes?"

Michelle does this thing of staring into space like she's thinking really hard and then she turns to George with a funny naughty look on her face and says:

"Give us a cigarette and I'll tell ya." And when she smiles I can see she's got something on her teeth, like braces only not so noticeable.

"Sorry, I don't have them on me." George is a bit taken aback.

"He hides them in our Grandfather's garden shed," I explain. "So nobody can get at them – including himself."

"Then we'll have to buy some ourselves," says Yvonne. "Who's got any money?"

"It's Sunday, the shop will be closed." Barry points out.

"Right, we'll have to get some from our parents. I know where Mum keeps hers I can nick one or two but any more and she'll notice. Who else can get some?"

"No Yvonne you can't. If you do I'm telling on you," says Zoe.

"Our parents don't smoke," I say, "Anyway I don't feel like smoking." I'm glad to opt out as this is getting serious – smoking is bad enough but smoking and stealing is too dangerous for my liking.

"I can get a couple from my Mum's handbag," says Barry.

"OK," says Yvonne. "Let's go and get them and meet up in St Mark's in ten minutes, by the Hanging tree."

And in a minute Yvonne, George, Barry and Michelle have gone down the ladder and left myself Patrick and Zoe looking at each other. In one way I feel a bit of a baby but I'm glad Zoe wouldn't do it either.

"They'll get caught and then there'll be big trouble," she says.

"Yeah we're better off not getting involved," I agree.

"So what'll we do now?" says Patrick.

"Nice Clubhouse, your Dad's done a great job," I say and then I remember I said that before.

"I have to go and do some homework," says Zoe. "See you later." And she disappears down through the trapdoor. I can't believe I just let her slip through my fingers we could have been alone here together if Patrick had left instead and I could have asked her about her standing at the window making X's with her fingers but she just went as if it never occurred to her to be alone with me now I have to try really hard not to look disappointed in front of Patrick but I'm feeling so sick inside.

"So Patrick, that just leaves us, what about a game of Cluedo in your bedroom?"

"Yeah, brill, come on!" And we're gone.

****

"You know what I heard in school today, in religion?" says Zoe, throwing little pebbles into the pond.

"You don't like Religion class much, do you?" says Yvonne.

211

"Well it's just that – some of the stuff they teach us is so ... weird! You won't believe this, but the Jews have this thing called the Passover, and on this day every year they have to sprinkle the blood of a lamb over their front door or else some avenging angel is going to come along and take the first born and kill it – that would be you Yvonne!"

"It's a pity we're not Jews then isn't it?" says Kieran. "Let's all become Jews."

"Brilliant idea," says Patrick, looking at Barry.

"Hey! Watch it!" Barry doesn't think it's a brilliant idea.

"Absolutely," I agree, looking at George and rubbing my hands together.

"Hey!" Neither does George.

"When I was younger I used to think I was going to go straight to hell when I died," I say and tell them about my First Communion day, ringing up the priest for confession over the phone which they find quite funny and laugh a lot.

"Yeah you hear some funny stuff in religion class," I continue. "Like about the Resurrection of the Dead. They tell us we're all going to be resurrected and get our bodies back and toddle off to live in Heaven. But you know what's really going to happen when you're resurrected from the dead? You suddenly wake up on Judgement Day and you've been dead for about ten thousand years just lying in your coffin, and you know the way the hair and the nails keep on growing after you die - "

"I didn't know that," interrupts Patrick.

"Yes it's true, I read that," says Kieran and everybody starts going, "Yuck!" and "That's disgusting!"

"Well," I continue, "Your hair is going to be a complete mess and your nails are going to be about six inches long and that's the way you're going to look for all eternity after the resurrection of the dead and life everlasting Amen. You're really going to need a haircut." Then they all join in:

"Yeah, you'll look like some of those guys on Top of the Pops," says Kieran.

"Yeah the Kinks or the Troggs or somebody," I add. And then Yvonne jumps up and starts messing up her hair with both hands and screaming:

"Today is Judgement Day, I've got an appointment with God at half eleven! I can't see him looking like this – he'll send me straight to Hell! I need a hairdresser quick! Help!"

"And I need a manicure!" says Zoe, "Look at my nails, they're six inches long, they haven't been cut for all eternity - yuck!" Then we all start saying things like:

"Yeah and then you'll be queuing up for the interview with God to decide who gets to stay in Heaven and who gets sent to Hell - "

" - And there'll be someone in the queue with a comb and you say, 'Hey - gives us a lend of your comb' - "

" – Yeah and he won't give it to you and there'll be a fight and everyone will join in trying to get the comb off this guy so they can comb their hair - "

" - Yeah and imagine the state of your clothes after lying in a coffin in a dirty old grave for thousands of years. You're gonna really look a fright!"

"You're gonna need a new suit and polish your shoes at least."

"And a hat if you're a girl, you know the way we have to wear a hat at Mass, it's probably the same in Heaven," Zoe says.

"Yeah, I'd say God likes hats all right," I agree, "You're really going to need a hat to get into Heaven. Come Judgement Day if you don't have a nice hat on you'll go straight to Hell." And we all crack up. I love these religious discussions with my mates, they're just the best ever.

****

"The meeting will come to order. The meeting will come to order!" Andrew is having trouble getting everyone's attention, you could say. Yvonne and Zoe are talking about what way they're going to get their hair cut tomorrow. Kieran is trying to explain to Barry and George all the different dental instruments of his father's he found in a big wooden case at the far end of the garage roof but both of them are completely ignoring him, as Barry and George are discussing which is better, Jimi Hendrix's version of "All Along the Watchtower" or Bob Dylan's original.

"I think he misses his little mallet," I say to Patrick beside me.

"Yeah, he should have brung it with him when we moved."

"I don't think 'should have brung' is correct Patrick."

"Oh yeah sorry – he should have brang it with him."

"Yeah ... we'll leave it so, but you're right," I agree. "And his block of wood."

"Remember the time he broke the block of wood in two, that was funny," says Patrick and starts laughing.

"Order! Order please!"

"Bag of chips."

"Salt n vinegar?"

"What about a fringe like mine?"

"No, I've never had a fringe, it wouldn't suit me."

"There's even an old-fashioned drill that was operated by hand, imagine that!"

"Yes but Hendrix's guitar and bass sound is so much better."

"It's an acoustic song. It shouldn't have all that guitar and bass."

"We have some announcements to make," Andrew says when he finally gets us to stop talking. "We have some important announcements – about the Beatles!"

"What?" someone asks.

"Firstly John Lennon and Paul McCartney have recently got married..."

"What - to each other?" Patrick asks and everyone cracks up.

"John has married Yoko - "

"No we're not sending them flowers, I don't care what you say," says Barry.

" – and Paul has married Linda ..."

"Or a congratulations card," George says.

214

"And we're not going to offer to babysit when they have children," I feel I might as well join in.

"Look, I was just letting you know in case anyone missed it. The other important news is that a new single was released at the end of May called The Ballad of John and Yoko. It's all about their wedding and honeymoon and it's supposed to be fab so you should all go out and buy it."

"Great! Banba here I come," I say.

"And there will be another album out at the end of the summer. No title yet but I will let you know. Now whose turn is it to buy the next album?"

"I don't like this taking turns buying their albums idea," I complain. "I had to buy the last one and it was rubbish – Yellow Submarine. The whole of side two is a load of junk from the movie, it's all orchestra stuff, not a single Beatles song."

"All right, in that case you can buy the new one too if you want."

"No, I want to buy it," says Barry.

"We want to buy it," says Yvonne.

"All right, all right, forget about that idea, I was just trying to save us money. You can all buy the new Beatles album if you want."

"Great!"

"I was going to anyway."

"Bet I get it first."

"I propose we all get different albums instead of just Beatles ones," says Barry. "And change the name, I'm sick of it being the Beatles Club. I want to call it the Rolling Stones Club."

"I think we should call it the Hellfire Club," says Kieran, "That's a real club that meets in the Dublin mountains and - "

"I want to call it the Barbie and Ken Club," says Zoe.

"What about the Billy Bunter Club," I propose, "And we all have to eat cakes and Jam Tarts."

"Jam Tarts!" laughs Yvonne. "Did you hear what your brother said? We have to eat Jam Tarts." And George starts laughing too, then Zoe, then Barry gives a snort, and first I think I've actually said

215

something funny until I realise they are definitely laughing *at* me this time and I've no clue what they're laughing at.

"What? What's so funny?" And looking around I see Patrick and Kieran and Andrew aren't in on the joke either and we just shrug at each other while the others go on laughing and saying things like, "Eat jam tarts – ugh! disgusting!"

"What's so funny?" I ask again.

"You'll find out, when you're older," Yvonne said, still smirking.

"All right come on now that's enough of that, we have to take a vote on something as serious as changing the name," says Andrew, "All proposals must be made through the Chair."

Andrew must have been distracted because he's obviously forgotten what happened the last time he said that but Patrick hasn't and immediately he's up and jumping on top of Andrew saying:

"Yeay, look at me, I'm sitting on the Chair!"

When Patrick finally lets him up Andrew's glasses are half off his face and he's covered in dust. He sits up and gives Patrick a look as he rearranges his tweed jacket and fixes his glasses.

"Stupid boy!" he says in his best Capt Mainwaring voice.

"I take it no one was serious about changing the name. In that case and since that's all the items on the agenda, I adjourn the meeting."

"Does that mean the meeting is over?" asks Barry.

"Eh – yes."

"Great, now let's do something a bit more interesting." Then we start our "What do you want to do" nonsense:

"What'll we do?"

"I dunno – what do you want to do?"

"I dunno – what do *you* want to do?"

"Well let's get out of here for a start, it's stifling," I suggest. It really is hot up under the roof of the Mullen's loft. "What about a game of French cricket on Temple Road?"

"Yeah – brill!" says Patrick beside me and the others reluctantly agree. This is something we've started doing recently, choosing Temple Road as it is so wide and there's even less traffic than on our road. We all agree so we head to our homes to get our bikes. Five minutes later we are speeding down to the end of the road, across the main road and freewheeling down Temple Road. We've got two tennis racquets and a couple of balls and the next two hours are spent firing tennis balls at each others' legs. When we've had enough we take shelter from the sun in the cool porch of St Philip's.

"Why does no-one go to Mass here?" asks Patrick, "It's much closer than Rathgar."

"It's Church of Ireland stupo."

"So? We're in Ireland and it's a church – why can't we go to Mass there?"

"Someone please explain to the idiot, I'm too hot and tired to bother."

"You see Patrick," I say taking his arm, "Once upon a time a long time ago there was a mighty king who ruled England – and Ireland - called Henry the Eighth. Now Henry didn't like his wife and he wanted rid of her but the Pope wouldn't let him so he told the Pope to get lost and he chopped his wife's head off and started his own religion called the Church of England. They're Protestants. Have you heard of Protestants?"

"Of course. Aren't they the naughty women who go out at night?"

"No they're something else. I'll explain about them when you're older."

"Thanks Karl."

So we're all sitting in the church porch with the cool tiles underneath and the cold stone to lean against it's like being in a fridge compared with outside and then George gets up and starts reading some notices on the notice-board.

"Hey, there's a garden Fete on here next week. Look – "Garden Fete in the grounds of St Philip's June 15th". Why don't we all go. It might be - "

****

"Fun here isn't it?" I say to Zoe beside me. "I'm glad it's just the four of us it's nicer sometimes without the Blaneys I mean Patrick's great but Barry can be a bit annoying ."

"*A bit* annoying! You can say that again." I'm so glad Zoe agrees with me, I don't like giving out about people behind their backs but it makes me feel closer to Zoe that she said that and it's just the two of us because George and Yvonne have gone off together and I don't want to even mention Rory. I can hardly recognise the garden of St Philip's, it looks so much bigger with all the stalls and tables and stuff around.

"Look at the two of them," I say, nodding towards George and Yvonne who are walking around the stalls ahead of us holding hands. I can't believe my eyes.

"I know," Zoe says, throwing her eyes up to heaven.

"When did they start doing that?" I ask.

"Remember the time they went into St Mark's with the cigarettes, when Michelle was here?"

"Yeah?"

"That night Yvonne told me she was with George and Barry was with Michelle but she wouldn't say what they were doing."

"What do you think they were doing?"

"Oh nothing much, just smoking, holding hands, kissing maybe. I couldn't care less."

"Yeah, neither could I." What the heck *was* he doing with her? I wonder. It occurs to me that this is the perfect chance to ask her about standing at the window making X's with her fingers and I'm just about to when she suddenly says:

"Oh look, a bottle stall, why don't we buy a ticket?" Zoe is running over to a stall with hundreds of bottles on it and there's a big wheel with numbers all around it.

"How does it work?"

"Well you have to pay a shilling or whatever it is and you're given a ticket. You may not win anything or you might get whatever bottle has your number, it could be something nice like that Fanta or it could be a bottle of furniture polish or – what else have they got there – Fairy Liquid or 2001 Carpet Cleaner – that's awful. Anyway, let's try it."

"OK," I say, reluctantly parting with a shilling.

"No it's all right, I have one," Zoe says.

"Let's buy one each then." We wait for the woman to finish spinning the wheel for the last customer who doesn't win anything and then she turns to us.

"Hello, what's it going to be? Are you feeling lucky? There's a big bottle of Fanta there if one of you gets the right number. How many tickets?"

"Two please," says Zoe taking my shilling and giving them both to the bottle lady. The bottle lady has big frizzy orange hair which looks like she's washed it in Fanta herself, and when I whisper this to Zoe she gives me a smile as she takes the two tickets. There's a lot more people buying tickets now so we have to wait for her to spin.

"What number do you want?" Zoe asks. "Twenty-five or seven?"

"I don't mind, you choose."

"I'll take seven then, it's my lucky number."

We're standing really close together because there's a bit of a crowd around the stall now and I can almost smell her smell and it's so exciting as the frizzy-orange-haired lady spins the wheel. I'm really praying that seven wins so Zoe can get a prize and I'm repeating 'Seven – seven - seven' to myself like mad .

"And the winning number is – 25!"

"Bad luck – sorry," I say before I realise that I've won. Zoe is jumping up and down.

"And No 25 is ... Oh my, this is a very good bottle of wine. Who's the lucky winner? Twenty-five! Who has number 25?"

I squeeze through the crowd and give the woman my ticket and I think she's looking a bit disappointed that I'm the winner.

"Oh, it's you," she says. "Sorry everybody, this boy has won the bottle of Chablis. That was the best bottle I had young man, I hope your parents appreciate good wine."

"Oh yes, both my parents are very fond of good wine. In fact Chab – that one - is their favourite," I reply confidently as I'm a bit worried she won't let me keep the bottle.

"All right then but be careful bringing it home. You don't want to drop it love."

"Oh that's all right, we don't have too far to go."

"Well done," says Zoe as we leave the stall.

"I should have told her I'm going to drink it myself."

"Yeah, serve her right, snooty old cow." And we both have a giggle. Up ahead we spot Yvonne and George at the hoop-la stall. As we arrive George has some hoops in his hand and he's trying desperately to ring a packet of twenty Rothmans at the back of the stall but he keeps missing.

"Here, give me some more money, I'll get them this time," he says to Yvonne after his last hoop is gone.

"Having fun?" I ask him.

"Don't distract me, I have to get them this time," George doesn't even look at us, he's too busy paying for more hoops.

"We've just been to the bottle stall," I tell him.

"Complete waste of money, you never win anything decent there. Fairy Liquid – can you believe it? Who would donate a bottle of Fairy Liquid to a bottle stall? Now watch this."

"Ahem," I say, standing there holding the wine in front of me.

"Actually, Karl won the very best bottle of wine there," says Zoe with a lovely little smile on her face. Thank you Zoe, I'm thinking.

"Yeah sure." George is still ignoring me and doing dummy throws at the cigarettes but Yvonne's looking at the bottle and says:

"Wow, look at that. It looks good all right. The label's all in French."

"OK, watch this – Oh no, just missed! Did you see that? It went over it and then jumped off again. *What*?" Yvonne's tugging at his sleeve.

"Your brother's just won a bottle of real French wine at the bottle stall and you can't even hoop-la a packet of cigarettes for us."

One look at George's face is enough as I show him the bottle.

"Let's go somewhere and open it!" says Yvonne.

"No way," I reply. "Sorry, but I'm bringing it home. This is for my Dad." We leave George and Yvonne trying to get their cigarettes and wander round a bit more before going home carrying my trophy very carefully.

"When I get home I'm going to go straight to Dad and give it to him and see what he says. I can't wait to see the look on his face." I say and Zoe says:

"I think he'll be pleased with you."

"Thanks, I hope so."

****

"Do you really think it's him?" I ask George in a whisper.

"Looks like him, doesn't it?"

"Yeah but it couldn't be. I mean what would he be doing here – on a boat about to go out to an island off the west coast of Cork?"

"He wants to buy an island. I heard it on the radio. I heard he was coming to Ireland looking for a remote island off the west coast to buy."

"Why would he want to do that?"

"Well for one thing he's just got married hasn't he, to that Japanese woman Yoko something. So he probably wants to settle down."

"Yoko Ono I think her name is. Settle down? Off the west coast of Ireland – are you mad? Who'd want to do that?"

We both look as closely as we can at the bearded man across from us on the ferry without wanting to stare but I still can't tell if it's really John Lennon. He's sitting about ten feet away from us, on the far side of the boat. OK the hair is right - long, brown, parted in the middle; the glasses are right - little round gold frames, and he's got a big beard like John had in his recent photos.

"Where *is* she then?" I ask George. "And stop staring."

"Where's who?"

221

"Yoky-bobs – if he's just got married why isn't she with him?"

"Oh, she probably gets sea-sick so he left her back in the B and B." My brother sometimes, he just never ceases to amaze me.

"And for another thing," he goes back to what he was saying earlier. "He probably wants some privacy, you know, get away from all the press and publicity after his wedding."

"Yeah, that was something: The Ballad of John and Yoko. Pity we weren't allowed buy that record, it'll be the only single we're missing."

" '*Christ you know it ain't easy'* – that's what did it."

"And '*They're gonna crucify me'*." Otherwise Mum didn't have any problems with it."

"What about the new one? Have you heard it?"

"What new one?"

"John has a new single out on his own, not the Beatles, just John and Yoko. Haven't you heard it? It's called "Give Peace a Chance".

"Why has he got a single out on his own?" This is news to me.

"Well he's sitting right there – why don't you ask him?"

"Very funny."

The boat's engine starts revving up and we pull backwards away from the dock, then spin round into the sun and head out to sea in between lots of little islands. Mum and Dad are behind us in their Aran sweaters, sitting close together holding hands which is nice, but there's no point in asking either of them do they think this guy is John Lennon. I make up my mind.

"There's only one way to find out. We'll have to ask him who he is," I tell George.

"Are you mad? I'm not just going up to a complete stranger and saying, 'Excuse me, are you John Lennon?' What if he's not him? What if it *is* him?"

"We'll never know if we don't ask. I'll do it." So I get up and stagger over the deck to the other side but the motion of the boat is making me fall all over the place and by the time I get half way across I'm too embarrassed to go through with it so I swerve and head for an unoccupied part of the bench and look out over the sea. From there I glance back at George who's making frantic gestures at me to get on with it so I start staring at the Lennon-looking guy, trying to attract his attention. Then something incredible happens, he actually talks to me, he says:

"Hi. Are you on your holidays?"

"Eh, yes, I'm here with my brother, that's him over there." I'm so nervous I forget about Mum and Dad.

"Are they not your parents?" he asks, and there's something about his voice that really sounds like John Lennon.

"Oh those, yes, of course, nearly forgot, yes that's Mum and Dad all right." And he actually gives George and then Mum and Dad a wave.

"Do you mind me asking ..." I start off. "It's just that ... you know you look a lot like one of the Beatles."

"Really, do you think so? Yeah a lot of people think that. People are always sayin to me, 'You look the image of Ringo'. Only jokin, it's John you're thinkin of, isn't it?" I nod and the more he talks the more he has this real Liverpool accent. "Yeah, I get that a lot." Then he says:

"Do *you* think I'm John Lennon?"

"I'm not sure. Are you?"

"Sometimes I'm not sure myself." He stares out to sea and when I look at him the sea and the sun are reflected in his round gold-framed glasses and his long hair is blowing over his face. Then he turns round to another guy standing just inside the hatch.

"Hey Derek, this kid wants to know am I John Lennon. What will I tell him?" And the other guy says:

"Tell him you're the walrus."

"That's it, I am the walrus, just like those ones over there - " and he points to a group of seals sitting on some rocks.

"There not walruses, they're seals," I tell him, and then I remember that it might actually be John Lennon I'm talking to.

223

"You're a smart kid. Go on, get back to your family, have a good holiday, it was nice meeting you." So I get up and stagger back across the deck to George and I've no idea what really happened and when George asks me was it really him I still don't know if it was or not. But then I take out my camera and pretend to take a picture of George but I'm really getting the John Lennon guy instead. A little while later the boat docks at the jetty on the island, we all get off and we never see him again, so I suppose I'll never know, but when I get my picture developed that'll prove it was him cause he looks just like him and no-one will ever be able to tell the difference.

****

"What day is it on?" I ask Mum as I finish drying up the dishes after lunch.

"What day is what on love?"

"The moon landing. I know it's the 20th but what day is that?"

"It's next Sunday."

"And we're going to watch it in Mrs Cullen's?"

"Yes. She's the only one around here who has a TV."

"Are you sure we'll be able to see it all right?"

"I don't know love, but the only other way is to get Dad's binoculars and look up at the moon yourself."

"Really? Would that work?"

"No, I was joking."

"Oh. Wouldn't it be better if we went home and watched it on our own TV. It's much better reception and we'd be comfier and then Dad wouldn't have to come down for the weekend."

"What do you mean Karl? Do you not like it here at the Cottage? You're not growing out of it already are you? No, you couldn't be."

"No, I still love it, it's just that ... you see all our friends on the road are at home for the summer, playing together, and I'll miss them. Sometimes it gets boring here on our own, just me and George."

"Well I'm sure you're not missing all that much, you see enough of those children God knows and they'll all still be there when you get back. Now run along and play."

That's the thing, I don't know if they'll all still be there when I get back, I'm thinking as we walk up the lane to Mrs Cullen's in the sunshine a few days later. The sunshine doesn't even make me happy anymore, the way I feel it might as well be raining. I don't even know if I want to be here at all. I mean, I do love the Cottage and I always will but while I'm here Zoe could be with you know who. What did she mean the day we left not to worry, that they would be having a great summer. All we did was go over to their house to say goodbye. And why did Yvonne say to George, "Well you know if the two of you aren't going to be around we'll have to find someone else to have fun with"? Who did she mean? Patrick is away at Irish College now so that leaves Barry, and why has Rory started hanging around so much now, he's not even in the Club. Why was he there the last time we went into St Mark's? And what were they talking about Zoe and him coming back from Vinegar Hill? Why did they walk slowly so they could be on their own? And then she hardly even said goodbye when we were leaving. I know her mother was there but standing in the kitchen like that it was like they couldn't wait to get rid of us, they could have brought us into the sunroom. And she didn't even give me one of her special smiles she just said:

"See you, have a good summer."

"Yeah, thanks, you too."

"Oh don't worry we will, won't we Yvonne?"

"Absolutely." And then her mother says:

"Who are you going to play with when George and Karl aren't here?" And Yvonne says:

"Oh we'll find someone." And of course George can't hide what he's feeling and says really crossly:

"Oh yeah, like who?" And then Yvonne comes out with it, right in front of her mother:

"Well you know if the two of you aren't going to be around we'll have to find someone else to have fun with, won't we Zoe?"

225

But she must have been joking, I mean she wouldn't have said something like that in front of her mother unless she was joking, would she? My thoughts are interrupted by a crackling voice from the telly:

"The Eagle has landed."

"What does that mean?" I whisper to George beside me, "Where's the eagle?"

"That's the name of the landing craft module yoke, the thing they land on the moon in, it's called the Eagle. Now be quiet."

I don't see why I should be quiet because everyone here has now burst into applause and cheers. It seems all the local farmers have taken the afternoon off from digging and ploughing and they're all in Mrs Cullen's kitchen around her rented TV watching the moon landing. There's some enormous men standing around and they're all wearing the same clothes. I mean I know I'm small but these men are like giants. Big black boots the size of Morris Minors, though they could do with a trip to the car wash, dark grey trousers, waistcoats and stripey shirts with no collars. Some of the men have braces and some of them have their trousers held up with string which looks so cool I'm going to ask Mum can I do that. They all take off their caps when they come in and roll them up into their pockets. Almost all of them are smoking pipes or making their own cigarettes with tobacco and little thin pieces of paper which they roll between their fingers it's amazing watching them. Mrs Cullen is sitting by the fireplace and even though it's the middle of summer there's a fire lit with a big black kettle hanging over it from the black bar - same as we have in our cottage but we never use and every now and then she fills someone's tea cup from the big pot. She doesn't have to lift it which is good it looks so heavy, she just tilts it up and pours out the tea. The TV is very hard to see because of the light coming in from outside, the amount of smoke in the room even though the door is open, and the grainy black and white pictures; they *are* coming from the moon though, I suppose, so I can't complain. It's not a colour TV like ours so when I come here to watch Batman it's in black and white and it's not as good as at home. But even if it was a colour TV it would still be in black and white because everything is black and white up there, the moon is white and the sky is black and that's all there is. Then there's another crackling voice from the telly:

"That's one small step for a man, one giant leap for mankind." Everybody is cheering again and they're all saying things like:

"There's a man on the moon."

"A man on the moon begor."

"Be the dad."

"What'll they think of next?"

"Aren't them Yanks the clever - " But I can't understand the next word.

"Be the hokey."

"Never thought I'd live to see the day."

So they all have another cup of tea to celebrate and some of the men pass around a little bottle which I think is whiskey to put in their tea and then it's time to go home. And when we go outside and walk down the lane to the Cottage Mum stops us and says:

"Look – you can see the moon, it's out already. Just imagine, there are two human beings up there walking around, isn't that wonderful?" And I suppose it is wonderful but all I can think of is where Zoe was watching the moon landing and who she was with. I look at George and wonder is he not worried about Yvonne, maybe she was with Barry. He's looking up at the moon and seems to be thinking hard about something, and then he says:

"Wouldn't you think they'd fall off?"

****

"Why don't you help Dad cut the grass?"

"Oh, I was just about to go up to Andy's. George has gone already."

"Well bring him back down here, he can help too. But hurry up, Dad's getting the lawnmower out and he'll be starting soon."

227

George is halfway up the road when I get out the gate so I run up and catch up with him.

"Mum says we have to help Dad with the grass and we should ask Andy to help too, good idea, huh?"

"Suppose so."

"There he is," I say as we turn the corner by the pussy willow in Andy's front garden.

"Where?"

"There - in the car. He's in his Dad's car, parking it." We stop and watch Andy as he reverses his father's Mercedes 250 up to the gates in front of his house.

"I can't believe he's allowed drive the car," says George. I think he's jealous.

"He's just turning it."

"Can you imagine me being let drive Dad's car?"

"I can imagine you driving it into the gatepost, no problem. Hi Andy, very neat parking there."

"Thanks," he says, winding down the window and pushing his glasses up his nose. "Here, get in."

"Really?" George's face lights up.

"I'll show you how the automatic works." The two of us run to get in, George just beating me to the front seat.

"See, if you put it in Drive like this," Andy says, jerking a big lever on the side of the steering wheel, "Then all you have to do is take your foot off the brake and it moves, see?" And the car smoothly glides forwards into the middle of the road as if by magic. He's not even moving the steering wheel.

"Wow!" says George.

"Wow!" says me.

"It's the automatic gearbox see, that's how it works, it's always on, so you just have to use the accelerator and the brake. You never need to change gear."

"How does it know that you want it to go backwards?" I ask.

"Well there is a reverse gear obviously, this one, look." And he jerks the big lever thing again and the car glides backwards to the gates.

"That's it, Dad wanted me to turn it because he's going out. What are we doing?"

"We have to help our Dad cut the grass, want to join us?"

"Yeah sure, just let me drop the keys back inside."

"No problem," we say and we all get out of the car. The doors all close with a deep, solid sort of clunk, not like the tinny bang of our ones.

Andy goes into the house and me and George are sitting on the little wall outside.

"You know who lives in there, in No 21?" I ask him pointing to the house next door.

"Who?"

"The McCarthys, and they have a little boy called Paul. Can you believe that - Paul! It's incredible - Paul McCarthy - that's nearly like Paul in the Beatles 'cept it's spelled differently. What a cool name!"

"Yeah sure, and in No 22 there's a little boy called John Lemon," says George crossly but then we look at each other and laugh.

"That's not bad for you – John Lemon!" I say, and we're still laughing a minute later when Andy comes back out and we tell him the joke as we head back down the road, accompanied for some reason by Dilly.

"What's Dilly doing?" I ask.

"She wanted to come with us," Andy shrugs.

"She wanted to come? How would you know?" I ask.

"You don't have a dog do you?"

"No – "

"Well then you wouldn't understand."

"OK, that explains it."

When we reach our drive I can hear the sound of Dad trying to start up the lawnmower and not having much luck. Round the side of the house and we can see him, shirtsleeves rolled up but still wearing his office trousers and brown leather shoes though he's taken off his tie. Just as well or he'd get it caught in the lawnmower and that'd be that. He's pulling away at the piece of rope that he uses to start the engine but it's not working. Every time he pulls it, it unwinds and he has to wind it up again. I can see he's getting very hot and bothered as Mum says. He's crouched over the machine, twisting the rope round again.

"We're here to give you a hand," says George helpfully.

"Brilliant! That's all I need!" I think Dad might want to be left alone, but George doesn't see it like that. Dad gives another mighty pull, the lawnmower gives a splutter and a cough and a shudder but that's it. Dad's left holding the rope and has to twist it up again. Dilly gives a little bark.

"What's that dog doing here? Oh hello Andrew, didn't see you there."

"Hello Mr Jones, hope you don't mind Dilly."

"Just make sure she doesn't get in the way of the mower, that's all. I know those poodles get funny hairstyles but she wouldn't want a haircut from my Strutt and Parker I'm telling you." Then he gives it another pull with the same result.

"Is there petrol in it?" asks George.

"Of course there's petrol in it. Do you not think I checked that?"

"Have you the valve open?"

"Of course I have the bloomin valve open."

"Have you the throttle on full?"

"Look," says Dad straightening up, "I know how to start the lawnmower, I've been doing it for fifteen years, it's just getting a bit temperamental in its old age like the rest of us, so if you don't mind just letting me alone to get it started I'd appreciate it thank you. If you want to help get out the wheelbarrow."

The three of us go into the garage and manage to get the wheelbarrow out. Dilly doesn't help as for some reason she takes a dislike to the wheelbarrow and starts barking like mad at it, though

230

you couldn't really call her little yelps barks, but I think they're beginning to get on Dad's nerves as I see him look up from the lawnmower and give Dilly a dirty look. Then with one massive tug which nearly sends him flying backwards he manages to get the thing started and it roars into life sending clouds of blue smoke into the air and producing a terrific smell of petrol. The noise and the smell are not to Dilly's liking however, and she sets up a continuous yapping as she runs around the strange monster trying to attack it. She's so funny we can't stop laughing at her. Not only has the lawnmower started, it's actually started moving. It's a really good one this lawnmower because not only does it cut the grass but you don't have to push it as it just goes itself.

"Hey look Andy, our Dad's got an automatic too," I point out as the lawnmower goes flying off on its own and Dad has to run to keep up with it.

"Yeah but I think we should get Andy to drive it," says George.

"Everybody out of the way I can't stop till it's warmed up," yells Dad and we have to keep clear while he does a couple of lengths of the lawn until he can get the thing to stop without cutting out. Finally he stops and it's chugging away sending out clouds of smoke and he's taking off the big bucket thing at the front that collects all the grass and calling for us to run up with the wheelbarrow. This sets Dilly off again and she's torn between attacking the mower or the wheelbarrow. In the end she decides to go for both and chases wildly round the garden taking turns barking at each of them.

"Can't you keep that dog quiet?" Dad calls out to Andy though really compared with the noise from the lawnmower we can hardly hear the poodle's yapping.

Having emptied the grass from the container into the wheelbarrow we give it back to Dad to reattach and off he goes again up the garden heading for the house, this time followed by Dilly snapping at his heels and having a go at chewing his trouser legs. The sight of Dad shaking his leg to get rid of the little poodle and occasionally launching a real kick at her is just too much for the three

231

of us and when he turns and comes down again we are all rolling around on the grass we're laughing so much.

"What are you laughing at?" he roars. "This is no laughing matter. Can't you keep that dog under control, it's a danger so it is, a hazard to life and limb, not to mention trousers."

This only makes us laugh even more but Andy gets up and after chasing her around the garden a few times eventually manages to grab hold of Dilly and put her in the wheelbarrow. Then he has a good idea and starts running around the garden with Dilly sitting in the barrow which she seems to like. Mum must have seen us because now she's coming out with her camera and the three of us stop for a photo with Dilly in the wheelbarrow. Then Andy and Dilly are off again, tearing around the garden, until the next time Dad needs to fill it up with grass. We take the box and George just tips the thing over Dilly's head and covers her with grass clippings. She yelps, jumps up, shakes herself and makes a dash for the driveway trailing grass behind her.

"She'll be OK," says Andy when he manages to stop laughing. "She'll go home and won't talk to me for a couple of days."

"I don't think she better help cut the grass again," says George.

"Yeah but she had fun chasing Dad and the lawnmower," I add. "I think Dad enjoyed it too, wouldn't you say?"

****

"Where did you say they are?" I ask Kieran. Myself and George and Kieran are sitting on the grass in Mullen's back garden waiting for the girls to come home so we can go into St Mark's together.

"Who?"

"Yvonne and Zoe – oh yeah, getting their ears pierced – how does that work?"

"Ask them yourself, here they are." And suddenly the two sisters come around the side of the garage, they're wearing what look like new denim jackets, but when they come closer I see Yvonne's is denim and Zoe's is corduroy. They are both amazing looking.

"Hey cool jackets," I say.

"Thanks," says Yvonne. "We got them for being so good and not crying when we got our ears pierced."

"Oh yeah, I heard. Show me." And they pull back their hair to reveal gold studs in each ear.

"These are just temporary," explains Yvonne.

"They're not real ear-rings – Mum got us nicer ones but we have to wear these for the first few days," adds Zoe.

"Where did you get it done?" I ask.

"Oh Mum did it in the surgery, they have everything in there."

"She numbed our ears first with some stuff," adds Yvonne."

"Then she stuck a really sharp needle in them."

"Yuck!" Did it hurt?" I ask.

"You bet," says Yvonne. "But as Michelle says, you have to suffer to be beautiful."

"In that case the two of you must be in constant agony," I reply and they both laugh.

"That's so sweet," Yvonne says. Then she turns to George. "Why don't you ever say things like that buster? Your brother is so sweet."

Now that we're all here, we all start walking out of our garden and head over to St Mark's. Nobody has to say anything it just happens automatically.

A few minutes later we are sitting around the pond and looking up at the trees which reminds me of what's been going on outside my bedroom window for the past few days.

"They're cutting down the pine tree next door, in O'Connell's. The smell is amazing."

"Why are they doing that?" ask Zoe.

"I don't know, ask Rory," I say, looking at her for a reaction. I still don't know if anything happened between them during the summer, all I know is she's not the same and I haven't seen her at her bedroom window since I got back. I really need to meet that blonde haired girl from Mass - if Zoe knew it might make her jealous and she would love me. She doesn't even look at me so I go on about the tree.

"The smell is incredible, that pine smell that you get at Christmas from the Christmas tree, only a million times stronger, and it's coming in my bedroom window all the time."

"I don't like the smell," says George sucking on a piece of long grass. I ignore him and go on:

"Only thing is though, the noise from the chainsaws is awful."

"Yeah, they're always cutting down trees in here too and we can hear it all through the house," says Kieran.

"Why won't they stop cutting down trees?" says Zoe crossly. "Trees are beautiful, how could anyone want to cut one down? Soon there won't be any left in St Mark's."

"Don't worry, there's plenty of trees in here," say Yvonne. "And there are more growing all the time."

"Yes but they're always building in here now, I hate it." Zoe is looking into the dark pond waters and she looks so sad I want to say something to cheer her up.

"Let's do our song," I suggest.

"Which one?" says Yvonne.

"Simple Simon Says."

"Naw, it's too much work, you have to do all those gestures, it's too hot," she complains.

"Oh come on, I'll start," I say and get up.

"Simple Simon says put your hands in the air..." I start singing and waving my arms around in the air. Yvonne, Zoe, George and Kieran just look at me like I'm mad.

"Oh all right, so you don't want to do that one. What about Strangers in the Night? Let's sing Strangers in the Night, come on."

"Strangers in the night, exchanging glances
Strangers in the night ..." I stop because I don't know the next words but Yvonne continues:

"Dropping their pantses." And we all crack up.

234

"Sing us a real song Karl," she says. "You're the only one who can sing. What about my favourite, 'Where do you go to my Lovely'. Sing that – please."

"Oh all right. I like it myself." And I start off:

"You talk like Marlene Dietrich
And you dance like Zizi Jeanmaire
Your clothes are all made by Balmain
And there's diamonds and pearls in your hair ..."

And when I get to the end of the verse they all join in changing the words as usual to:
"I want to look inside your bed.*"*

"Hang on, hang on," says Yvonne, "There's another one I love, it's by this black woman and she's listing all the things she's got:
"I got my arms, got my hands, got my fingers got my legs
Got my feet got my toes got my liver ..."

" 'Got my liver'?" says Kieran, "Ugh, that's disgusting!"

"It's not disgusting, it's a great song, I wish I knew all the words," says Yvonne. "There's one line that goes:
"I got my SEX!" It's so cool. I'm going to learn the whole song and sing it at Sunday dinner. That'll really drive them mad. Oh Zoe what about this one - " And she starts singing *'In the year twenty-five twenty-five'*, Zoe joins in and when they come to the line *'Everything you think do and say is in the pill you took today'* they both start falling about laughing and so does George but I've no idea what they're laughing at as usual.

I think of another favourite of ours and say:

"What about: *'Oh I could hide 'neath the wings'* - "

"Wait," says Zoe, "You forgot to do 'What number is this Chip?'"

"Oh yeah, here goes: What number is this Chip?"

And they all shout: "Seven A!"

And I say: "All right, just cause I'm short I know" and then I start singing again:

"Oh I could hide 'neath the wings
Of the bluebird as she sings
The six o'clock alarm would never ring"

And they all join in for the chorus of:

"Cheer up sleepy Jean
Oh what can it mean for a
Daydream believer and a
Ho-ome coming queen"

We're so loud I look up at the building beside the pond to see if anyone is watching us but the windows are all empty, there's no one visible anywhere in the hospital or in the grounds, just us, me and my friends singing our favourite songs by the pond in the sunshine on one of the last days of summer, and it's the best ever. But now as I lie in bed thinking about today it's just a memory and it feels like it never really happened. The summer holidays are nearly over and I have to go back to school on Monday. I cannot believe they really happened, it seems like the summer was all a dream, a dream or a memory. It's like I can remember it all without ever having actually experienced it. Maybe that's what life is like too – just a memory of things that never really happened.

****

"Out of the way I can't see!"

"You get out of the way – *I* can't see!"

"Dec, you're scrum-half."

"Knew that."

"Stop pushing."

"Who's out-half?"

"Ivan."

"Am I on?"

"Who's full back?"

"New guy, McDonagh."

"Am I on?"

"Who's on the wings?"

"Wingers are O'Meara left and Jones right."

"Brilliant."

"Who are we playing?"

"De La Salle."

"Where?"

"Cabra."

I stay just long enough to get a glimpse of my name opposite number 14 on the sheet with U12 B's at the top just to be sure and wriggle out of the crowd around the noticeboard.

At least the match wasn't away and at least it's not a Sunday even though I have to get the bus home I'll be home by six in time for The Flintstones and tea and even if I have to stand here at Hanlon's Corner for another say fifteen minutes I can still be into town by five cross O'Connell bridge over to the 14 bus stop five minutes even if I go into that shop and get something maybe a Curley Wurley then wait for the 14 I'll easily be home by six maybe even before that if only this bus would come the 39A I hate having to wait here the cold damp air is clinging to my face like wet swimming togs it smells of rotting leaves and old brown mushrooms I'm always on my own here no one else goes home this way at least it's not dark yet it's only October how long is it till Christmas? November December two months and about two weeks where's that stupid bus the last Club meeting we had Andy didn't like it and left - it's funny how we've all started calling him Andy now - he didn't want to start playing Truth or Dare I didn't either at first it's a bit scary but it's better than talking about the Beatles all the time I mean I love the Beatles and I always will but sometimes we need something more interesting than just -

"First item on the Agenda. The Beatles new album, Abbey Road. By the way, does anyone know why it's called Abbey Road?"

"Oh God!"

"Here we go."

"Who cares?"

"Is it because you can buy it in Dolphin Discs and they've got a shop on Abbey Street?" asks Patrick.

"That's Abbey Street not Abbey Road silly."

"Oh yeah."

"I'd like to be
Under the sea
In an octopus's garden
In the shade"

Patrick starts singing and we all join in, all except Andy who's trying to explain that it's called Abbey Road because that's the name of the road that the recording studios are on and that's the picture on the front cover where the four of them are crossing on the zebra crossing but nobody's really listening.

"You know Paul is really dead," says George.

"You don't believe that do you?" says Barry.

"Everyone knows it, there are clues everywhere. There's another one on the front of Abbey Road. You know the Volkswagen Beetle that's parked there? The number plate is 28IF, that means Paul would have been 28 *if* he had lived. That proves it."

"Yeah sure," says Barry," And if you play Sgt Pepper's backwards you can hear John saying, 'I buried Paul' but what he's really saying is 'Cranberry Sauce'."

"Why would he say 'Cranberry Sauce'?"

"I heard it was 'I'm very bored'!" I say.

"At least that makes sense, I know how he feels," says Patrick.

"Can we get on with the meeting please?" says Zoe.

"Right," says Andy, "So hands up who bought it in the end?"

We all put our hands up except Barry who says:

"Hands up? Hands up! Why do we have to put our hands up, we're not kids, we're not in school, when is he ever going to learn?! Why do we have to go on having these meetings?"

"These Club meetings *are* getting boring," agrees Yvonne.

"Well what else can we do?" asks Andy. "Do we need another name change?" Everyone's silent for a moment and I'm singing to myself:

"Sexy Sadie
What have you done?
You made a fool of everyone"

"Yeah we could call it the Sexy Sadie Club," says George. "Hey, why don't we do that again, like when Michelle was here? What do you call it - Truth or Dare?" I've no idea what he's talking about.

"I'm bored. I think I'll go and read some magazines," says Kieran. And he gets up and climbs down through the trapdoor.

"What time is it?" says Patrick.

"Time you had a watch," replies his brother. Then Andy does his usual:

"If you vant to buy a vatch buy a vatch and don't be vatching all the vatches in the vindow" but I can see his heart isn't really in it.

"I've got some homework to finish, I better go too," says Patrick and disappears down the ladder.

"So who's on for Truth or Dare then?" Yvonne asks.

"No thanks," says Andy. "I don't like that sort of stuff. Let me know when you want another Beatles Club meeting." And he goes down too. So the rest of us are sitting there looking at each other wondering who's going to go next.

"Who else is going to leave? No? No?" says Yvonne, looking at me and Zoe. "Barry? No? OK, Truth or Dare. Where's the bottle?" And she gets up and looks in behind some old boxes and pulls out a bottle of Coke and an opener.

"Who's that for?" I ask.

"For all of us," she replies with a strange smile of her face as she opens the bottle and takes a swig.

239

"Things - " she says and passes the bottle to George who also takes a swig, says, "Go - " and passes it round the circle and as everyone takes a slug out of it they complete the famous Coca Cola slogan: "Better - With - Coke" until we have all had some and the empty bottle has come back to Yvonne. She then very carefully lays it on its side in the middle of the floor.

"What is she doing now?" I ask, looking around at the others. "What's that for?"

"To spin of course," answers Yvonne. "If you want to play it properly you have to have a bottle to spin to see who has to answer the question. And a Coke bottle is best because look – it's curvy here - so you get a really good spin with it."

"Have you been doing this before?" I ask but they just ignore me as usual.

"Right, I'm spinning," says Yvonne. "Hang on, where are the questions?" She has a list of questions which she said she got from a girl in her school. This is really scary I don't want to think about the rest of it and I don't know if I want to do it again where's that bus? By the time I get home it will be dark walking up the road with the street lights on the way they overlap like sets in Maths going from one street-light to the next without stepping in a shadow when I was small I was able to climb up those lampposts right up to the bar at the top Mum explained what the bar is for it was when they were gas lamps and a man had to come and light them every evening and he would lean his ladder up against the crossbar is this it? yes a 39A thank God upstairs seat at the front great I'll be home in time as soon as I get in the door I'll go and have my bath I don't like having a shower after rugby in front of everyone then I'll come down and watch The Flintstones and Mum will be making the tea and Dad's Army is on after tea I love that Corporal Jones saying "Permission to speak Sir" and Sgt Wilson saying "I say would you mind awfully just lining up in two neat rows that's awfully nice of you" and tomorrow we'll watch Disney and then go down to the playroom and listen to records or maybe go out to the garden and play for a while and when it's cold and dark outside we'll all come in from playing in the garden and

240

we'll take off our coats and hang them up on the pipes by the big old boiler which will be humming away like it does and the girls will have this amazing smell they have when they've been outdoors that's absolutely the best smell ever and the sky will be getting dark outside the window of the playroom and I'll be so happy being with my friends but sad and lonely too because tomorrow is Monday and I have to go to school and won't see them for another week then we start playing again and talking and listening to records and I look up at the clock on the wall and it's ten to six and I feel this panic in my heart because there's only another ten minutes left before they have to go and the fun will be over for another week with nothing but school and homework all week and I watch my friends get their coats and go out the back door saying goodbye to Mum on the way and the pain is almost unbearable loving them so much and having to say goodbye and tonight I'm standing at my bedroom window before I get into bed and the window pane is really cold as I put my forehead against it and my breath is making a foggy circle on the glass so I rub it with the sleeve of my pyjamas and I'm waiting until the light in the girls' bedroom comes on and - there it is – I know it is her and I can see her coming to the window and standing there looking at me and she knows I'm looking at her too and now we are making X's with our fingers again crossing them like this sending each other kisses before we go to sleep though I still haven't kissed her properly and at this rate I probably never will.

****

"OK we're going to have a Two Little Boys competition," says Yvonne. She's sitting on the worktop in our playroom with her legs dangling over where I do my homework. She's got her old jeans on and her plimsolls.

"What? I hate that song. What are you on about?" complains Barry.

"Me too," I say, agreeing with him for once. "How did it get to be the Christmas No 1? Who here bought it?"

"I didn't."

"No way."

"I certainly didn't."

"My Mum likes it but I don't think she would have bought the single," says Kieran.

"My school bought it and gave out a copy to everyone who has a brother so me and Barry got one." Patrick is looking sheepish and trying to dodge blows from his brother.

"I told you not to tell anyone! I'm going to kill you later!"

"Aha! So you do have a copy of it!" I claim, "Two in fact!"

"Yeah maybe, but we didn't buy them. Anyway I'm going to burn mine the next time we have a fire."

"So, Yvonne, what are you on about? A Two Little Boys competition?"

"Yeah you see we've got two pairs of two little boys, you and George and Barry and Patrick, so each pair of brothers has to sing the song and then me and Zoe decide who's best."

"You must be joking, I'm not doing that," says Barry. "In fact I'm not even staying here to listen to anyone else doing it. I'm going home to listen to some Clapton. See you." And he turns round and heads out through the kitchen.

"He has a point, you have to admit," I say to Yvonne. "I mean, it really is a hideous song."

"Come on you two, you and George are the only brothers left, you have to sing it for us." Then George makes up his mind for us.

"I can honestly say that I will never ever sing that song for anyone as long as I live."

"I don't mind singing it," says Patrick, and off he goes:

"Two little boys had two little toys
Each had a wooden horse"

"No stop, please," I shout, "That's enough!"

"What is this lecture we're going to anyway?" asks Kieran.

"It's a Science Lecture, you'll love it," I reply.

"Yes but what kind of Science lecture? Physics? Chemistry? Biology? What?"

"Ah well you'll just have to wait and see. A bit of everything I'd imagine."

"Where's it on?" asks Zoe.

"The RDS," says George. "Your Mum and our Mum are bringing us but we can swap around in the cars.

"Do you want to come Patrick? There's a spare ticket because Andy can't come."

"Sure, I'll just go home and ask Mum." And off he trots.

"You two are coming, aren't you?" I ask Yvonne and Zoe.

"Suppose so, but we're not very good at Science."

"No, well, there probably won't be too much Science in it. Anyway you won't have to do anything, just sit there and try and stay awake."

"When's Michelle coming up again?" asks George.

"Tomorrow. Is tomorrow New Year's Day?" says Yvonne.

"Well let's see, today is New Year's Eve, so that would be about right," I say but then I regret it because it sounds a bit sarcastic and mean. "Did you hear we're going out to dinner tonight with the O'Briens?"

"Really? All of you – with your parents too?"

"God no, just us, me and him," says my brother.

"Where are you going?" asks Zoe.

"Place in Stillorgan, just before the new shopping centre. It's called the – what's it called?" George turns and looks at me for information.

"Something Mews. Beaufield Mews I think."

That's it all right "The Beaufield Mews" it has it in big letters that look like handwriting on the white end wall. The whole place looks like a stables which is exactly what it is, as Andy explained to us in the car on the way here.

"Don't park there, park over there look, there's a better space. Mind the tree! There is an Antique shop here too so when we've had our dinner we can look at the antiques," says Andy's Mum turning around from the front seat where she has been helping Mr O'Brien with his driving. She's just had her hair done I'd say, for the occasion,

243

being New Year's Eve, and it's a rather fetching shade of Lilac. George and myself are in our Sunday best, I'm wearing my blue coat and George's cowboy boots because we've both grown out of our own. Andy's got his new boots with the elastic sides and George is wearing his school shoes and blazer.

"How was the Science Lecture?" Andy asks when we are sitting at our table. "They went to the Science Lecture in the RDS today. Pity I couldn't have gone but we had to visit Aunt Emily didn't we?"

"Family always comes first," says Mr O'Brien. "I'm sure the Joneses appreciate that."

"Oh you didn't miss very much really, just a lot of Science stuff," I say so he's not too disappointed.

"Yeah but there was this brilliant bit where he did an experiment," says George before I can stop him, "And he asked for a volunteer from the audience and we were sitting near the front so genius here shoots up his hand and the lecturer picks him and he goes up and he's standing on the stage and we're all looking at him trying not to laugh and he asks Karl his name and what school does he go to and Karl tells him and then the Lecturer asks him is he frightened of electricity and he says not really and the guy tells him to put his hands on this big shiny steel ball he has on the desk and he does and - "

"And my hair stood on end," I interrupt so George can't say it.

"And when he's finished and the guy sends him back to his seat his hair is still sticking up and he doesn't even know what everyone is laughing at, it was hilarious."

"And at the end they all got a go to put their hands on the ball and make their hair stand up, even the girls' hair went right up on end," I add.

"You see what I missed?" says Andy unhappily.

"I am sure your Aunt Emily would have appreciated your sacrifice Andrew. Family first, friends second, as I keep saying. Andrew knows that and if you two remember it you won't go far wrong, now let's hear no more of it."

Then the waiter arrives with the menus and we look at them in silence for a moment. Family first, friends second, I repeat to myself, remembering a conversation I had with Mum this morning when I told her that Mrs Blaney was a really good swimmer just because Barry had been going on about it and she got upset and said I seemed to have forgotten that she swam for her University and did I mention that to Barry and I couldn't answer because I knew I hadn't and that was so disloyal to Mum that for a moment I hated myself for it.

"What's this – *mooles murn-something*?" I say, trying to forget about it.

"That's French, it's mussels," explains Mr O'Brien. I study French in school but they never taught us that. I whisper to Andy beside me:

"This kind of muscles?" And point to my upper arm.

"No. They're shellfish," he replies.

"Oh like George, he's really shellfish sometimes." But Andrew doesn't really laugh at my jokes, not like Patrick, he's too serious, and all he says is:

"You're better off skipping the starter and going for a steak, the steaks here are excellent."

"This is lovely thanks very much Mr and Mrs O'Brien," I say when my steak arrives.

"Thank you for coming," says Mrs O'Brien.

"And a very Happy New Year to us all," adds Andy. "A new decade starts tomorrow, imagine that, the 1970's. I can't believe the Sixties are over, it was our decade, the one we grew up in. I wonder what on earth the 1970's will be like."

"No one can tell," says Mr O'Brien. "All we know is that by the end of the decade you will be 26, you will be finished college and be working, you may even be married!"

Andy looks completely shocked.

"I really don't want to think of that," he says, and I have to agree with him. The Sixties *was* our decade, we did grow up in it, and now it's over. It makes me quite sad but happy at the same time, and as I give Mrs O'Brien a smile she puts her hand on mine and says:

"By the end of this decade you'll be 21 – imagine that Karl."

"Imagine that," I repeat, and in spite of her silly hair and the way she gives out to Andy's Dad when he's driving, I can't help liking her.

"What about me?" says George, "I'll be 23."

"You'll be a big boy," Mrs Barry says, smiling at him.

"He's a big boy already," I joke though it's true, he's got enormous recently, and we all laugh.

"I think this calls for a toast," says Andy, "Has everyone got a drink?" We have because his Mum and Dad are sharing a bottle of wine and the three of us have Cokes. Andy is looking round at all of us and I can see his eyes behind his thick old glasses and the little brown squirrels are there all right and they're hopping around like mad.

"To the 1970's," he says and we all raise our glasses and clink them off each others'.

"To the 1970's," we all say. And I wonder to myself what will the new decade be like and if it will finally happen in

1970

"Michelle's here again, I've just seen her."

"Well yippee! What is so great about Michelle anyway?"

"Are you joking? She's beautiful."

"Is she? You know she has braces on her teeth?"

"They're not braces, it's just a retainer, it comes out, it's so cool."

"A retainer is cool?"

"Yep, sure is."

"Anyway, aren't you supposed to be ... you know ... with Yvonne?"

"Yeah well. Come on out, they're all hanging round outside Mullen's gate, I saw them from my bedroom."

Two minutes later we're in our coats and gloves crossing the road outside our gate. Everyone's there all right, all dressed up in their winter clothes, Mullens, Blaneys, Andy, Michelle – and Rory, what's he doing here? Zoe and Michelle are talking together, Patrick and Andy are playing the "can't say yes" game but Patrick keeps forgetting not to say yes, Rory and Barry are talking about – let me see, yes it's Eric Clapton, and Yvonne is watching us cross the road.

"We were just about to come and get you," she says. "Come on, we're all going into St Mark's."

Zoe doesn't even say hello to me but it's probably because everyone is there. We go through the Mullen's drive and into their back garden to head over the back wall at the corner where they burn their rubbish.

"Any jam tarts here today?" asks Rory, at least I think that's what he says though I can't understand it and I remember they were laughing at the same thing in the Club but I don't have time to ask anyone because Patrick is punching me on the arm pretending to want a fight.

"Come on, come on," he's saying, "Let's be havin you." But I'm trying to listen to Yvonne who is poking around in the half-burnt rubbish with a stick and saying:

"No don't think so, she must be finished." And now they're all climbing over the wall, there's a big drop on the other side and you have hold on to the metal pole that's there keeping up the fencing for the raspberries so it takes a while. Pretty soon they're all on the far side except for me, Barry and Rory. Just as me and Barry are about to get up on the wall to climb over, Rory holds us back.

"C'mere," he whispers, "Wait till you hear this."

"What," says Barry, and the three of us are standing beside the rubbish dump as Rory looks around as if to make sure no-one's listening.

"Wait till I tell you: You know what she does, she stands at her bedroom window at night and sends kisses to me across the street! Like this with her fingers." And he makes an X sign which makes me nearly get sick into the dump.

"Who - Michelle?" asks Barry.

"No, Zoe. I think she must fancy me." When he says this I feel a pain in my heart like I have never felt before and I nearly cry out. I feel so stupid standing here while this creep is telling Barry how she sends kisses at him when it's really me she's sending kisses to.

"Are you serious? She does that?" says Barry.

"You bet, she's really keen."

Then they start climbing over the wall and they're still talking but they've lowered their voices so I can't hear any more and they're sniggering disgustingly. I couldn't join them so I stay at the bonfire dump staring into the ashes and the rubbish feeling more sick than

I've ever felt in my life, thinking is it possible she might be doing it for him? I know where his bedroom is, it's on the front of the house just like mine, only nearer to Mullens. Maybe she *is* doing it to him and hasn't even seen me standing at my window further up the road? Is that possible? No - I'm not that far away from Rory's, she must have seen me. Or maybe it was a different night. Does she do it for him one night and for me another, depending on which of us is standing there? Could she do that? None of this makes sense and the thought of it is driving me insane.

Come on, you can't stay here, I say to myself and climb over the wall. As soon as I'm in the grounds I can see George, Yvonne, Michelle, and Barry have all lit up cigarettes and there's a cloud of smoke coming from up ahead of me. I run to catch up in time to hear Rory with one of his jokes.

"Have you heard this one?" he says. "A fart is a message from the heart to tell the bum there's more to come – pretty good huh?" Kieran and Barry and George start laughing but Michelle makes a face and says:

"Ugh, that's disgusting!"

Then Rory starts talking to Zoe, telling her he's got an air rifle and how he likes to shoot pigeons, and I can't believe Zoe would be impressed by somebody shooting pigeons, it's so cruel. He's wearing this big Army coat I think it's called a trench coat after the trenches in the first world war and he's really tall now, taller even than George or Andy, and as we pass the Nissen hut I think of Zoe years ago being afraid of the Nasties as she called them and now she's talking to someone who looks like one. I'm too depressed to make a joke about it I just can't believe what's happening, it's like we never went to the Fete together and now I don't even know if she was making X's with her fingers to send to me or to him, I don't understand it and I'm really really worried. We go over to the pond and then we keep on going till we reach the little chapel with the flowers and candles inside and then as usual we stop.

"What are you stopping for?" Rory demands.

"We never go any further than this," says Andy.

"Why not?" says Rory.

"It's too close to the hospital, there's too many people that way," says Andy.

"And the Greeners," adds Kieran, at which Rory gives a snort.

"The Greeners – really? You're afraid of the Greeners?"

"We're not afraid, we just don't want to get caught," says Kieran. We're all standing round the little chapel now and I'm wondering what's going to happen.

"Well I'm going on, anyone want to join me or are you all too scared?"

"I'm not," says Andy, "I'm heading back." And for a moment we're all looking at each other wondering if anyone's going to follow Rory. Andy has always been our leader and we've always done whatever he suggested, not because he's a bully or has to have his own way like Rory, but just because he's two years older than George or Yvonne and much older than the rest of us and we trust him.

"Anybody coming?" Rory asks again and I'm really scared that the others will follow him and leave Andy though I know what myself and Patrick are going to do but the funny thing is, no one moves, so Rory just blinks his reptile eyes a couple of times and shrugs and says:

"You can get over the wall at the end here, I think I'll go home and shoot some more pigeons. See you round." And he heads off down the path.

"Not if we see you first," says Yvonne under her breath.

"God he's so creepy that guy," says Michelle, and she gives a big shudder.

"Actually," says Barry, "he's a friend of mine."

"Why don't you go after him then?" Kieran says.

"Couldn't be bothered," says Barry but I can see from the way he's looking at Michelle the real reason why he's staying. I don't care, I'm just glad that we all backed up Andy and that Rory is gone but I'd really like to know what Zoe is thinking. Then it hits me, the only way to find out what someone is really feeling is:

250

"Truth or Dare!" I blurt out without even thinking and everyone turns to look at me. "How about a game of Truth or Dare."

"Are you feeling all right?" asks George. "You never wanted to play before." And then I look around and I see Andy looking at me like he's really disappointed in me and I hate having said that but it's the only way I can find out how Zoe feels. It doesn't matter to him, he's never felt like this about anyone.

"I'm not playing that," says Kieran, "It's a stupid game."

"Yeah, nor am I," says Patrick and then says to me, "What you want to suggest that for?" The look on his face makes me feel really guilty.

"Everybody knows how I feel about that game," adds Andy.

"Well we don't have to if you don't feel like it," I say lamely trying to backtrack.

"No you've said it now, off you go back to the Clubhouse and play your Truth or Dare," says Andy, and I can see what's going to happen. He's staying in St Mark's with Kieran and Patrick and the rest of us are going to head back to Mullen's garage, and then I instantly realise what I have just done and it shocks me. I've succeeded in doing what Rory failed to do a minute ago; I've split up the gang and it makes me feel sick and ashamed.

"All right," says Yvonne, "Let's go back to the Clubhouse and do it."

All the way back to the Mullen's wall I want to turn round and go back to Andy and the boys because I feel like I really belong with them and not with the others, and another thing suddenly strikes me: there are now six of us, three boys and three girls, and I'm beginning to think I'm way in over my head.

Back upstairs in the loft Yvonne goes in behind the junk cupboard and produces the old bottle of Coke. It's got the list of questions rolled up and stuck in the top of it. Nobody has said a word pretty much all the way back and now we're sitting cross-legged in a circle in silence while Yvonne straightens out the carpet in the centre so it's flat and places the bottle on it. She looks around.

251

"No boys or girls together, it has to be boy girl boy girl so you two swap round." I was sitting beside George so now it's Yvonne George Zoe Barry Michelle me Yvonne.

"Right, same rules as last time," she says. "When the bottle points at you first you decide if you want a truth or a dare but you can't do two of the same in a row. I spin. Anybody got a cigarette? Thanks" as George hands her one from his packet. "Here goes." Zoe is sitting opposite me and as her sister reaches in to spin the bottle I'm pretty sure she gives me a little smile which is nice because I'm really scared.

The bottle spins round a few times and stops pointing halfway between George and Zoe and they argue as to who it's pointing at so she spins again. This time it's pointing directly at George. Yvonne flattens out the list on her knee and asks him:

"Truth or Dare?"

"Truth," he says.

"Have you ever had a crush on anyone here?" asks Yvonne.

"Only you my darling," he replies in a funny voice and we all laugh. She spins again. This time the bottle stops at Zoe.

"Right little sister, truth or dare?"

"Truth."

"What is the most embarrassing thing that ever happened to you in school?"

"When I was in Kindergarten I did a wee in my pants."

"Hey Kindergarten doesn't count, that's baby stuff," objects Barry.

"It's still school, that's Ok," says Yvonne who really seems in charge here. Looking at her reading the questions off the list with the cigarette dangling from the corner of her mouth I've never seen anyone so cool in my life but I'm still terrified.

"Right, here we go, big spin – yes – Barry!" It's definitely pointing at him so he can't argue.

"Truth or dare?"

"Oh give me a dare then." I suspect Barry doesn't like answering questions about himself.

"Right, dare – I dare you to imitate a hen laying an egg."

"Aw, that's too easy!" we all say as Barry starts flapping his arms and making clucking noises and then stands up a bit and drops a packet of cigarettes onto the carpet underneath him.

"Oh look, I've laid a packet of Rothmans," he says. "Think I'll have one."

"Right, give me the bottle, we need to keep moving here." And Yvonne gives the Coke bottle a big spin and it comes to rest pointing at Michelle.

"Ok country cousin, what's it going to be?"

"Oh I don't know, don't care really, truth so," Michelle says in her lazy country drawl.

"Right. Who was the first boy you kissed and where was it?"

"Oh that was in the hay barn at home last summer, he was one of the local lads, Pat."

"Was it fun?" Yvonne adds.

"I remember the hay was very tickly and got everywhere," Michelle laughs and for the first time she begins to come alive for me.

"And did Pat give you a *pat*?" asks Yvonne.

"I've answered my question, that's enough, spin the bottle."

"Right Karl, I'm going to get you now," and everyone looks at me. I'm trying hard not to look scared but I think she has a knack of spinning so that she can make it stop wherever she wants. Luckily she spins a bit too hard and it comes back to her.

"Hey, you can't ask yourself a question," says George.

"It's just the next one on the list, same as anyone else. I'm going to take a truth: are you afraid of any animals? Yes I'm afraid of mice, next."

"Aw!" some of us complain. "That was too easy."

"It's on the list," she says and spins again. This time it *is* me and as she consults the list Yvonne is giving me this really sly smile.

"Right little Karl, truth or dare?"

I don't know what to choose. Everyone is looking at me. I can't think. I'll go for truth - no, dare, no -

"Eh truth please."

"OK, do you have a nickname and what is it?" Oh God I should have gone for dare.

"I know this one so you have to tell them," says George.

"What? How do you know?"

"I heard in it school, go on tell them."

"Here, on the road with you, I don't have any nickname."

"And in school?" prompts Yvonne.

"I've answered the question," I reply. "I don't have to say any more."

"You've answered half the question."

"But you have a nickname here," Zoe suddenly says and I look over at her. She's mouthing what looks like –

"Oh yes, I do have a nickname now that I think about it; you should know - it's 'Little Karl'."

"Yes but in school they call him - "   I stare and point at George and he suddenly stops and doesn't have the nerve to continue; even he isn't that bad.

"Ok, ok, we'll accept that," says Yvonne. "And we'll come back to the other one later." I breathe a sigh of relief but I'm still giving my brother very clear warning looks.

Yvonne takes the bottle and gives it another spin but I'm not paying much attention to the next few spins. I know one of them is about sleeping positions and we all spend about ten minutes showing each other how we all sleep. Then there is this unbelievable one about wiping your botty standing up or sitting down and no one will answer it except Michelle she doesn't seem to mind at all and says:

"I wipe my bottom sitting on the toilet and if anyone wants proof they can watch me." Everyone is staring at her and around at each other and we cannot believe she has said this. Then Yvonne gets another one herself that's really funny, it's a Dare and she has to hug anyone in the room and tell them she loves them, so she gets up on her knees and reaches out to her left and George opens his arms expecting it to be him, then she goes right past him and hugs Zoe and tells her she loves her. The look on George's face is priceless. He's next and he has to lick someone's toes as a Dare and of course he picks Yvonne's;

254

Michelle is dared to take off her socks and put them on her hands for the rest of the game; Zoe is dared to stand up and recite a poem and she says a few lines from that poem that starts, 'My heart leaps up when I behold a rainbow in the sky' before getting stuck; and Barry has to tell the truth about whether he ever stole anything; he says "no" which no one believes. Then Yvonne gives me another look and I'm really sure she's going to get the bottle to stop wherever she wants. Sure enough it's me and I have to take a Dare.

"Ok. I dare you to kiss somebody on the lips," she says and everybody gasps. I can't stop to think about this one, it's going to be like jumping off the diving board in Butlins I've just go to do it without stopping to think so I immediately turn to her and kiss her very quickly and firmly on the lips. Everybody is shocked and as I sit back down again I look over at Zoe, she has her mouth wide open in disbelief. Barry and George are laughing and cheering and for once I don't think they're laughing at me.

"Well Karl, that was very well done, no one can argue with that one," says Yvonne and she's actually licking her lips and pretending to fan herself with the list. "Next one coming up," And I can't believe it but it's me again and this time it has to be another Truth.

"Right Karl – no more 'Little' I think after that - tell me the truth: Do you have a crush on anyone here?"

I can feel everyone's eyes on me and I'm getting really hot, in fact I might be going red –

"Oh look I think he's blushing," says Yvonne. "He didn't blush when he kissed me! Come on, answer the question." I look over at Zoe but I've no idea what's going through her mind.

"I suppose so," I reply.

" 'I suppose so' isn't an answer. Yes or no – do you have a crush on Zoe – I mean on anyone here? I said on anyone here all right – could be anyone! Could be me after that kiss! Well, have you?"

"Yes," I answer reluctantly.

"Thought so," says Yvonne. "That's all right Karl, nothing to be ashamed of. Next." And as she starts spinning again I look up at

Zoe but she's not looking at me, just following the bottle as it spins round and round. Amazingly, it stops pointing right at her.

"What are you on – Truth or Dare?" asks Yvonne.

"Truth!" says everyone, "And make it a good one," adds Barry.

"Right little sister, tell me the truth if you please: Do you have a crush on anyone?"

"On anyone here?" Zoe asks.

"No just anyone."

"But that's different from the question you asked Karl," says George.

"It's what it says on the list. So answer the question: do you have a crush on anyone?"

"Yes," says Zoe, "Now spin the bottle." And even though I'm sitting opposite her and looking straight at her she never looks at me and at first I think she's talking about me and then, like a knife going into my stomach, the realisation hits me that it's someone outside, it's not me, and if she had been asked if she had a crush on anyone *here* she would have said 'no'. The rest of the game passes in a blur and I just can't wait till it's over to get home and hide in my bedroom. Lying here in bed now I'm thinking there is still a chance that since she said she does have a crush on someone that maybe it is me but she wasn't at her window tonight even though I waited for ages for her so I still can't be sure and now I'm beginning to feel things inside that are really horrible and it's making me scared and really really sick. And I still can't stop thinking about what Rory said in the Mullen's back garden by the rubbish dump. I've been thinking about it every minute and the best I can come up with is that maybe he was peeking out through his curtains and saw her sending kisses to me and thought she was doing it to him but she didn't even see him. That is the only hope I can get from it though I know it's not much.

****

256

Oh God no, Richard Burke beside me has just made a stink again, they better not think it was me. Now Peter Brown behind me is coughing and making choking noises and going "Euch!" so I turn round.

"It wasn't me!" I shout-whisper, "It was him!"

"Uhhh, that's disgusting," Peter says right out loud and now Mr Gregory our Maths teacher has stopped writing on the board and is staring at us.

"What's going on down there? Pay attention."

"Someone just made a stink Sir," Peter is never afraid to come right out and say something.

"Thank you Mr Brown for bringing that to our attention, now if you don't mind perhaps you might like to repeat what I was just saying."

"Eh, well it was about, you know, what you were saying about ... you see I couldn't really concentrate, with the smell you know Sir, it was hard to breathe, I was afraid I was going to lose consciousness Sir." Everybody roars laughing.

"One more word about that and you will be going straight to the Headmaster's office. Do you understand me?"

"Yes Sir."

"Burke!"

"Yes Sir," says the culprit beside me.

"Please remind Brown what I was just saying."

"Eh yes Sir it was about the triangle Sir ... "

"Yes - and?"

" ... and it has three sides Sir ..."

"Yes - and?"

"And they're all equal Sir."

"Brilliant - and what is that called?"

"Eh ... eh ..."

"Oh - anyone? Can anyone enlighten Mr Burke as to what a triangle with three equal sides is called?" Nearly everyone puts up their hands it's so easy.

"Sir, Sir, Sir ..." we all shout.

"You - O'Malley, what is it?" Gregory picks on the one boy who doesn't have his hand up.

"Eh ... I know this Sir, is it ... eh equi something Sir?"

"Yes - equi what?"

"Eh equidistant Sir?"

"No it is not equidistant. There is no such thing as an equidistant triangle except where it dwells in the darkest recesses of your fetid imagination. You - Cochlane."

"Is it isosceles Sir?"

"No it is not an isosceles triangle. This is getting worse. You - Jones."

"I think it's an equilateral triangle Sir."

"You think right, has everyone got that? An equilateral triangle is a triangle with all sides equal in length. Now pay attention to this: see this triangle here - " And he rubs out the triangles he has been drawing on the blackboard sending clouds of white chalk dust up into the air filling the space in front of the board and streaming up to the ceiling there's a tiny ray of sunshine coming in the corner of the window and all the chalk dust rushes over to it and starts dancing around in the sun they must love the sunshine the tiny bits of chalk because they've all gone over there and there's none left anywhere else in the classroom outside the window there's those ancient dirty old buildings that are hundreds of years old and have never been cleaned not even the windows there's three small ones because it's the side of the house not the front the ones on the front are big enough all right very tall and with ten or twelve little panes that's a joke - sit down I know you're a pain but I can't see through you - but these windows only have six panes two on top and four underneath and I can see the chimneys about twenty of them all the houses around here have hundreds of chimneys one for every fireplace in the house that's what makes the buildings so dirty I suppose so many fires burning all that coal and years ago little boys used to have jobs cleaning them because they were the only ones small enough to get up the chimneys that must have been a horrible job Mr O'Regan told us about it in history class and said we were so lucky not to be living in the 19th century

258

that was a hundred and fifty years ago because we wouldn't be sitting in a nice classroom getting a good education we'd all be out working and -

"Some of you smaller ones would be climbing up and down chimneys all day long for a penny a day and only one meal a day of a bowl of gruel how would you like that Jones?" Mr O'Regan says.

"I wouldn't Sir," I answer quickly before he finds some reason to give out. Mr O'Regan's got a really bad temper and when he shouts we all go quiet and sit there in our desks afraid to move or even look at each other and especially not look at him because if he catches you looking at him he'll pick on you and ask you something really impossible to answer not easy stuff like about the triangles -

"... and this one is the isosceles triangle – Cochlane have you got that? – see, it's got two longer sides the same length and one short side that's the base of the triangle ..."

- but I don't care right now because today is Friday and tomorrow there's no real classes only singing and painting and drama until 12.30 then we go home I can't wait.

∗∗∗∗∗∗∗∗∗∗∗∗∗

The last time I was here was that time with Michelle playing you-know-what and kissing Yvonne. Well I'm better off out of things like that, that's for sure. Patrick is joking with me like old times and trying to get me to play paper rock scissors which he's just discovered, Yvonne and Zoe are looking through a copy of Jackie, George is reading a copy of Beatles Monthly which he borrowed from a guy at school and still hasn't let me look at, and Andy is trying to teach Kieran how to click his fingers but he can't. Everyone seems back to their normal selves and happy enough in fact in spite of the terrible news we are here to discuss. I'm sure all of us have heard it as it's been on every news programme on TV and radio, as well as in all the papers since the day it was announced.

"Order! Order!" Andy starts off but nobody bothers to crack the usual old jokes and we just stop talking.

"Well I'm sure you have all heard the news. Last Friday the 10th of April the Beatles announced that they were splitting up. Or rather Paul announced it but we have to take it by now that it is true and it has happened and nothing can get them back together again."

"Not even if you write them a nice letter?" says Barry sarcastically.

"Oh shut up Barry will you?" says Yvonne.

"Look, I couldn't care less that the Beatles have split up, they were never that good in the first place and there are far better bands still   around."

"What?" shouts everybody.

"How can you say that?"

"They were the greatest ever!"

"No band will ever be as good as the Beatles!"

"Look, they produced a few good albums, now they're gone, big deal, move on. The Who are just as good as them now."

"The Who?" says Patrick beside me.

"Yeah, The Who," I reply, seeing what's coming.

"That's what I asked you – the who?"

"Yeah The Who," I repeat.

"Who?" he says again and he cracks up laughing. "What a stupid name for a band – and my brother thinks they're as good as the Beatles!"

"Order! Order! The point is ... the point is ..." says Andy finally getting some attention, "That if there is no Beatles then there can't be any Beatles Club. I mean, we are called the Beatles Club but if the Beatles are no more, then there's not much point in us having a club is there?"

"There's loads of other great bands around – the Stones, The Kinks, Led Zeppelin, Cream, there's even a great new Irish singer called Van Morrison." Barry knows them all.

"Maybe there are," says Andy, voicing what we are all thinking, "But none of them are the Beatles and we're not about to dedicate a club to any of them are we?" We all know that is true and what's more, we can see what's coming next.

"So as the chairman of the Beatles Club it is my sad duty to propose a final motion: the dissolution of the Club and winding up of activities including all future meetings. Seconded?"

"What does disoll – whatever you said mean?" asks Patrick.

"It means the club is finished, over, finito," I explain.

"Aw – that's really sad, do we have to?"

"That's what we are going to take a vote on if someone seconds the motion," says Andy in his most business-like tone.

"Can't we change the name to something else and go on meeting?" asks Patrick, "I love these meetings, especially up here. Why can't we go on meeting up here anyway?"

Andy looks around at all of us. "I understand what Patrick is saying and it's a fair point. We changed the name once before so we can do it again. If anybody has any good ideas as regards changing the name and continuing the Club now's your chance to say it."

"No!" says Barry immediately. "I've had enough of it. Unless we call it the Hard Rock Rhythm and Blues Club."

"NO!" everybody shouts.

"All right then – forget it."

"Any other ideas?" asks Andy. We all look around at each other and I'm desperately praying that someone will come up with something we can agree on to keep us together. I see Yvonne lean over and whisper something in George's ear which makes him smile. Andy's beside her and I think he heard it because he gives them a look and immediately says:

"Any genuine ideas, I mean."

I can't think of anything myself even though I know this might be the last time we are all together up in the Mullen's garage loft. But I have to say something and all I can think of is:

"Do we need a name? I mean, do we need a reason to meet up here and talk and have fun?"

"Well of course we can all go on meeting and playing to-gether..." Andy starts saying but then I think he realises it sounds silly and stops. After all he's just turned seventeen, George and Yvonne are nearly fifteen, it's not like when we were all kids. After a second he looks round again.

"No? In that case I am calling on someone to second the motion."

"Seconded," says Barry.

"All those in favour?" Everyone puts up their hands except me and Patrick.

"Against?" Me and Patrick sadly and uselessly put up our hands half way.

"The motion is carried and I hereby dissolve the Beatles Club. No further business. Now if you'll excuse me I've - " and Andy starts heading for the trapdoor but not before we all see him wipe away a tear from under his tortoise shell glasses.

"Was he ...?" Yvonne whispers and gestures, looking around at all of us and now it's beginning to hit us as Andy goes down the ladder and we hear him walk to the garage door and go. It's not just the end of the Beatles, and it's not just the end of our Club. Something else has gone, we have lost something that has kept us together for so many years. The 1960's are over, the Beatles have split up, and now our Club is gone, and we just sit there for a few minutes, together but no longer together, our world breaking apart. Then slowly and silently we make our way one by one through the trapdoor and down the ladder and without a word of farewell to each other we all go home.

****

"Do you want to listen to records or look at H and E?"

"I don't know – what do you want to do?"

"There's a new H and E in, it's incredible. Do you want to see it? There's a woman with the most amazing tits in it."

"What if we get caught?"

"My folks don't even care – they know I look at it."

"Yeah all right," I say though I don't really want to, so we go into the front living room where the good record player is and where they have the magazine rack and the wire thing for holding all the

262

records and the funny fireplace that's long and flat but doesn't have a mantle-piece like all of ours. Barry told me his Dad designed it himself because he's a modern architect and in a drawer under the record player Barry pulls out a small magazine and we start looking through it.

"Cool, aren't they? Look at this one. Nice tits huh? Look at the size of that guy's mickey, I wish I had a mickey that size - wow!"

"Yeah, but why don't we just listen to some records," I suggest because I'm really not feeling too good looking at this stuff and I'm getting that sick feeling in my tummy again like when I saw that picture in the Sunday Times of the woman with no top on so I say:

"What about playing me some of your favourite rock albums – Cream or Hendrix or something!" I've really no interest in this music but it's better than looking at people with no clothes on, I mean that's really weird.

"Yeah all right, if that's what you want. Are you sure you don't want to look at this?"

"Yeah, pretty sure thanks."

"OK, what about Electric Ladyland or – come on in next door – I know what you'll like, I have the new Stones album, forget about the Beatles, this is where it's at – Let it Bleed. Oh yes you are in for a treat!"

"Great."

"Wait till you hear Gimme Shelter!"

"Cool."

"And You Can't Always Get What You Want!"

"Brill."

****

"When are we going back to school?" I ask George. We're in the playroom having breakfast.

"Monday of course."

"Only tomorrow and Sunday left then. Is Michelle still here?"

263

"Since when are you interested in Michelle?"

"I'm not, but I thought if she was we could meet up for a ... while ..."

"Why would you want to do that?"

"Well ... I don't know ... maybe to have another game of Truth or Dare or something."

"A-ha! So that's it. You're hooked aren't you? That didn't take long. I warned you it's dangerous stuff, you don't want to mess with it. Why do you want another game of Truth or Dare anyway – want to kiss Yvonne again, well you can lay off that for a start, I don't want you muscling in there, not that you could anyway, she could never be interested in you, not when she has me. Hang on, it must be Zoe. Oh yeah I get it, you want to see if it's you Zoe has a crush on? Well why didn't you just ask? I can tell you right now it's not you, she's changed her mind about you, says you're too young and too small. Now it's Rory she has a crush on. Sorry and all that."

"How do you know?" I am barely able to whisper.

"Yvonne told me, she'd know of course wouldn't she?"

Yes, I have to admit to myself, she would know. So that's it then. And in two days' time I have to go back to school. It's too much. Not him, anybody but him, he's so old, he's so big, he tells dirty jokes, he dresses like a Nazi for crying out loud. He's just not her type, not my Zoe's. I'm not that much younger than her, just a year. How could she think that I'm too young for her? He's too old for her. OK I'm smaller than her all right, there's nothing I can do about that, but not much smaller and I will grow. But not him, anybody but him. Oh God Zoe! Zoe! How could you?

****

'Symptoms' – that means things that tell you what's wrong with you. 'Swelling or lump in the breast'. 'Blood in stool' – what on earth does that mean? 'Sudden and inexplicable loss of weight'. 'Lethargy or loss of energy'. 'Chronic pain in head or abdomen'. And loads more – what is this and why has Dad got it pinned up inside his wardrobe? Is

264

there something wrong with him? I know what these are symptoms of – cancer. His sister auntie Eire died of cancer and he's afraid he's going to get it too, so he's got a list to check. That's all, nothing to worry about. Unless he's got the list because he has some of the symptoms already and he's worried he might get more. I better not say anything to either of them I don't want them thinking I was poking around in his wardrobe I was only looking at his ties I could say that but I still wouldn't want him to know I saw the list so I better not. Oh God now I'm worried. What if he has cancer? He looks healthy enough. Let me see, lump in breast – I've no idea if he has a lump in his breast, he hasn't lost weight still as chubby as ever, he seems to have plenty of energy, he doesn't appear to have a pain and I don't understand the others. So what does that mean? Is he OK? Maybe I'll ask Mum. The garden looks nice from here we're so high up you can see into the overgrown garden over the back wall at least we haven't lost the ball in there again. If I look right I can see into the crazy old guy's garden I shouldn't call him that it's not fair he's probably just old and lonely and doesn't like kids coming into his garden to fetch their cricket ball. And if I look left I can ... all those times we used to play together when I moved here first just because he lived next door I was always a bit scared of him and his house I used to think it was bigger and darker than mine just like he was bigger and darker than me and that time he dropped the drain on my hand was it really an accident and the time in the cloakroom with his game bombers that was disgusting and making mud pies round the back by the old conservatory till Mum found us there one day covered in mud and sent him home now he's got an air rifle and shoots pigeons and sometimes he even shoots at cats if they're far enough way not to kill them he told me I bet she doesn't know that and if she did she wouldn't ... maybe I should tell her but then she'd know that I was jealous or she might think I was making it up and she wouldn't believe me but she couldn't have a crush on him how could she? not my Zoe it's not possible I won't believe it.

****

265

As I walk through the old hospital grounds I see her once more rising up out of the morning mist the sun just coming up over the little red-brick gate lodge by Vinegar Hill and catching the top of her head where her auburn hair is flowing lightly gently over her face her freckles lightly dancing on her nose and her sunflower eyes gently glowing as she reaches out her hand to me and I walk through the long grass towards her knowing it's a dream and knowing it's real too and when she takes my hand she kisses me lightly on the cheek and smiles her special smile and we walk on together towards the pond where we sit by the water's edge and throw the tiniest little pebbles into the water so they barely make a ripple before they sink slowly down we can see them gliding down to the bottom the water is so clear and the sunlight is shining through it making it translucent so we lie together silently in silent ecstasy fifty years of memories floating through our hearts a lifetime together a whole world of love and joy shared between us and in the afternoons behind drawn curtains watching something on TV we hold hands and laugh glancing at each other every time we laugh and sometimes we exchange little kisses on the cheek or on the lips and in the darkness her eyes are just the dark centre parts of the sunflower but still as beautiful and darkly deeply unknowable and this is our life all our life all we are to know and feel for all time and when I awake she is still with me filling my heart with love and I know she will be mine forever for all time.

****

It's hot on the bike at this time usually it's first thing in the morning twenty to eight when I'm cycling to the Convent and it's freezing I hope I don't start sweating take it easy then after this bit it's all downhill these Easter ceremonies are a pain but I have to do them I can't stop thinking about that time the last game of Truth and Dare when Yvonne asked Zoe straight out do you like Rory or Karl I wonder had George said anything to her to make her say that or did she just do it for me but even though Zoe complained that the question

266

wasn't on the list Yvonne made her answer and I was holding my breath I couldn't even look at her I was so nervous and I was dreading what she'd say and what would I do if she said him I'd have to get up and leave but she said "Karl" and I looked up at her and she was smiling at me as if to say "relax" and the very next spin was me and it was a Dare and Yvonne said immediately, "I dare you to kiss Zoe" as if on purpose and I leaned right over to her and kissed her on the lips just like I did that time to Yvonne but it was much nicer because it was Zoe and she smiled again when I did it I think as if to say she liked it but I should have left Mullen's earlier I knew what time it was I just couldn't stop and let them go on doing that without me that was incredible this afternoon I wish I didn't have to leave to come here I must have kissed Zoe for a whole minute nearly the last time but they didn't time us to the very end it was unbelievable and then she started kissing my neck I hope I don't get a love bite I hate that other word hickey you only get one if she sucks your neck she wasn't sucking it only kissing very lightly and gently and then she touched it with her tongue and it felt so good but I wonder what French kissing is like none of us have done that yet not even George and Yvonne I don't think and then I kissed Michelle too it's really funny the way Michelle takes out her retainers to kiss I like her now I wasn't sure at first but I don't like it when the others kiss Zoe she doesn't mind but I know she likes kissing me best because she told me and it's only me she sends kisses to at night from her window and she'd no idea how Rory got the idea it was him she told me that time we were going into St Mark's and Yvonne had the bottle in her pocket and we all knew where we were going and what we were going to do and Yvonne said "Hey I've got a new name for the Club. Let's call it The Kissing Club - but don't tell Andy!" And everybody laughed and then she said to George "Do you think he heard us that time up in the loft?" but I didn't laugh because it made me feel guilty again because I love Andy but I can't help it I love kissing the girls too and it's brilliant when Michelle is here but she only comes at the holidays and I didn't see Zoe at all hardly since we went back to school in January till last week when we went to that place inside the trees The Den only the six of us

267

Zoe Yvonne Michelle George Barry and me and when you're there no one can see in and the grass is short and flat so we can put the bottle down and it spins really well I love spinning it myself and if I'm really careful I can get it to stop wherever I want I like kissing Michelle too because her lips are really soft and she smells and tastes different and she lets me put my hand on her breasts but only on the outside not on the inside like Yvonne does hers feel so warm and soft like a balloon with warm water inside it better stop thinking about that I'm nearly there Oh God I wonder is it a sin no one ever said it was or told us we shouldn't be doing it but then no one knows what we get up to in St Mark's or in their bedroom if they did maybe we'd be in serious trouble here's the gates and they're open already great just cross the road and straight in I know how to do it this year. I know exactly how to do it so I won't get it wrong and end up giving it to the priest back to front or inside out like I did two years ago I didn't have to do it last year I suppose they didn't want me messing it up again but this year I've practised it enough times I just need to concentrate so I know when to do it I hope there's another Disney on Sunday afternoon I don't care if it's a cartoon or not it's just so incredible sitting there with Zoe whose turn is it for the couch pretty sure George and Yvonne had it last week so we get it this week brill I love holding her hand watching TV that movie Singin in the Rain was great there's nothing to worry about with Rory she doesn't even like him it's better this way with George and Yvonne together and me and Zoe and after that there's the kissing the cross bit and I have to go round after the priest and wipe the cross where they've just kissed it before the next person kisses it that's after Communion that's easy then there's the incense burning in the Ceborium but Ken holds the incense boat so I don't have to worry about that and the smell is incredible when the priest swings it to and fro and makes the fire inside glow red hot but the rest is just a normal Mass apart from this Gospel that goes on forever I know I should be listening to it but I've heard it a million times St Peter denies Jesus three times and the cock crows it won't be finished for ages ... I can see Mother Superior behind the bars why did she say that to me that they were all praying for my mother I know

268

she's got a tummy bug and that's why she's lost weight and she was in hospital for a few days having tests but she's all right now she told us she was fine right the Gospel's over I better pay attention after this I have to get the cloak that's it there's the catches one in each hand into the centre genuflect up the steps hand it to the priest back down he's put it on perfect where was I in a minute it's the Eucharistic Prayer it's No 1 that's the really long one anyway it's Dad they should be worried about he's the one who has the list of symptoms inside his wardrobe door and it's his family that are more likely to get it because of Eire and Seamus dying so why was Mummy crying that time I came into the house to go to the bathroom upstairs because Patrick was in the downstairs cloakroom the house really cool and silent after all the heat in the garden though I can still hear the voices of my friends outside laughing and shouting and I hear this sound as I'm coming up the stairs but at first I can't understand what it is I've never heard her crying before she never cries she's always happy and I'm standing really still on the little landing and listening and it's definitely her crying all right and I'm holding my breath so she doesn't hear me she's in her bedroom what is she crying about it must be Dad it must be because Dad is sick and maybe even has cancer and that's why she's - should I go in and comfort her and see if she's all right or should I pretend I didn't hear anything maybe she wouldn't want me to know she was crying because that would upset her more she's like that she wouldn't want me and George to be worried so she'd keep it to herself what will I do maybe I should just go to the bathroom and then make a noise coming out and see if she hears me but when I come out there's no sound from anywhere in the house I don't even know if she's still in her bedroom so I go back downstairs and out into the garden to play with my friends and when I see her again she's fine though maybe her eyes are a bit red I don't know now it's Communion the Nuns first I'm glad I'm not holding the patten Ken's going to do it the church is so full it'll take forever holding your arm out like that it gives you a cramp it's not so bad wiping the cross after they kiss it because you're moving your arm more I'm really knackered after that flogging my arm is falling off stupid git just stood there as if he couldn't feel a thing like it was a fly swatter I was belting him with and not my favourite whip the twelve-tailed one with the lead pellets and the stars at the ends he just stood there never seen anything like it but now he's suffering I doubt he'll make it up the hill don't want to wear him out so he's half dead when I get him up might let this old geezer give him a hand with the cross till we get up if he's near dead when I crucify him he'll be gone as soon as we get the cross up gotta drag it out as long as I can make him suffer by Jupiter that crown of thorns was a nice touch Pilate appreciated it hope he remembers it can't wait to get those nails into his wrists know exactly where to put them that's gonna hurt no need to tie him down first he's half dead already just stretch out his arm just about here should do where's the nails what a beauty must be near a foot long where's my hammer right stay right there don't move an inch till I get my ham- what the hell - what is he - how did he get - who is that I don't believe it he's up and that one I've seen him before he's one of his disciples so-called I don't believe it he must have bribed the other guard and they've all scarpered they're gone the lot of them - Jesus Christ the guard that fella Judas he's the one we paid off that double-crossing two faced git the old man who was carrying the cross and them women - they're all half way down the hill and no one to stop them by Jupiter I'm dead when Pilate hears of this he'll crucify me in his place I might as well just kill myself now oh God there's Mother Superior she's looking at me she looks worried what is it really going on at home which of them is sick better say a prayer please God don't let Mum or Dad be sick and don't let either of them die please God I'll be good I'll do anything you want I'll even give up playing kissing games that's it I'll give up starting now I promise I'll never kiss the girls again not even Zoe if you just let Mum and Dad be all right and not die please God in the name of the Father and the Son and the Holy Ghost Amen.

****

"Not much time left. Who will we try first?"

"Andy?"

"OK, but if he's not in we go to Mullen's."

"All right, but they're probably washing their hair, that's all they seem to do these days any time we call." We go out the gate and head up the road. It's late afternoon and we've been out all day with Mum and Dad for Sunday lunch.

"What about Let It Be?" says George.

"What about it?"

"Are we going to buy it? Will we ask Mum for the money – or it could be a joint birthday present, what about that?"

"I don't mind, I don't care really."

"What do you mean, it's going to be their very last album ever, we have to buy it."

"It doesn't bother me if I don't have it, it's just not the same any more without the Club, you know? I mean, what's the point?"

"Oh forget about the Club."

"Yeah well you get it then."

"OK, I'll get Mum to give it to me for my birthday if that's the way you feel about it."

"Why aren't you friends with Donal any more?" I ask as we pass his house.

"What do you mean?"

"I never see you talking to him. He went down the road last week and passed us and didn't even say hello."

"Oh yeah, well ... remember when Mum and Dad went away – to India? And I stayed in his house."

"Yeah, I stayed in the Mullens' - what about it?"

"Well we didn't really get on and when Mum rang up to see if I was OK I told her I didn't want to stay."

"What?"

"That's why she got Orla to babysit and we both went home."

"I don't believe it!"

"What? It's no big deal."

"No, it's just that, I thought it was because of me and Kieran."

"What – you didn't get on either?"

271

"Not really. I threatened to suffocate him with my pillow."

"That was nice."

"Yeah, really nice. I thought it was my fault."

"When are you finished school?" he asks a minute later when we're nearly at Andy's house.

"Next week. Friday's the last day."

"Last day in Junior School, imagine that. I still remember the first day we went in together. Seems like years ago."

"Seems like no time ago to me. Anyway it *was* years ago, four years ago to be precise."

"We met one of the priests going in the gate, remember, and you thought he looked nice."

"Killer Crowley."

"How did you get on with him afterwards?"

"He sent me out and got me biffed. Last month. The one and only time I ever got biffed in the whole of Junior School."

"Are you serious? That must be a record, no one goes through Junior School without getting biffed loads of times." For a moment I think back to that day standing outside my classroom door trying to hide in the doorway to keep out of sight, my heart nearly stopping every time I hear a door open somewhere, terrified it's the Prefect of Studies and he'll find me, looking at my watch every few seconds willing the minutes to pass faster. Only ten minutes. I was only outside that door for ten minutes but it seemed a lifetime. I think a little bit of me is still there and always will be, and then with one minute to go before the bell just as I was about to open the door and ask could I come back in he passed by coming down from the top floor - not the way I expected at all - and took down me into his office.

"You're generally speaking a good boy Jones, you've a good record, academically and in your behaviour. Why, I don't think I've ever had to discipline you, is that right?"

"Yes father," I reply, convinced that he's not going to do so now either.

"Why did Fr Crowley send you out?"

"I was fighting father." I wasn't really fighting, and it wasn't even my fault, but I couldn't be bothered trying to explain.

"Fighting in class is a very serious offence, if you had said anything else I might have been able to exercise some leniency although it is exemplary that you didn't make excuses or prevaricate. Neverthe-less I must discipline you as we cannot allow any expression of physical violence in this school."

What about this then? I felt like asking as he took out his biffer and I held out my hand. I was curious though, as I'd never experienced it before and wanted to share some of the pain that I had seen my classmates suffering so many times. Two slaps in quick succession follow, both equally painful, and the funny thing is, in between he touches my finger tips to steady the hand for the second blow as he takes aim, but it feels almost like a caress and that's the worst part of it, not the touch as a betrayal, but the mere fact of being touched at all. Suffering the scalding lash of the leather is bad enough, but being touched on the fingertips by this loathsome creature is worse. I just keep thinking of Zoe and her kisses and caresses and how she will kiss my hands when I tell her and heal them with the loving touch of her lips and I know he can't hurt me.

"What are you thinking about?" George asks me. "Where are you? On another planet?"

"He's not in, is he? I mean we've rung three times. Let's go."

"Suppose so." We walk back down the road passing a couple of young girls on roller skates in their school uniforms. Their legs look so skinny under their school skirts.

Five minutes later we're getting the same treatment outside Mullens' back door and no amount of amusing myself with the silvery doorknob is helping.

"Will we try St Mark's?" I ask.

"Come on then." And we both head past the garage and down the path by the lawn. As we pass the rubbish dump at the corner of Mullen's vegetable patch I remember when we all passed here at Christmas.

"What are Jam Tarts?" I ask.

"Jam Tarts?"

"Yeah, Jam Tarts. Rory said it when we passed here, and you were laughing about it in the Club. What's so funny about Jam Tarts?"

"Oh you're too young."

"What? Just tell me will you?"

"No. Why don't you ask Mum?"

"As if I'm going to ask Mum what Jam Tarts are, she'll tell me they're small round pastries filled with jam."

"Ask her about the Facts of Life then."

"Jesus I know all about that stuff, I just don't know about Jam Tarts."

"All right, do you know about periods?"

"In Maths?"

"No not in Maths you little genius, in women."

"In women? What in women?"

"It starts when they're twelve or thirteen. Every month they bleed ... you know ... down there. So they have to use these things called sanitary towels to mop up the blood. Then they have to be burned you can't throw them in the bin they're too dangerous and they really stink so they have to be burned. Mrs Mullen burns hers here."

"And they're called Jam Tarts?"

"Yeah, good name isn't it? Come on, I think I can hear them over by the pond."

"That's awful. The poor girls." He climbs over the wall and I wait a minute looking at the dump and thinking about what happens to women every month, it may even have started happening to Yvonne and Zoe, and I think about their two younger sisters and the two girls on roller skates with the skinny legs and all the other little girls in the world that this terrible thing will happen to, and it seems tragic to me, and it seems to me that all girls are tortured and heroic creatures to suffer such humiliation and still be able to smile at life.

That's what I'm still thinking about when we get through the laurel bushes and we're at the pond. Everyone's here, except Andy and thankfully not Rory either. George has gone over to Yvonne; Kieran, Barry and Patrick are sword fighting with bits of long grass

274

like little kids, and Zoe is sitting on her own over to the left where the pond curves round and gets bigger. I'm looking at her and wondering how I can get over to her. She's wearing her summer sandals and her frayed blue jeans shorts and a new pink top and a little bit of sun is shining through the trees onto the water in front of her and reflecting onto her face and her hair making it shine like a golden halo in one of those religious paintings in the Convent, only more real.

"How did you get over there?" I call over to her.

"Round the back," she replies, pointing behind her, but there's another, shorter way to get to her, by the edge of the pond. There's no real path at all, the only way to do it is by holding on to the overhanging trees at the water's edge. I look over at Zoe, wondering should I risk going by the water's edge and again I notice the light all around her. It's that special light that comes from the setting sun, when it's going down at the corner of the road, or in that part of St Mark's past the haunted chapel where none of us has ever been. I've seen it from my bedroom window but only in the Spring and early Summer, before that and after that it's not the same. If we're in St Mark's when it comes I can see it here too, shining through the trees behind the Nissen hut, and all over the field between the gate lodge and Vinegar Hill. It's not a strong bright light like you get at midday, it's soft and gentle and it is so special that I can taste and smell this light when it comes into my bedroom or when I'm here in St Mark's. That's easy but sometimes I can almost touch it too, like you can touch a painting, and I reach out my hands to feel it in my fingers and I think I can, but maybe that's just the wind. That's the light that Zoe is sitting in at the water's edge, and that's the light that I am walking in as I start over towards her, that surrounds us both as I try to reach my Zoe.

The first couple of yards are easy but then the trees come down lower and I have to be careful. There's a willow here and I grab hold of some of its trailing branches to pull myself round and then suddenly I feel myself falling and hitting the water. As I go under I can see the blue sky receding from me as the green pond water closes over my head it is like being buried alive only in water instead of in earth the green gets darker and darker as I sink lower and then I feel a bang on the back of my head that doesn't really hurt but makes everything go black and in that blackness I can see myself in the bath at home and Mum is washing my hair and she's just pushed me under the water by mistake and now we're in her little Mini in the flood and we're sailing downstream towards the sea and now the sea is crashing over my Dad's car as we drive back to the Cottage late at night filling the car with water and dragging us away over the fields and now I can feel my wellies clinging to my legs and dragging me under the surface of the pond with a funny squelchy noise and I am once again in my dreams holding my breath and kicking for the surface but it's too far away so far away I cannot even see its light and I know I won't be able to hold my breath long enough to reach the surface but then I will wake up out of breath but safe in my bed so when my lungs are bursting I take a breath but it's not like my dream I can feel the cold black water filling my lungs and I know I will not wake up safe in my bed ever again and I have to get out of here or I will really drown and really die but I can't I don't know how to I can't even see the surface and I'm sinking further down into the dark green black water and I know I'll never get out and I'm going to really drown and die here in the pond but then I suddenly feel my body being lifted up by many hands up out of the dark water into the sunlight again and laid on the grassy bank in the sunshine.

"Is he alive?" I hear someone ask as if in my dream and then a host of familiar voices crowding round me, my friends.

"No, he's dead. He's not breathing."

"Better give him the kiss of life. Anybody know how?"

"George you do it."

"I told you, he's dead, there's no point. And anyway I'm not kissing him, he's my brother!"

"Out of the way. I'll do it." The voice I hear and recognise through my semi-conscious state is Zoe's.

And then I feel her lips on mine, those familiar unforgettable lips, soft and warm, and she is blowing air into my lungs, her breath from her body into mine, filling my lungs with her life-giving breath, and I start coughing and roll over and spit out half a lungful of water back into the pond and then I lie back and look up into the sunflower eyes of my beautiful, loving, life-saving Zoe. She helps me sit up and someone slaps me on the back as I continue to cough and splutter and Zoe is rubbing my hands and:

"You have to do this to get the circulation going," she's saying.

"Good job with the kiss of life little sister, where did you learn to do that?"

"I saw it on Blue Peter."

"Really? Amazing! You really are going to be a nurse when you grow up."

I start coming back to normal and look around me.

"Who pulled me out?" I ask and then see George, Barry, Kieran and Patrick standing around in soaking wet trousers.

"You all jumped in?"

They nod.

"It's not so deep," says Barry.

"No, it only comes up to your knees," adds George.

"Well on me it's nearly up to my waist," laughs Patrick, "But it was so much fun, hey - why don't we get in again?"

"Brilliant idea," says Barry and in a second they are all back in the pond splashing around and having a water fight while I sit on the bank with Zoe rubbing my hands and Yvonne saying:

"Idiots."

"*You're* not getting back in again," says Zoe to me. "You've had a shock and need to rest. You're staying right here with me." And she gives me a kiss on the cheek.

I look at my brother and my friends splashing each other in the pond and say to the girls beside me:

"Aren't they the best ever?"

"Maybe, but they're going to get into big trouble when they get home that's for sure, and so are you, come to think of it," says Yvonne.

"Naw, they can just say they saved me from drowning. You know, Andy was right after all."

"About what?"

"It *is* better to be nearly drowned than nearly saved."

****

Sometimes it's good to just get on my bike and race up and down the road, I am completely in control and completely free. I can feel the power of my legs turning the back wheel and I can go anywhere and stop any time I want. Turning the handl bars upside down was really difficult and took ages but it was worth it because the bike looks so cool now, just like a motor bike, well the handlebars do anyway and even though it's George's old bike it's better than my old one that I got for Communion, that's way too small for me now. I know I'm not supposed to ride on the footpaths but this isn't really I just go up on it at the driveway and if I'm going fast enough I can take off where it slopes up again like this but I have to pull on the handlebars a bit too like -

"Out of the way! What are you doing?"   Oh God Barry has just come out of his driveway.

"Sorry! That was close, well done for not hitting me!"

"Thanks for nothing, you nearly knocked me off my bike!"

"Sorry!"

"Right, you're a goner. Just for that I'm going to challenge you to a game of cornering, starting now. I'm on."

"Great!" I love cornering and I'm pretty good at it because I can go real slow and almost stop on my bike without having to put my foot down. Also I'm fast at getting away like this.

"It's no good with just two, where's everyone else?" I ask after a while.

"Patrick should be out in a minute – oh, here he is now. Patrick, go in and get Kieran out here, tell him we're having a major cornering championship."

"Brill! We haven't played in ages."

Pretty soon we're all out on our bikes on the road. Even George has joined us and when we play Joneses against Blaneys it turns into a classic game of cornering like we haven't played in years. But before we're finished Yvonne appears at her front gate and calls George and Barry over to her.

"What?" I ask, as George and Barry suddenly head off down the road. "Where are you two going? We're not finished the game." George doesn't bother turning round but shouts back two words in explanation.

"Shop. Ciggies."

"Oh brilliant!"

"What? Where are they going?" asks Patrick as he comes back down the road.

"Looks like they're running an errand for her majesty there," I say with some sarcasm.

"Yvonne?" says Kieran, joining us.

"Yes, she seems to be out of cigarettes."

"This I've got to see, what are we waiting for, let's go!" And the three of us take off down the road, Kieran doing a wheelie on his Chopper. He's got some old playing cards clipped onto his back spokes they must have been there for years and when we go down the road the sound from them is incredible. At the end of the road we fly round the corner and can see George and Barry side by side up ahead of us. George has his hands in his pockets as he cycles along the main road. Then they see us and put on some speed but we're already on top of them and the five of us are like the gang of bikers in that Marlon Brando movie, The Wild One. We have the road to ourselves and we're all over it. Around the next left and we're on the road Miss Carey's was on which we cross without slowing and pull up on the footpath outside the shop, parking our bikes with the pedals leaning against the curb or up against the wall.

"They're for my mother," I hear George explain to the shop-keeper as I'm looking through the paperbacks on the swively stand. Some of them have really sexy covers.

279

"They're for my mother," I hear Barry announce a minute later and I nearly laugh.

I buy a packet of Love Hearts and we head outside and back onto our bikes. George and Barry have already lit up and as they cycle back along the main road their cigarettes burn brightly and send off sparks like miniature versions of the moon rocket.

Back on our road we stop outside Mullen's as Yvonne and Zoe are there, leaning up against the gates. There are two or three dogs wandering around.

"What kept you buster?" Yvonne says to George. "I'm dying for a fag, come on." And she turns up her drive heading for her back garden and the wall that brings us into St Mark's. We all lean our bikes up against the Mullen's gates and watch as George and Barry follow Yvonne and Zoe up the drive and through into the back garden. Just then Mrs Blaney comes out and asks Patrick to come in for his bath. He gives us a shrug and leaves.

Myself and Kieran head into St Mark's and pretty soon we're all sitting around in the Den. Yvonne, George and Barry are smoking their Rothmans and I'm offering my packet of Love Hearts around and I make sure when I come to it that Zoe gets the one that says, "I Love You." She smiles at me and pops it in her mouth.

"You know Mini's in heat," says Yvonne. "That's why all those dogs are there. She can't be let out for a month." I've a vague idea what she's talking about but I decide to ask anyway:

"Why a month?"

"That's how long she's in heat for."

"So?"

"So if she's let out a dog will mate with her and she'll have pups and we don't want pups," says Zoe, who obviously knows more about it than I do.

"What does mate mean?" asks Kieran. Even I know that one.

"God, don't you know anything?" says Yvonne, "Ask Mummy."

"Mating is when they – you know – get it on," says Barry, making suggestive gestures which I don't think Mrs Mullen would have used.

"They go for a ride," George says helpfully.

"Do humans do it the same way as dogs?" asks Kieran .

"Of course, we're all mammals," says George, "Don't they teach you anything in school? The man puts his mickey into the woman's whatsit, you know, her Middlesex, and that's it."

"*Middlesex* – what the heck is that?" I ask him.

"Oh that's a joke someone made up in school, you know what I mean."

"How long does he have to leave it in for?" Kieran asks. Now that he's started he seems determined to get to the bottom of this. I'm quite happy to stay quiet as I figure I might learn something, or at least fill in some of the gaps. Funny thing is, none of them seem sure of the answer to Kieran's last question.

"Oh about a minute," says George.

"A minute?" says Barry. "I thought it was a half an hour."

"Half an hour?" says Zoe, "God, you'd get so bored lying there for a half an hour. Can you at least read a book or watch TV or something?"

"Don't worry little sis, you won't be bored," Yvonne says with a funny sort of smile on her face.

"You don't just leave it there," says George, "It goes in and out, like when a dog grabs you around the legs and starts humping your leg, it's like that."

"Oh is that what a dog is doing? How disgusting!" says Zoe.

"You know Debbie was a mistake," says Yvonne.

"Yvonne! You're not to tell them - Mum said!" Zoe seems pretty upset about something.

"So what, it doesn't matter. That's why she's so much younger than the rest of us."

"Yvonne!"

"They thought Mum was too old to have babies and they were still doing it and she got pregnant and Debbie came along."

"I'll kill you when we get home. And then I'm telling Mum!"

"Well I'm glad she did," says Kieran, "I love Debbie, and I'm glad she was born even if she was a mistake. I couldn't imagine the family without her, it sort of finishes it off properly if you know what I mean." And we all think about this for a minute and it seems like Kieran is right.

"You should have seen Mum's boobies when she was feeding Debbie, they were enormous!"

"Yvonne! Stop it now this instant!"

"All right, but they were."

"Where does the 42 bus stop?" asks Barry. "About here!" he holds out both hands in front of his chest.

"That's not funny!" Zoe scowls, "That's the kind of joke Rory would come out with."

"Little amuses the innocent," says Yvonne. Then she starts pointing at all of us boys and asking, "Are you innocent? Are you innocent?" and we don't know whether to say yes or no.

"I know *you* are," she says to Kieran. Then she stands up and starts doing what looks like some kind of chest expanding exercises and chanting:

"I must I must increase my bust!" and we all laugh, but George has to go one better of course and comes out with this:

"Three months later began to show
Six months later began to grow
Nine months later out it came
A little hippy swinging a chain."

"Thanks George, nice one," I say sarcastically. "I really wanted to hear that. Have we all heard enough about the Facts of Life? Can we go home for tea now?" and we all get up and start walking back home through St Mark's.

****

282

"What's this movie called again?" asks Zoe.

"Gigi!" the three of us say at the same time.

"Oh – what's it about?"

"Gigi!" we all say again.

"It's about this girl growing up in Paris a hundred years ago," I explain to Zoe quietly, whispering in her ear as she sits beside me on the big black couch in the Mullen's front room. The room is so big the couch doesn't have to be up against a wall it's right in the middle of the room halfway between the door and the TV. Their other TV is broken, the one in the sunroom, so we are in here. Yvonne and George are beside us nearer the window and George has his hand up Yvonne's top. I don't because Zoe doesn't have any yet so we're just holding hands.

"Are you sure they can't see in the window?" Zoe asks.

"Of course not, it's the net curtains, they're impossible to see through from outside.

"How do you know? I can see out no problem. And Dad's right there, just outside the window, weeding the flowerbeds."

"Right, get your hand out, just in case," says Yvonne sitting up. "Ooh it's cold now, put your hand back in." George happily obliges.

"Hang on, where's he gone now? Is he coming in?" And no sooner has she said that than the drawing room door opens and Mr Mullen is standing behind us. I notice George very slowly removing his hand.

"What are you watching? Oh that must be Gigi. Look at Maurice Chevalier, he has these dreadful false teeth that keep falling down when he smiles, watch him and you'll see what I mean."

"Eh - did you want something Dad?" Yvonne asks.

"Oh, yes, I was going to tell you I have to go to the garage to get some petrol for the lawnmower so keep an eye on Debbie, you know your mother's having a lie down." Yvonne turns around and replies:

"Yes of course Dad. Leave it to us, you go off and get your petrol. Don't you worry, we'll keep an eye on her."

Mr Mullen leaves the room and a minute later we hear the engine of his Audi start up and see the car moving out the gate.

"Come on quick, I'm dying for a drink," says Yvonne jumping up out of the couch.

"What have you got?" George asks. I've no idea what they're talking about but I could swear she said she was dying for a drink.

"You know, the banana wine. Come on, quick!" She dashes out the door and by the time we have followed her into the sunroom she is already in the wine cellar, a kind of narrow room about three feet wide halfway along the right-hand wall, and she's standing there slugging away at a bottle with a nice yellow label with a picture of a bunch of bananas on it.

"God I needed that," she says, wiping her mouth with the back of her hand. "Anybody want some?"

Of course George can't resist and takes the bottle from her and starts knocking it back.

"Hey! Don't drink so much – they'll notice!" shouts Zoe.

"No they won't, relax, they never drink the stuff anyway. It's really good, isn't it?"

"Delicious," agrees George.

"I can't believe this," I say and look at Zoe despairingly.

"This is why we're being sent to boarding school in September," says Zoe miserably. "It's all her fault, because she's so ... oh God!"

"I didn't know you were going to boarding school in September!" I say, panic grabbing hold of my heart and squeezing it tight.

"I'm sorry, I was going to tell you. We only found out last weekend." Zoe looks really sorry.

"But what about ...?" What I want to say is, 'What about us?' but Zoe understands.

"I know, I know," she says. "It's terrible."

"How is it my fault?" says Yvonne. "They always said we'd go to boarding school when you had to go into senior school. That's the only reason. I'm fifteen and you're fourteen little sis, we're not

284

kids any more. Now, give me one more slug then I need a fag."
Yvonne takes the bottle again and takes another drink.

"OK come on - St Mark's. Where are my ciggies? Have you
got any, buster?"

"Yup, got a new packet yesterday," says George, "Let's go!"

"Are you mad?" screams Zoe, "You can't go in there now –
we have to look after Debbie till Dad comes back – remember?"

"Well we don't all need to stay, you can look after her and tell
Dad I've gone out. See you. If you want to join us for a game when he
comes back you can." Yvonne leaves the bottle back on the shelf,
hiding it behind some red wine, and she and George go out through
the French windows into the sunshine.

"Oh, I'll kill her some day," Zoe is really annoyed. "Where is
Debbie anyway? I better check her bedroom and see that she's all
right. Go on back into the TV, I'll be down in a minute."

So I'm keeping an eye on Maurice Chevalier's dentures as he
sings, *"Ah yes, I remember it well"* when Zoe comes back in. She's
looking a bit hassled.

"Look, do you mind going into St Mark's and I'll meet you
there in half an hour? I have to do something for Mum. Please?"

"Yeah sure, no problem. Where will we meet?"

"I suppose they're gone to the Den so we might as well join
them there. Is that all right?"

"OK, see you there."

I give her a kiss and walk out through the French windows and
down the lawn. When I get to the Den I can see George and Yvonne
sitting on the grass, smoking cigarettes. The old Coke bottle is on the
ground beside them.

"What's that for?" I ask.

"I brought it. Just in case you two wanted to join us," says
Yvonne. "But since you're here we might as well have a quick game."

So the three of us sit down, fairly evenly spaced and we start
playing Spin the Bottle. Only thing is, when it's George's turn the two
of them get stuck into each other for about five minutes French

kissing and everything, and when it's my turn all I get is a peck on the cheek. After a few turns of this I get fed up.

"Look I know where I'm not wanted, I'll see you round." And I head back towards the Mullens' garden thinking if Zoe comes in I will meet her at the back wall. But before I reach her wall I see her climbing over. I am just about to call her when my heart stops as I see Rory follow her. I duck in behind a tree and wait to see which way they will go. Luckily they go straight ahead and don't see me. I cannot believe that this is happening and that Zoe is with him again. I don't want to follow them in case they see me so I just stay where I am and watch them going through the trees behind the Nissen hut. When they are out of sight I stay leaning against the tree unable to go anywhere or do anything. My mouth is dry and I can't close it. I just keep saying to myself over and over, "I don't believe it, not again, I don't believe it." But then I hear a shout and another one. It's Zoe's voice and she's screaming, "Stop!" and "Leave me alone!" I run through the trees and I'm in the clearing behind the Nissen hut in a minute. Rory has Zoe by both arms and he's shaking her and trying to kiss her while she keeps turning her head away to avoid him and shouting "Stop!" all the time.

"Rory!" I yell as soon as I come into the clearing. They both stop and look at me.

"Right, take your hands off her – NOW!" I say with as much authority as I can manage. "Let her go!"

"And you're the one who's going to make me I suppose?" he sneers.

"That's right, I'm the one."

"All right, let's see you." And he lets go of Zoe's arms and pushes her away to one side as I launch myself at him. I am so enraged that I don't really know what I'm doing, I just know I have to fight and I fly at him with my arms and fists flailing around blindly.

A few minutes later I am lying on the ground battered and bruised with blood coming from my eyebrow and nose and Rory is standing over me.

"If you want some more of that just let me know. And as for you, you're not even worth fighting over." And he stalks off. Zoe rushes to me and starts kissing me and wiping my face with her hanky at the same time.

"Oh you poor thing! You poor darling, are you hurt? Look you're bleeding, oh that brute." And then as she raises my head and holds me with both hands she says:

"You saved my life, just like I saved yours. Isn't that wonderful? Are you all right?"

"Yes really, I'm fine, not hurt at all."

"I'm so sorry, that was all my fault. He came into the house, just walked in, he was standing in the sunroom when I came down from Mum and I was about to go out to you. I told him I was meeting you and he said fine he'd come in with me because there was something he wanted to talk to me about. Then we got in here and he grabbed me and started trying to kiss me and then you came along thank God."

We are still sitting in the grass in the middle of the meadow and I decide we might as well stay there. We're kind of leaning against each other's knees and facing each other, she's got her hands on my chest playing with my silver locket. The sun is shining on her hair and when she looks up it fills her sunflower eyes with the most dazzling light.

"Zoe?"

"Yes."

"Are you mine now?"

"Yes."

"Forever?"

"Yes."

"No more ... no one else?"

"No, only you. I love you."

"Do you really?"

"Yes, let me prove it to you. I've never done this with anyone else before, I always wanted you to be the first." And now she is putting her lips to mine and for the first time I can feel her tongue against my lips parting them and sliding into my mouth I reach my tongue forward and touch hers and her tongue pulls back and she takes her lips away from mine and laughs a little laugh and her face looks so strange and wonderful up so close and her sunflower eyes are so big they're like a whole field of sunflowers waving in the sunshine I feel I could get lost in them but then she kisses me again with her lips touching my lips and again she gently puts her tongue inside my mouth and our tongues touch again and it is like we become one our tongues dancing around each other melting into each other my whole being dissolving into hers becoming one body one soul it is like nothing I have ever felt before in my life and I never want it to end it feels like there is no one but us in the whole universe and I want to stay like this with Zoe for all eternity but suddenly I hear something terrifying – I can't believe it but it is - the sound of my father's voice and he's shouting "George! George! Where are you?" and "Karl! Come here! Karl!" There is something in his voice I have never heard before that is terribly frightening it seems to be coming from the Mullen's wall and now his shouts are getting closer I can't believe it but he must have climbed over the wall I don't know what my father wants or why he has come into St Mark's where he has never set foot before but now I remember my vow at Easter during the Good Friday ceremonies that I wouldn't kiss a girl again and I think of my mother crying alone in her bedroom and the nuns saying prayers for her and I suddenly realise what is happening and I am horrified at what I have done and even Zoe's loving hand on mine cannot save me from this for I know that I have done something terribly wrong and I am going to be terribly punished…

1984

The interview process went on longer than Dr Thompson had expected, mainly due to the unusual talkativeness of his patient. Eight days of sessions had gone without any hitch – no breakdowns, no show of temper or aggression, not even an interruption to the steady flow of his patient's narrative – so that by the end of the first week the services of Nurse Ryan had been dispensed with, leaving just Nurse Mullen behind the two-way mirror. In fact it was becoming increasingly harder for Dr Thompson to equate this mild-mannered, soft-spoken young man with the same person who just a few months previously had gone out into the garden shed of his family home, picked up a short-handled axe, returned to the house where his father was watching television, come up on him from behind and buried the axe in his father's head.

Nurse Mullen continued to sit in the observation room each morning, silently witnessing her childhood friend recount their past, and every evening she was given a copy of the transcript to take home and read. They had no consultation during this period, Dr Thompson and the nurse, he wanted to leave everything to the end, but he did think that she seemed very subdued, deeply thoughtful, possibly even troubled when each session ended and she left his office. The only disappointment as far as Dr Thompson was concerned was that the patient stopped his story in 1970 at the age of 12 and no amount of prompting, asking questions, or more strenuous interrogation techniques would persuade him to continue. In the end the doctor had to accept that all he had to work with was the patient's pre-teenage years. Two weeks after the first session he called Nurse Mullen into his office for a full discussion of patient Karl Jones.

The transcripts of all Jones's sessions lay on the desk between them. Dr Thompson gave the nurse a reassuring smile and began.

"Firstly, Zoe, I wish to say how deeply grateful I am to you for attending these sessions, and for reading the transcripts of them. I know it has taken up a considerable amount of your free time these past weeks and I assure you that has been noted on your file and will not be forgotten. Now, you have heard our patient give a very full and precise account of approximately seven years of his childhood and then, unfortunately as you know, he clammed up and couldn't be persuaded to utter another word. It is a pity, but these things often happen in treating psychiatric patients and we must learn to accept

289

them and work with what we've got. So, firstly I must ask you, have you read the whole transcript?"

"Yes doctor."

"And what is your overall impression?"

"It's all lies Doctor," the nurse said immediately. "Well, not all, some of his account of our childhood, what I remember of it anyway, is pretty much as it happened. But *he* wasn't like that, he wasn't like that at all. He was always difficult, always aggressive. He was the way Barry is in his story. Only worse. He was always telling us to shut up and calling us stupid and idiots and being really insulting and horrible."

"Really? How remarkable. Please continue."

Nurse Mullen took a deep breath. "He mentions something that occurred as far back as 1964 but in the opposite way to how it really happened. It was Karl who injured Rory's hand with the grate of the drain and not the other way round. He deliberately dropped the grate on Rory's hand and hurt him badly. Rory told me so himself.

"Interesting. Tell me, how do you remember him as a child?"

"I think you could say he was ... troubled. Very strange, unhappy, withdrawn, and prone to fits of temper, though he wasn't really violent when we were together, as a group. As I said, he was like the way he describes Barry, that's the way he was himself. Barry was actually a very happy, funny boy, Karl was the aggressive one, always fighting and calling everyone 'stupid'. And he was ... dirty ..."

"Dirty?"

"Sexually. He was creepy, always spying on me, looking out his bedroom window over at ours, me and Yvonne's, blowing me kisses at night. We'd laugh at him, but it wasn't really funny. And then after his mother died of cancer that summer – 1970 it was – he really started to fall apart. He got himself expelled from school and soon after that they moved house and I didn't hear anything for a few years. Then Yvonne met George in town one time and she asked him how Karl was, and he admitted he wasn't well but that was all. George went on to be a successful accountant but Karl never went to college

290

and didn't even have a job. We heard nothing for years until now – and this ..."

"Interesting then that he sees himself so differently, if this transcript is anything to go by. An extreme case of identity substitution possibly. But his account is so plausible, so real."

"It's all nonsense doctor, he was never like that, none of this ever happened, not the way he describes it, it's all his imagination. Except for the religion – he was very religious all right, and when he wasn't serving Mass in his convent he was always praying."

"How did the others get on with him?"

"Well he always hated Rory for no reason. He picked a fight with him once at the pond, got him in the water and nearly drowned him holding his head under. We all had to pull him off. And that bit at the end, that's all a lie, I remember that day very clearly, Rory and I were walking in St Marks and Karl came up and attacked us, he flew at Rory like a madman, quite the opposite to the way he describes it, Rory had to protect me. That was when his father came into St Marks and took him away. His mother was dying and he had to go into the hospital, that's where she was – in St Mark's, the same hospital where we had played for years. The truth is he had a very unhappy childhood and he did his best to make us all unhappy too."

"Then his account is meaningless, completely worthless. How did Shakespeare describe life? 'A tale told by an idiot, full of sound and fury, signifying nothing'. This is a tale told by a psychopath, full of joy and beauty it is true, but signifying nothing." He looked at the script in his hand and shook his head in disbelief, then asked the nurse another question.

"What about your own personal relationship with him, do you mind if I ask you about that?"

"I suppose I felt sorry for him, we all did in a way, because we knew he wasn't normal, wasn't of standard mental capacity as we would say. When children are small they don't notice these differences but later on ... when he was so aggressive ... it was hard to like him."

"And yet in his subconscious or his imagination or wherever *this* came from, he believes you were in love with him. Tell me, did he show any signs of being – in love, or infatuated with you?"

"Just in that creepy way."

"Fantasising obviously, reinventing the past to absolve himself of guilt perhaps."

"It's all in his imagination. I never loved him as a child, I didn't even like him much. It would have been impossible to love someone like him. It was never him, it was always my husband, it was always Rory."

"Excuse me, are you saying you married the Rory he talks about, the Rory from your childhood?"

"Yes, we were married six months ago."

"Well, well. And do you think that the patient would have been aware of this? Did you put notice in the paper or would he have heard of it somehow?"

"It's quite likely, you know this city it's a small place. Oh my God no! You don't think that he did that because of me – because I got married to Rory ...?"

"No, no, of course not, please don't think of it. A mentally ill person is entirely unpredictable and is liable to act in the most unaccountable manner. It was obviously building up over many years, anything could have set it off. I am making a tentative preliminary diagnosis of a delusional mania with a Father-God substitution complex. He was already associating his father with God and this set up a latent Oedipal desire to kill his father in order to revenge himself for what he saw as a betrayal by God. This desire was building up in his subconscious for ten years before he committed the murder. In killing his father he killed the God who, as he saw it, had betrayed him by letting his mother die of cancer. There was nothing you or anybody else could have done. If we had better early intervention services available he might have been cared for in a more timely manner which could have prevented this tragedy, but you must not blame yourself in any way." He paused for a moment.

"I want to thank you for your assistance which has been extremely helpful. Tell me, where did you go for your honeymoon?"

"We just had a week touring around the country, we didn't have time for anything more."

"I am going to recommend you have two weeks paid leave starting from today. I will speak with Professor Jacobson about it. Organise something special, get out of the country and have a proper honeymoon. You deserve it."

"Thank you doctor, I don't know what to say, you are so kind."

"Not at all."

"What will happen to him doctor?" Nurse Mullen asked with a concerned look on her face.

"At this stage it's too early to tell. Isolation for the moment. Medication of course, see how he responds to treatment. There have been huge leaps in psychopharmacology recently, some of the new neuroleptics are showing very promising results in cases like this. But I think he will be here for a very long time to come. That's all I can say." He stood up and reached out his hand.

"Goodbye Zoe, and again thank you for your invaluable help."

"Goodbye doctor, thank you so much ... thank you."

The doctor called his secretary who came in and took a quite emotional Nurse Mullen out of the office. That evening Dr Thompson drove his car out through the tall steel gates of the hospital and went home. He was looking forward to seeing his wife.

****

Cold tap hot tap wiggle my toes and here come the waves one little mini wave every time I move a toe the water's getting cold when's Mum coming back where are my toys to play with they took away my little sailing boat and my Noah's ark and my elephant and giraffe tomorrow's Sunday we can go to the park after I serve Mass and play on the swings and in the afternoon there'll be Disneyland on TV whose turn is it to get the couch we'll pull the curtains and it'll be really dark and in the dark I'll slip my hand into Zoe's hand and we'll watch the cartoons and she'll sit really still not moving at all but sometimes she laughs at the funny bits and then she looks at me and smiles her special smile and my heart fills up with that funny lovely feeling and I want to die I'm so full of love for her and I lean over and give her a kiss and even in the dark I can see her sunflower eyes darker now but still as beautiful and I know she is mine my own lovely beautiful girl my Zoe my Zoe.

****

A few days after Dr Thompson's last interview with Nurse Mullen a short press release was issued to all the national newspapers saying that the doctors and staff of the Central Mental Hospital were shocked by the discovery that, despite their best efforts to observe strict rules of patient supervision at all times, Karl Jones had been left unattended for a moment while taking a bath and had drowned.

THE END

Printed in Great Britain
by Amazon

85005255R00167